Amanda Cinelli was born into a large Irish-Italian family and raised in the leafy green suburbs of County Dublin, Ireland. After dabbling in a few different careers, she finally found her calling as an author when she won an online writing competition with her first finished novel. With three small daughters at home, she usually spends her days doing school runs, changing nappies and writing romance. She still considers herself unbelievably lucky to be able to call it her day job.

USA TODAY bestselling author **Natalie Anderson** writes emotional contemporary romance full of sparkling banter, sizzling heat and uplifting endings—perfect for readers who love to escape with empowered heroines and arrogant alphas who are too sexy for their own good. When not writing, you'll find her wrangling her four children, three cats, two goldfish and one dog…and snuggled in a heap on the sofa with her husband at the end of the day. Follow her at natalie-anderson.com.

FAKING IT

AMANDA CINELLI

NATALIE ANDERSON

MILLS & BOON

First published in Great Britain 2024
by Mills & Boon, an imprint of HarperCollins*Publishers* Ltd,
1 London Bridge Street, London, SE1 9GF

www.harpercollins.co.uk

HarperCollins*Publishers*, Macken House, 39/40 Mayor Street Upper, Dublin 1, D01 C9W8, Ireland

Faking It © 2024 Harlequin Enterprises ULC.

Fast-Track Fiancé © 2024 Amanda Cinelli

Billion-Dollar Dating Game © 2024 Natalie Anderson

ISBN: 978-0-263-32019-0

08/24

This book contains FSC™ certified paper and other controlled sources to ensure responsible forest management.

For more information visit www.harpercollins.co.uk/green.

Printed and Bound in the UK using 100% Renewable Electricity at CPI Group (UK) Ltd, Croydon, CR0 4YY

FAST-TRACK FIANCÉ

AMANDA CINELLI

MILLS & BOON

CHAPTER ONE

NINA ROUX KEPT a polite smile in place until she'd gained a safe distance from the hot overhead lights of the press tent. The rain-soaked paddock of the Elite One Monte Carlo circuit was relatively deserted in the aftermath of yesterday's disastrous race during which ten drivers had crashed. Thankfully there were no significant casualties, with the exception of one career-ending injury for the lead driver of Falco Roux. The team in which she was currently the first reserve driver.

She wasn't so callous as to say she'd been waiting for this moment, but, as a reserve driver, the only chance she'd ever had to get actual race time was at the expense of one of the lead drivers on the team. She had sat patiently during the morning briefing from management, proudly wearing her standard polo shirt and crisply ironed chinos in the team colours of white and maroon. It had seemed straightforward, to promote her into a permanent seat for the remaining seven races of the season. To give her the chance she had earned and one she deserved after graduating top of the academy at eighteen, followed by five years of hard work in testing and development. Much longer than most other drivers had to wait when they performed at her level. Team members had shaken her hand, and she'd felt a sense of bubbling excitement grow within as they'd readied for a 'surprise announcement' that would be delivered during a live-streamed press briefing.

She had imagined how they might announce it. Would they lead with her being the first Roux to earn a seat on their family's team since her brother's ill-fated attempt as a race driver ten years before? Or go with the more shocking fact that she would be the first woman to take a permanent seat in Elite One since her aunt, Lola Roux, had dominated the sport twenty-five years ago?

In the end, they had discussed none of those things... because it had turned out that Nina wasn't the subject of this surprise announcement after all, but rather the sign-ing of a completely new driver. Not only that, but a driver who was the grandson of the owner of their biggest rival team, Accardi Autosport. Apollo Accardi, a champion-ship-winning driver who had stunned the racing world by disappearing from the sport six years ago.

The announcement had come from their new team owner, Tristan Falco, via video link, his handsome tanned face and perfectly coiffed dark blond hair filling the screen as he performed his most basic of duties from somewhere far away. Likely upon one of his famous su-peryachts, surrounded by glamorous guests and merri-ment. The potential return to Elite One of the legendary driver had been whispered about all season, and she'd foolishly believed the rumours too good to be true. But Apollo Accardi had indeed made his return, and with it had taken her chance to secure a seat for the rest of the season. She'd get a drive for the next few races, but, once Apollo had arrived and familiarised himself with the car, he'd complete the rest.

As the details of the shocking announcement had been talked through and not one of her teammates had spoken up at the injustice of it all, her chest had tightened with despair and anger. She'd found herself standing suddenly, ignoring the quick warning look from their head of PR as she'd mumbled her excuses and made her exit. Her knees had threatened to buckle with every step she took, cameras flashing wildly to take in her reaction. Watching for the woman they'd nicknamed the ice princess to scowl or tantrum or make a scene that they could gleefully publish on their various websites.

So she'd smiled.

She'd smiled as she'd walked calmly past the line of journalists and through the belly of their impressive track headquarters, only breaking into a run once she'd reached the empty front foyer filled with their legacy of Elite One driver and constructor championship trophies as well as posters and flags in white and maroon. Colours that had been made famous by *her* family name alone for more than half a century until one impulsive playboy billionaire had seemingly swooped in and made her reckless big brother an offer he couldn't refuse. Even when she'd emerged into the rain outside, she hadn't slowed down. Her feet stomped along the tarmac, keeping time with the furious beat of her heart.

She waited until she was a safe distance towards her own secluded motorhome at the edge of the Falco Roux buildings before she released a growl that had been building in her chest. Video link. The biggest disaster that had hit their team in years and their billionaire owner hadn't even bothered to be here in person. Tristan Falco had been almost completely absent from every race and meeting from the moment he had taken the reins from her older brother, Alain.

Famous for his skill in acquisition, rebranding and subsequent big-figure sales of struggling corporations, Tristan Falco likely believed that his usual routine would work just the same here in the pinnacle of motorsport racing. But as evidenced by their recent slide of steadily declining popularity and investments, it was not. She seemed to be the only one willing to tell him why, which she would do if the man weren't utterly impossible to get a meeting with.

If her frustrations with management hadn't already been at boiling point, perhaps she could have held it together today. For any other team, Nina would have been impressed and excited. Nabbing a huge name like Apollo…it likely had cost Falco more than a quarter of their year's budget to achieve. But *she* was the reserve driver, a position she'd held for far longer than any other driver she knew with adequate licence points to drive in Elite One. It was unacceptable. And it was exactly the kind of move that she'd needed in order to make the next difficult decision about her own career.

What was that saying? The definition of insanity was doing the same thing over and over again and expecting a different result. She knew now that there was no other option for her here, not if Falco was prepared to pay an external driver probably triple her salary to come in and learn their car from scratch. The car she had been instrumental in developing alongside the team she'd known from birth. The car she had set their track record in at the end of last year during their winter break. She had taken first place in this year's Legends race, for goodness' sake, after being chosen as a second driver by former Elite One world champion Grayson Koh.

If all of that wasn't enough...nothing ever would be.

It was a gift really—perhaps she had held on too long to familial loyalty. Her charity girls' driving academy was already on the verge of bankruptcy since her shares and inheritance had been lost in the months of financial woes that led to her brother accepting the buyout. She understood why Alain had done it, or at least she had tried to over and over after she'd realised that he had got her inadvertently to sign away every cent in what she'd believed was an effort to save them. Instead, reckless and selfish as he was, Alain had sold their legacy to Falco and left her with nothing. The last she'd heard, he was currently living it up in Ibiza on one of the yachts owned by none other than Tristan Falco himself. Probably another little perk that he'd secured in the secret negotiations that had led to Monaco's oldest and most historic team, Roux Racing, being renamed Falco Roux.

She slammed the door of her private motorhome, turning around just as the door swung inwards. Astrid Lewis, Falco Roux's head of PR, entered, her green eyes sparking with fury behind her designer horn-rimmed glasses. The woman was a silhouette of perfectly coiffed rage and Nina was the sole recipient.

'Before you say anything, I did the right thing by walking out of there.' Nina turned away, still intent on getting changed and leaving as quickly as possible. The press wouldn't follow her to her late aunt's home in the south of France, and she knew better than to assume she would be left alone if she remained in Monte Carlo any longer.

'Your contract requires you to remain in the press tent for the entirety of each sitting. We just announced a major development in the team line-up following the worst driver injury of the season, Nina.'

Nina bit the inside of her cheek, forcing herself to hold her tongue. She knew better than anyone what happened when she allowed herself to speak freely. Keep calm, she told herself. Calm people didn't lose their jobs. It wasn't that she was unable to control her temper, it was simply that injustice was her biggest trigger. She believed in working hard and reaping a fair reward for her efforts. She *deserved* to be the one in that seat for the remainder of the season instead of just the next few races. She had been the one pushing the team to make upgrades. She had spent hundreds of hours with the engineers during development and they had ended up with the best car they'd had in a decade and were maybe even on track to win a constructor's championship.

She'd put every ounce of herself into being a hardworking team member, believing the results of her talent and drive would be enough. So no, she wasn't going to sit and listen to her team wax lyrical about how excited they were to welcome their new driver to the Falco Roux family. She wouldn't smile and wave and play the good girl a second longer. She had done it for the entirety of her career so far. She had followed every rule and toed every line and look where it had got her.

Superstition and loyalty had led her to sign a ridiculous contract that kept her locked into Falco Roux until she turned twenty-five. But she knew now, she couldn't stay that long. She wouldn't waste two more years in a place that seemed determined to use her and benefit from her talent while giving her none of the recognition or opportunity. Maybe another team would treat her with more respect, give her more actual access to opportunity instead of constantly holding her back with excuse after excuse.

And there was only one man who could set her free.

'I don't like that look in your eye, Nina,' Astrid said warily. 'I know that this might seem unfair, but I promise you there is a plan. Tristan Falco knows what he is doing—'

'Do not mention that man's name in front of me. Not when he hasn't even had the decency to speak to me in person *once* since he took my family's company from under me.'

To her credit, Astrid pursed her lips and remained silent. Good, too, because Nina didn't want to take out her frustrations on the other woman. They might not technically be friends, but Astrid had never steered her wrong in the years since they had both started as newbies on the male-dominated team. Nina as a brand-new test driver, Astrid as a PR assistant.

'Please just tell me what you plan to do.' Astrid sighed wearily. 'And if I need to take measures on my end to counteract any potential damage.'

Just as she'd opened her mouth to offer benign reassurance, Nina's phone beeped, grabbing her attention. A slow breath escaped her lips as she read the text message. A smile slowly spread across her face as she realised it was exactly the news she'd hoped for. She'd nabbed a last-minute invitation to an exclusive event taking place in Paris later that evening. If she left now, she could just make it. She could take matters into her own hands and show Tristan Falco exactly who she was.

'There will be no damage,' she said carefully, putting the last of her things into her gym bag before turning back. 'Not if Tristan Falco is as good a businessman as he claims to be. Now if you'll excuse me, I have a flight to catch.'

* * *

By the time Nina's limousine pulled up in front of Paris's stunning Musée des Arts Décoratifs, the sky over the city had faded to a pleasant brushwork of purples, pinks and oranges. The one benefit she enjoyed from the four years she'd spent at an elite all-girls boarding school in the Swiss Alps was the network of powerful women she now had dotted all across the globe. One of whom was Hermione Hall, a fashion stylist who had served to get her access to this particular event. Considering the ticket she'd nabbed was for a model who'd fallen sick at the last minute, she'd also been required to sport an haute couture gown for the evening.

Nina took one last look in her compact mirror at the finished result of the past hour of lightning-fast make-up and dress alterations. Fashion-world people truly were magicians—there was no other explanation for how they had managed to transform her from a tired, unpolished mess to whatever illusion of glamour this was. Her gown was a kind of powder-blue lace and tulle creation that clung to her body like a second skin from neck to mid-thigh, before flowing out into a long train behind her. A white glittering mask covered her from above her eyebrows to below her nose with glittering diamond appliqué making her sparkle as she moved in the light.

To most people, one couldn't get much luckier than getting the opportunity to dress up and play the part of a supermodel for one night. But she was a naturally introverted person with a rather complicated history with the press, and stepping out onto the red carpet outside the museum was quite frankly Nina's idea of hell on earth.

A wall of photographers and journalists seemed to command the throng of glamorous A-list carpet walkers in a shocking wave of sound that temporarily held her frozen still with its urgency. Anonymity wasn't necessary for her plan tonight to work, but she couldn't deny it was a lot easier to hold her head high without the weight of her family's world-famous downfall hanging over her.

The hum of voices tumbled over one another as she took a few shaky steps forward, feeling the comforting glare of the event's security guards ensuring nobody got too close. The theme of the Falco Diamonds showcase was a summer masquerade and, once she'd made it halfway down the carpet without slipping, she focused on locating the only person she actually cared about seeing tonight. She was so distracted by the long line of famous faces that she almost missed him entirely.

'Tristan, over here!' a photographer called out, soon joined by an echo of others, all scrambling for the perfect shot of the man of the hour.

Nina's breath caught as a man passed close by her, his sleeve just slightly brushing the skirt of her dress as he stepped out into the glare of the camera flashes. In a sea of black, his tuxedo was a brilliant white that seemed to make his dark blond hair and tanned skin glow. He wore no mask on his face. He stood a full foot taller than everyone around him, his blue eyes smouldering at the cameras as if he were some kind of fallen angel, sent to earth make every other human feel inferior. He owned every inch of the red carpet as a quartet of beautiful women posed and clung to his impressively muscular arms.

Who on earth needed to bring four dates to an event? She felt a flash of irritation as the women smiled and simpered up at him, while he all but ignored their presence. She knew that Falco carefully curated his wild playboy image and possibly was not actually involved with all four of the women. But the way their hands roamed over his torso as they moved as one spoke of a certain intimacy.

Was that even possible?

She was staring openly now, wondering at the...*practicality* of one man entertaining four women at once. Then again, if the rumours about Tristan Falco's insatiable appetite for bedroom gymnastics were true, perhaps this was the minimum number of participants required to maintain his attention. It had been all over social media when his girlfriend had left him a few months ago for his cousin—maybe one woman wasn't enough for Tristan Falco. Her inexperienced mind and overactive imagination attempted to conjure up an image and she couldn't help it, she laughed out loud with surprise at the absurdity of it.

There was no way her laugh could have been heard over the din of the crowds around them and yet she felt a prickle of awareness skate along her skin before she looked back up to see that she had become the sole focus of one man's attention.

She felt frozen in place as Falco's gaze blatantly dipped to languorously take in her figure before rising back up to meet her eyes with exaggerated slowness. The slow smile that transformed his lips was pure sin, his midnight-blue eyes sparking with the kind of devilish glint that she would have to be completely naïve not to understand.

'Miss Roux?'

She felt as if she were breaking out of a trance as she blinked, turning to find one of Hermione Hall's assistants standing by her side looking impatient.

'You need to get inside or all of the best pieces of jewellery to accompany this gown will be gone.' The woman urged her ahead and Nina dutifully followed, ignoring the strange prickle on the back of her neck as she moved inside the entryway.

For a man renowned for his wild playboy lifestyle and love of excess, Tristan Falco was never anything but fully in control at all times.

But tonight, he was distracted.

He usually adored playing host, a role that he had been raised in as the only son of a world-famous Argentinian diamond heiress and global fashion icon. His mother had taught him how to work a crowd and how to use his charm and good looks to build a fortune of his own. He had long been a success in his own right, with his carefully curated image paving the way for his skills in the business world to slide under the radar just as he liked it. But that success had come with a certain level of disconnect.

He had long grown used to suffering through the company at A-list events, with people clamouring for his attention while he worked through his mental list of business connections and takeover bids. And of course, lately, with dodging the more and more overt attempts his mother was making at finding him a wife. Recent scandals in the press regarding his love life had done him no favours, but ever since her retirement as CEO of her beloved company, Dulce Falco had decided the time had come for her only son to settle down and give her grandchildren. Not even planning her own upcoming wedding in Buenos Aires had distracted her.

He loved his mother and didn't want to worry her…and having a wife and family of his own was an idea he had actually gradually been warming up to in recent times, not that he'd admit it. Until his ex had run off with his cousin and the ensuing scandal had served as a reminder that men like him were not built for domesticity.

Grabbing a second glass of champagne from a passing waiter, he tried to focus on his task list for the evening. He felt…on edge and it had nothing to do with the pressure he was under to marry and everything to do with finding out the identity of the mysterious beauty he'd seen outside.

Time and time again he had found his eyes searching for the woman in blue in the crowd, catching glimpses of her progress in between interruptions from his own less than captivating companions. She had been allocated a tiara from the exhibit to match the gown she wore; he knew the one from the antique jewellery collection being exhibited tonight by Falco Diamonds. He wore the matching crown on top of his own head, chosen weeks ago by his personal styling team.

As he downed the remnants of his glass of champagne and gestured for a refill, his eyes roamed the cavernous museum hall once more, taking only a few moments before finding the object of his thoughts.

She stood under one of the domes at the centre of the nave, her white mask glittering under the light show that had begun on the ceiling and upper walls. Utterly still, she gazed up at the cascade of blooms and stars that pulsated and blossomed above them. Around her, countless A-list attendees schmoozed and networked, but her gaze remained focused upon the lights above as though she were in a trance.

Or perhaps, just like him, she wished to be anywhere else but here.

It was easy to imagine slipping over there and introducing himself with his usual charm. He would tell her the story behind the inspiration between their headpieces, his own based on a coronet worn by the King of old Sardegna and hers the beautiful princess who became his queen. He would compliment her dress as he gazed into her eyes; they had seemed dark and soulful from what he could make out under the mask she wore. From there, the game of seduction would begin and it would be only a matter of time before he was peeling her out of that blue lace and she was crying out his name.

He cleared his suddenly dry throat, shocked at how quickly his thoughts had descended into depravity. His libido had barely stirred all evening as his four beautiful dates had made a show of flirting and touching him at every opportunity. He hadn't bedded a woman in months, hadn't felt genuine interest in even longer. As if to prove his point, his last remaining neglected date finally reached her limit and sighed loudly before stalking away in search of more attentive entertainment. The distraction caused him to lose track of the blue-lace beauty once more and he cursed under his breath.

'Tristan, why am I not surprised that you chose a crown?'

His entire body stiffening at the familiar feminine voice, he turned to find scarlet-tipped nails clawed upon his white tuxedo sleeve. His ex-lover Gabriela, owner of said claws, leaned in for the customary Argentinian greeting of one single kiss upon his right cheek. Before he had a moment to prepare, he was engulfed in her cloying scent. A scent that had once seemed seductive and warm, but now served only as a reminder that the prettiest flowers were quite often the ones that held the most venom.

'You managed to snag an invite.' He smiled, steeling

his jaw against any hint of the anger that seeing her here at his event provoked in him. 'What a surprise.'

'Surprise? Don't tell me Vic hasn't spoken to you yet?' She sighed, turning just as they were joined by another person he would rather claw his own eyes out than speak to tonight. His cousin.

'He's impossible to track down.' Victor Falco laughed, the humour not quite meeting his eyes as he looked anxiously between Gabriela and the man they'd both publicly humiliated just a few short months before. 'I was wondering who had selected the King's crown piece. I should have known it was you.'

'I thought the sapphires would bring out my big, beautiful eyes,' Tristan gritted.

'Bring out your massive ego more like,' Victor teased, but the once easy joking between them was no more, and so the barb only rubbed.

Tristan resisted the urge to growl, taking a sip of champagne. 'How could anyone have an ego with you two always nearby, primed to kick them back to earth?'

Victor opened his mouth as if to retaliate, only for the tension to be broken by the return of one of Tristan's dates, who insisted upon hand-feeding him a chocolate-covered strawberry. A second date appeared toting a fresh flute of champagne, both women leaning in to drape themselves across his arms.

'Good to see you're not too heartbroken, anyway.' Gabriela let out a delicate sniff of disbelief.

'Amazing what inheriting control over a multibillion-dollar corporation will do for one's sex appeal.'

'Charming as always, Tristan.' Victor frowned repressively. 'I had thought recent events might have made you more serious.'

'Which events are you referring to, *primo*?' Tristan said darkly, his body tensing at the disapproving tone of his cousin's voice. 'The fact that my mother chose *me* as her replacement on the board…or the fact that I had to take that seat under a cloud of scandal caused by you?'

The air between them seemed to crackle with a sudden intensity. Victor was only a couple of months older than him, hardly the voice of wisdom. They had been more than family. Tristan had once counted him his closest friend. But at some point in the past year, Victor had grown increasingly distant towards him. And a large part of the reason for that distance currently stood between them with a shiny diamond ring on her finger and her hand delicately cradling her stomach. Her very obviously *rounded* stomach.

'I see congratulations are in order,' he said, pasting on a serene smile even as his gut roiled.

'I thought Victor had already told you.' Gabriela breathed the incredulous words, which seemed surprisingly genuine, while Victor simply gritted his jaw and brooded.

'How could I have told him when he avoids me at all costs?'

'Well, now I know.' Tristan shrugged, downing the remainder of his champagne. 'I see a large diamond ring as well, so it seems my cousin was an easier man to pressure than me. Bravo.'

Gabriela inhaled a sharp breath, painted lips parting in a mixture of shock and anger. Tristan felt another uncomfortable twist in his gut as he watched Victor lean down to his fiancée, touching a hand possessively to his unborn child as he whispered something into her ear.

With a final sharp look in his direction, she turned and walked away. Disappointingly, Victor did not follow.

'This is neither the time nor the place for our personal issues.' Victor muttered angrily. 'This exhibit honours our family's legacy and you show up in typical playboy style with an orgy of partners.'

'I will not apologise for the fact that I am in high demand,' Tristan felt his mouth tighten with a cruel smile. 'Since you so selfishly took yourself off the market, my workload has doubled.'

His cousin shook his head, eyes narrowing. 'Your mother told me what you promised her, along with taking the helm.'

'That's my business.'

'So it's true?' Victor's brows rose. 'You're finally going to settle down with a wife and family?'

'I'm going to give my mother the grand wedding she craves, with the perfect bride.' Tristan tugged at his collar, feeling it tighten around his neck like a noose. He inhaled and pasted on his most rake-like smirk. 'I never promised anything about settling down.'

'You've already found the lucky lady in question?'

'You seem very interested in my love life, cousin; have you already tired of the last fiancée you stole from me?'

There was no trace of mirth in Victor's eyes as he stepped forward, closing the small space between them. 'You weren't engaged. I've tried to explain countless times. Gabi and I never set out to hurt you.'

For a brief moment, he imagined the satisfaction he would get from punching his cousin squarely in the jaw. But ultimately he decided that the sight of Victor clutching at his own broken nose, while highly deserved and overdue, would not be worth the ruination of his pristine white tux.

'As I've said, I'm over it,' Tristan snapped, pulling his arm away. 'Now, if you'll excuse me, I have a fiancée to track down.'

He walked away, leaving his cousin stuttering with outrage while he moved along the lavish gallery under the pretence of greeting the other guests, but, really, he was hunting. His skin vibrated with awareness as he scanned the crowd gathered around the cases of priceless jewels, his steps slow and measured. A shimmering cloud of blue caught his attention like a moonbeam in the darkness and he looked up, catching sight of her in the reflection of the glass case in front of him. He looked over his shoulder, just in time to see her slide sideways behind a mannequin.

Interesting.

Testing his theory, he moved along the crowd to another case, and sure enough a shimmer of blue followed a few moments later, partially obscured by a large wall of diamond-encrusted flowers. Curiosity burning now, he continued to amble slowly along the crowded floor, calmly waving off the calls of attention from various business contacts. A few moments were all he would need to ascertain who she was and assuage this fixation. Then he could return to the event clear-minded and hopefully with a plan in place for his mystery lady later tonight.

His pulse quickening, he made sure she still tailed him as he made a series of turns until he reached an empty hallway. There, he slipped through a balcony door…and waited.

CHAPTER TWO

SHE HAD LOST HIM.

Nina looked from one edge of the darkened terrace to the other, squinting in the low light. She'd spent the past hour discreetly tailing Tristan Falco from afar, waiting for an opportunity to sidetrack him and make her move. For someone who had avoided the paddock as a new owner under the guise of being far too busy, the infuriating man had a remarkable flare for striking up a conversation with every passer-by with a pulse. Not only that, it was very clear that he was hosting the entire event.

Her irritation had grown as she'd watched him glide effortlessly between the influential guests that filled the long gallery, a grand crown atop his head as if he owned the entire museum. Which he did not. She had already done a quick search on her phone to check. The Falco family were probably the biggest benefactors, with their historic jewellery and gem collection being one of the grandest exhibits in Europe.

She had already been exhausted after the weekend of racing events, followed by *that* press conference and the subsequent mad dash to get here, and she was now feeling the effects. Her insides felt too tight, her thoughts moving too fast. Events like this served only to remind her of her childhood in Monte Carlo, back when the Roux name had been a golden ticket to every elite event in the city. Her mother had wanted to parade her only daughter around in all the latest fashions like a doll, then grown furious when Nina had struggled to behave correctly. She'd been told she was too sensitive. Too different. *Too much.*

But, for Nina, the high-society world had been what felt like too much. The scratchy clothing, the dancing, the unwritten rules, the constant noise and banal chat. The only way she'd managed to cope was by zoning out to the happy place in her mind, imagining she was navigating the trickiest chicane in the Circuit de Monaco or flying along the final straight to victory at the Autodromo Accardi.

On the track she wasn't too sensitive or weird or wrong. Her attention to detail and her immovable focus were what made her a damn great driver. The only time she'd ever felt *right* was behind the wheel of a racing car with her aunt Lola's words ringing in her mind, to ask herself not *if* she could become a world champion but *when*. She refused to lose that determination and let a bunch of clueless men in suits break her down. She wouldn't let them win.

A balmy breeze blew across her flushed cheeks and she prayed she wouldn't cry. She ached to remove the false lashes on her lids, feeling rather like a prisoner in a cage of modern beauty standards. The haute couture gown was too heavy and felt like sandpaper on her skin. Bracing her hands on the stone balustrade, she drew a hearty breath and growled with frustration, letting go of some of her tightly held restraint in the solitude of the dark terrace, adding a string of curses under her breath for good measure.

'Looking for someone?'

Nina jumped, peering over her shoulder to find a man looming in a shadowy alcove beside the doorway she'd just exited through. A loud squeak escaped her lips as her body seemed to react of its own accord, her hands slipping on the balcony ledge, sending her sliding sideways until her hip bone thumped painfully into the cold stone.

When she looked up, the man had moved out of the shadows, a familiar sapphire-encrusted crown glinting atop his head and white tuxedo jacket glowing in the moonlight.

Falco.

Her eyes narrowed upon the man she'd been seeking for much longer than one night, the man who had hijacked all of her plans and taken her dreams, stamping them under his shiny billionaire shoes. He stared at her, eyes hooded and the hint of a smirk dancing upon his full lips. He really was sinfully handsome, for a spineless jerk.

'Why yes, as a matter of fact.' She stepped forward. 'I'm here to—'

'Take off your mask,' he interjected silkily.

Nina inhaled sharply. 'Excuse me? That's not exactly—'

'Take off your mask…*por favor*.'

'Do you always bark commands at strangers in the dark by way of greeting?' she snapped.

'Only if said stranger has unashamedly stalked me from the moment she arrived at this event.'

She felt her cheeks heat, another flare of irritation at herself for how utterly terribly this plan was going.

'Did you hope for me not to notice your eyes on me, *belleza*?' He took another step forward. 'Or is this all part of your game for me this evening? Because I'll admit I'm hoping for the latter.'

Belleza? Her game? What kind of riddles was this man talking in? She opened her mouth to speak, only to feel a warm fingertip press ever so slightly against her lips. Eyes wide, she fought the urge to bite it off.

'There is no need to be embarrassed,' he continued, oblivious to the danger his digit was in. 'I admire a woman who sees what she wants and tracks it down un-apologetically. I noticed you from the moment that you stepped onto the carpet outside. I found myself...irre-vocably intrigued. I know everyone here. But you are a mystery.'

'Everyone here is wearing a mask,' she pointed out. 'Everyone except you, Your Highness.'

His smile widened at the sarcastic honorific, his ego clearly enjoying a thorough stroke. Her mind's eye im-mediately conjured an image of herself smacking that smile from his pompous, arrogant, perfectly sculpted lips. She paused at that last descriptor, wondering why look-ing at those lips made her feel too warm all of a sudden. He noticed where her gaze had wandered and his smirk turned utterly sinful.

'Take off the mask,' he murmured again. 'Or are you waiting for me to remove it for you?'

'I dare you to try.' She spoke through gritted teeth.

'Do you realise your eyes practically glowed just now?' he mused, pursing his lips as he trailed a fingertip along the edge of her mask. 'Quite an achievement, consider-ing they are such a deep brown that they're practically black. Like tourmaline...or the rarest obsidian.'

The sudden bubble of laughter that escaped Nina's

throat took her by surprise, but once she released it she could no longer hold back.

'Something amusing?' he asked, his charming mask slipping ever so slightly.

'It's just…the pretty Spanish endearments, describing eyeballs like rare gems et cetera. Do you speak to every woman you meet with such flowery words?'

'Are you trying to puncture my ego on purpose?' He feigned injury, pressing a tanned hand to his chest. 'Or is this how you flirt?'

'I think you know that I'm not here for vacuous flirtation.'

'No, I can tell that you're different. You're here with a purpose, aren't you?' he said softly. 'How lucky that we find ourselves having a rare and magical moment on this deserted terrace.'

'Of course.' She let out another tinny breath of laughter. 'I'm different. I'm *special*.'

'You are…certainly fascinating,' he countered. 'And not at all what I expected to find when I lured you out here.'

'I was not *lured*, I followed you.' She paused, a blush climbing her cheeks at the immediate expression of victory on his smug face. Damn him. Fully tired of this *game*, as he'd called it, she swept the white mask from her face and waited for his immediate recognition and apology. None came.

His eyes roamed her face, the tense silence that followed making her feel as if she were under a microscope. When he finally spoke, his voice held an odd rasp, as though it vibrated directly out from the depths of his chest.

'*There* you are, *belleza*.'

* * *

There was something familiar about her. Something he couldn't quite put his finger on. As though they had met before, but he knew all too well that if they had, he would have remembered her. He was not a man prone to fascination. He had become jaded with the frequency of intimate situations such as this, of people practically throwing themselves in his path once they had heard the rumours of his sensual prowess. Rumours that had begun during a particularly intense time in his life and had never quite left him.

Of course, many of the things that had been said about him were completely true. But that was beside the point.

Perhaps that was why this delectable woman was making him feel as if his chest were suddenly too tight beneath his skin. She was young and beautiful and yet she seemed entirely unimpressed by him, almost irritated by his silky words and practised compliments. It was refreshing… And did absolutely nothing to calm the raging heat that had been steadily building within him from the moment he'd seen her delicate features up close.

Without the mask, the full perfection of her face had assaulted him, those focused obsidian eyes perfectly framed by dark brows and delicately rounded cheeks. Her lips were lush and full, certainly kissable, but it was the small dimple in her chin that caught his attention most. A stubborn chin, currently tilted up at him as if to emphasise that very fact.

She hadn't made any move to push him away, or go back inside, so he knew that her protestations were likely a part of her gambit. Perhaps she had heard the rumours that he was seeking a wife and was fearlessly offering herself up for the cause.

He would reward her bravery, quite thoroughly if given the chance. Images of peeling her out of that sparkling blue confection sprang to his mind, not doing anything to help the rather *pressing* situation threatening below his belt.

'Nothing to say?' she asked, a strangely expectant expression on her pixie-like face. The make-up she wore was pronounced, too pronounced for his liking. He had the sudden urge to see her freshly washed, scrubbed free of any excess. In his shower preferably after a night of vigorous lovemaking.

'I would offer up more compliments, but you've made it clear you have no need for them. Instead, let's talk about why you're here,' he said simply.

'I would think it's quite obvious why I'm here,' she answered softly. 'You're a notoriously difficult man to pin down.'

'And you believe that you are the woman for the job?'

'I wouldn't have come all this way if I didn't. Of course, I'm quite busy and would have preferred for you to come to me…for us to have discussed this in a more appropriate setting. But this will have to do.'

Tristan smiled, surprised at how very much he was enjoying her directness. For a man in urgent need of a fiancée to put his mother's matchmaking to rest, he couldn't do much better than this woman if he'd tried. He wouldn't do something so foolish as to actually *marry* her, of course. But he could enjoy exploring this hypothetical negotiation of theirs for a little longer.

'A more formal setting?' he asked silkily. 'The nearest courthouse perhaps?'

'There's no need to rush straight to legalities. I heard you were a more skilled negotiator than that?' She looked away, a small frown appearing between her brows. 'I'm not interested in a public spectacle. I followed you here tonight to discuss the benefits for us both in getting this done quickly.'

Again, words left him for a moment. He simply stared, utterly baffled at the rush of exhilaration coursing through him. She was speaking of marriage, for goodness' sake. He should be running a mile. Just what kind of spell had she put over him?

'Are you expecting a proposal right here on this terrace?'

She frowned at his words. 'At the very least I'm expecting an attempt at negotiation. A display of your notorious skills before you allow me to walk away. Because, trust me, I am fully prepared to do that.'

'You would deny yourself the experience of my…*skills* so easily?' He stepped forward, close enough that the skirt of her dress pooled against his knees. 'Are you not curious to see me in action?'

Her eyes widened, her neck lengthening prettily as she looked up at him through hooded lashes. Ah yes, the guile of innocence… Not one of his favourite performances but one that he could appreciate, nonetheless. Here she was waylaying him with the hopes of dazzling him into a proposal and when all else failed she would play the naïve damsel, completely unaware of her sensual prowess.

'I'm sure you're quite impressive,' she said breathlessly, her eyes still trained on his lips. 'I don't want to walk away, allow me to be perfectly clear on that point. But I know that you'd be a fool to let me go. I know how valuable I am.'

'Like a rare gem, in fact?'

Her nostrils flared, one pointed finger rising to poke

him in the chest. 'Don't mock me, Falco. I'm not here to play.'

He grabbed her hand, holding it captive against the spot where his heart beat frantically against his ribcage. Those obsidian eyes glowed up at him once again with irritation and he was done for. He'd give her whatever she wanted just to see that passion in another, more intimate setting.

'*Playing* is the best way to negotiate, *cariña*.' He laid a single tentative kiss against the inside of the wrist he held captive. 'It's my favourite way, in fact. But we will need to take this meeting somewhere more private if I hope to give you my full attention.'

'Somewhere private,' she repeated slowly, her eyes glued to the point where his lips still pressed against her skin. 'Okay…'

'I can have my driver meet us out front in five minutes,' he murmured, urgency rapidly taking control of his libido as he slowly drew her closer. 'And I can have you naked and calling out my name in ten.'

She looked up at him, and he caught a brief view of her eyes widening in surprise before he lowered his lips to hers. The heat of her mouth against his was like a fire in his blood and he suddenly doubted if they would make it to the car at all. It felt like a lifetime since he'd experienced this kind of unbridled desire for a woman.

He paused, realising she hadn't moved since he'd kissed her—in fact, she was as still as a statue. He moved to pull back, only to hear the smallest moan escape her lips. Her hands slid up to wrap around his neck and suddenly she was kissing him back frantically, albeit with very little control or finesse.

A roar of victory coursed through his veins and he

scooped her up, pressing her back against the stone balustrade and tilting his head to gain deeper access. He needed to taste every inch of her and have her do the same to him. He needed her wild for him. As though she heard his thoughts, her tongue delved into his mouth in a perfect imitation of his own, giving just as good as she got. Just as he'd thought, she was a little firebrand. *Dios*, but he was half tempted to take her right here on the balcony, no questions asked. He didn't even know her name.

Perhaps he'd keep it that way, keep the air of mystery between them for tonight, then once they'd both been thoroughly satisfied he'd deal with the aftermath. The real world could wait. Everything could wait.

Vaguely, he was aware of a sudden flash of white light. His mystery woman froze in his arms and for a moment he wondered if lightning had struck. How very poetic that would be. But as a second burst of light surrounded them, his sex-addled mind finally processed that it was the unmistakable flash of a camera bulb. Rearing back, he turned just as a third flash bathed the terrace with white light and briefly illuminated a young woman holding up a phone on the next terrace.

'Mierda,' he growled, gently lowering his equally kiss-addled companion down to her feet before moving quickly towards the iron railing that separated the two balconies. The woman with the phone had already begun running in the opposite direction, but if they moved quickly his security team might catch up to her. He had to, if he wanted any chance of stopping those photos from getting out. His promise to his mother ringing in his ears, he made the call and felt his chest release slightly when he was assured that his team were on the case. It would be fine, everything would be fine and he

would still be free to continue exploring his little inter-lude with the woman in blue.

That particular thought renewing his lust, he spun around to find the terrace was now empty and all trace of his mystery woman gone.

CHAPTER THREE

NINA UPPED HER maximum speed on the treadmill, pushing herself into a sprint. She was all alone in the Falco Roux private fitness facility, with most of the team taking a rest day. With the idea of rest being utterly laughable, she'd chosen to complete a punishing session of strength and mobility work. She pushed herself past her usual limits, making the excuse that she needed to get some heavy cardio in after a long night travelling back to Monaco from Paris. In truth, she was simply trying to take a break from the constant notifications on her phone and the threat of Astrid Lewis appearing like an anxious PR damage-control fairy behind her at any moment.

She had messed up, royally.

The photos of her and Tristan Falco kissing had appeared on a gossip site late last night and had spread like wildfire across social media within hours. Even with all the money that Tristan Falco had, no one could stop the power of the Internet. They were the top trending topic on most social media sites and if he hadn't known who she was last night, he certainly did now with headlines like *The Roux-mours Are True* and *Falco's Driving Her Crazy* titillating the masses. She'd stopped looking after the first few, utterly unable to stare at another image of her one moment of weakness.

She wasn't even quite sure how it had happened. She wasn't the best judge of context most of the time, but add in the kind of intense charm that Tristan Falco exuded and, quite simply, her mental processing had been compromised. He'd mistaken her for someone else, that much was for sure with the kind of things he'd been saying. But who he might have mistaken her for was an utter mystery. She had gone over and over their conversation in her mind, trying to pick at which point things had begun to unravel past her control.

Her mind conjured up an HD slow-motion reel of the moment his lips had touched the inside of her wrist and she was shocked at the immediate flush of warmth that swirled behind her bellybutton.

Yeah, that had been the start of it, all right.

One thing was for sure, the rumours about ultimate playboy Tristan Falco were not at all false. And apparently, she had come perilously close to experiencing his skills first-hand. Even the small taste she had received had felt like being hooked up to a live electricity source. He was brutally intense, and she had never reacted to anyone physically like that. Not a single person.

It was why she'd never felt any urge to go on dates, or pursue flirtations with the many guys who'd expressed intense curiosity about thawing the so-called Elite One Ice Princess. It wasn't an act or a measure of self-preservation; she simply wasn't interested. She was always in control and she never forgot who she was and what she wanted.

Well, almost never.

Punching the speed even higher, she ran and ran until she thought she might come close to pulling a muscle and then she stopped and cooled down, staring out at the view of the harbour for a long time before forcing herself to go and shower. She lingered longer than usual under the hot spray, once again feeling lucky that she was the only female driver on the team and had an entire bathroom to herself. She'd managed to avoid the rest of the team since arriving at their relatively deserted headquarters, but she was no fool, she knew that she couldn't avoid them for ever. Any respect she'd had as a driver was now compromised, with her name being dragged through the mud.

The idea that she'd been seen *kissing* their new playboy owner… Scandal like that was bound to cause trouble. Would all of the work she'd done to be seen as an equal to the male drivers be reset and disregarded? Reputations were everything in this high-drama sport and she had just painted a target on her back. She'd already been branded as a pay driver, a term given to minimise the talent of drivers who were related to their team owner. But she'd proven herself time and time again as she'd risen up through the ranks, showing her skill while still acknowledging the enormous privilege she'd experienced as a member of the Roux family.

There was no fancy term she knew of for a driver who was perceived to be sleeping with the team owner, but she was pretty sure the public would come up with plenty. None of which would be remotely complimentary to her.

With a single kiss, Tristan Falco had possibly landed the final nail in the coffin of her short-lived career. Or perhaps she had done that herself by allowing her temper to take hold and travelling to Paris to confront him incognito. He hadn't forced himself on her after all. She could have stopped him at any moment. Much as she'd like to pretend that she hadn't been in full possession of her senses, in fact the opposite was true. A handsome man had shown her the slightest bit of attention and she'd melted into his embrace like butter. She'd been painfully aware of every touch, every look, every slide of his lips against hers.

She was twenty-three and hadn't experienced a true kiss of passion until last night. She wasn't embarrassed about that fact—her lack of experience wasn't something she thought about often at all. It was easy not to think about sex when you didn't particularly feel or engage in sexual attraction. But with Falco, she'd felt far too much. Now she wondered, if they hadn't been interrupted, would she have stopped him at all?

Her nipples pebbled painfully and she blamed the air conditioning, shaking off her thoughts as she stepped out of the shower. Her reflection in the mirror was a cruel reminder of the real reason Falco hadn't recognised her when she'd removed her mask last night. Her black hair hung limply to her shoulders, not quite curly but not quite straight either. Dark circles underlined her red-rimmed eyes, framed by a face most in the media had delighted in describing as plain and uninteresting.

Most people outside the media described her that way too. They seemed to make a point to comment on her supposed lack of femininity, analysing her ungraceful gait and her far too casual dress sense. Traits that the men in her industry generally did not have to accentuate or play up to. She'd long ago stopped bothering to challenge their boring ideals.

Still, she couldn't help but wonder would the playboy find her so *fascinating* if he could see her now? She pushed the thought away, reminding herself that Falco's opinion of her did not matter. What mattered most right now was to try and figure out a way to see if anything in this workplace nightmare was salvageable. Perhaps she could use this to get her contract fully cancelled, maybe get in ahead of the news to one of the other teams, offer to sign a scandalously low contract with them... Even as the thought crossed her mind she pushed it away, knowing that the legal ramifications would bankrupt her if she tried to do that.

'You *are* fascinating,' she told her reflection in the mirror. 'Fascinatingly gifted at tanking your own career.'

A knock on the door startled her out of her thoughts and she rushed to wrap a towel around herself before answering, betting it was Sophie come to chastise her for working too hard. It took her a moment of stunned blinking to realise that the handsome blond besuited man standing on the other side was not her trainer, but Tristan Falco. With a squeak, she threw the door closed again.

'I've already seen you, so there's no point in hiding. We need to talk.'

She held her breath, pressing herself back against the cool tiled wall and fighting the urge to groan at her own terrible life choices. Realistically, how long could she hide in here before he gave up? Her gym bag with all of her things was on the other side of the door and he knew she was in here. She wasn't the only one who'd been dealing with a personal PR nightmare for the past twelve hours. He hadn't come all this way for a casual chat.

As if to prove that point, he rapped on the door once again. 'Nina. We don't have time for this. I'm here to discuss urgent matters.'

Her name in his silky voice sent a shiver down her spine—of trepidation, she was sure. This man was her team owner, her boss's boss. The person who controlled every cent that kept the racing team she loved alive. Like it or not, she had to at least try to plead her case to him. She had to fight.

'Do you plan to hide in there all day?' His voice was a rough rasp on the other side of the door, his impatience clear. 'Your little photo stunt in Paris has created a situation that requires immediate action.'

Irritation won out over modesty and before she knew it, Nina was flinging open the door to face him once more. '*My* little stunt?' she fumed. 'I'm not the one who was comparing my eyes to diamonds and bragging about my *skills*.'

His eyes briefly lowered to take in her towel-clad form before his jaw set and he met her gaze head-on. 'I didn't know who you were.'

'That says more about you than me, considering you've owned my family's racing team for more than a year.' She ignored the wave of embarrassment threatening to drown her and focused on her anger and indignation. 'I never court the press and I had nothing to do with that photo. I followed you because you are impossible to meet with and I needed to convince you to cancel my contract. That's the only reason I went to Paris.'

Falco's eyes narrowed, a hand absent-mindedly rising to scrub along the shadow of stubble along his jawline. 'Did you kiss me in the hope I would fire you?'

'No.' Nina gasped, her cheeks heating. 'And you kissed *me*.'

His eyes darkened. 'It's irrelevant who initiated it… because your contract is not up for negotiation. Surely you know that. You're the only remaining family member working in a team that thrives on superstition. A team that I've been trying to rescue and bring back to glory, but been met with public resistance at every turn. I may not be a racing expert, but I've done my research. The only thing that has *not* been against us is having you locked into a five-year term.'

Nina closed her eyes, knowing that he was right. Knowing that the superstition the Roux fans held was ridiculous, but that didn't make it any less real. It had been the only reason that had kept her here over the past couple of years since her brother had brought their family's finances to the brink of collapse. They had only ever been without a Roux on the team for a handful of seasons, and each one of those had been plagued with crashes and incidents bringing them nothing but ruin.

'Perhaps you should have thought of that before you signed Apollo Accardi instead of promoting your hardest-working and best-performing reserve driver.' Nina stood up tall, wishing she'd at least been wearing her gym shorts for this altercation. But she was here now, so she might as well say her piece.

He tilted his head to the side, surveying her with keen interest. 'You expected the promotion to fall to you instead of a former world champion with years of track experience?'

'I expected at the very least an attempt at showing me some respect, some form of communication to explain why the usual protocol was being changed to make way for a completely new driver mid-season instead of the obvious replacement, yes.' Nina stood her ground, ignoring the flash of awareness in her gut that she felt with his eyes on her. 'But it really shouldn't have surprised me, considering the way you do business.'

Tristan tried to ignore the way Nina's cheeks flushed as her temper rose. The woman was furious with him, that much was abundantly clear. Suddenly her aloof attitude from the night before made infinitely more sense. She'd been in a mask and haute couture, but as he'd surmised—scrubbed clean, she was still strikingly beautiful.

Pulling his attention back to the conversation at hand, he tried to resolve his unusually scattered thoughts. He'd come here to ascertain if her appearance last night had been with the intent to sabotage the team, or deliberately cause a scandal. Now that he was relatively sure it had been a misunderstanding on both of their parts, he had an even more difficult job to do—convince her to help him.

'Exactly how do I do business, Miss Roux?' He purred, 'Please, enlighten me.'

'You buy up failing companies and sell them off, with very little close contact or sentiment,' she responded easily. 'That tactic might work in a hedge fund or a faceless corporation, but it won't work here. You may have put your name up front, but Roux Racing was built on passion and loyalty.'

Passion. Loyalty. The way she said the words with such conviction, it was clear she truly believed them. Perhaps in this case, she was right. 'My ownership style is not why you weren't consulted on the Accardi deal. We secured the signing of the decade that will give us a psychological and strategic edge against our biggest competitor. Surprise was essential.'

She didn't answer him immediately, instead she grabbed her gym bag and disappeared momentarily into a screened-off area, no doubt to change into some clothing. He took the chance to steer the conversation to his ultimate goal. To the reason why he'd chosen to race here himself today, instead of sending his PR team in his place to clean up the mess. Tristan Falco never missed an opportunity to capitalise on a business opportunity, and Nina might not know it yet, but their kiss had unwittingly become the answer to both of their problems.

'Speaking of passion, Astrid has informed me that the photo of us kissing has officially gone viral.' He waited a moment, taking a seat on the long bench that lined the wall of the dressing room.

She reappeared from behind the screen in a pair of white gym shorts and a loose-fitting Falco Roux polo shirt. 'You say that like it's a positive thing.'

'Actually, my team seems to think it's the answer to all of our PR issues.'

Nina immediately stiffened and shook her head, jet-black waves shaking gently with the movement. 'For you, perhaps. I'm sure the comments about me aren't quite the same.'

He slid his phone out of his pocket, pulling up the curated list of comments that Astrid had forwarded him an hour before. They included gushing viral clips from critics and romantics and superstitious old-timer racing buffs alike. The list also included an unheard-of increase in the sale of Falco Roux merchandise, stock and race tickets over the past twelve hours, which was predicted only to grow as the news continued to spread. He watched as Nina read through the data, her keen eyes rising back to his with stunned understanding.

'These comments…they're all positive. Happy, even.'

'Apparently the fans love us together. And the stockholders love it when the fans are happy. This is great for the team.'

She crossed her arms. 'So this is why you came here. To ask me to go along with a lie for publicity?'

Tristan crossed his arms. 'I expected a true business

mind would see this as the golden bargaining opportunity that it is.'

'You're suddenly open to negotiation?' She paused, one cynical brow quirking.

'My offer is simple. Stay. Play the paddock romance out until the end of the season and you're free to go.'

'Just like that?' She moved to the end of the bench, her hands twisting over and over in a strangely entrancing motion. When her eyes met his, they were stark. 'What if I say no?'

Tristan paused, measuring his words carefully before he spoke. 'If you try to leave for another team, then this goes exactly the same way it has gone for every other driver who has tried to break their contract. No special treatment.'

Nina closed her eyes. She knew what that meant. Legal battles, public defamation, and her reputation as a spoilt princess would become even more prominent. But there was still a chance she'd be bankrupt even if she saw the full contract out. Reserve drivers' wages didn't pay nearly enough to cover the her annual racing licence fees and other costs, not now that she was maintaining the cost of running the girls academy fully by herself. She'd have to downsize, maybe even close down for good and disappoint all of the talented young girls around the world who looked up to her and relied on her guidance.

Nina ran a hand through her hair. 'So my choice is to stay put for the next two years and waste more time as a reserve, or compromise my integrity by playing the part of the billionaire owner's girlfriend for the next few months. That's great, just great.'

'Fiancée,' Tristan said silkily, his eyes pinning her in place.

'What? Why?' Nina felt her words tumbling over her tongue but was powerless to stop them. Nothing about this interaction was anywhere close to being in her comfort zone and it just seemed to be getting worse with every new piece of information he divulged.

'My mother has recently been pressuring me to marry, and until last night I was in the market to fulfil that wish. If we go ahead with encouraging this PR fire for the next few months, it'll give me time without her breathing down my neck. I need it to benefit me as well.'

The mention of his *needs* made her breath catch and her traitorous imagination run wild with images of what such needs might entail. She pushed them away, trying to focus her business mind on the offer as a whole. Trying to make sure she wasn't being led astray.

'If I say yes, what would this deal entail?' she asked slowly, nibbling on the edge of a fingernail. 'Just holding hands in public every now and then?'

'Initially, we would just continue to stir speculation, capitalise on the current interest by being seen often together in the public eye.'

'And once that part is done?' she pressed.

'We would eventually announce our engagement and use our individual images to benefit one another: my presence at more of your races and your presence in my upcoming Falco Diamonds centenary campaign, that kind of thing. I will also require your attendance as my fiancée at my mother's wedding in Buenos Aires, but we'll be there for the Argentinian race, anyway. Don't worry; behind closed doors, this relationship will be purely platonic. It'll be safer for us both that way.'

'So it wouldn't be a big commitment, then. Timewise, I mean?' she asked, mulling over the potential pitfalls and struggling to find any that weren't in favour of agreeing to this mad plan. 'With your decision to bring in a completely new driver mid-season, I won't have much spare time, Mr Falco.'

'You'll make time for me, *Nina*,' he said calmly, without missing a beat.

Nina ignored the thoroughly inappropriate pulse of awareness that thrummed through her at his words. 'With all due respect, *Tristan*, as a professional driver, I have a very demanding job.'

'Duly noted, but as my *fiancée* you will go where I go. Starting right now.' He eyed her Falco Roux polo shirt. 'You might want to change. I've made a lunch reservation at Blu Mont.'

'I haven't actually agreed to anything yet.' She looked down at her shorts and running shoes. 'And besides, I find it hard to see how anyone with a pair of eyes will believe that you're planning to marry *me* whether I'm in my uniform or a ballgown.'

He stepped closer. 'You'd better start convincing yourself, then. Because once you agree, this deal begins immediately.'

CHAPTER FOUR

IF HE'D THOUGHT the sight of Nina braless in her slightly translucent Falco Roux polo shirt had been a distraction, nothing could have prepared him for how she looked in a pair of jeans. She'd brushed her hair out so that it flowed around her face and donned a simple white T-shirt and red leather jacket. It was laughable that some of the media articles he'd read had referred to her as plain—considering his blood pressure hadn't quite stabilised since he'd walked in on her in nothing but a towel.

Some casual lunches and sightings of them together in public would be just enough to add more fuel to the fire before they officially confirmed their relationship to the press at a more strategic time. Astrid had been specific in her directions, and he trusted his PR manager implicitly, which was why he'd told her the truth. She was the best in the business, and if anyone could use this situation to their benefit, it was her.

He knew all too well that the key to selling a narrative was in the details, and so as he directed Nina to precede him onto the exclusive restaurant's very publicly visible seafront terrace he made sure to touch her elbow and guide her with his hand in the small of her back. Once she was seated, he trailed his fingers along the back of her chair, leaning down to lay a gentle caress upon her cheek before taking his own seat.

As he predicted, she was a little less relaxed about their ruse, those expressive eyes throwing daggers at him across the table every couple of moments as she intently focused upon her menu and not him.

'Have I done something to upset you, *mi cielo*?' he asked, reaching a hand out to cover hers with his own. She pulled away, hastily taking a long sip of water.

'The photographer isn't here yet,' she said quietly, returning her attention to the menu.

'This isn't just about appearing in more photos. Everyone who sees us should be under no illusion that we are an item.'

'These people are all looking at you, they barely even know who I am. Nor do they particularly care.'

'You're the daughter of one of the most famous families in Monaco.' He frowned, noting the way her hands anxiously twirled her napkin around her index finger.

'Infamous,' she corrected. 'We fell out of favour with the public long ago, as you well know.'

He knew a lot, of course. As part of acquiring a company in debt, it was his job to dig deep and know everything about what had got them there before he committed and planned his strategy. He knew about her great-grandfather's brilliance as an auto engineer and how he'd founded and ruled his empire with an iron fist, raising an army of his own children to carry on his legacy with their innovative designs and racing wins. Her own father had been a truly terrible businessman plagued with a catalogue of personal vices, and her aunt, Lola Roux, had been a racing legend in her own right before she'd died in a tragically ironic car accident.

Most recently, her reckless brother, Alain, had been happily draining the last of their funds for his lavish lifestyle, ending with him losing everything to Tristan in a high-stakes poker match. Said poker match was how Tristan had inadvertently ended up in his current position as the new team owner. What had happened, and the deal he'd made afterwards with Alain to try and save the Roux company, was not public knowledge and iron-clad non-disclosure agreements had been signed, but still he wondered just how much Nina knew, and if she potentially shared any of the vices of her more scandalous family members, other than the obvious thrill for speed.

'You believe your family's financial downfall has made you less interesting to the press?' he asked. 'That's not how it works.'

'My mother was the most in demand with the press, but, of course, they took an interest in me for a while once I was old enough and began attending parties.' Nina took another sip of water, pursing her lips into a thin line. 'They would take strategic shots of me at bad angles to make it look like I was some kind of party girl. Like mother, like daughter. But I didn't want to be a society princess. I preferred working, being on the track. Once I stopped attending any events or socialising outside work at all, they switched to the unlikable, plain Jane, ice-princess angle. Quite predictable really, yet I much prefer it.'

He surveyed the measured lack of interest on her face, and the way she pressed her fingertips down flat into the tablecloth. She spoke of the press's interest in her calmly, but he had always been an expert in reading people. Everything about this bothered her. The press, public opinion... He knew the look of someone who had suffered.

But he would not have expected that of the spoiled society princess everyone had described to him.

He had spent his entire journey this morning from Paris to Monte Carlo trawling through her social media and various news articles. To learn about her, not for personal reasons, but in an effort to gauge how he might fix the PR nightmare he'd realised was about to unfold.

There had of course been coverage of her academy successes and the handful of Elite One Premio races she had taken part in as a reserve driver.

But most of the articles he'd seen had focused on a few years in her late teens, most specifically upon a photo shoot she had taken part in a few years back. A rather risqué photo shoot, by most people's standards, and it had shocked him to see that the brand involved was Roux Motors' now defunct luxury car brand.

The New Generation Never Looked So Good! the advert had proudly proclaimed, while showing a fresh-faced, bikini-clad Nina draped over the bonnet of a sleek silver coupe.

The press had taken an interest *'once I was old enough'*, she'd said. Old enough for whom? The girl he'd seen in those photos had looked as though she'd barely finished school. She had come to Paris, to the museum event, incognito, choosing to sneak her way in to confront him rather than using her family name as a bargaining tool. She had asked him to release her from her contract, to allow her to start over elsewhere. None of those actions matched up with the image of her that he'd assumed was accurate.

'Nina…' he said quietly, reaching a hand across the table to grasp hers. 'Could you please try not to look like you're being tortured or blackmailed into having lunch with me?'

She made a non-committal noise, stabbing her fork

into her salad. 'I've no idea what you're talking about. I'm having a wonderful time. Thank you so much for giving me the option of having lunch with you in public, Mr Falco.'

'I really think you should call your fiancé by his first name, don't you?' he reminded her, fighting the urge to laugh aloud at the saccharine sweetness in her voice.

'Tristan.' She met his eyes with challenge.

'Can I take that as confirmation that you accept the terms of the deal?' He waited, his hand still extended towards hers across the small table. Slowly, her fingers uncurled from her fork and moved towards his. Her skin was silky soft as she placed her much smaller hand into the palm of his and he wasted no time in closing his grip around hers with triumph.

'I accept,' she said calmly. 'Pending an official contract outlining the details of the arrangement in full.'

He nodded his own agreement, making a mental note to have the terms drawn up immediately. Further conversation was first interrupted by the arrival of their steaks and then subsequently by a business acquaintance who stayed a few moments to arrange a meeting. He was a hard man to pin down, as everyone seemed to say.

When the other man raised a brow in Nina's direction, Tristan made a show of linking his fingers through hers to leave no question as to the nature of their relationship. The media loved a possessive caveman, didn't they? He was simply playing to the cameraman he had seen arrive midway through their food.

That was also why he insisted upon taking her hand as they exited the restaurant terrace and guiding her along the promenade that lined the seafront.

Nina hesitated, glancing anxiously at the slim watch

on her wrist. 'I told you I don't have much spare time. I'm racing for the next two weekends until Apollo is ready. I have to get back to headquarters to test out some new strategy in the racing simulation equipment.'

'Surely you want to linger here a few minutes for a prolonged goodbye?' he said smoothly, running a hand along her shoulders as he turned to pull her against him and whisper near her ear. 'Two photographers, just over the wall. Don't look behind you.'

She nodded, seeming to brace herself before relaxing slightly. 'I forgot, sorry. Tell me what you need me to do.'

Tristan closed his eyes against the onslaught of inappropriate thoughts that immediately followed her innocent words.

Think of the deal, Falco. Focus.

'Wrap your arms around my neck and look up at me. Like you can't resist me,' he murmured, sliding a hand tightly around her trim waist. Again, her body tensed before she did some more deep breathing and followed his command. Another woman might have slowly slid her fingertips along his shoulders, teasing him into a sensual haze. Not Nina; she might as well have been performing a Swedish massage, for all the grace she put into her grip. Once she'd settled her hands into place, she met his gaze with an irritated huff. He smiled, a small sound escaping his lips.

Nina instantly tensed up. 'What? Am I doing it wrong?'

His mind tripped over the question, at how odd it seemed for her to be uncertain of something so simple. Surely she had been in a lover's embrace before?

'You're supposed to *melt* into my powerful embrace, not attempt to wring my neck.'

'That doesn't make sense. Humans don't melt,' she argued.

'*Dios.*' Tristan leaned his head forward, pressing his cheek against hers to avoid bursting into laughter at the utter ridiculousness of the situation. 'It just means to bend, to relax into me.'

Nina frowned, turning her face away from him. 'I can't see how anyone will believe we're in the midst of a whirlwind romance when we can't even stand close to one another without arguing.'

'They say intense, combative relationships are often the most passionate.'

'Or the most toxic,' she countered.

'Perhaps.' He pulled her into his arms once more, not missing the slight hitch in her breath as her chest met his. 'Good thing our intensity is all just for show, then, hmm?'

He thought he heard a faint growl under her breath before she gave in, allowing him to rest her head against his chest while he wrapped his arms around her. With one hand, he moved her hair aside while the other ran a slow path up beneath her leather jacket to stroke along her spine. The thin cotton of her T-shirt was soft beneath his hands, his fingertips tingling as he slowly slid them up and down with measured slowness. She might not have melted, but she certainly relaxed into his touch, her breathing becoming more shallow. She practically vibrated at the caress, her body moulding to his own.

She was like a little cat, he smiled to himself, all claws and teeth until she was stroked into submission. But he barely had a minute to savour his win before she disentangled herself from his grip and they turned to find a mother and her young daughter standing nearby. As Tristan watched in fascination, Nina Roux transformed from the awkward, prickly woman determined to hold him at arm's length to something else entirely. Her voice softened and her eyes sparkled as she spoke to the young girl and signed a number of items with her scrawling autograph.

After a quick chat with the girl's mother about signing up for an upcoming academy open day, they were alone again once more but the haze of their embrace had long gone and been replaced by that same tension he'd felt during their lunch.

Tristan insisted upon driving her back to headquarters, refusing her thinly veiled lie that she needed to walk back on Sophie's orders to make up for missing her afternoon session in the driving simulator.

'Your busy schedule didn't seem to mind a little detour for fan adoration,' he said silkily as the sun-soaked Monte Carlo coast whipped past them.

'I like making time for the kids.' She shrugged. 'They're easier than the adults most of the time.'

'The open day they asked about, it was for a youth academy?'

'The Lola Roux Racing Academy, yes. I founded it a few years back to get more girls into the sport. We have a few training facilities set up around Europe and they do global mobile recruitment drives and scholarships too.' She'd almost forgotten about the upcoming virtual open-day event and quickly opened up her phone to tap a few notes into her schedule.

'A colour-coded schedule. Interesting…'

She looked up to find Tristan's eyes still firmly on the road, but a small smirk on his lips. Feeling self-conscious, she tapped her screen closed. 'Colour-coding makes it easier for me to follow. I like to be organised.'

Truthfully, she *had* to be organised or she didn't function, but she didn't need to tell him all of that. He didn't need to know how she had only two speeds as a professional athlete, workaholic or burnt-out mess. She put a lot of effort into remaining firmly on the working side, so that no one had to see how hard she fell when things came to a stop.

'Do you fund the academy yourself?' he asked a few moments later, spurring her out of her thoughts.

'We originally had support from Roux Racing, but that was cut a couple of years back. It's a big reason why I need to win more races but, for now, yes, I fund it myself.'

He nodded, hands gripping the wheel even tighter. 'You do most things by yourself, from what I can tell.'

'Perhaps I just know that I'm reliable,' she countered.

'And everyone else isn't?'

She remained silent, refusing to rise to the bait of another argument with him. Not when she was still recovering from that embrace on the pier. The way he'd enveloped her in his arms first, then begun stroking her back, and she'd just melted like putty in his hands.

'What about you?' she asked as he brought the car to a stop in front of the gleaming glass façade of the Falco Roux headquarters. 'You seem quite content to run things from afar while you maintain your role of wild playboy. Do you honestly think the media will believe that I've somehow tamed you?'

He turned in his seat until he faced her, midnight-blue eyes sparkling in the late afternoon sun. 'Everything about me is curated; they see what I want them to see. I am in control of the narrative at all times and that is how I prefer it.'

'Does anyone know the real Tristan Falco?'

'Why…do you wish to disassemble me like one of your engines? Find out what makes me tick?'

'I don't care what makes you tick,' she said, inhaling a sharp breath when he leaned forward, placing a kiss upon one cheek then moving slowly to the other side of her face to do the same. A traditional goodbye gesture she'd made herself a thousand times in her life—so why did it feel so intimate with him? The scent of his cologne filled her lungs before she had a chance to defend herself, making her stomach swirl again in that unsettling way it had on the terrace in the Paris museum the night before. He was deliberately disarming her, that was the only explanation for it. He was clearly trying to make this temporary fake fiancée ruse as uncomfortable as possible for her.

'You're getting better at that,' he murmured, pulling away.

'Better at what?'

He smiled, revving the engine loudly to life. 'Lying.'

She schooled her expression so as not to give away how utterly unsettled she felt about everything that had taken place between them in less than twenty-four hours. How on earth was she going to survive another three months like this?

'I'll be in touch about our next date.'

'My schedule is full. As I've said more than once, there is no time.'

'And as I've also said before, you will make time for me.'

His parting words had her grunting and growling the entire climb up the steps to headquarters as she wondered what on earth she had just agreed to.

CHAPTER FIVE

AFTER WRAPPING UP three very successful practice sessions on the first day of the Italian race weekend, Nina had half convinced herself that the previous weekend had been a dream. Despite his threat, Tristan had not been in touch to demand any more of her time, nor had he appeared at the track during any of the press conferences that had taken place yesterday.

Conveniently, their playboy team owner had left Nina alone to issue a litany of *'No comment'* and *'Next question'* after every journalist's probing and snide remarks about the speculation surrounding their public displays of affection.

The Falco Roux team principal was an older man named Jock, a man who already begrudged Nina's presence on the team at all. As predicted, the recent events had only worsened his treatment of her. Her fellow drivers and team members, thankfully, had interjected a couple of times to remind the press that their new team owner had not attended any races yet so far and had very little to do with the day-to-day running of the team. This was after one particularly barbed comment from a news reporter asking if she didn't think her family name had already given her enough privilege in Elite One.

Usually, she shrugged off the overwhelmingly negative

opinions of herself as a pay driver, but being accused of using her *body* as a way of climbing the industry ladder felt different. It had got under her skin, making her feel shaky and tight. A feeling that she struggled to throw off, even today on the track as she moved through their strategies and worked on a few last-minute issues with the car.

She had seen the other team drivers and crew looking at her and whispering when they thought she wasn't looking. It didn't take much to imagine what they might be thinking. Despite the overwhelmingly positive public reaction to the romance, from a professional point of view, some people were uncomfortable with the notion. Billionaire playboy or not, Tristan was older than her by twelve years and he was essentially her boss. And despite his assurances that he would swing the narrative, Tristan had done nothing to protect her from the backlash so far. On the contrary, he'd practically fed her to the wolves.

Friday of the race weekends was often a strange mix of on-track and off-track commitments, followed by whatever events and public appearances were required of her in the evening. She took her time showering in her modest hotel suite, taking advantage of the sleek high-pressure shower and steam room to try to blast away some of her stress. She didn't have a high-maintenance beauty regime by any standards, but as she took in her reflection in the mirror, she had a feeling that her usual routine of moisturiser and mascara wasn't going to be enough to mask the sheer exhaustion on her face.

At least the cocktail dress the PR team had sent up was a delightfully lightweight and comfortable satin stretch material that wouldn't irritate her skin for the entire evening. She couldn't avoid heels, but compromised by sliding a pair of simple black flats into her clutch for when the discomfort became too much and she could slip away. Which she fully intended to do as early as possible.

There were three events on the roster from what she could remember, a charity meet and greet, a dinner with their Italian investors, the Marchesi family, followed by a rooftop cocktail hour and dancing.

With the track qualifying sessions beginning tomorrow, it was accepted that the drivers could leave at their own discretion once their minimum appearance had been made. Appearances meant photographs, lots and lots of them—and as far as she knew, Tristan Falco was still in hiding. Perhaps she'd imagined the entire debacle at the beginning of the week, or perhaps he'd taken her advice and realised that she was far more trouble than she was worth. That a match between the two of them would never convince anyone.

Perhaps he'd simply found someone else to fulfil his temporary fiancée needs. Perhaps she was about to be fired, after all. Her stomach tightened at the thought.

Her security guards escorted her in the lift down to where a sleek limo awaited her outside, a much more extravagant ride than she was used to being assigned. Her curiosity was short-lived, however, as the door opened when she was a few steps away and out emerged the object of her thoughts.

Tristan Falco had come to Milan after all, and that meant the deal was still on. She didn't know whether the sudden tightening in her stomach was from fear or anticipation as he leaned forward to place a kiss upon her right cheek. Again, the smell of his cologne was surprisingly pleasant, as was the weight of his hand upon her waist as he looked down at her.

'Miss me?' he asked.

'It's been five days.'

'You poor thing, you've kept count.' The tilt of his head and slight smirk to anyone else might seem like a gentle lovers' back-and-forth. No one looking on would know that Nina was desperately resisting the urge to smack him in the face.

'If I were to keep count of how many race weekends you've actually attended, I wouldn't need to go further than my thumb. That is, if you actually plan to attend the race.'

'After the spike in sales this week, I'm under strict instruction from Astrid Lewis not to miss a single race weekend for the rest of the season.'

Of course, he wasn't here to watch her race or cheer her on or anything of the sort. His appearance here was entirely to do with the optics of this nonsensical PR stunt his team was executing. Apart from the speculation around their relationship, the other main news point in the motorsports world was Apollo's decision to return to Elite One for his family's rival team. It was an action that no team had ever seen in the past, a driver bearing the name of a historic team signing for their family's biggest rival.

Of course, no one was talking about the fact that Nina had spent four days this week with the team as they began the monumental task of readying their new driver for the second half of the season. With the Belgian Premio next weekend, followed by Spain the weekend after, and then the three-week summer break, Apollo's first race would be a historic one, starting as it was with the revival of the Argentinian Elite One Premio in Buenos Aires. She doubted that Astrid had to coerce Tristan to attend *that* race.

'I know I haven't been around anywhere near enough.

Thankfully I have my beautiful fiancée to step up now and give me all the harsh truths I've needed to hear.'

'I wasn't trying to be harsh.'

'I know,' he said with a slight smile. 'It took a moment for me to realise that; it's just your nature to be rather...'

'Blunt?' she offered defensively.

'I was going to say boldly honest,' he said, his gaze holding onto hers for a long moment before he continued. 'I'm not here to fight. I'm actually here to take care of some very important business.'

Nina looked out of the window as the car slowed. They were in the very heart of Milan where some of the most expensive and grand fashion houses had their flagship stores. The limousine pulled to a stop outside an ornate historic-looking triple-storey store, one that bore the Falco crest.

'We are not here for me, Nina, we are here for you,' Tristan said once they were inside.

'Me?'

'I hope you don't mind but when we planned tonight's look, I specifically told the team to leave out jewellery for this reason.'

Nina stilled. 'You planned my...wait, you're choosing my clothing now as well?'

'Your personal trainer Sophie was kind enough to give me some guidance on your rather specific taste in clothing. The material is to your liking, no?'

He had picked out her dress. Suddenly the silken slide of the material against her thighs as they walked along the central aisle of the cavernous store felt intimate and seductive, rather than comforting. Much like the man himself. There was nothing about Tristan Falco that was comforting at all.

'So you're here to drape me in your diamonds like a walking advertisement, is that it?'

'Actually, we're here for a ring. Your engagement ring, to be precise.'

If Nina had been a cartoon character, she was pretty sure this would be the moment when her jaw would drop comically to the floor. As it was, she just about managed to keep herself from tripping over her own shoes. Had he picked out the damned heels as well?

'I thought… I assumed that we wouldn't be announcing that part so soon.'

'We won't be announcing anything. You'll be seen tonight wearing an appropriately eye-catching diamond on your left hand. Gossip will do the rest.' He waited a beat, his eyes searching her face with a frown. 'You look surprised, *cariña*. Surely you didn't expect the CEO of Falco Diamonds' fiancée to walk around without a gigantic rock on her finger?'

'No, I suppose not,' she murmured, her fingertips suddenly feeling tingly and numb as she fought not to twist them in her lap. Her mother had taught her, forced her not to fidget when she was uneasy or nervous. She'd learned how to keep her breathing even and steady, how to periodically meet the gaze of important people so that she didn't seem shifty or untrustworthy. But she had never been trained how to respond in a situation like this.

As she sat frozen still, the world's most untameable bachelor slid a tray of antique diamond rings in front of her. In her peripheral vision, the store manager and sales assistant looked on with whimsical smiles as though they were observing a truly romantic moment between a couple in love. She supposed that was why Tristan reached over and grabbed her hand gently, sliding his thumb across her knuckles and leaning forward to move a lock of hair from her forehead.

'I asked them to bring this one up from the vault.' He held up a small red box, separate from the tray of glittering pieces the manager had placed between them. The box snapped open, revealing a truly gigantic black diamond surrounded by a coronet of brilliant white gemstones. 'But you are the one who must wear it, after all. So take your pick from everything you see here.'

She hardly remembered what she did next, but one moment Tristan was smiling with triumph and the next he was on one knee before her. He slid the black diamond ring slowly onto her finger while a gentle round of applause sounded out from their small audience.

'Perfect,' he murmured, meeting her eyes for one scorching second before turning to ask someone to bring a tray of earrings and necklaces to match her newest accessory.

He insisted upon draping the jewels around her neck himself. With the mirror in front of her, she watched as he slid her hair to one side and did up the clasp at the back of her necklace. His eyes met hers with a silent question through the reflection in the mirror. Nina glanced at him, then quickly away as her breathing began to feel a little tight.

To all the world right now, she had just become the future Mrs Falco, and she couldn't even look her fiancé in the eye without having a mild panic attack. What on earth would she do when he eventually had to kiss her again?

Tristan could not say that he had ever imagined how a proposal of his own would go, but this certainly had not been it. Nina had looked as though she was breathing through a rather painful dental procedure during their entire ring selection, elevating into a mild state of frozen panic once he had actually placed the diamond upon her finger. Things had not improved much since they'd made their way out of the jewellery store to pose briefly for a small crowd of photographers. Nina had brushed her hair out of her face with her left hand as he'd instructed her to, and they had travelled to their first event of the evening in silence. He lost sight of her soon after arriving at the charity event, with his presence being required for a series of minor television interviews and hers for an Elite One photo call with the other drivers.

His own interviews were predictably focused on getting him to release any details about his relationship with Nina, which he handled with ease, taking enjoyment out of toying with his word selection. His team had not had to coach him much on the art of selective information sharing; Tristan had always viewed his relationship with the press as a game of sorts, a series of chess moves, using them as he pleased. It had worked in his favour so far, but when he'd seen some of the articles and social media posts that had been released about Nina during the few days since their scandal had gone public, he'd immediately booked for his private train car to take him from Paris to Milan.

Even now, not knowing where she was or what questions she was having to field alone made him feel like the world's biggest jerk. He'd played it cool, but sharing more than he'd intended during their last encounter had made him feel off balance, and so he had done something he never usually did. He'd ghosted her.

It wouldn't happen again. From this moment on, he

intended for them to act as a team, whether she liked it or not.

Teamwork seemed to be a concept that Nina was quite familiar with, judging by her current cosy pose with her co-driver, Daniele Roberts. The Scottish-Italian heart-throb had been one of their team's biggest assets over the past year, and Tristan knew Nina had played an expert game in defending him into first position in a race earlier in the season, when their lead driver had been unwell. Tristan might not have attended that race either but he had kept tabs on the results and highlights, as he had done for every other racing weekend this year. As he watched, Roberts leaned in and whispered something into Nina's ear, making her laugh loudly before she composed herself back into a serene smiling position for the camera. Once the photographer had finished up, she turned back to Roberts, lightly punching him on the arm.

Their interaction was so friendly, so *easy*, it caught Tristan off guard. She wasn't cranky with the other man, nor was she picking apart his words or studiously avoiding his gaze. In fact, she seemed to be actively enjoying their conversation as the two moved to the side of the room seeking a more private spot.

He immediately felt his body tense as if to launch into pursuit, but before he could he was interrupted by a familiar bellowing Italian voice. Valerio Marchesi had once been his biggest rival when they had both attended boarding school, a rivalry that had lasted until they had bonded over their shared traumatic experiences and Tristan had eagerly helped the other man to access some therapy and begin to heal. That healing, along with some other, more shady and dramatic occurrences, had led to Valerio marrying Daniela Avelar, who stepped up now to give Tristan a familiar kiss on the cheek.

'I heard the most delicious rumour this week, Falco,' Valerio said, a mischievous smile lighting up his face as he slid onto a barstool alongside him and demanded the full details of how Tristan had gone from a devoted bachelor to being engaged to a racing-car driver all in a matter of a few days.

'It seems your fiancée is a little busy at present,' Valerio said wryly, glancing at the spot where Tristan was very much still keeping tabs on Nina and her teammate. 'I do love to see you finally getting your comeuppance.'

He was vaguely aware of the fact that his friend referenced a night in the past, where his wife had asked Tristan to play the role of her date to prove a point. A night that felt like a lifetime ago now that Valerio and Dani were very happily married with two children. But he didn't have time to rehash the past, not when his fiancée was being pulled into a deep embrace by a twinkly eyed dandy in plain view of the entire room.

His friends' laughter quickly blended into the background noise as Tristan made his way across the gallery towards where Nina and the other man had retreated. As he got within earshot he heard the Scot ask, 'So you're not even sleeping together yet?'

Tristan's blood boiled as he crossed the rest of the distance between them with two long strides. Feeling a hint of satisfaction as Roberts's smirking expression faltered when he caught sight of Tristan standing over Nina's shoulder.

'That seems like a very personal question, Mr Roberts.' Tristan smiled wolfishly, leaning down to press a lingering kiss upon Nina's bare shoulder before sliding a hand around her waist and meeting the other man's eyes. Instead of looking shaken or uncomfortable, Roberts seemed only to smile wider.

'It's just locker-room banter,' he said, his trademark broad grin pasted upon his handsome face. The driver's playboy reputation rivalled even Tristan's own if the tabloids were true. But Tristan had always liked Roberts's upbeat charisma, until this very moment in fact. Because right now he wanted to wipe that smile right off his face.

'You like to be treated like one of the guys, isn't that right, Roux?' Roberts said.

Nina let out a small huff of laughter, at the same time attempting to subtly slide her waist out of Tristan's grip. He held on even tighter, splaying his hand across her abdomen and noting that his finger-span almost covered her from hip to hip. Below the belt, his body reacted primitively to that knowledge, but above the belt he remained stony-faced and focused on staring down the man who seemed intent on challenging his patience.

Nina sucked in a swift breath and looked up at him for a split second before turning back to answer Roberts. 'I think we both know I am far superior to all of you, but yes, the banter is fine.'

'Well, she's *not* one of the guys. She's my fiancée.' Tristan offered a charming smile of his own, through rather clenched teeth. 'And I take offence to you probing for the intimate details of our relationship.'

'He wasn't probing about our intimate details,' Nina said drily. 'He was just probing about yours. He's quite curious about your bedroom prowess, it seems. That's actually been the most common question I've been asked this week. Is it true that Tristan Falco is a magician in the bedroom?'

Tristan choked. 'A magician now, is it? Last I heard I'd been compared to a deity. I've been downgraded, it seems.'

Roberts laughed aloud and then had the good sense to slowly retreat from their conversation. Leaving them alone in the corner of the gallery.

'I don't think the caveman performance is quite necessary for this ruse to work, do you?' Nina turned from him and surveyed the crowd in the gallery below.

'I believe I was pretty clear that I would be the one to decide what is necessary.'

'Ah yes, how silly of me to forget. I have simply to endure your brooding looks and act as a walking jewellery stand.' She sighed, her eyes lingering for a moment longer than necessary upon the area below his belt buckle. 'I should have assured Roberts that there is no chance of me ever experiencing the truth behind those rumours of your…prowess.'

Tristan froze, not quite believing his ears. Surely he had misheard her, or misconstrued her intention. Surely she couldn't mean…?

'Deity…' she mused thoughtfully. 'It's like everyone is asking me about the supercar parked in my garage, and I'm expected to brag…even though I'm not allowed to drive it.'

Tristan startled. 'Nina…what are you—'

'Oh, relax, I'm not actually propositioning you, Tristan. No doubt my brother has already warned you off too.'

'Your brother has no say in who I do or do not take to bed.'

'Well, *he* thinks he does.' She wandered to the next painting, her gaze roaming over the paint strokes absently as her voice tightened with a hint of emotion. 'He hasn't spoken to me in fourteen months, did you know that? Then today I saw he'd left me a voicemail, no apology or explanation, just warning me not to sleep with you.'

Tristan ignored the pang of guilt in his gut at the knowledge that he alone knew the truth of why her brother had left her alone for that long. But he couldn't tell her yet…and how very unfair that was—for both of them. All Tristan could hope was that when Nina did finally discover the truth about what he'd done, she'd see that Tristan had acted in the Roux company's best interests and understand the reason for his silence. Instead he simply said, 'He's just being protective of you.'

'He used to be,' she said, turning to face him once more. 'I only wish he was half as protective of our family's legacy and my inheritance as he is over my virtue.'

Tristan laughed at the outdated term. 'Your virtue? You make it sound as though I'm some kind of devilish rake and you're an innocent debutante.'

A strange look came over her face, and she took a few steps away, looking up at a nearby painting. 'My reputation is my virtue, I suppose. Just look how easily people assume that I must be some kind of calculating seductress, because I've managed to pin down the world's most untameable bachelor.'

'I suppose that makes me the devil in this scenario?' He paused, realising he didn't like that contrast between them one bit. 'Are you wondering if I plan to seduce you, Nina?'

'Are you?' Her eyes pinned his without missing a beat, holding him captive with their unfathomable depths that seemed to always see far too much.

He made a weak attempt at charm. 'What would you do if I said yes?'

She shrugged. 'I walked away easily enough after your first attempt.'

Whatever he'd expected her answer to be, it wasn't that. Ignoring the now persistent ache below his belt at the turn this conversation had taken, Tristan leaned back against the balcony rail and surveyed his pint-sized fake fiancée. There was no trace of mirth in her delicate features, nor any indication that she might be testing him or making fun of him. She was absolutely serious. He was struck suddenly by how young she was. And how old and jaded he felt in comparison. He'd flirted and toyed with plenty of women in his life, but with her…it wasn't the same. There was no guile in her words, no double entendre or expectation.

Having her look at him this way… It made him feel as though he'd had his clothing peeled off piece by piece, leaving him with nowhere to hide. It irritated him that she could influence him with so little effort. It wouldn't do.

'Are you challenging me, *cariña*?'

'Of course, you would see it that way. Your reputation precedes you on such a scale it borders upon a cult. I'd be lying if I said I wasn't curious to see if any of it is true or if it's just more of your…*spin*.'

'You believe that I've hired women to stalk me and break into my hotel rooms on purpose?'

'No.' She paused, thoughtful for a moment. 'But I believe you do nothing to discourage it. If this were a real relationship, I would never have a moment's peace.'

'If this were a real relationship, I'd make sure you only felt peace. You'd be so relaxed you'd practically float from my bed, out into the world.' He let his voice drop to a murmur as he fought not to step closer.

Her pupils dilated, a slight blush appearing high on her

cheeks. She opened her mouth to respond, then closed it and looked meekly away as they were called to rejoin the party for more photos. Tristan felt a thrum of satisfaction rush through him. His little cat might play tough, but she wasn't unaffected by him. Not at all.

CHAPTER SIX

TRISTAN WAS NOT present at the Belgian Premio events the following weekend, nor did he show up for Apollo Accardi's first official training sessions in their Monaco headquarters over the week that followed. Nina threw herself into her own training, determined to finish out her last stint as second driver in Barcelona with her head held high.

Her agent had contacted her this morning with the news that representatives from Accardi Autosport were seeking a new driver for next year's season now that their long-time champion was retiring. She'd hesitated but told them to put her name out there. When her deal with Tristan was concluded, she'd be out of contract at the end of this season after all, so she needed to keep her options open.

But the guilt weighed heavily on her mind as her team smiled and joked while they gathered at the marina to travel from Monte Carlo to Barcelona. They'd been treated to a night on a Velamar superyacht, likely courtesy of their main sponsor as a thank-you for their fantastic result in Italy. Of course, the vessel they were directed to was the largest one in the bay, a world-famous superyacht design that she remembered was called *La*

Sirinetta II, but a different name was pasted on the bow of this one.

The Falco Experience.

Tristan appeared on the welcome deck dressed casually in a pair of tan linen trousers and an open-collared polo shirt. He greeted each of the team by name, leaving her for last as everyone else hustled to get on board and find their room for the night. The ship was huge and had more than enough bedrooms for them all, but, still, she was amazed that he'd so easily decided to open up his precious vessel to them all. It wasn't usual for the team owner and drivers to travel along with the mechanics and administrative staff, but then again not much about Tristan's ownership had been traditional so far.

The team was awash with excitement as they were greeted with fruity cocktails and canapés while Tristan played gracious host. After he greeted her with little more than a quick peck on her cheek and then instructed her to continue on to her guests, Nina quickly realised that he intended to keep the distance between them.

It shouldn't have bothered her that he'd become so distant again after their night of flirtation in Milan. She'd all but dared him to seduce her after all, hadn't she? Sure, she'd tried to pass it off as casual flirtation but she knew better than anyone that she was utterly terrible at lying. She'd thought about being seduced by Tristan Falco more times in the past three weeks than she'd ever dare to admit. Thinking of him had become some kind of sickness, affecting her focus on the track and infiltrating her very steamy dreams at night like a constant itch that she was forbidden to scratch.

She'd always hated being told that things were forbidden. It was rather like placing a giant flashing button within her reach emblazoned with bright letters that commanded: Do Not Touch—even though she was a dedicated rule follower by nature, all she wanted to do was touch it.

She knew that when he'd first proposed this deal, he'd said it would be safer for them both to keep their arrangement platonic behind closed doors. But deep down, she didn't truly believe that was the reason he'd shown no sign of wanting more once the cameras panned away and it was just the two of them. Apart from the fact that she was a driver on the team he owned, she knew that aesthetically she was miles away from the kind of women she'd seen draped on his arms at that event in Paris. She wasn't tall or willowy, she didn't laugh prettily at his jokes and compliment him on his charms.

Once again…she was too much.

Determined not to allow him to see how self-conscious that realisation made her feel, she focused on chatting with her team and smiled when Astrid Lewis appeared to greet her. Astrid's appearance at social events had become more and more rare lately. Her son, Luca, was an expert in everything Elite One and had never missed a single race until he'd started school last autumn. Nina had spent some time with them in their home in London before the season started and discovered that Luca had been diagnosed with autism. This had stunned her because of how often in the past Astrid had compared her sensitive, serious little boy to Nina herself. Nina had always felt a deep connection to Luca, and knowing more details about how he experienced the world only made her love him more.

But when Astrid had gently suggested that Nina perhaps should look into the experiences of some late identified autistic adults she'd found online, the moment had become a little awkward between them. It had played heavily on her mind since, but she shook off the memory and embraced her friend.

'Please tell me you're not here to add to my schedule,' Nina asked quickly. Every time Astrid approached her with an eerily calm look in place it usually accompanied bad news of some sort.

'Tristan said he told you about the Falco Diamonds centenary campaign that was in the works?'

Nina fought the urge to groan. 'Yes, I remember.'

'The actual campaign will be shot in Buenos Aires next month, but the PR team wanted to go ahead and do some tests while you're at your photo shoot in Barcelona this week.'

Nina frowned, remembering that she was scheduled to shoot as a cover model for a magazine. 'Do they want to do this at the same time as the shoot?'

'That's up to you, I would say perhaps all together might suit better with how much energy these things take from you. But here's the thing… The magazine got wind of all of this and now they want to include recent events in the narrative. More specifically, they want to involve Tristan.'

As if summoned by his name, Tristan appeared at Nina's side with two flutes of champagne in hand and offered her one. 'Who wishes to involve me and in what?'

Astrid quickly went through the proposed feature from a prominent sports and fitness magazine that had shown interest in featuring women in motorsport and using Nina as their cover star.

'This all sounds excellent, but I don't see why I would

be needed.' Tristan frowned. 'Unless you mean they wish to use some Falco pieces as part of the shoot?'

'I definitely want us to include Falco Diamonds in some way, to really emphasise that connection between the two brands. I think it's a great idea to push a united image for people to see. We also need to find a suitable location on short notice. But what I really wanted to ask was… They wanted to see if you'd consider taking the photos yourself, Tristan,' Astrid said.

'Absolutely not.' Tristan's face tightened. 'I'm sorry to disappoint there. But the location and the diamonds, I can arrange. I've been meaning to check in on my uncle's estate while we're here anyway. He left it to me, rather than my cousin, Victor. My uncle was more like a father to me, and I think he knew I'd preserve it just as he wanted. He had a classic car collection that would work well as a backdrop.'

Nina felt the tension coming off him in waves as Astrid walked away, leaving them both alone. She took a sip of champagne. 'I didn't know you were a photographer.'

'Briefly…a very long time ago. After my uncle's untimely death I travelled for a while. I dabbled in portrait photography and published some work in a few magazines under a pseudonym.'

She saw the flash of pain in his eyes at the mention of his uncle, and thought of him, travelling the world in his grief and finding beauty where he could. 'You don't take photos any more?'

'No,' he said simply. 'Not in the past few years anyway. I still have most of my equipment but… I just don't have the time any more.'

'One should always make time for hobbies you enjoy.

Or do you only think of finding pleasure in bed these days?'

He smirked. 'We've barely been alone for three minutes and you've already mentioned my sex life. That must be a new record. You truly are obsessed.'

'That's probably accurate,' she muttered under her breath.

'What was that?'

'Nothing… I was just thinking…you *should* shoot the photos yourself,' she blurted, immediately regretting her words when his eyes flashed a warning at her. He shook his head, downing the rest of his champagne flute in one mouthful.

'It's just an idea.' Nina shrugged one shoulder. 'Astrid is very observant, and she knows that I'm usually quite awkward about these things. It might help to not have a stranger behind the lens.'

'Nice to know I'm not a stranger now at least.' He smirked. 'But no, I have to be back in Paris once the race is through. It's a prominent magazine, they will have a reputable photographer in charge. You'll be fine.'

She nodded. 'Makes sense that you plan to leave so quickly.'

'Makes sense how exactly?'

'Well, after I expressed my curiosity in Milan… You've kept your distance.'

'Perhaps I've just been busy.'

'You were flirtatious, until I mentioned that I was not entirely opposed to exploring the attraction between us and then you backed off.'

'Nina…'

'Don't worry, I'm not about to express the same interest again. I have some self-respect, Tristan. It's just infuriating dealing with people's assumptions about me. When the truth is utterly laughable.'

'The truth?'

'The media have gone from painting me as an ice queen to wondering if I am some kind of secret sex goddess because I've "pinned you down".'

His eyes darkened and he muttered hoarsely, 'A sex goddess?'

'It's the natural fit for a man described as a deity in the bedroom, no?'

'Sounds like a match made in heaven.'

Nina rolled her eyes, turning to brace her hands against the railing and look out to where the sun was beginning to dip against the horizon, turning the water a beautiful mixture of orange and yellow. She was aware of Tristan moving closer behind her, but, still, her breath caught when she felt his arm brush against hers. He wasn't touching her, but he wasn't exactly keeping his distance either. Her skin thrummed in response and she fought the urge to remain still.

'You believe that me keeping my distance means that I was turned off by your honesty?'

'Weren't you?'

A low chuckle escaped his lips and she saw him shake his head gently in her peripheral vision. 'I find your honesty to be the single most entrancing thing that I've encountered in recent memory, Nina Roux.'

She inhaled a soft breath as he moved closer, his eyes raking down over her skin in a look so scorching hot he might as well have been undressing her with his hands.

'You think I don't want you?' he murmured. 'You think that I don't obsess over all the reasons that I want to touch you? And all the reasons why giving in to that impulse would ruin us both?'

'But…why?'

'Apart from you being twelve years younger than me, and the fact that I'm technically your boss, I pulled you into this ridiculous deal in the first place, dangling your freedom from your contract in front of you. For me to seduce you would be taking advantage of you.'

She found she wasn't bothered by the age gap or the fact that he was her boss. 'What if I wanted to be seduced? Is that against your rules?'

'Nina…' he warned.

She moved closer, testing him by reaching up to place both of her hands on his shoulders. He could move away if he wished, or he could tell her no. But the burning desire she could see in his eyes told her that he wouldn't do either of those things. Feeling emboldened, she reached up and was delighted when he immediately lowered his head to hers in response. He let her control the kiss, making himself pliable under her hands and lips as she explored him. He tasted just as delicious as she remembered, the sensations of the breeze upon her hair and his hands snaking around her waist to pull her closer against his hard body were like heaven. She heard a moan, and realised it came from her own throat.

Kissing Tristan again was as explosive as she knew it would be. It was the kind of feeling she usually got only when driving full throttle around the track, as if she were flying through the air. It made her stomach twirl and her thoughts turn blank. All she could feel was him, all she could think about was how it felt and how badly she wanted more.

So much more.

He pressed her back against the railings, pressing himself against her, and she could feel the hard ridge of his erection against her abdomen. She was wearing jeans, and he was wearing linen trousers, but still the intimacy was almost too much for her. They might as well have been completely naked for all she knew, the way her insides turned to molten fire, and she ground back against him.

Her sensual movements made his body harden even further against hers, and she heard a low growl in his throat as he speared his fingers through her hair and took control of the kiss, deepening it and taking her just as she wished to be taken. This was what she needed, exactly this.

Too late, she heard footsteps coming down the steps and they paused just in time to see Astrid's shocked face before the woman turned and quickly exited the way she'd come.

Nina pressed both hands against her face, groaning. 'Oh, my God, did that just happen? She's seen us.'

'She did,' Tristan said, standing up to his full height and putting some distance between them.

'It's okay, everyone else thinks that we're engaged anyway. Of course, Astrid knows the truth, but I doubt she'll make a big deal of it.'

'That's not why I'm annoyed right now, Nina,' Tristan said. 'Every time I am alone with you, I lose control. It's not acceptable. I never lose control. We set parameters for this arrangement and you…keep pushing.'

'You're right. I deliberately pushed those parameters. And I won't apologise for that,' she said defiantly.

'You won't?' he asked, raising an eyebrow.

Nina's heartbeat fluttered at the heat still evident in

Tristan's gaze. 'No. I'm very attracted to you and I was curious.'

'Damn it.' He moved closer, licking his lips as he stared down at her. 'Damn *you* with your curiosity and your refusal to accept the word no.'

'If you had actually said no at any point during the past ten minutes I would have stopped,' she said as sweetly as she could manage.

'Hell would have a better chance of freezing over, kitten.' He was upon her again, his lips crushing hers against his as he pulled her close and kissed her senseless once more. Until she was breathless and aching between her thighs.

'I only have so much willpower, Nina. Are you sure this is what you want?' He growled the words in between kisses.

'Yes.' She moaned against his plundering mouth, gasping as he stroked her sensitive nipples through the material of her bra and T-shirt. She felt as though she'd played with fire and now she was getting an up-close-and-personal demonstration of what it felt like to go up in flames. His hands explored her willing body inch by inch, his mouth not breaking their kiss. But when his fingers began to toy with the top button of her jeans, Nina felt the first flicker of uncertainty freeze her up. Of course Tristan noticed the moment she stopped enthusiastically kissing him back.

'Sorry, I got carried away.' he murmured. 'Maybe we should take this somewhere more private?'

Nina shook her head, feeling reality come crashing back with all the subtlety of a cold bracing shower. She was on his yacht, with their entire team nearby. Plus, even if she did throw caution to the wind and go back to his bedroom with him, after all her talk tonight of seducing him, he would be expecting her to be experienced. Not a nervous virgin who had absolutely no idea what she was doing.

'Can we pause for a moment?' she asked quietly.

He nodded, taking a step back as if needing that physical distance between them in order to bring his desire under control. The knowledge that he wanted her just as badly as she wanted him was a heady kind of power that made her feel alight with passion.

'I want this. Very much,' she assured him a little nervously. 'It's just…a little fast for me. Also, this weekend is really important and I can hardly focus around you as it is.'

'Are you saying I'm jeopardising your race? I'm very flattered.'

'Of course you are. But yes, I think perhaps we should pause this…until afterwards?'

'Only if you promise to schedule me into your diary at the earliest opportunity,' he murmured against her cheek. 'In bright red pen. I don't know why, but I'm rather obsessed with your colour-coding.'

She smiled, feeling a blush in her cheeks. 'For the next three days my focus is on the race, but after that I'm yours.'

The moment she spoke the words, he froze, his hands tightening upon her waist for a split second. 'Cristo, you could drive a man wild saying things like that.'

She hadn't intended to drive him wild, but if the consequence of speaking honestly was him kissing her like this, she'd continue to give her thoughts free rein. 'I feel like I should be honest that, um… I don't usually do this. Like, I've never—'

He continued to kiss a trail down the side of her neck, so she wasn't entirely sure if he'd heard her. A series of low murmurs was all he said in response.

'Let's get you to bed, Nina. Before I'm tempted to tuck you in myself.'

He walked her to her bedroom door and lingered for a long moment, one hand braced quite attractively on the doorjamb as he stared down at her with possession.

'Three days,' he repeated.

'Three days.' She nodded.

The executive box of the Spanish Premio was filled predictably with people that Tristan did not know. He knew of them, of course, politicians and celebrities schmoozing with one another in the hopes of gaining influence. Likely some of them might actually follow the sport, but Elite One race weekends were as much about the experience and atmosphere as the racing after all. He'd deliberately procured a spot near the back of the room, away from the windows, once the race had begun an hour ago.

Even after years of therapy following the aeroplane accident that had killed his uncle and almost killed him too, the sound of roaring engines still managed to set his teeth on edge. But he was managing it, as he always did. He was a master of the public performance, after all, his guests simply seeing their bored owner schmoozing and wishing he were anywhere but here. No one knew the truth was that the very idea of Nina whizzing around that track at such high speeds was almost more than he could bear.

She would laugh, of course, if she knew that he held her skill in complete regard and truly hoped that all of her dreams on the track would come true…if only it didn't involve actually putting her life in the hands of a car.

The car was in great shape, and according to the mechanics on the team downstairs their strategy was sound and both of their drivers were in fighting form, as was evidenced by their current positions in fourth and fifth place out of twenty.

The Accardi team were in first and second, and had been for most of the race, but Nina's expert defending and Roberts's aggressive driving style had already moved them through several impressive overtakes. As he listened to the commentary he heard them each move up another spot.

'Do my eyes deceive me?' a British voice sounded out and Tristan looked up to see Astrid's smiling face approaching him. 'Tristan Falco, in the flesh at a race weekend. Don't tell me you're actually following my advice.'

'Actually it was Nina who convinced me that I was actively impeding growth by not showing my full support to the team.'

Astrid smirked. 'Yes, I noticed she seems to have made *quite* the impression on you.'

Tristan cleared his throat, tugging at his suddenly tight collar as Astrid continued to give him an all too knowing look.

'You know, Tristan, I wasn't quite sure at first if this plan would work but the narrative in the media has felt like a real romance. You're doing a great job of making it look that way anyway. Even in private, it's quite the dedication to the cause you're both showing. Just…be careful with her, okay?'

Tristan thought of Nina's hesitancy three weeks ago when she'd agreed to this deal, how he'd insisted he wouldn't allow the lines between them to become blurred. How he'd been so confident in assuring her that everything between them was just for show. The trouble was, the more time they spent alone, the more they both seemed to forget. Or at least their bodies did anyway.

The attraction he felt to her was like nothing he'd ever experienced before. It was all-consuming, bordering upon an obsession at times, and he'd even found himself checking in on her at training or showing up at her hotel to take her for lunch over the past few days. She had taken it all in her stride, of course, giving him no indication of how she truly felt. But still, her words on the yacht had stuck with him.

'My focus is on the race, but after that I'm yours.'

She hadn't meant it in the way that his primitive brain had taken it. That she would be *his*. That he would possess her, finally. But to all intents and purposes, she would be in his bed at least. He fought to control the sudden reaction as his body got tighter.

'I heard an interesting rumour,' Astrid said, reminding him of where he was and helping him to refocus his thoughts.

'A good one, I hope.'

'An important one, for sure… Accardi have their eyes on Nina.'

Tristan paused with his glass midway to his mouth, his eyes snapping up to focus on his PR manager. 'Over my dead body.'

Astrid pursed her lips, tilting her head at his rather emotional reaction. 'I thought you might feel that way. But, as it stands, under the terms of your agreement with her, you're going to free her from her contract at the end of the season, aren't you?'

'Yes, but they don't know that.'

'Are you planning to keep her, Tristan?' Astrid asked, her bespectacled gaze as shrewd as ever. 'Because after the decisions made by this team in the past month, I don't think Nina is planning to stay.'

'That's not the point. The point is that this is blatant retaliation by Enzo Accardi for us signing his grandson. And he is not going to use Nina as a weapon to play games with me.'

'You do realise this is Elite One, yes? The most game-playing of all the motorsports. It's all drama, Tristan. The racing only takes up five per cent of the entertainment. Nina wants to leave anyway and just think of the media storm that would follow.'

He knew Enzo Accardi, and he also knew the stories about the old man and how lecherous he was, how ruthless and underhanded. There was a good reason why Apollo had refused to ever race for him again. To think that Enzo might get his hands on Nina… To think what kind of hoops he might require her to jump through in order for her to achieve her dreams…

Suddenly he realised the decision to pass Nina over in favour of signing a much more experienced driver for the remainder of this season had been completely the wrong call. He'd thought he'd been doing the right thing for the team, but he could see now with gut-churning guilt and horror that this should have been Nina's season with her team, and they were practically allowing their biggest asset to walk into the arms of their vilest competitor. Despite it being an obvious retaliation on Enzo's part, the senior Accardi would not be pursuing Nina for his team if she weren't also one of the most prominent rising stars on the track. All he could hope was that his mistake wouldn't prove too costly—for Nina, for the team…and for himself. He knew now that her skill was practically unmatched, along with her even, cool temperament. If she'd been in the number one Falco Roux seat today, she would already have been ahead, but she continued to stay behind their primary driver, defending him and allowing him to rush towards victory.

As he listened, the crowd went wild as a commentator announced Roberts overtaking into second place right behind Accardi's number one driver. Unable to look away, he moved closer to a nearby monitor and watched as the cameraman zoomed in on where Nina and Accardi's number two driver were now battling it out for third place. His whole body tight as a string, he watched as she edged and weaved behind the other driver as they both hurtled in the rain towards the next turn much too fast.

No! Surely she wasn't planning to… Tristan fought the urge to shout at the screen, controlling his own panicked reaction. But hell, it was a hairpin band on a downhill slant, and surely it was impossible to keep the car under control… But he watched as, to his amazement, Nina feinted in one direction and then, in a move so skilled and sleek the entire crowd gasped, she slid neatly between the other car and the apex of the track to steal neatly into third place.

He was by no means an expert in motorsport, but whatever that was, it was pure poetry in motion. The woman had a gift. A smile transformed his face and he couldn't help a bellow escaping his chest as he cheered along with the rest of the garage. It was the final lap, and all going well they would have two team members on the podium for the first time. The first time in fifteen years, the commentator announced wildly.

Tristan turned to their team principal, slapping the man on the back and listening as the R & D team continued to monitor their drivers and ensure they kept their positions towards the finish line.

But as Nina pushed to the max around the final lap, the Accardi driver behind her gained pace and grew reckless. Disaster came swift and ruthlessly, as it often did. One touch of his front wing against Nina's rear tyre was all it took, sending both cars into a helpless spin.

'No! I've lost it, I've lost it.'

Her frantic voice was the last thing Tristan heard as her car hydroplaned at speed before careening into the wall.

CHAPTER SEVEN

THE MEDICAL TEAM was quick and efficient as usual in tending to the minor bruising that Nina had incurred when the other driver had hit the back of her car. Incidents of any kind were treated with severity in Elite One, a sport that prided itself on the huge safety improvements they had developed for drivers and crew over the past couple of decades. In no time at all she'd been signed off to return to her hotel, accompanied by her trainer, Sophie, who would stay with her for the night in case of concussion.

Nina had had multiple crashes in her career, as most drivers did. She'd adhered to her safety protocols and kept her cool, much to the compliments of the team, but still…knowing she'd been so close to her first podium finish hurt more than any amount of bruising or damaged pride. She knew that she didn't have a concussion, but still she was happy for Sophie's company on the long walk out past the roaring crowds and into a car.

She had foolishly expected Tristan to rush to her side, considering he'd been right above the crash site and had likely had a full view of the entire incident. But he hadn't appeared in the medical bay, nor had he shown up to check on her in her motorhome with the rest of the management team. She'd been half tempted to text him, to chastise him for jeopardising the legitimacy of their precious ruse. What kind of fiancé didn't rush to his lover's side when she'd been injured?

Her needy thoughts had felt silly and pathetic, and she'd angrily shrugged them off, instead opting for the far more mature option of ordering multiple fried foods and desserts to her hotel room, much to the eye-rolling of her beleaguered trainer.

'I'm just saying there are healthier forms of ice cream on the market now,' Sophie grumbled as they stepped out of the car service and into the foyer of the team hotel.

'I don't want healthy, I want sugar,' Nina gritted, laying a gentle punch on her long-time friend's elbow. 'If you're nice to me I might even share.'

'Looks like someone else might have a different idea,' Sophie said cryptically. 'Like maybe a little Argentine tango for two?'

'Tango is always for two, that's a given.' Nina stopped speaking as she caught sight of the *someone else* Sophie had just referenced.

Tristan strode across the hotel foyer, directly towards her. When she'd briefly imagined him rushing to her side while the medic had checked out her bruises, she'd envisioned a little more swoon and romance, but instead he came to a stop in front of her, a scowl transforming his usually flirty features.

'The doctors cleared you?' he asked, mouth tight with tension.

'I'm completely fine. I just need to go to bed.'

'We were supposed to attend the big party, but I offered to stay with her in case of concussion,' Sophie said awkwardly, looking from Tristan's furious face to Nina's impassive one with rampant curiosity.

'There's no need for you to miss the event. Nina will be staying with me.'

'I most certainly will not be—'

'Nina,' he gritted, turning a forced smile to Sophie. 'Thank you for getting her back safely. Enjoy the party.'

To her horror, he simply grabbed her by the elbow and directed her towards the private elevator that led to the penthouse suite, leaving Sophie waggling her eyebrows gleefully in their wake.

'Stop manhandling me. You're walking way too fast.'

He paused, looking down at her with a stricken expression before returning to a slightly more gentle form of manhandling, straight into the lift.

'This elevator only goes to the penthouse. Your things have already been delivered to my bedroom,' he stated, punching the only button on the dial and exhaling a long breath as the elevator stuttered and then began to move smoothly upwards. 'Don't fight me on this. I'm already only just about holding it together as it is.'

'I'm sorry if you had plans to socialise and be photographed this evening, but I don't see how my injury has to change any of that.'

Midnight blue eyes narrowed upon her. 'You think I'm bothered about us missing a photo call right now?'

'Aren't you? Your top priority is your reputation, that's what this little fake engagement ruse is all about after all.'

'That was before…' He paused, eyes closed and a pained expression on his face. For a moment she wondered if he was about to pounce, as he had that night in Milan when she'd dared him to. But all too quickly, the elevator doors slid open to reveal a long hall and two security guards. Tristan greeted the men by name, guiding her down the ornate hallway to a set of tall double doors.

The grand royal suite inside was as lavish and need-lessly large as one would expect. It was modern and airy, but still held an air of history, as though it had been recently vacated by the kings and queens it had been named for. Priceless gold-framed artworks hung on every wall, and the ceilings were high and ornate with tiny cherubs carved into the moulding.

'My own room was perfectly fine,' she couldn't resist griping as she followed along behind him through the cavernous hallway. 'You could fit the entire team up here and still have space for a ball.'

'I'll get right on that, once I've made sure you haven't passed out from your injuries.'

'I'm fine.' Tiredness washed over her and for once she didn't feel like fighting him. 'You don't have to watch me, but I suppose that's what my fiancé would do.'

'I don't care what I should do right now. Not when I've just watched you smack into a metal wall at almost three hundred kilometres an hour.'

'It wasn't that fast. I had just decelerated from a turn, remember.'

He narrowed his eyes wildly upon her once more, his deft hands pausing inside the first-aid bag he'd produced.

'I've already been checked and cleared by the medical team, Tristan, no cuts and no visible wounds of any kind, other than minor bruising.'

'I know. I spoke to them over the phone and had a second opinion phoned in by my physician in Paris.'

'You did?'

'Yes. I did.' He met her eyes, his mouth opening for a second as though he might add to that but, instead, he just went back to gathering more medicines and an ice pack from the case.

He guided her into the massive master bedroom, insisting that was where she would sleep tonight. Growing more groggy and tired by the minute, Nina didn't argue when he kneeled down to remove her running shoes and helped her peel off the cotton yoga pants and baggy T-shirt she had hastily changed into after the medical team had finished scanning her entire body for internal bleeding and fractures. As calm and cool as she pretended to be, hitting the wall at such high speed was not a minor thing.

In fact, it was the one incident she had managed to avoid her entire career thus far, having only heard anecdotal accounts from other drivers about the shocking pressure of the gravitational forces that came with travelling at exceptionally high speeds. If you put a solid metal barrier in front of that speed unexpectedly, well... She had been incredibly lucky today.

Maybe that sense of relief was why she didn't stop Tristan from fussing over her pillows as she took the pain relief medication he'd laid out. He guided her back against the pillows he'd adjusted but then surprised her by lying down next to her on the bed.

'Get comfortable here, because you are not leaving this bed.'

Nina rolled over to her side so that she could look at him, wincing when even that hurt. 'Don't threaten me with a good time, Falco. Your three-day wait is up—am I finally about to get the full playboy experience?'

He turned to face her, and for the first time she realised that he had removed his suit jacket and tie. She took in the bared skin on show, the strong column of his throat and the top of his tanned chest beneath. When she looked up to see his eyes had darkened upon her, she swallowed audibly.

Tristan made a low tutting sound, reaching out to place the back of his hand against her now flushed cheek. 'Utterly insatiable...even with a possible mild concussion. Is that truly what you're thinking about right now?'

'You made me promise you, after all,' she whispered, shivering as his knuckles trailed down to skate along the side of her neck and bare shoulder.

'Even I have my limits when it comes to focusing on certain situations.' His brows furrowed, his hand sweeping down the outside of her arm where light bruising was already beginning to appear.

'How can someone be so fearless and strong, and still be so utterly breakable?'

She wasn't sure if he had intended to speak those words aloud, and the sudden strain in his voice hit her squarely in the chest. She realised then that his snappy, irritated caretaking was not exasperation as she had assumed, but possibly...worry? For her?

'So you've skipped out on your big event to tuck me into bed?' she asked quietly.

'You need to rest. And I'm here to make sure that you actually do that.'

'You've waylaid all my self-destructive plans for the night, I assure you. Sophie is likely very relieved. I told her I planned to order every dessert on the menu and then eat every single one while watching as many romantic comedies as I can find. She hates romance almost as much as she hates refined sugar.'

'But you don't?'

'Romcoms have always been my go-to for when I'm overwhelmed. They're like medicine, they help me calm down and…regulate.' She used the last word deliberately, gauging his reaction to the rather clinical term. She'd often wondered if her personal collection of unique strengths, differences and challenges were perhaps symptoms of something more. Something that her parents hadn't noticed or hadn't known to look for. But after seeing Astrid on the yacht, she'd done a little research and it turned out she ticked quite a number of boxes.

Tristan frowned. 'I can see how that would help. I usually prefer action-adventure-type films, but my mother and I would watch all the classic romantic comedies together to learn English. I had quite an interesting vocabulary for a number of years.'

'You're close with your mother,' she said tiredly, her eyelids drooping as she fought off sleep. 'I have no idea what that must be like. That kind of…easy love. I didn't have that with mine. We're too different, I think.'

'It's not always easy,' he said honestly. 'Back then it was even easier, when we had my uncle to play referee between us. But yes, we were always close.'

She didn't miss the furrow in his brows at the mention of his uncle, nor the way he quickly got up off the bed and set about ordering them both a copious amount of dessert from room service. She focused on staying awake as long as she could, but eventually not even the sugar or her favourite romcom could do the job.

She slid into a dream-filled sleep where Tristan watched over her like a guardian angel, his strong hands gently petting her hair while he whispered passionate words in his native tongue. Dream Tristan smelled just as divine as the real-life version and she allowed herself to burrow her face into his skin, breathing him in with a groan of approval. How easy this would be to get used to, she mused as she crawled up higher against his solid male chest and felt his low rumble of amusement as her lips clumsily pressed against his.

'You make me wish this were real,' she murmured, half on a sigh. 'Making me…want you.'

'I'm right here, *mi querida*,' her dream lover whispered against her mouth. 'I'm yours.'

Tristan opened his eyes to the sight of sunlight streaming in through the windows and Nina fast asleep in his arms. He'd managed to sleep the whole night through somehow, despite the little minx's determination to press every inch of her lithe body against his. Testing his muscles, he was pretty sure he hadn't moved once through the night. A quick look at his watch showed it was just dawn.

He had done his best to keep Nina awake and talking for as long as possible until her eyes had begun to droop and she had become completely unintelligible. Once he was sure that her sleep was safe and not one born of deep concussion, his own body had eventually begun to relax. That was, until she'd begun mumbling and moaning in her sleep, seemingly determined to have her way with him. Her clumsy kiss and sleep-induced longing had kept him awake far longer than he'd like to admit as he pondered his own tangle of emotions. Adrenaline really was the best form of sleeping tablet and he'd eventually fallen asleep with her nestled safely in his arms.

But now that he was awake, the anxiety from the day before came back in full force. After Nina had hit the wall and everyone had gone into a panic, Tristan's anxiety had taken over and he found himself needing to retreat so as not to do something reckless. He never knew when his panic would impede his day-to-day life. It had become such an immovable part of him over the past decade since the accident that had ended his uncle's life prematurely. His beloved uncle, who had been such an important father figure to him, as he'd never known his own. A man who'd fallen apart after the death of his wife, a wonderful woman Tristan had also loved dearly. He'd never been able to reach his uncle through the years of deep grief that had followed. His disengagement with life meant he should never have been flying the plane he'd crashed, killing himself but thankfully not Tristan, the only passenger on board. He closed his eyes, feeling the familiar tension in his chest rising as his ears imagined the sound of screaming jets and rushing air.

His post-traumatic stress disorder was something he managed, but not something he would ever be free of. The aeroplane accident would always be a part of him, even if it had taken him a number of painful years to accept that. Still, old wounds flared up hard and he was using every one of the tools and strategies he'd ever learned to keep himself in check.

Carefully, he disentangled his arm from beneath Nina's head and slid backwards until he could quietly slip out of bed. He still wore his clothing from the day before minus his shoes and coat, but the collar of his shirt felt too tight and he resisted the urge to rip it off himself in one move.

He hardly remembered getting on the phone and bellowing at his own private doctor in Paris for a second opinion on Nina's injuries. The small number of executives who had followed him from the guest spectators' suite had looked upon him with shock and possible fear, he'd likely seemed so unhinged. It was a part of himself he'd worked hard to keep under wraps, so uncomfortable he was with the unpredictability of his own reactions once he'd been triggered. And so Tristan had been forced to leave the paddock to calm down, once he knew that Nina would be following him quickly enough.

Making his way through to the living room area of his suite, he quietly called through to the concierge and ordered coffee and breakfast to be sent up shortly. Nina would need to wake in order to take her medication and she couldn't do that on an empty stomach. The domesticity of that thought made him pause but strangely, for once, it didn't make him want to scream and run. He wanted to care for Nina in a way that he had never felt the urge to care for anyone before. It was a feeling that he couldn't quite explain away with simple sexual attraction.

Sure, he very much wanted to bed her at his earliest convenience, but he also wanted to make sure that she was eating enough and that she wasn't working too damned hard. She was too independent for her own good, and was always thinking of the team and her charity, never about herself.

She could have *died* yesterday.

And yet all she'd been worried about once she'd emerged from that car was missing out on the damned podium place. It had made him feel so furious and helpless—two emotions he greatly disliked feeling. Well, he'd taken control of himself now and he'd decided she was going to be forced to rest and to prioritise herself for once. Even if she fought him tooth and nail the entire time—in fact, he hoped she would. He loved it when she fought him.

This tangle of thoughts held him frozen in place on the balcony as he stared out at the sun rising above the city of Barcelona. He almost didn't hear the terrace door sliding open behind him until Nina appeared by his side, wrapped in a fluffy white robe.

'I wasn't going to wake you until breakfast arrived,' he said, gesturing for her to take a seat alongside him.

'It's gorgeous.' She sighed, her eyes glued to the sky putting on a show as the dawn broke fully. 'It's the most stunning thing I've ever seen.'

'It really is,' Tristan murmured in agreement, his eyes not leaving her face. She turned to look at him, a slight blush creeping to her cheeks.

'How's the pain?' he asked, scanning her face for traces of discomfort.

'I feel rather how one would expect to after slamming into an immovable object at high speed.'

Tristan winced, turning back to look out at the domes of the roofs in an effort to distract himself from the overwhelming urge to demand she never set foot in a race car again.

'Sorry, Tristan, I'm honestly fine. I've never hit the wall before, not that hard anyway. But we are trained to encounter all emergencies, so I knew what to do to keep myself safe. The cars are safe, our apparatus is safe… I'm safe too.'

'Luckily,' Tristan growled. 'This time.'

Her lips pursed tight. 'Luck does have a part to play in it. But I'd also like to think that my skill and my commitment to using the correct techniques at all times are also in my favour. For the number of races I've started, I've got an exceptionally low damage record.'

'I'm not saying that you're not skilled, Nina. You didn't cause that incident yesterday. I've already asked the team principal to issue a protest to the stewards to get that bastard suspended.'

'You did what?' She gasped, wincing a little at the pain in her shoulder as she turned to face him.

'We all saw how he attacked you, recklessly trying to move ahead when he didn't have the room. He will be severely penalised, if I have my way. He's lucky if that's all he gets away with. I just don't understand how you can get back in the driver's seat after an event like that.'

'Because it's my *job*, Tristan.' She tilted her chin up defiantly. 'I just as easily could have miscalculated during an overtaking manoeuvre and caused *them* to hydroplane. Would you seek to have me suspended from the sport if that were the case?'

He remained silent, holding his tongue at what he wished to say. What he wished to demand. If their engagement were real and they'd been planning to intertwine their lives, perhaps he might have spoken those thoughts aloud, but it wasn't his place. Maybe it wasn't his place either way. It *was* her job, after all.

But no job was worth more than one's life. His uncle had learned that the hard way.

They were interrupted by the sound of a knock at the door and the next while was a pleasant distraction of a delicious breakfast, which they both practically inhaled, neither of them having eaten since early the evening before. Once they were pleasantly full and their plates had been cleared away, Nina stood and announced that she was going to get ready.

'Get ready for what, exactly?'

She looked at him, hands on her hips. 'I appreciate you taking care of me last night, Tristan, but we both have separate plans. You need to be back in Paris today and I have to pack for the photo shoot. And I'd like to get a workout in before I leave.'

'First of all, you are on bed rest. And secondly, I will not be going to Paris. I'll be escorting you to the Falco estate.'

'You will? Does that mean that you've decided to do the photo shoot?'

'No,' he growled. 'It means that I will be coming with you, and I will oversee the photo shoot to make sure that it goes according to my specifications.'

'I rather feel like you are babysitting me.' She narrowed her eyes at him. 'But okay, then.'

'That's it?' He narrowed his own suspiciously. 'No five-minute sermon about how you don't need to be babysat by me and how I'm stifling your independence by ordering you around?'

She smiled. She actually smiled at his outrage, the little brat.

'No argument. I'll go back and then we can leave.' She sauntered over to the bathroom, pausing for a split second at the doorway. 'You know, I think I kind of like it when you order me around.'

She smirked, disappearing into the bathroom and leaving him to groan into his own hands with the effort of not following her.

After being firmly denied her suggestion of a gentle swim before they left, Nina remained quiet and on edge for most of their journey as they travelled north along the Spanish coast. Resisting the urge to ask the hundred burning questions that entered her mind, she almost picked through the skin on the beds of her nails as they began to move further and further away from the city.

Going without heavy exercise for two days straight might not be much to most people, but, as someone used to a certain amount of challenging physical activity per day, the lack of release was rapidly sending her anxiety levels through the roof.

Sophie had sent her a number of probing texts to see if she was doing okay, her trainer likely remembering how easily Nina had slid into burnout after her neck injury a couple of years ago. The long period of bed rest and slow torturous rehabilitation had been painful on so much more than just her injured body. She had always known that she didn't cope well with slowing down, but now, looking at her difficulties through a new lens, she realised that it was possible her neurodivergent brain actually *needed* to keep busy. That maybe it was okay that she relied so heavily on having measurable goals to focus on and tasks to hit in order to feel any semblance of balance. Perhaps there was no need to feel so ashamed of how rigidly she clung to her schedule. Much like the temperamental vehicles she drove, if she stopped too suddenly, she risked fully losing control.

'Still cranky?' Tristan asked, breaking her out of her own thought spiral.

For once she was actually grateful for the distraction. 'Just trying to ascertain if you always drive at this speed, or if you're crawling along in the slow lane just to irritate me.'

He smirked, his hands drumming a beat on the wheel as he slowed even further. 'Maybe I like to enjoy the scenery when I travel. Live in the moment.'

'Well, you'll have a lot of scenery to enjoy, seeing as we likely won't arrive until tomorrow.' She pressed the button on the dash to try and find some music to distract herself, only to be met with her least favourite big summer dance tune. She winced, turning the volume back down.

'My radio, my rules,' he scolded, turning the dial back up and singing along with the overdramatic tune. He sang well, annoyingly well. Of course he had been blessed with the voice of a fallen angel as well as having the looks of one. Still, she had to turn her head to watch as he bellowed the fast-paced Spanish lyrics, describing the famous singer's scorn after her lover had strayed. He knew every single word. She thought of how intensely he'd reacted after her accident.

Was it possible that he actually wasn't quite the paragon of calm that he pretended to be? This man sang the song with a quiet passion that made her skin prickle and her heart throb. He *felt* the lyrics. Too soon, the song came to an end and she felt as if she'd just witnessed yet another tiny glimpse beneath the mask of Tristan Falco. Something even wilder and more intense than the devil-may-care playboy he presented to the world.

The Falco estate was as grand and exaggerated as she expected it to be, with a sweeping tree-lined drive that seemed to go on for miles before the actual house came into view—well, Tristan had referred to it as a house but as they grew closer, she could hardly believe her eyes.

'Is that a freaking castle?' she asked.

'The main house dates back to the seventeenth century, yes.' Tristan smiled. 'My uncle had a flair for the dramatic, and once he saw this place nothing else would do.'

Nina had grown up in luxury and was no stranger to the opulent grand estates of wealthy families, but the Falco estate was nothing like she had ever seen before. After parking in the middle of a grand courtyard, com-

plete with legitimate antique marble statues and a man-
icured garden that would make a king weep, Tristan
greeted the couple who managed the estate year-round
and linked his arm through Nina's as they were given a
grand tour.

He introduced her as his fiancée, of course, which the
housekeeper and her husband acknowledged with delight, asking if the wedding was to be held upon the estate. Without missing a beat, Tristan mentioned that his
mother would likely insist it took place in Buenos Aires.
It was just part of their ruse, she reminded herself. But
still, hearing him mention their non-existent wedding
plans shifted something in her stomach.

Her sense of awe quickly overrode her unease at their
deception as she was guided through the most stunningly
preserved historic estate she had ever seen. She was given
the full history by the very animated groundskeeper, his
wife interrupting every now and then to correct him if
he got the dates wrong. The majestic manor house was
located in the most exclusive area of Barcelona's north
coast, less than an hour from the city centre. Surrounded
by beautiful garden and lush forests, it was gloriously private with breathtaking views of the Mediterranean Sea.
They were shown around more than ten spacious suites
inside, then guided outside where there were a large ball-
room and chapel hidden in some lush forest, as well as
a long swimming pool and a handful of smaller villas.

The main building was comprised of several outbuild-
ings that formed a fortified enclosure. It had been re-
formed over time while preserving and enhancing the
architectural wealth of the original stone features. Its
charm lay in the perfect fusion of its historical charac-

ter with the more modern touches that added comfort and luxury.

Tristan seemed on friendly terms with the staff, which surprised her considering she had read he'd grown up mostly in Buenos Aires with his mother, with the exception of his teenage years when he'd attended a boarding school somewhere in Europe. She knew so little about him, she realised.

The couple didn't live on the estate, she learned, they instead ran a small restaurant in the nearby town along with their grown-up children. They invited them to come for dinner that evening, before bidding them farewell and leaving them alone.

'So this place just sits here empty, year-round?'

'My mother has held a few events here over the years but, yes, since my uncle's passing, no one has lived here. This was his home and he commuted to the Falco headquarters every day. He even converted one of the villas on the property into a home for me. He loved it here. He had horses and dreamed of running his own personal tours for the public, free of charge, when he retired.'

But when they reached the end of the stables where a large building bridged off in a long rectangle, Tristan paused. Nina looked up, not missing the shutters that seemed to instantly come down, hardening his handsome features.

'His garage,' he said, reaching into his pocket to extract a key and placing it in her palm. 'He had a few cars, so, while we're here, you may as well select which model you would like to use for tomorrow.'

'You don't want to choose it with me?' she asked, confused.

He shook his head, already turning away. 'I need to

do a walk around of the few setting locations while there is still light. The magazine's team will be here early in the morning; it will save us time if they know where to set up.'

She nodded, watching him stride across the lawn. The doors to the garage were automatic and slid upwards with ease once she turned the key. She had only a few seconds of squinting into the darkness before lights flickered on overhead one by one, until the entire cavernous space was lit, revealing much more than the small collection of cars Tristan had intimated was in there.

Nina's heart pumped in her chest as she began to walk along the rows, not quite knowing where to look first as she was met with what had to be around fifty perfectly preserved classic cars. Each one of them bearing her family's symbol on their bonnet.

'My God,' she whispered, spotting a particular model given pride of place on a raised podium at the end of the hall. For a moment she contemplated dropping to her knees, feeling as though she had entered a hallowed space of some sort. She supposed, to people who worshipped cars, it didn't really get much better than this.

The first edition Roux Motors coupe was one she had never actually seen in person, as only five had ever been built. Two had met their fate in fiery crashes in various parts of the globe and the other two that she knew of had been sold to collectors' museums in Asia. This particular car had passed through a number of nameless private owners, as far as she knew. It had been the car used in a very famous film with an equally famous lead actor playing the role of a spy.

She ran her fingertips along the buttery soft column of the steering wheel, noting the fresh smell of leather polish and the lack of dust upon the bonnet. If this garage had been left unattended for as long as Tristan had said, that meant he was employing someone to keep them valeted. A person would only do that if they also cared about the vehicles within. No harm would come from letting a collection like this gather a little dust. But she could tell by the gleam on each of the cars, and the scent of pine in the air, that this collection was beloved. Polished and ready for display, as though the previous owner had never left.

The way Tristan had spoken of his uncle, the fact that he had been given his own home on the property... It spoke of a very close bond between the two men. Tristan had even said he'd been more like a father to him. And to think that Tristan had almost lost his life in the same aeroplane accident that had killed someone so important to him... It was more than she could bear thinking of.

When she finally tracked him down, he stood in the courtyard with an impressively large camera in his hands as he surveyed a particularly ragged-looking fallen tree trunk in the woodland that bordered the property.

'You see one you liked?' he asked, the sound of the camera shutter flicking periodically as he changed view and moved back and forth a few steps.

'I feel like I just went to church.' She came to a stop by his side, peering over his shoulder to take in the image he'd captured of a butterfly landing on one of the craggy branches.

'I thought you'd feel that way. Half of all the Roux Motors' models ever made are in there, if not more,' Tristan murmured, clearing his throat as he continued to glower down at the fallen tree. 'He was only missing four that he wanted, before he...well, before. When the news broke that your father was selling his collection, he was one of the first to bid.'

She pursed her lips, remembering that chaotic time when her father's scandalous gambling debts and impending bankruptcy had been all over the news. The Falco plane crash had happened that same week. In another universe, how might it have gone if instead of Alain taking the helm, Tristan's uncle had bought them out and preserved Roux Motors with all of the passion she'd felt in that garage?

'He used to joke that he would name the first car he produced the Dulce Diablo after my mother. My mother always teased him for his collection and how much time he spent there, leaving all the party invitations to her. But he was obsessed.'

'I would have got along quite well with him, I'd imagine,' Nina mused, sitting down upon the thick trunk of the fallen tree. 'We'd have shared a bond in our fascination over cars and engines…and you.'

'You're fascinated with me, hmm?' Tristan asked, holding the camera up to his eye again and flicking the shutter a few times.

'I am. Hopelessly so.' Nina felt the air shift around them from his difficult past, the sunlight dappling her skin as if to remind her that she was in fact here right now. Living in the moment, as he'd said before. He was so tense, so burdened by the memory of being here in this place. Maybe she could help him with that, give him some new, happier memories. Making the decision to be brave, she slid down one strap of her dress.

CHAPTER EIGHT

BEING BACK IN the home where he had shared so many happy memories with his uncle and aunt before they'd both died had already put Tristan on edge for most of the day. But that was nothing compared to the torture of watching Nina slide down the straps of her summer dress. The loose cotton material easily skimmed over her toned curves, before sliding down to pool around her ankles, leaving her in skimpy underwear.

'Shoes on or off?' she asked meekly, kicking the dress to one side and leaning back against the tree trunk.

'Shoes?'

She smiled, gesturing down to the trainers she still wore. 'The magazine wants me to be in swimwear tomorrow, so I feel like these should come off too, no?'

The simple *yes* that escaped his lips was little more than a croak, and he cleared his throat, frowning down at the display of his camera to click a few random buttons. He was doing absolutely nothing productive of course; with his automatic high-grade apparatus a lot of it was done automatically.

'Is that completely necessary?' she asked, raising an eyebrow.

He grunted a reply, getting down into a crouch in the grass. He narrowed his eyes on her, suddenly realising what kind of game his little cat was playing. He'd denied her request last night, not willing to risk her injuries might be more serious than either of them had assumed. But now, apart from a little light bruising here and there, she was most certainly fighting fit and determined to break down his chivalrous control in whatever way she could.

'Lean back and arch your neck,' he growled, satisfied, when she looked up at him with surprise.

'Like this?' She leaned back in the way he'd directed, attentive and serene as he instructed her to place her body this way and that, then to move one ankle over the other.

'Soften your lower lip, *querida*,' he breathed. 'Yes, that's it. Now…look directly at me. Don't look away until I tell you.'

'Or else, what?' She narrowed that onyx gaze on him.

'Perhaps I'll decide that this photo shoot needs even less clothing.' Through the lens of the camera, he zoomed in, seeing the very moment that her pupils dilated and her nostrils flared.

Little minx. He'd bet she was imagining it right now, him ordering her to strip off her underwear, exposing her bared flesh to him and his camera. They were all alone out here after all… He could easily follow through on his threat. The idea of it made his blood thrum in his ears and he almost entirely lost focus on his act of taking photos completely. Nina wasn't doing too much better as she fixed her lust-hazed eyes on him, her arms beginning to shake with the effort of leaning back on the rough surface of the tree trunk.

'Breathe, Nina,' he murmured, moving a few steps closer and continuing to click, at speed. He caught the moment her eyes turned sultry, and the blush that had been kissing only her cheeks swept down to cover her chest.

'You're a natural at this…so beautiful.' He ignored the tightening of his raging erection, focusing on her, on nothing but her as she obeyed his instructions. 'Good, Nina. So good.'

She practically blossomed under his praise, her nipples tightening into little peaks beneath her bra as she thrust her breasts forward and spread her legs wide of her own accord. She posed herself this way and that, loosening up under his gaze.

He had never actually done a posed photo shoot with a model this way. He'd always preferred to find his subjects in real life, unaware. Catching the little moments of honesty. But this, whatever they were doing here, felt like a perfect meeting of the two styles. A mixture of instruction and honesty that made his skin feel too tight and his heart beat too loud in his ears. He had held himself in check with this woman for weeks on end, determined to deny his own pleasure. While it seemed she had slowly realised that there was one thing she wanted from their deal, the one thing that he had told her he could not, should not, give her.

Dropping the camera down to his side, he replaced the mechanical gaze upon her with his own and saw her beautiful features soften even more. She didn't move out of her pose, the one he'd put her in. Like the cat he'd compared her to, she lay in wait. Those onyx eyes didn't leave his as he took one step closer followed by another and another until he had her pressed up against his chest. His lips found hers as if he were a magnet and she his true North, and he plundered and possessed every inch of her mouth before coming up for air.

'You drive me wild,' he rasped, fisting his hands in her hair to keep her in place or to keep himself tethered perhaps. He felt out of control, more out of control than he'd ever been, but he welcomed it. He welcomed the adventure that was Nina… The passion and the infuriating fire that she had brought back into his life replacing the numbness of mediocrity and boredom. It would reappear all too soon once they went their separate ways again.

Sliding his hands down along her sides, he allowed himself to stop overthinking everything and simply feel. The sensation of her silky-smooth skin under his fingertips was heaven, as was the delicate way she rocked her pelvis against his erection. Needy moans escaped her lips as she peppered his throat with hungry kisses.

'I'm supposed to be the one seducing you,' he growled.

'Says who?' She looked up at him through long sooty lashes, a sensual smile on her lips.

'You really liked it when I ordered you around.'

A fresh blush crept up her cheeks, and she tilted her head down bashfully.

He put one finger under her chin, encouraging her to look back up at him. 'Those photos are all yours, by the way. To keep or delete as you wish. I don't need a photograph for what's already burned in my memory, *querida*. But I do need to get you to a bed fairly soon.'

'A bed…*yes*.' She whispered the words in between moans and delicious whimpers as he bent his head to busy himself with one taut nipple through the thin material of her bra. Forcing himself to move, he stood back up, took her by the hand and led her towards his villa.

The journey from their little interlude was a complete blur and Nina soon felt her frantically aroused body pushed back onto Tristan's huge four-poster bed, giggling wildly as his equally frantic form spread over her.

He murmured pretty words against her mouth, his hands clumsily working to undo his belt. The room was dimly lit with the curtains drawn, but she could just about make out his muscular form as he straightened to pull off his T-shirt and shuck off his jeans. He was upon her again in an instant, his hot skin sliding against her own in the most blissful sensation. Her entire body felt like a livewire that had been activated. She wanted him everywhere.

'I'm afraid this first time might not last very long.' Gently, he spread her thighs wide and Nina gasped at the sensation of him *right there*.

'I don't want to crush you…you're sure your injuries aren't—'

'Tristan. I'm fine. But if you stop right now, I swear…'

He laughed, lying on his side to pull her against his chest as he ripped open a foil packet and slid protection over his length with impressive speed. With one hand, he pulled her thigh up so that her body half straddled him. She'd done some research to feel more prepared but this position was not one she'd ever seen in a movie or read about in a book. It felt impossibly intimate with his eyes on hers and almost every inch of their skin touching. His erection was hot and heavy against her entrance as his finger traced a slow circle right where she needed it.

'Please,' she begged, grinding herself against him. 'Oh, my God.'

'Slow…slow down, *por el amor de Dios*, or I swear I won't last more than five seconds.'

'You said you never lose control.'

'I say a lot of foolish things around you.' He caught

her mouth in another punishing kiss as he pressed forward, sliding the very tip of himself inside her. The slight stretch felt uncomfortable but not overly so and with his lips devouring hers so passionately she quickly forgot to worry about pain, eager for more. With his eyes on hers there was nowhere to hide, but she didn't feel self-conscious, she felt beautiful. She felt desirable and sexy and right. More right than she'd ever felt, even behind the wheel.

The combination of him at her entrance and against her clitoris was magic and she quickly felt her legs begin to tremble with the onset of release. He didn't speed up, nor did he look away or react as she whispered a series of curses and prayers in French. He was right there with her, holding her with his quiet strength as he ruthlessly worked her body in a perfect rhythm until she broke apart.

Her orgasm was a slow earthquake that swept up from her toes to her chin, wiping out every coherent thought she had and turning her into a shaking mass of limbs against his chest. She was vaguely aware of his lips pressing tenderly against her brow and of the fact that he hadn't seemed to experience the same release as she had.

'That was…perfect,' she whispered, unable to stop the smile that spread up to her cheeks.

'Perfect,' he murmured. 'I need to hear you come again before I do, but I need to be fully inside you.'

'That wasn't…fully inside?' she whispered, shaking herself out of the haze of her post-orgasmic bubble.

He let out a husky laugh, already bracing himself over her and spreading her thighs wide. 'My ego needs no further stroking, *mi cielo*, I'm already on the edge as it is.'

Nina tensed up, trying to find the right words to tell

him that *fully inside* might not be an option just yet, but all thoughts left her as he gently slid his thumb over her still-sensitive core in a slow firm circle. All thoughts subsided, replaced by a heady rush of sensation and heat that made her groan aloud. This man was going to overdose her with orgasms before the night was through, she was sure of it. She looked up at him, pleasure drunk, and was struck anew at how handsome he was. Seized with a sense of bravery, she told him as much in a breathless voice that sounded nothing like her own.

He smiled. The next thing she was aware of was him pressing his length into her with one smooth thrust.

The pain was so sharp, so sudden that Nina whimpered, a guttural sound escaping her throat as she braced both hands against his powerful chest with the urge to push him away. Tristan immediately froze, brows furrowed as he settled himself and his massive member right where it was apparently attempting to split her apart.

'You...you're too tight, *belleza*,' he gritted, a slow breath hissing through his teeth as he held himself frozen in place.

'You're too large,' she countered. 'Oh...my God.'

'Not that large.' He shook his head slightly, a horrified expression transforming his face. 'Nina, are you...? Is this...?'

'My first time, yes,' she finished for him. 'I'm okay, it's already feeling better. Don't stop.'

A low series of curses followed, his brow dropping to press against the junction of her neck and shoulders. *'Dios... Nina.'*

She placed her hands on either side of his face, lifting him until his tortured gaze met hers. 'I'm fine now. Don't you dare stop.'

His expression hardened, a vein popping in his temple as he visibly wrestled with emotions she couldn't quite name but would hazard a guess about. She'd thought he'd understood her lack of experience, but she should have made it crystal-clear to him. But even so, she would not apologise for how tonight had gone. Nor would she change any of it. Unless he walked away right now—*that* she would not recover from too easily.

He didn't seem fully deterred by her revelation, not judging by how his length still pressed hot and hard inside her. Plus, it didn't seem to hurt quite so much now that they'd taken a small breather. Curious, she experimented, tightening her inner muscles around him with a slow squeeze. Tristan's eyes drifted closed so she did it again, this time eliciting a low growl from his lips.

'You're trying to kill me.' He groaned. 'You needed me to be much more gentle with you. I shouldn't have—'

'I don't *want* gentle, Tristan.' She moved again, a swift tilt of her hips to grind up against him. She was clumsy and unpractised but not entirely without skill, it seemed, as his eyes opened again and he finally, finally began to move once more. Slowly at first, but his restraint quickly faltered as his breathing grew more ragged. She felt the power in every thrust, as though both of them were fighting against one another but somehow moving perfectly in time. Like a dance. As though every other interaction they'd had had been building towards this.

Was this what their fighting had been about? Perhaps she had never hated him at all.

There was no other word for how it felt to have him taking her this way other than complete possession and it was over far too soon. She gasped and climaxed for the second time and, with a loud roar, Tristan shuddered against her and collapsed, his breath fanning against her cheek for a second before he gently withdrew. He lay on his back alongside her and they stayed like that for a long moment, their chests rising and falling in tandem.

After a long silence, Nina felt him move away. A click of the bathroom light followed and the running of water. He returned moments later, gently guiding her so he could use a warm compress to cleanse between her legs. When he pulled the towel away, a small amount of blood stained the white cotton. Squinting in the low light, she saw the furrow between his brows and the tension in his shoulders. She wanted to soothe him, to reassure him that tonight had been perfect. She wanted to apologise for being too shy to tell him that she hadn't technically had sex before, but that she was glad he'd been her first. She wanted him to kiss her again and tell her that he was glad too.

'Sleep.' He spoke softly, but made no move to join her again in the bed.

Nina watched as he pulled on a robe and walked to the high balcony windows that overlooked the coastline, his broad silhouette framed in the light of the moon. She fought off the sleep that threatened to claim her. It wasn't meant to feel this way, getting her wish. She was supposed to feel empowered and satisfied, having very thoroughly got the Falco experience.

He'd been everything she'd fantasised about and more, but a whole new ache had been opened up within her, entirely unrelated to the dull throbbing between her legs. She realised with alarm that the ache had now settled in her chest, bringing with it a longing for the man who seemed so intent on holding her at a distance while he possessed her every waking thought.

She wanted much more than to be just another woman

who'd lost herself in his bed. She wanted him to lose himself with her. To need more of her, just as she seemed unable to stop needing more of him. All these thoughts seemed so urgent as he turned around, walking back over to the bedside to quietly ask if she was okay. But that dreamy haze still pulled at her mind and all she managed was a husky 'thank you' before she fell into a deep, satisfied sleep.

CHAPTER NINE

NINA'S SLEEPY THANK YOU rang in Tristan's ears long after she'd dozed off and left him alone with his thoughts. She'd been a virgin. A virgin in his bed and he'd had no idea. He'd trusted the chemistry between them, been blinded by his own lust so much that he'd missed all of the signs. Now he could see that, while she might not have specifically referred to herself in such terms, she'd tried to let him know that she wasn't experienced.

Still, he was furious with himself.

The image of her face wincing with pain after he thrust inside her would be burned into his memory for ever. He'd taken her without any finesse, so eager he'd been to possess her. He'd hurt her...

Hour after hour in the dark, he wrestled with his unsettling thoughts until he gave up and slid back into bed alongside her. Staring into her sleeping face, he realised why he was so angry with himself for not seeing the signs of her inexperience. It wasn't about his ego or his reputation in the bedroom. When he was with Nina, none of that mattered. It was because he cared. She was rapidly beginning to matter to him in a way he couldn't look at too closely. It made his chest feel tight, his throat dry and painful as he reached out to run his knuckles over the silky skin of her bare shoulder.

The idea that she'd seen tonight as a temporary experiment of sorts did nothing to ease his temper. He'd have to set her to rights on *that* tomorrow. Once he'd cooled off. Maybe even once they'd made love again and he'd shown her exactly how it should have been the first time and how he planned for it to be every time after that for the foreseeable future if he got his way.

With that thought settling with some satisfaction inside his chest, he pulled her sleeping form against his chest and let her delicious scent carry him off into a deep sleep.

Nina didn't know what a person was expected to feel or say the morning after having sex with a fake fiancé, but after Tristan's silence the night before she didn't plan on sticking around until he woke up to find out.

The morning sun was pleasant and warm on her face as she took a long walk through the tree-lined woods that surrounded the castle grounds, letting the effect of gentle exercise in nature smooth out some of the knots that had taken up residence in her muscles. Sex was a more strenuous workout than she'd anticipated, she thought with a small smile as she set about grabbing some coffee and fruit from the long buffet table that the housekeeper had set up for the crew.

She briefly greeted the few who had arrived early to set up the shoots for the day, then decided it was best to keep out of the way until someone told her otherwise. Still, her nerves tightened and she felt more twitchy and uncomfortable with every second she tried to remain calmly seated on the patio that overlooked the pool. Dark sunglasses shielded her sensitive eyes from view at least, so she whiled away some time with a game on her phone until the sound of heavy footsteps grabbed her attention.

Tristan's powerful form made its way across the flagstones of the pool area, his eyes unmoving from where she sat, like a laser focused upon its target. Nina sat up a little straighter in her seat, resisting the urge to run away and avoid him a little longer. He hadn't been able to hide his dissatisfaction last night, but she shouldn't be surprised. Would he be heartbreakingly kind and let her down easy? Would he pretend it never happened? She didn't know which was worse.

In the end he simply stood and glowered down at her once he reached the opposite end of the low table she sat at. His breath came heavily, as though perhaps he'd run some of the short distance from the villa.

'Good morning,' she said, her voice a slight croak when he continued to simply stare down at her without speaking. 'Did you…um…want some coffee?'

'What are you doing?' he said, his voice low and perilously near to a growl.

'I'm waiting for the photo shoot to begin. I like to be on time.'

His jaw worked for a second, his gaze moving to rove down over her bare legs and feet before he scrubbed a hand over his jaw. 'Have I woken up in some alternate dimension or did we not make love last night?'

'We did,' she said, steeling herself to simply lay it all out there since he seemed hell-bent on doing so. 'If you're wondering why I left, I thought perhaps some space might be needed today, to avoid any uncomfortable conversations. As you can see, I'm completely fine and not going to spend the day crying or whatever you might think virgins do in the aftermath of being…deflowered, or whatever they call it now. I don't regret it and I don't want you to feel obligated to be kind to me.'

Tristan stared down at her, a muscle ticcing in his jaw. 'Nina, kindness is the bare minimum I should treat you with. *Dios*… I was simply taken off guard by your lit- tle…deception. But I see now that I wasn't careful enough with you. I didn't intend for you to feel you had to run away from me.'

She folded her arms across her chest. 'Deception? Is that how you view what happened last night?'

'You weren't completely honest with me. I could have hurt you, badly. I *did* hurt you.'

He had no idea how much he was still hurting her, she thought balefully as she felt a lump in her throat. Stand- ing up suddenly, she resisted the urge to run and stood her ground, hands on hips. 'I may not have proclaimed my virginity from the rooftops, but I was not dishonest and I didn't deliberately deceive you. I expected some- one of your vast experience to be able to read between the lines, that's all.'

'Que?' He paused, dark blond brows rising almost to his hairline. 'Are you saying that you blame *me* for what happened?'

Nina picked up her empty coffee cup and bowl, mov- ing swiftly down the steps towards the castle, forcing him to keep pace with her. 'I don't see why blame has to be placed anywhere. We are two grown adults who had sex. It was all…perfectly fine and consensual.'

One moment she was racing ahead of him, the next he'd moved to block her way through the archway to the kitchen building with one muscled forearm. She looked up, finding his handsome face staring down at her with abject incredulity.

'Fine and consensual,' he echoed, eyes not leaving hers.

'Exactly.'

'So if I were to suggest we make it a regular thing, you'd slot me into your schedule?' He ran a hand along the side of her face, brushing aside an errant lock of hair. 'Tell me, Nina—which colour-coded category would sex with me fall into? Orange for social events? Or perhaps blue for personal well-being?'

'I'd probably say red for fitness regimen,' she snapped, praying he couldn't hear the rampant hammering of her heart as she tried desperately to appear as calm and controlled as possible.

He bared his teeth in a smile that still didn't quite meet his eyes. 'Ah, of course, we worked up quite a sweat, didn't we, *querida*? I'm glad I was of service to you, then.'

She blushed, turning her head away in an effort to escape this ridiculous game he was playing with her. He was angry about the whole virginity detail, that much was certain.

'It's irrelevant, because you made it perfectly clear from the start that we *won't* be making it a regular thing. And for what it's worth I agree—it's best not to complicate our arrangement any further. Now, if you'll let me go, I need to go and have some cold pointy diamonds draped all over me.' She pushed at his chest to no avail, looking up to find him glaring at her, ice-blue eyes narrowed with tension. He licked his lips and for a moment she thought he might do something utterly ridiculous, like kiss her until she couldn't stand up. He could—they were still playing the part of blissful lovebirds, after all. But in the end, he simply gritted his jaw and moved aside.

He was being punished.

By whom, he wasn't quite sure. He had been the one to agree with Astrid that they use Nina for the jewellery

124

campaign while they were here, after all. But as Nina walked back out onto set in the world's tiniest flesh-coloured two-piece swimming suit, draped in Falco diamonds, he rather felt as though he were being tortured.

Her tanned skin glowed under the late afternoon sun, with summer having finally decided to make an appearance. She didn't glance his way as she was shown around the set that took up most of the lavish stone courtyard, smiling and nodding as the team discussed the vintage car they'd be using for the day. A model that she was expected to pose upon while draped in Falco diamonds, the director had explained to him only moments before. His gut churned as he recalled the similar photo shoot she'd done in that magazine several years ago, but he forced himself to remain still, to not interfere.

She was not a damsel in need of rescuing, as she'd told him. She had consented to act as a model, knowing full well what it might entail. But as she finally looked up and met his gaze, offering up a small polite wave before turning her back, he fought the urge to growl.

It wasn't that he'd expected clingy tears upon waking this morning, but when a man awoke after the most peaceful sleep of his life to find that his bed partner had already fled the scene after their interlude... It had got under his skin. He still felt completely on edge after last night, his ego and his control rubbed raw. For all of his grand ideas about maintaining their professionalism and distance in the wake of their lovemaking, he was the one having to refrain from jumping up, throwing her over his shoulder like a caveman and depositing her back into his bed for the rest of the afternoon.

As he watched, the director's assistant instructed her to move, draping the thin silk wrap she'd been provided with over her shoulders to cover her mostly naked flesh. She moved with ease, her athlete's muscles bunching up and flexing as she slid herself into place, perfectly following the direction. However, was he imagining the slight look of discomfort in her tightened features as she settled herself more fully upon the hard edge of the car's bonnet? When she moved again, the director's assistant sliding her a couple of inches to the right and removing her wrap again, she winced and readjusted herself.

Tristan's stomach tensed with awareness at the sudden possibility that she was uncomfortable with far more than just her body being on display. He'd been careless last night in bed with her; surely she would've told him if she was too sore to do the shoot today?

Even as the thought occurred to him he shrugged it off, knowing that was exactly what Nina would *not* do. She would insist upon working past her own limits, ignoring her own feelings, much too stubborn for her own good.

As the director called out for her to change position once again Nina's face tightened, and this time a low hiss escaped her lips before she straightened and posed once more.

He'd had enough.

'Cut!' he called out loudly. 'Stop everything. Stop.'

'What? We're in the middle of a take,' the director shouted, gesturing wildly with her hands.

'I need to speak with my fiancée,' he growled, striding across the set until he reached her side in a few short steps. Nina looked up at him, her arms crossed defensively over her chest. 'We haven't finished yet, Tristan. You can't just yell out cut because you wish to speak with me.'

'I can and I am,' he insisted. 'Be honest with me, please—are you in pain?'

Her mouth tightened, her gaze slipping to look away, past his shoulder. 'It's no more than I can handle. Go back to your chair.'

'Everyone, take an early lunch in town, my treat. My housekeeper will escort you.' He gripped her waist gently, lifting her slim weight up against his chest. 'You... come with me.'

Thankfully she didn't fight him when he insisted on draping her silk robe back around her shoulders and gathering her into his arms. The journey from the courtyard back to his villa was a blur as he fought the red haze of rage that had settled over him. Rage at his own PR team for suggesting that she model his diamonds when the focus should have been on her role as a woman in motorsport, rage at the magazine's decision to have her pose semi-nude, but most of all rage at himself for allowing it all to happen. Because he knew that he had put her in this situation, the same situation her parents had once put her in. He should know better.

When they finally entered his bedroom, she kicked her legs, fighting her way into a standing position before tightening the belt on the flimsy robe.

'I hope that you have a good explanation for why you just did that.' She stood, arms crossed, black eyes narrowed upon him like a furious queen.

The fact that she had been nicknamed with ice in mind was so utterly laughable, not only because he had experienced her fire first-hand, but because her passion and strength burned hotter than anything he had ever seen. His attraction to her was so much deeper than the quick sexual gratification she had accused him of pursuing.

'Tristan, you can't just shut down an expensive photo shoot with no explanation. People are going to talk and make assumptions.'

'Let them,' he said, scowling at her. 'I don't care about their opinions.'

'The whole point was to mingle our two families' brands and meet somewhere in the middle. Fashion and racing.' She shrugged one slim shoulder. 'I wouldn't have agreed to it if I didn't feel totally comfortable.'

'Did you?' He stepped closer. 'Because from where I was sitting you looked pretty damn uncomfortable.'

'Is that what this is about? Your conscience at hurting me last night? Because, honestly, I've heard that discomfort in those circumstances is pretty unavoidable. It really doesn't matter.'

'It matters to me,' he insisted, tightening his hold on her wrist and pulling her closer. 'You can act as unaffected as you like, but, from a purely physical point of view, I should've taken better care of you. I would have done it so much differently if I'd known.'

She paused, her gaze softening at his regret. 'You would have?'

'Oh, yes,' he said, inhaling a deep breath of her inimitable scent. 'I would have taken my time. I would have made it so much better for you. You have no idea how good it would have been.'

He ran his cheek against the soft skin of her neck, breathing her in and feeling her shiver in response. She was always so responsive, so honest. Perhaps that was why he'd flown into an immediate fury upon waking up alone in his bed this morning. Her scent had surrounded him, but her warmth had been long gone and the idea that she'd left him…that he might never get to touch her again… It had been unacceptable.

'Let me put this into terms you'll appreciate,' he murmured softly. 'You see, you expected the Falco experience, but I didn't have all the details. If I'd known exactly what I was going into, I would have changed my tactics and strategy in order to achieve the best result for you. Your pleasure is what's most important to me, and the sound of you in pain… I can't get it out of my mind. I need to replace it with the sound of your pretty moans as you come. With the sound of you calling out my name in ecstasy. I'm a perfectionist, *querida*, so please let me make this right.'

'You're not playing fair.' She gasped as his erection made contact with her hip.

He took her face into his hands, meeting her eyes. 'This isn't a game. Not here. There are no cameras, no audience to pretend to. Whatever this is from now on… It's just between me and you.'

CHAPTER TEN

IF THIS WAS a punishment of sorts, please sign her up. She wanted him never to stop.

He laid her back on the bed, kissing a path from her inner ankle up past her knee, slowing down all the more the closer he got to the apex of her thighs. Then, to her frustration, he moved to the top of the opposite thigh and began a slow path downwards again. At her whimper of discontent, he chuckled darkly.

He rose up onto his knees, gazing down at her with a look of what she hoped was deep admiration, but she couldn't quite tell. He got back into place between her thighs, sliding her underwear down slowly until she was fully bare to him. Smoothly, he sucked on his index finger, taking the glistening digit and sliding it down in a line between her intimate folds. Nina moaned as he began a slow silky torture between her thighs, until she practically begged him to insert that tricky finger. He refused of course, leaning down to blow cold air upon her tortured flesh.

'I told you, it's too soon for that. You need time to recover. This is just about making you feel good, Nina. I'm going to make you feel so good.'

Nina gasped as Tristan's lips pressed against her core, his fingers spreading her wide as he leaned in to kiss her silky hot skin. It felt absurdly intimate and intense and for a moment she wondered if she might push his head away, but as he licked and laved her just in the perfect spot she seemed to melt. Her body relaxed, mind emptying of all thoughts other than, *Yes!* and, *More!* and, *Please, Tristan, oh, please...*

After a time she realised that those words were actually escaping her own lips on small gasps and pleas for mercy as his gentle teasing kisses became more demanding. He worked her body as though he knew every inch of it. He was a master of pleasure, and she was fully at his mercy, coming apart at the seams.

The orgasm that built within her seemed to overtake her entire body, tuning her nerve endings to a fine point and then breaking her apart with an explosion of heat and wave after wave of delicious pleasure. After a few breathless moments of delirium, she regained an awareness of her surroundings and realised he hadn't made any move to continue as they had the night before.

'Still tender?' he murmured against her inner thigh, stroking a hand along her still sensitive skin and making her shiver.

She shook her head to signal no, because the ache in her core had shifted into something very different from the reminder of her first time. Her hips shifted against him, her throat working with the effort not to beg for the scorching stretch of relief that she craved.

Tristan's eyes darkened, seeing far too much as he rose to his knees above her on the bed. 'The crew will be returning from town soon...but I think we have time for a shower.'

'Together?' she asked, picturing the intimate slide of hands along wet flesh and feeling her cheeks heat.

His smile was devilish as he lifted his head, a man thoroughly satisfied with his work. 'This was a good start. But I'm going to need to gather more data if I'm expected to formulate an accurate strategy.'

'How much more?' she asked, trying not to show how ridiculously turned on his racing terminology made her when used in this context. It was perfect, he was perfect, and he wanted this just as much as she did. It was almost too perfect to believe, but she could worry over the potential risks and consequences later. Much later.

'As much as you can take, kitten. If you think you can handle me?'

A flush of arousal pooled low in her belly and she knew she was in trouble, but she'd always been powerless to resist a challenge. Tristan Falco was like the thrill of the track distilled into human form and if she wasn't careful, she'd lose herself in his wicked games.

She smiled back, her limbs heavy with pleasure as she accepted his hand and allowed him to lead her to the bathroom where he proceeded to show her exactly what kind of data he intended to gather from her until they were both weak limbed and thoroughly late to finish the rest of the photo shoot.

Over the course of the afternoon, Nina felt Tristan's eyes on her and her body seemed to be experiencing a constant low hum of awareness in his presence. If anything, it only enhanced her confidence for her poses. Usually she felt awkward and ridiculous during photo shoots like this, but with Tristan's gaze devouring her, she came alive.

The magazine photographer deferred often to Tristan's expertise and while he didn't actually take any photos of her himself, he did offer up some great ideas to change the direction from the earlier, more sexual poses to something edgier and infinitely more unique. He had an artist's eye, she realised as he instructed the crew to drive the car back into the long expanse of the garage for some of the shots and incorporate a stack of spare tyres and mechanical tools in the foreground to represent Nina's knowledge of the industry she loved.

As they gathered to see a preview of the photos, Nina felt surprisingly satisfied with looking at herself in the images. She looked powerful and sexy, as if the woman and the athlete had been given equal space to shine. The Falco Diamonds team also joined them for a few hours and were quick and efficient in completing their objectives for their campaign.

When Tristan announced that part of the Falco experience included being whisked away by him on a yacht for a couple of weeks, Nina found herself agreeing. She was technically still on bed rest, even if there might not be much resting being done while in bed with Tristan... But, for once, she allowed herself to play hooky from her strenuous schedule. After assuring Sophie that she would meet her in Argentina for the next race, she threw caution to the wind and accepted Tristan's invitation.

'I'm just saying—you definitely cheated,' Tristan growled, his breath still coming hard and fast in the wake of a late afternoon lovemaking session. Nina smiled, remembering how he'd reacted after she'd beaten him at chess for a fifth time and he'd responded by pinning her down and punishing her with kisses that had eventually devolved into them retreating to his master cabin for several hours.

'I never cheat,' she teased, rolling over to tuck herself

into the side of his chest. 'You simply aren't up to my skill level yet. But don't worry, I'll be very gentle with you next time.'

'Little minx.' His laughter rumbled against her skin and she smiled at the easy intimacy they'd fallen into over the past few days spent alone. He'd taken a much smaller vessel out and insisted on only a skeleton crew to give them as much privacy as possible. It was as if they'd stepped into a dream.

Since they'd set sail on his yacht, the world's wildest playboy had thrown himself into showing her exactly how he had got his reputation. He made love to her in the morning as the dawn light crept into the opulent master cabin. He seduced her on the top deck in broad daylight after plying her with strawberries and champagne. The shameless man had even infiltrated her daily workout, in the gym filled with specialist equipment that he'd had inserted into the yacht specifically for her to use.

She couldn't complain though, because he was certainly keeping her in shape on her time off. With both their bedroom activities and the myriad excursions he arranged for them, like snorkelling off the coast of Corsica and a hiking trip along Sardinia's Montiferru mountain trail. For someone who'd travelled throughout much of Europe and beyond as a part of her job, she realised that she had been far too insular in how she spent her time away from the track. She ate at the same restaurants, walked the same paths and generally put all of her energy into driving all of the time. Even the few friendships she'd had had waned and dissipated since she'd removed herself from the public spectacle of being another Roux family scandal.

But spending time with Tristan felt like stepping into

a dream, where none of that mattered. Sure, the sex was becoming addictive, but even more intoxicating were the moments where they simply spent time together, just existing. She'd told him more about her past, her relationship with her parents and how they'd barely spoken to one another—or to her and Alain—since her mother had remarried. In turn, Tristan had shared his experiences of growing up with a single mother and his regret at never having the opportunity to know his father, who had died shortly after Dulce had discovered she was expecting him.

As well as personal conversations, they didn't shy away from talking about work, with Tristan surprisingly eager to discuss his ideas for the future of Falco Roux and her usually countering with how he was entirely wrong. He respected her expert opinion, she'd quickly realised, and so she eventually felt safe to share with him her belief that their management team was riddled with misogyny and inequality. He'd been furious that night, their peaceful meal at an Italian marina derailed while he'd asked for more details and had taken notes of names.

The whole thing had made her feel strange but relieved that she'd spoken up and that she hadn't been immediately shot down. Tristan was aware of his privilege as team owner and as a man among men and, even long after she'd settled him down with kisses and caresses back in the comfort of their quiet cabin on the yacht, she'd caught moments of unrest in him as he'd stared broodily out at the ocean.

After that day, she'd steered clear of any more talk of Falco Roux, trying to redirect him towards more playful avenues of entertainment. Hence why, today, she'd suggested they play chess. He knew only how to play at a basic level, so naturally she had beaten him time after time. But he was an entertaining opposition. He was not a sore loser; he threw himself into the game and into the mental back-and-forth that he seemed to intuitively know she enjoyed most.

But even as she lay in the wake of their lovemaking and tried to tell herself to relax and enjoy this temporary break for what it was, the reality of their situation was always looming on the horizon like an elephant in the room that neither of them wished to address first. Lying in bed with him like this, she felt as if she were just waiting for the other shoe to drop. For something to ruin this interlude and remind her of all the reasons why it would only end in heartbreak.

But no, that wasn't possible because her heart most definitely was not involved. She tended to get overly attached to people sometimes when she really liked them, that was all. It was just infatuation and endorphins from amazing sex. Maybe that was why she had begun to daydream about floating down the aisle in a flowing white gown. No amount of chemistry and infatuation would change the fact that this wasn't a real engagement and there would be no real wedding bells chiming in their future. She was too young and too busy with her career dreams to be having such absurd thoughts. Right?

'You seem preoccupied,' he murmured, pulling her closer against him. 'I thought I'd worked hard enough there to calm your mind for a bit.'

'Nothing calms my mind,' she said honestly. 'I only ever get a brief respite before it's right back to full speed again.'

'Sounds exhausting.' He chuckled. 'But it makes sense.'

'How so?' She turned to look up at him.

'You couldn't do the job you do without an enormous amount of focus and knowledge. You're talented and you work hard, of course, but you're also gifted, from what I can tell. You don't just know the sport, you live and breathe it.'

She hesitated for a moment, then decided to tell him what she'd begun to suspect about herself. She told him about what she'd learned of autism and neurodivergence and how it often ran in families for generations undetected for a variety of reasons. By the time she realised she'd been talking uninterrupted for far too long, she felt a little ridiculous and poised to apologise and change the subject, only for Tristan to surprise her once again.

'I can see it.' He smiled, one hand smoothing down over her hair. 'The way your mind works has fascinated me from the moment we met. Like you see the world in high definition, no detail missed. But I can see how that would be an intense way to live.'

Nina sat with the strange feeling of being finally *seen* and tried to repress the emotion that had filled her chest. There was no way he could know what just listening and validating her wild new feelings and thoughts would mean to her, but even if he was just being kind…it was more than she'd ever experienced before.

'I think I've always been different in a way no one around me could understand,' she said quietly. 'Except maybe my brother. He's different too, in his own way. He knows just as much as me about racing, and he even got a seat after the academy at eighteen. But where I thrived with the consistency and the heavy workload, he struggled and turned to partying to cope. He couldn't keep up with the pressure to perform in Elite One, so they let him go.'

Tristan seemed to stiffen at the mention of her brother, his gaze slipping away from her as they listened to the peaceful lapping of waves on the outside of the yacht.

'Alain is a troubled soul,' he offered vaguely.

'He is. I think that's when he started to lose control. He wanted to join the R&D team, maybe be team principal someday. But he felt ashamed of not living up to the family name or something. And then I started doing so well in my racing…' She frowned, thinking of her own single-minded nature and how obsessed she'd been with graduating top of the academy. Had she ever asked her brother how he was? 'I don't think I was a very good sister to him.'

'You can't blame yourself for the actions and struggles of the people you love. Trust me, that way lies only suffering.' Tristan sighed, seemingly agitated by her admission. 'Your brother is a grown man. He will either figure it out, or he won't. Either way, none of that is on you.'

'Spoken like someone with a similar experience?' she asked, curious.

For a moment she saw a strange emotion cross his features, and his throat worked as though he was about to speak before he stopped himself. 'I won't pretend to know why your brother did the things he's done. Just as I had to admit the same about my uncle. He became severely depressed after his wife, my aunt, died of cancer; he became disassociated from the estate and impossible to reach emotionally by those closest to him, and, with his refusal to help himself, he left a lot of people hurt and angry in the process. In the end, his total immersion in his grief to the exclusion of all else killed him, and nearly took me with him. I couldn't save him, nor could my mother or Victor. I don't think anyone could.'

'You're very wise, Tristan Falco,' she mused, running a hand along his chest.

'Is that your way of calling me old?' He growled, pulling her on top of him. And just like that, they both made a silent agreement to avoid the darker turn that their conversation had taken and throw themselves back into the fantasy of it just being the two of them alone in their bubble. And while Nina was grateful, she still couldn't shake the feeling that something had shifted between them, that the path ahead had become infinitely more perilous.

CHAPTER ELEVEN

BY THE TIME the day came for them to travel with the team to Buenos Aires, Nina found herself wishing for more time off for the first time ever. Usually, she hated the three-week vacation that took place in the middle of each Elite One season, but this one, now more than half-way through, was possibly the most enjoyable holiday she'd ever had. Tristan was fun and charming and educated, and while having sex with him was rather amazing, even by her very inexperienced standards, conversation with him was just as stimulating. It was a pity reality ever had to intrude.

The commercial jet that Tristan had chartered for their entire team to travel upon together was top of the range and included a handful of private cabins for the owner and the management of the team, along with the three drivers travelling together. From the moment they'd boarded the jet, Apollo and Daniele Roberts had disappeared into their cabins. As had the team principal and the other members of the board who were travelling with them. Nina had brought her things into her own cabin area and then immediately gone in search of Tristan, who had gone to speak with the pilot. When he re-entered his cabin to find her sitting upon his makeshift bed, he did not look as seductive and relaxed as he had when they'd awoken upon the yacht earlier this morning. Instead, he had a tightness about him.

'Is everything okay?'

He nodded, putting his hands into the pockets of his trousers, then taking them back out again to place them upon his hips and stare around the small cabin walls. He looked rather like a lion in captivity, she thought, as if he were pacing behind the bars of his cage and wishing to be anywhere but here.

She had never considered the fact that flying might be difficult for him, considering his accident. It was hard to see past the calm, confident mask that he portrayed to the world. Surely he would have told her...but as she thought back, there was no denying he avoided flying. In all their time together, he had opted for private train cars, yacht travel, he had even driven for hours on end in lieu of the much faster option of helicopters or jets.

'Do you struggle with air travel?' she asked gently, standing up to place one hand on his chest.

'I manage okay.'

'Tristan.'

'Nina, I don't need your pity right now.' The words came out of his mouth harshly, and she tried not to take offence. He was feeling whatever he was feeling and she wouldn't judge.

'Let me help.'

A small laugh escaped his lips, and he scrubbed his hand over the stubble upon his jaw before finally meeting her eyes. 'Nothing helps. The terror is the same every time. The memories, the intrusive thoughts... It feels just like it did... That day.'

'The day of your accident,' she finished for him.

'Yes, the day of the...crash.' He inhaled, releasing his

breath slowly before lowering himself down into the seat opposite hers.

Nina leaned forward, placing both of her hands upon his knees and squeezing gently. 'That must be an incredibly difficult thing to manage, all by yourself.'

He nodded once as he stared determinedly at the window. 'I didn't remember much of the accident itself for weeks afterwards, a temporary blackout of sorts. It's quite common, apparently. But I had dreams, and in the dreams… I heard the noise of the engines getting louder, the sounds of screaming, the rushing of wind. Everything after that… I lost. I woke up in a hospital bed with my mother sobbing by my side telling me that my uncle was gone. For a long time what I felt was anger. And a lot of confusion as to why I'd survived when he hadn't. I was young, selfish and more expendable than he was in the grand scheme of things.'

'You survived something truly terrible. That's not something anyone could predict or control.'

'Therapy helped me to see that eventually. I've worked through every stage of grief in the past decade but eventually I decided to help myself and step up within the Falco company and take the reins. But the flying… Still brings me to my knees every time.'

Her heart ached for the brave man in front of her and the senseless pain that he'd been put through. Life could be so unimaginably cruel sometimes, but she felt such relief that he had survived that accident. She would guess his mother felt the same relief too. As the pilot came online to say they were about to take off, Tristan closed his eyes.

'Let me stay with you?' she asked gently. Knowing that if he asked her to leave, she would.

'Please,' he said simply.

That one word lit up something in her chest, warming her through as she took the seat alongside him and they both did up their belts. As the plane ascended, Tristan's breathing became laboured but his hand didn't drop hers. She remained silent by his side as he worked through it at his own pace, not rushing him or trying to guide his panic. Just letting him be.

When a flight attendant came to interrupt them, Nina politely shooed them away, placing the 'do not disturb' sign upon the outside of the cabin door, and waited.

Tristan became aware of his surroundings in flashes of colour. The white of the closed cabin door. The blue of his jeans. The dark curtain of Nina's soft hair as she leaned over him and wrapped him in her embrace. He pulled her onto his lap, tightening his grip on her as he inhaled and exhaled deeply.

As the panic faded, there was only her. Only Nina. She peppered his face with kisses, gentle at first, but quickly he felt her breath hitch and her hips jerk.

'Is this still a part of your plan to distract me?' he asked.

She laughed against his cheek as he trailed his own kisses down the side of her neck, but he felt the speed of her arousal in her heartbeat against his lips.

'I've clearly unleashed a sex-mad woman, *mi amor*.'

The endearment slipped from his lips as smoothly as air and he felt her stiffen momentarily, her eyes gliding to his in a question he answered quickly with a deeper, much more demanding kiss. His heart hammered in his chest, not with anxiety but with the utter unpractised uncertainty that came with every interaction with this maddening woman. She made him feel godlike and uncertain all at once.

'You just *love* to flatter yourself,' she breathed, fighting to hide a groan as his hands cupped her breasts through the stretch material of her T-shirt.

'Tut-tut. Always fighting me.' He smacked one palm lightly upon her behind in faux punishment. 'Why do you have to wear such sensible clothing?'

'You'd prefer if I walked onto the plane in a diamond-encrusted thong?'

'If I had it my way, you'd never be clothed. Ever.'

'That might get in the way of safety regulations when I drive.'

The reminder of her safety, of her career, made him want to hold onto her even tighter. It made him feel as if he was losing control all over again, only this time it had nothing to do with his traumatic past and everything to do with the very perfect, very alive woman straddling him. He leaned his head between her breasts, fighting off the urge to make demands he knew he had no right to make.

'What are you thinking?' she whispered, her soft, perfect lips tracing a path along the side of his neck.

'I'm just thinking, these tight-fitting yoga pants pose a challenge to the very despicable things I want to do to you. A challenge…but not an impossible one.'

He showed her just how very possible it could be, while the hum of the jets coupled with the closed cabin door provided just enough privacy to conceal her loud groan as she sank down onto his length. Her eyes met his in innocent question as she tested her movements and he was reminded once again how new she was to this. How he was the only person who ever had seen her this way, so wild and hungry for release. How it made him feel possessive, as though he'd stumbled upon a rare gem in the rubble and he needed to keep it all for himself.

Dios, she was…unmatched. And he was becoming completely undone just by looking at her as she braced her hands on his chest and began to grind her perfect body over him. The pressure of keeping quiet made everything more intense and he lost control at the exact moment she came apart.

Afterwards, he kept her on his lap, his hands stroking through her hair as she asked questions about his home city of Buenos Aires, about his family and his childhood. He knew she was still distracting him, but he was grateful for it as he described his father's close-knit family and how they compared with the much more crusty, upper-class Falco clan. How the world had reacted when Dulce Falco had recently announced her engagement and upcoming wedding after decades of being a content widow. How, in the wake of his public cuckolding by Victor and Gabriela, Dulce had decided that matchmaking was all the support he needed. His mother had always been a big character in his life and something warmed within him when Nina openly chuckled at his description of the recent bizarre and hilarious matchmaking attempts he'd endured at his mother's behest.

'It makes sense now, why you needed a fake fiancée so quickly,' she mused, the aftermath of her mirth still spilling from the corner of her smiling eyes.

'Yes, but she will demand the real thing soon enough. She's found love again and has settled into retirement so naturally she's now decided I have to give her the big society wedding and the grandchildren she craves. Getting married herself clearly isn't enough.'

Nina stilled in his arms, her lips curving down. 'What about what you want?'

'I made my mother a promise that I would settle down

this year, mostly just to stop her worrying about me.' He shrugged. 'But the more I think of it, the more I realise my playboy days had become less and less fun even before the drama with my cousin. Maybe…the reason why I've not fought back on this is because, deep down, I think I want it too.'

His own words hit him with the weight of truth he couldn't bear to look at too closely, not when he had just come down from the adrenaline of the past hour of anxiety and connection and openness. It was all suddenly too much and yet not nearly enough as he gathered Nina closer into his embrace and urged her to sleep. His exhausted mind drifted off quickly, where he was joined in his dreams by a bride that bore a striking resemblance to a certain raven-haired racing driver.

CHAPTER TWELVE

As a town car drove them through the heart of Buenos Aires, Nina fought off the waves of anxiety that made her chest feel tight and her skin prickle. Preparing to attend Dulce Falco's wedding and be introduced to Tristan's entire extended family as his fiancée was quite a jolt back to the reality of their ruse after the past two weeks spent in a bubble of their sensual explorations. Tristan had reassured her more than once that his family would be too thrilled to meet her to suspect the truth, but she was less certain.

On the yacht, it had been only them and the insatiable attraction between them. But from the moment they landed and the Falco family's small army of assistants appeared with a change of formal clothing for them both, she was reminded that she was very much expected to play a role here in front of people who knew Tristan the best—and she was no actress.

He'd told her they had the wedding's formal rehearsal dinner to attend the moment they landed, but still she hadn't been quite prepared for the level of pomp and circumstance surrounding his arrival back into the city. It had been a number of years since he'd visited Argentina, he'd explained quietly as they'd landed, and she'd looked out of the jet window to spy a small crowd of people had lined up around the fence of the runway of the private airfield. If she'd thought Tristan Falco was famous in Europe, it appeared he had an even more godlike status in his home country.

She'd taken her time donning the stretch satin golden sheath gown she'd been given along with matching gold diamond earrings and necklace. The material was a perfect fit, soft and seamless, and she'd smiled, knowing Tristan must have passed along her specifications. When she'd emerged back out onto the main area of the jet, Tristan had been fully dressed in a sleek black tuxedo and talking through their event schedule with his family's event co-ordinator. He'd seemed distracted as they'd been brought out to the limousine, even as he'd taken a moment to compliment her ensemble before being interrupted once again with some details about the wedding ceremony they would attend the following afternoon.

They hadn't actually discussed the parameters of their deal, now that they'd ventured into spending each night in one another's arms. Once the season ended and their three months were up, would she leave the team and become a stranger to him once more? The realisation that he still intended to fulfil his mother's wish of finding a bride and having a grand wedding had been a stark one on their flight over and she'd spent hours trying not to think of it after Tristan had fallen asleep.

He would find someone easily once she was gone, that much was for certain. But as for her...she couldn't quite imagine herself ever falling into another man's arms without comparing them to him. To her first lover. Over the past two weeks, something within her had begun to change and unravel. She'd begun skipping workouts and training exercises in favour of spending as much time as she could in Tristan's arms. Instead of mulling over circuit layouts and strategies when her mind was idle, she thought about midnight-blue eyes and how his smile lines transformed his entire face when he laughed.

Armed with a wardrobe of gowns for the handful of events over the coming days, Nina reminded herself to be on her guard. The Falco family were the highest of Buenos Aires society, and not only were they old money but they were also fiercely traditional people, which she found out quickly upon being introduced to his grandmother, Valentina, his mother, Dulce, and his soon-to-be stepfather, Agustin, at the extravagant rehearsal dinner being held at an opulent hotel in the heart of the city.

'You are a racing driver?' Valentina asked her shrewdly, holding her hand and looking at her face as though trying to peer into her very soul. 'That little hobby will have to stop after the wedding.'

Nina stiffened, looking up at Tristan beside her as he coughed and immediately intervened.

'Abuela, Nina is very prominent in the motorsport world. It's not a hobby. It's her career,' he explained gently.

The older woman tutted. 'That's too dangerous a career for the mother of your children, my love.' And with that, the elderly woman walked away.

Tristan looked down at her with a wince. 'I love my family, but you see now why I don't come home very often?' He laughed.

She attempted a laugh of her own, but the interaction shook her. And she felt even more on guard as she was introduced to the rest of the family one by one. His mother was a face she had seen countless times while growing up; Dulce Falco was a worldwide fashion icon.

But here in her home city, surrounded by her loved ones, she wore very little make-up and a simple flowing gown of white linen embroidered with traditional Argentinian artwork. She looked rested and peaceful, the antithesis of the sleek, professional fashion mogul that had dominated fashion magazines and social pages for the previous four decades.

'So, this is the woman who has finally stolen my son's heart,' Dulce pronounced as she pulled Nina into a full hug. 'You are just as beautiful in person as you look whizzing around that racetrack. I've watched your last couple of races out of interest, and I've got to say—you are ferocious.'

Nina blushed. 'Coming from you, that's a huge compliment.'

Dulce waved a hand at the flattery, raising a brow in her son's direction. 'So ferocious, in fact, that I wonder why a certain team owner hasn't ensured that you are the one to lead Falco Roux to victory in this Argentinian Premio race.'

'Mama, we just landed. At least let a man eat before you begin taking him apart piece by piece.' Tristan sighed dramatically, then smirked and grabbed his mother in a deep hug.

Nina watched the open affection between mother and son and felt a twinge of jealousy. Any hugs or praise she'd ever received as a child had been veiled in expectation or judgment or had been a simple show for the press. Her parents had been selfish people, driven by their own individual agendas, and watching Tristan interacting with his own family now she could see the difference in how she had been treated. She had always just assumed that every family had their issues, but perhaps her own had been a little more problematic than she'd realised. Perhaps she was a little more affected than she'd realised too.

Much to Tristan's grandmother's horror, his mother insisted that Nina and Tristan sleep together in his childhood room once they all returned to the Falco family's grand town house after the evening of spectacular food and schmoozing was done.

Well, they described it as a *room* but, in fact, it was more of a penthouse apartment with a master bedroom and a study and a living room that overlooked the entire city of Buenos Aires. With jet lag weighing heavy upon her, she welcomed Tristan's suggestion that they go straight to bed. But as she followed him slowly into the master bedroom, she found herself pausing in the doorway.

'What's wrong?' he asked, frowning in the middle of removing his bow tie.

There was nothing wrong, of course. This entire day, the entire past two weeks, had been perfect, but with every moment she spent in his life and in his bed as his fake fiancée the lines of protection she'd drawn around her own heart grew thinner and thinner.

'I just wonder…if perhaps we should sleep separately.'

'And why would we do that?' He took a step towards her, his handsome features tightening with concern. 'Do you *want* to sleep separately?'

'No, of course not.' She shook her head.

He reached her side in a few easy strides, his hands sliding up her bare arms and coming to rest upon her cheeks. 'Then let's not,' he murmured against her lips. 'I feel like I've barely touched you since we landed, and we've barely had a moment alone. I've been counting down the moments till I had you all to myself again. Sleep here, where you belong. With me.'

She ignored how his words made something deep within her chest sing with joy, telling herself that he simply meant he didn't wish to sleep alone. Truthfully, neither did she. She'd thought about it over and over and if she had to choose between ending this now for the sake of self-preservation or risking her heart for a few more weeks of pleasure, she'd choose the latter. Even if it hurt, at least she'd know she had him, even just for a little while.

'There won't be much sleeping if I'm in bed with you.' She laughed, then gasped as his lips slid down to the most sensitive part of her neck.

'Get into bed, let me debauch you a little. Then you can sleep.'

And so she did, ignoring the alarm bells going off in her mind as she imagined this was a real love affair and her real fiancé was making love to her in his childhood bedroom while they tried to keep quiet. She let Tristan's touch still her overactive mind as his attempt at letting her sleep turned into slow, languorous lovemaking that carried on well into the night.

Tristan walked his mother down the aisle to marry the man she loved so dearly, who had made her so happy, and was proud to say that only the smallest tear slid down his cheek as he placed his mother's hands into the shaking one of his stepfather. Agustin leaned across and placed a kiss upon his stepson's cheek, whispering words of thanks into his ear. As Tristan sat down beside Nina, she quickly gripped his hand in hers and he realised that she too was feeling the emotion as his mother gave an impassioned speech about the longevity of love and how short people's time together in this world was.

The celebration that followed was one of the grandest that their home had ever seen and Tristan revelled in having all of his relations together under one roof. They feasted like kings, with a famous local chef having been hired to create a unique twist on the traditional wedding buffet of *carne asada*, roasted pigs and freshly prepared fish. *Empanadas*, *provoleta* and *chimichurri* were also in abundance, along with copious bottles of the famous Falco reserve Malbec, some of which Nina sampled with gusto despite technically still being deep in her training regime as a reserve for the race the following weekend.

After Dulce and Agustin completed a beautiful first dance, they urged Tristan and Nina to join them and what followed was possibly the most hilarious attempt at instructing his fiancée in the Argentine tango. She begged him to stop, but eventually devolved into laughter as he careened her around the dance floor to the tune of the band's dramatic music. Their guests laughed heartily at the display, and as he looked down into Nina's sparkling eyes, he was helpless to do anything except capture her lips in a deep kiss. She kissed him back, despite the loud tutting from his grandmother, and his mother whooped loudly with delight.

When his stepfather asked to take Nina for a dance, Tristan took his mother to sit down and rest her weary feet. He guided her to the side of the open-air dance floor, where they sat together and Tristan watched as Nina bravely attempted a simple waltz.

'Good thing her driving isn't impeded by her two left feet.' His mother laughed good-naturedly.

Tristan smiled. 'She's making a great attempt though,

to her credit. She's a perfectionist, so admitting her faults is hard for her. I'm not sure she knows she doesn't have many of them, though.'

He turned to find his mother looking at him with a strange smile on her face.

'I was going to wait until my wedding festivities were over to have this conversation with you, but I see now that I should probably just get it out of the way.'

'What's wrong?' Tristan asked.

'Nothing, at least I hope not. When you told me you were engaged to a woman I'd never heard you mention to me, or even seen you photographed with, naturally I was a little suspicious. So I did some digging... And I discovered your little PR dilemma and realised what you'd done in coming up with this little deception.'

Tristan frowned. 'You did, did you?'

'I know you better than anyone. I know when something is off...so, you see, I was preparing myself for your acting skills—and hers too. I'd already written my speech, about why lying to your mother in her old age is a despicable act, even if I knew you'd have some kind of ridiculously guilt-ridden good intentions at heart.'

'Mama.' Tristan turned in his seat, wanting to explain himself.

She raised her hand to stop him, then placed it firmly upon his knee, meeting his eyes. 'My son, I was waiting to see how far you would go with this ruse just to please me. But now that I've seen you together, I can see that you've dug yourself into a much deeper hole than you had intended.'

'I don't know what you mean.'

She smiled knowingly, looking up as her new husband twirled Nina in a circle and her laugh rang out across the dance floor. 'I think you know exactly what I mean, darling. She's perfect for you. You are both so madly in love with each other. I think perhaps we should have saved today's wedding for you.'

Tristan thought about the idea of walking Nina down the aisle today, while his entire family looked on. The sensation in his chest was one of absolute primal possession and the need to see that happen. Was it true? Had he fallen in love with his fake fiancée? He, the wildest playboy, a man utterly allergic to commitment... But then again that wasn't *quite* true, was it? He had never openly courted the idea of settling down, but he hadn't been averse to it, once upon a time.

It was only since watching his beloved uncle deteriorate into a man he didn't recognise, and seeing the utter devastation that came with losing the one you loved, that Tristan had made some kind of subconscious decision not to forge any more connections of his own in case he got just as badly hurt. Not even Gabriela had touched his heart that deeply. He realised now that it had been only his pride that was stung by her and Victor's betrayal.

'Tristan... I want you to be happy. You deserve a great love just like the one that I once had with your father. And like the one I have now, since I finally let myself be loved again. I've watched you hide yourself away over the past decade since your uncle's death, blaming yourself for not being able to reach him through his depression, and trying to put yourself in a glass cage of sorts, where your heart could be seen but not touched by anyone.'

'Mama, please let's not talk about this today.'

'If not today, then when?' she asked firmly. 'I lost my brother that day, just as you lost your father figure, but ever since then I've felt like I've only had half of you too.

Then Gabriela and Victor dented your smile even more, and I could have killed them. I didn't invite them here today because I thought it would be painful for you. I want you to know that you matter most to me and even though you keep telling me you're fine, I know you. But now, this beautiful girl…she's reawakened something within you that's been lost for a long time, my love. She's brought you back to life.'

His mother's words rang in his ears long after the dancing had come to an end and their guests had begun to filter out. Soon, the only ones left were him and Nina, all alone in the dim lighting as the servers moved to clear away the chairs and tables.

'We should go up too,' Nina said, her cheeks still pink from the exertion of her night's dancing attempts. She wore a spectacular gown in deep red, a gown made for tango, and so when the low strains of music filtered up from a speaker in the main house, he pulled her close for one last dance of his own.

'You look beautiful,' he whispered against her cheek, sliding them into an easy movement.

'You're not so bad yourself.' She laughed, sighing when he dipped her back in the lamplight in a classic tango pose. 'I wish I were better at this. I wish I could do it for real.'

She was talking about the dance, of course, but something in Tristan's chest tightened at her words and what they evoked within him. 'You can…if you take a chance.'

'I think it has more to do with practice and skill.' She raised a brow.

He rolled her over his arm, stepping around her and pulling her back up against his chest. 'This is a dance about trust, about passion.'

'And speed and precision too, surely,' she argued, her foot stepping squarely upon his and making him wince.

'That too.' He chuckled, lowering her slowly over his arm so that her back arched and her breath caught. 'But mostly…it's about giving in to your deepest desires…letting go of all restraint and trusting your partner enough to catch you when you do.'

They stood for a long moment in the pose, with Nina's eyes not leaving his as he slowly pulled her back up to standing.

'I want to let go,' she whispered softly. 'I want to believe that I can…that it won't just lead me to a path of regrets. But I've never been a good partner…in the dance, I mean.'

He looked into her eyes, knowing that she hadn't just been talking about the dance, just as he hadn't either. But he couldn't think of the right words to say without sounding entirely mad. Trust me, Nina. Stay with me. Marry me.

He closed his eyes, remembering how important her racing career was to her, how she'd said she never wanted to be seen as a society princess, like her mother. She was still young, quite a bit younger than him. He had been her first lover, for goodness' sake. Marriage and motherhood were likely long-term goals for her, if they were even on her radar at all. Surely he was being selfish by wanting to keep her?

Not to mention he had yet to reveal the truth behind his deal with her brother. Non-disclosure agreement or not, he had to be fully honest with her if he had any chance of proposing they keep their arrangement going past the end of the season. Would she ever be able to forgive him for keeping secrets from her? Would she understand why he'd done it and that it had been the only way to save the Roux company from bankruptcy and complete collapse? He'd stayed silent, according to the conditions of the NDA, but it had become increasingly difficult as the guilt had started eating him up inside. And now he'd run out of time.

But he had to try. He had to hope that once Nina understood the full implications of his actions, she'd forgive him. Because he knew now with full certainty that, despite everything standing against them, it was the only thing he wanted.

He wanted Nina Roux in his life for real.

The Falco Aerodrome was an impressive new circuit that had been purpose-built for this year's Elite One Premio race by Tristan himself, which he proudly talked her through as they took a tour of the paddock. Nina had noticed that Tristan had seemed extra attentive in the two days since the wedding, but she'd put it down to the abundance of amazing sex they'd been having. But with the race now only a few days away, she knew she had to get back to her routine as soon as possible and try to regain her focus.

When Tristan was called into a meeting up in the executive boardrooms, she took the chance to take a tour of the Falco Roux garages where their team had already begun to set up in preparation for the upcoming race weekend. She was in the middle of inspecting an upgrade she'd overseen on their engine injection system when footsteps pounded down the tarmac outside and a man appeared in her peripheral vision. She stood up, expecting to see one of their mechanics, but instead froze with recognition.

Her brother stood in the entryway of the garage, his dark hair and eyes so like her own as he looked awkwardly around before stepping inside.

'Alain.' She gasped in shock. 'What…what are you doing here?'

'Falco stopped answering my calls, and I needed to speak to you about this in person.'

Her stomach tightened at the look on her brother's face, all elation at seeing him melting away. He wasn't here to apologise to her for what he'd done or even to cheer their team on. He was here with the exact same look on his face as he'd had on the day when he'd told her about the sale of the Roux company.

'What would you need to speak to Tristan about?' she said coldly. 'You already walked away from all of this, Alain. You abandoned ship.'

Alain sighed heavily, running a hand through his hair in a gesture that reminded her so much of their father. He was like him in many ways.

'He hasn't told you anything about the deal we made yet, has he?'

'I know how easily you sold our family company to him for a tidy sum, practically bankrupting me in the process. I trusted you. I thought you were trying to save the company, not ruin it.'

Alain shook his head, a hollow laugh escaping his lips. 'I never went to him with the intention of selling. We were going to go bankrupt whether I sold or not. You have to believe that I wanted to save our family's legacy, Nina. Your legacy. I know I've made so many mistakes.'

'Understatement of the year,' Nina muttered.

'You're angry at me, and that's fair. But I'm not the man you knew any more—the party boy, the wastrel. My recovery has taught me to accept the consequences of my actions and I guess now is the time I start doing that.'

Recovery? The consequences of his actions? Who on earth was this man and where was her brother? 'What are you not telling me?'

'The company was in bad shape when I took over from dad, but I made it all worse. I got into serious debt, Nina. Gambling debt. I refused to admit that I had a problem, until I got into a very high-stakes poker game with Tristan Falco.' Alain shook his head, walking as if to go towards the small bar at the wall before turning away with a hiss of breath. 'Old habits...'

Nina looked at her brother then, really looked at him and saw how much weight he'd lost since she'd last seen him. He looked...healthy. Not like a man who'd been partying on a yacht in the Mediterranean for the entire summer. His eyes were clear, he was clean-shaven and well dressed and, above all, he appeared sober.

Much like with their mother and father, the tradition of excessive partying, including drinking and gambling, among other vices, was not generally spoken of in their family. Nothing was mentioned other than clothing styles and newspaper articles and how they appeared to the outside world. They were a rotten apple with the prettiest, shiniest skin.

'That was my rock-bottom, Nina. I bet our family company in a poker game.'

'How could that be true? How would no one know?'

'Because Tristan took pity on me. He agreed to stage it as a takeover, and we signed a non-disclosure agreement to keep it all under wraps. He gave me a year to sort myself out. He cut a deal, to freeze our shares while he took control of the majority and worked on bringing the company back to solvency. He always intended to give it back.'

She reared back, totally shocked. 'Why would he do that?'

'I still don't know. He said he had a sentimental attachment to the brand.'

Instantly she recalled the garage full of Roux motorcars his uncle had collected, and she ran an agitated hand through her hair.

Alain was still talking. 'I think the guy just has a hero complex, to be quite honest. Who was I to argue? Don't look a gift horse in the mouth and all that. He got me into a discreet programme. There is an island off Greece that's notorious for helping wealthy addicts get clean while also forcing us back to our humble roots. I've cleaned beaches, I've power-washed streets, I've helped the homeless... At some point I finally accepted that I am an addict and that I always will be, but that doesn't make me a lost cause.'

She felt a painful tweak at what he'd been struggling with. 'Alain, I never thought you were a lost cause. I know we fought but that doesn't mean I don't still love you.'

'Nina, please, this isn't even the beginning of me making amends with you. I was so selfish. I don't know how our parents didn't ruin you too, but you are such a good person. You didn't deserve any of that.'

'Neither did you.'

That simple, brief acknowledgement of their shared childhood pain felt like a knife sliding out from her ribs a few inches. She knew that there was more to be said between them, much more, but perhaps here and now was not the time. She still had to wrap her head around what Tristan had done...and what he'd been keeping from her.

'Why tell me now?'

'I saw the rumours of your engagement to Falco on social media and I just saw red. I don't understand what kind of game he's playing with you, but as soon as I could leave Greece, I had to come. To protect you.'

She looked over Alain's shoulder to see Tristan striding towards them, a stunned look on his face. Tristan, the man who had been lying to her all along... Or perhaps she'd simply been lying to herself about the kind of man she'd thought he was? She felt like such a fool. Excusing herself to Alain, she took the coward's way out and fled.

CHAPTER THIRTEEN

NINA WALKED QUICKLY away from the garage until she found herself wandering along the path that lined the empty racing track. She didn't even know where she was going, she just needed her body to move so that her mind could work through her own confusion. A hand landed upon her shoulder and she spun around with a squeak. Tristan stood before her, his face a mask of pain.

'You're running away without even allowing me a chance to explain?'

She could have said yes, because she needed time to think, to try to understand why he would have lied to her about her own brother's actions and how he'd come to be their team owner. But instead she felt the embarrassing build-up of tears in her eyes. 'You lied to me.'

'I was waiting to tell you myself,' he began, then stopped. 'I'm sorry. I wanted to tell you so many times, believe me. But apart from the legal agreements we signed, I also wanted to give your brother time and privacy to recover, as he'd asked.'

'I just don't understand any of it.' She shook her head. 'You knew you were lying to me about my brother. And yet you still kept it from me. You knew that he planned to come back once he'd recovered and take back the helm of the company himself, and yet you were about to let me accept a deal from Accardi and leave Falco Roux!'

'I would have told you before you took any deal from that licentious old man. Even despite the non-disclosure agreement I made with your brother, I intended to find a way to tell you the truth before you actually left Falco Roux. I only signed Apollo for the rest of this season, thinking it was the right thing to do for the team. I assumed your brother would want to make the decisions about his own drivers when he took over again.'

'You can see why I find that hard to believe, right?'

'That's fair.'

'None of this is fair. I'm so sick of this. I'm so unbelievably sick of having my future decided upon by men who have assumed all the power behind my back. I'm so sick of working so hard *all the time* and ending up right back where I started. I trusted you.'

He took a step towards her, closing the space between them. 'You can still trust me. I made a mistake. Regardless of the NDA, I should have told you sooner, I see that now. But your brother insisted that you not know. Don't let this ruin what we've started between us, Nina. I meant it for the best, to try and help save your family company. I want to make this work. Us. I want to earn your trust back and show you just how serious I am about never breaking it again.'

She bowed her head, wanting that explanation to be enough. But deep inside her, something had split apart at his deception. He'd known far more about Alain than he'd admitted. He'd known he was only caretaking the Roux company until Alain was better. He'd seen how upset she'd been about being forced out of a main driver's seat, and, despite him erroneously thinking that signing a more experienced driver for the rest of this season was the right thing to do, he'd done nothing to reassure her that it wouldn't be for ever. He'd lied by omission, but still it was like a knife to her heart.

'Don't let this come between us,' Tristan pleaded, his voice tight. 'Don't walk away from what we've started to build together, Nina, because I know you feel it too.'

'We both know that this was just a performance,' she whispered.

'It's not,' he growled. 'Not for me, anyway.'

'No, Tristan, I'm not looking for you to placate me or lie for my benefit any more. I know exactly what this deal was when we entered into it. A sham to hold your mother off a little longer. A PR exercise to raise the company's profile with fans. It's just I wasn't expecting to feel so…affected.'

'That's good,' he rasped, taking a step closer.

'Is it?'

'I mean…it's good to know I'm not the only one living in torment.' He reached out to touch her, then paused as if rethinking the movement. 'We spent every single day of the past two weeks together, you in my bed, learning about one another and it still wasn't nearly enough for me. I have absolutely no idea where I stand with you. Yet, my mother took one look at us together and immediately knew the truth.'

'What is the truth?' she asked shakily.

'That I've fallen in love with you, Nina,' he said, his voice rough, and his eyes trained intently upon her. 'I've fallen in love with everything about you and I want this fake engagement to be real. I love your focus, your ambition, your willingness to fight me at every turn… And of course your body and your ability to drive me wild with just a look.'

Nina's breath caught in her chest; she could hardly believe what she was hearing. 'But the deal, the rules. Your secrets and lies…'

'Forget the rules, forget everything. I thought I was doing the right thing all along, but I think I was only trying to fool myself. I realised in the moment I saw you hit that wall, that nothing I felt for you was simple. I think I fell in love with you that night, holding you in my arms while you monologued about your favourite movies. I'm so sorry I didn't tell you about the company, but I can't go back, Nina…only forwards.'

'You might think you're in love with me, but you barely know me. If you did, you'd never have lied to me.' She shook her head, taking a few steps away. Her heart was hammering in her chest so hard she was surprised she still stood upright but she needed to have this conversation with him. She needed him to understand. 'You've been put under a lot of pressure by your mother to find someone to love. And with your ex getting engaged to your cousin, that had to have hurt you.'

'This isn't about any of that.' He took a step closer, an expression of desperation on his face. 'Look, I can see now that this was a lot to put on you so suddenly. With Alain here, and after learning what I did, maybe we should wait to talk until later, once you've had time to think about it.'

'No.' She pulled her hand away from his, and hated the immediate look of hurt in his eyes. 'Waiting isn't going to solve any of this, Tristan. We've got so tangled up in the haze of the past couple weeks I don't know which way is up any more. I don't know what is real and what is fake and what is simply induced by spending time with your wonderful yet slightly dramatic family, who I adore.'

'They adore you too,' he said hoarsely.

'Please, stop. I can't think straight with you looking at me this way.'

'Sometimes thinking straight is the least helpful thing we can do. Not everything can be made logical and clear-cut, Nina. Sometimes a person comes storming into your life when you least expect it, bringing parts of you back to life that you didn't even realise were dead. Let's do this for real, let's get married and build a life together.'

Nina closed her eyes, wishing she could trust this. Trust *him* after what he'd done. He'd just said he loved her. She'd dreamed of hearing those words from his lips. She wished that she could simply take his hands and throw herself into his arms, throw caution to the wind. She could just imagine it now: a big white wedding, his entire family would be overjoyed. The media would love it. A whirlwind romance… Just like the one she'd grown up as a product of.

Her mother had married her father in the eye of a media storm, never as happy as when she was the centre of attention. Every step of their relationship had been scrutinised and followed until her mother had become unrecognisable. Her father had walked away from his marriage and children unscathed, unchanged by the media's opinion, which had largely been aimed at her socialite mother and her supposed sins. Could she do that? Could she trust that whatever this intense connection with Tristan was, she wouldn't be swallowed whole by it?

Her aunt Lola's words rang in her ears.

'Only trust yourself, Nina.'

'I can't,' she whispered, squeezing her eyes tight as if

hoping, if she tried hard enough when she opened them, all of this might have just been a bad dream. But it wasn't, and she eventually opened her eyes to see Tristan staring at her as if she were a stranger.

'You can't?' Tristan shook his head. 'Or you won't?'

'I struggle with trusting people, Tristan. I didn't have the same loving family upbringing as you but I know that relationships can be hard to maintain. And if they start out based on lies and deceit—however well meant—what does that say about our future? We've only been together for a short time, and most of that was just for show.'

'It might have started that way, but these past couple of weeks have been real,' he urged. 'Just give us a chance.'

'I can't.' She felt her entire body shake from repressing the tears that threated to spill from her eyes. 'I'm sorry.'

Tristan wondered how things could go downhill so quickly. For the past two days he'd been hopeful that Nina might understand why he'd done what he'd done, and had been imagining proposing to her all over again. This time for real. But here she looked at him as though he were a stranger. He should have told her about his deal with her brother sooner, he knew that. But he'd signed that NDA in all good faith, and the longer he'd waited, the deeper the lie had become. And now, seeing the hurt on her face, he wished so hard that he'd done everything differently.

No business deal was worth her pain. Nothing was.

'Even if you had told me the truth right from the start…even if we'd got past all of it, do you really think we would ever have worked as a couple?' Nina closed her eyes, and his chest tightened as he saw a single tear snake from her eyelid down across her cheek. She had never cried in front of him, he realised. She held herself together so tightly, never showing weakness, rarely allowing anybody a glimpse underneath the surface armour to the tender vulnerability beneath.

But over the past few weeks he had slowly dug beneath that armour. She'd *let him in*, damn it—and look how he'd rewarded her trust. Not for the first time since they'd met, he felt like the world's biggest bastard and he reached up with a shaky hand to brush away her tears. She let him touch her, but he knew by the stiffness in her shoulders that it was not an indication of forgiveness. She had told him she struggled to trust, had she not? She had cut people out of her life for far less than this. She burned bridges because it was easier than allowing people a second chance to screw her over again.

'Tell me how to make this right,' he growled, refusing to admit that he had irretrievably broken whatever fragile thing had begun to blossom between them. Refusing to give up on them, even if she was already fading away from his grasp before his eyes.

The silence that stretched between them felt as if it went on for hours, every second ticking down like grains of sand. When she finally spoke, her voice was barely a murmur and her eyes were far away.

'Tristan, this would never have worked out anyway. It was only ever meant to be temporary. Maybe this is what I needed to hear today, to stop feeling this foolish hope.'

'Hope is good,' he rasped, holding himself still as she pulled free from his arms.

'Sometimes hope is just prolonging the pain of something that was always inevitable. We're so different. You're handsome, outgoing and charismatic and I'm…a plain workaholic ice queen.'

She raised her hand to silence him when he immediately rushed to deny her words.

'It's taken me a long time, but I like who I am. I like being obsessed with fast cars and metrics and studying engines until my eyeballs hurt. I like the danger too, Tristan. None of us would be in this career if it didn't give us a thrill. You can barely stand the thought of my job. You flinch every time I mention getting behind the wheel again. Your fears are real and so valid and I feel like—'

He flinched at the hitch in her breath as she paused, shaking her head.

'I feel like if we use hope as the glue to see where this goes, we will only hurt each other very badly in the end. I don't want to hurt you. But is it any better for me to twist myself into smaller pieces, just to keep you comfortable?'

Tristan closed his eyes at the harsh truth in her words. Yes, his fears over her dangerous career were vast and definitely had the potential to pose an issue between them. But was it fair for her to use it as an argument against them together when she hadn't even given them a chance?

'No.' He shook his head. 'I don't accept that, Nina. My fears, while legitimate and a hurdle, are something that I can work on because I would *choose* to work on it for you. That's what you do when you love somebody. You grow, you change, you choose to put eachother first.'

'Maybe I'm just not built that way.'

'We are not born knowing how to trust. It's something you have to learn to do, just like being in love. And I think you *do* love me, but you're angry and afraid to take a chance.'

Her jaw tightened, and her eyes briefly met his. She made no move to refute his words and for one wild moment he thought she might jump into his arms. He prayed she would.

But just as quickly, he seen her shut down once more as she shook her head sadly and looked away towards the deserted racing track.

'Okay,' he said softly, cold seeping into his bones despite the balmy evening air. 'I won't stand here and beg, if you've already made up your mind.'

He felt the last fragile slip of hope slide through his fingers as he took a step backwards and she didn't make a single move to follow him.

CHAPTER FOURTEEN

THE DISTANCE FROM her hotel bed to the bathroom and back was the most movement Nina accomplished over the following two days. With her phone switched off, and a strict do not disturb sign on the door, she ensured herself some peace. At least externally.

Internally however, she was a hurricane of emotion that she couldn't quite separate or work through. She cried silent tears when notes appeared under her door on two separate occasions from Alain. A small package arrived too, a basket filled with her favourite romcoms and chocolates. No note accompanied the gift, but she knew Tristan had sent it, even before she opened up the simple hotel card to see his sprawling initials on the signature line. She didn't have the appetite for romance or sugar, instead choosing to leave them propped upon the desk in the corner of the room as a reminder. A reminder of what exactly, she wasn't quite sure…why not to trust anyone, perhaps?

Tristan's words rang in her ears.

'We are not born knowing how to trust. It's something you have to learn to do, just like being in love.'

She knew that people made mistakes. She'd made plenty of mistakes herself in her life. But being lied to and deliberately misled was another thing entirely. Alain had always said she was too rigid in her views, and perhaps she was. She had always been so sensitive to injustice, finding solace in the solid concept of right and wrong. But with her heart broken and her future in the sport she loved uncertain, she just didn't have the energy to make sense of it all. She'd gone from hating Tristan Falco to falling in love with him in a matter of weeks. Surely falling back *out* of love could be achieved simply? Even as she grasped at that thought her chest tightened and her body seemed to push it away. Somehow, she knew that this would not be so easily healed.

She slept for what felt like weeks, the only indication of day bleeding into night coming from a thin slit in the curtains and the glow of the single hotel clock upon her bedstand. It was a slippery slope, allowing her overwhelmed mind to rest this way. She knew from experience that giving in to this kind of exhaustion could lead to a dark place she would only struggle more and more to pick herself back up from.

The next morning, a knock sounded upon the door, one that she did her absolute best to ignore as she burrowed her face deeper and deeper beneath the pillows. Until a familiar voice intruded upon her thoughts.

'You'd better open this door, superstar. Or I'll be calling some hunky Argentinian fireman to chop it down for me.'

Stiff and cranky, Nina forced herself across the room to throw open the door and was practically attacked by the blonde ball of energy that was Sophie. 'You're not supposed to get here until tomorrow.'

'You turn your phone off for *two freaking days* and expect me not to rush here early?' Sophie practically shouted, then she paused and looked around at the chaos of the darkened bedroom. 'It smells like something died in here.'

Perhaps something did… Nina thought mournfully.

'Nope. Stop whatever it is you are thinking right now. I know that face.' Sophie placed her hands on both sides of Nina's cheeks, forcing Nina to look up into her eyes. 'When's the last time you trained?'

Nina shook her head, pulling away to sit down heavily on the side of the bed. 'I'm not driving this weekend; I'm not needed here. I don't know why I don't just go back to Monte Carlo.'

'Dear God, would you listen to yourself? You are a superstar, and superstars need to train. Whatever personal stuff has gone on, it's not worth giving up your career for.'

'What have you heard?' Nina asked roughly.

'Nothing. But I can piece two and two together and get four, darling. I know that whatever has happened, you'll think through it ten times better after running your backside off and cursing at me through your own sweat.'

Nina groaned, pressing her eyelids into her hands. Sophie was right, of course. Her brain craved movement and order to keep regulated. Everything she was feeling was far more intense and unmanageable as a result of her staying here, isolating herself in this room. But she was so tired… So tired of trying so hard all of the time and still ending up right back where she always started. Alone, betrayed.

Sophie kneeled down in front of her, her blue eyes wide and worried and her jaw set in that way Nina knew too well. She was the best trainer in the industry—Falco Roux was not paying her nearly enough. She always knew exactly what to say.

'Okay, thank you for coming to get me.'

'I'll always have your back.' Sophie smiled, leaning in to give her a deep hug. With a polite sniff, she whispered in her ear, 'But I think you need to have a shower first.'

Nina arrived on the morning of race day at the brand-new Argentinian track to find the garage in utter chaos. At least half of the team was missing, and as she wandered around in confusion she spied the team principal, Jock, sitting on the floor with his head in his hands.

'What is it? What happened?' she said, looking frantically around at the worried faces that greeted her.

'They're all dropping like flies, that's what,' he said, running agitated hands through the little hair he had remaining upon his head.

Sophie appeared at her side, a worried frown creasing her forehead. 'They went out to eat at a restaurant last night, with Daniele Roberts. At least a quarter of the team have food poisoning. Some of them have gone to hospital. Including Roberts.'

'Oh, God, is he going to be okay?' She felt her heart drop. 'How bad is it?'

'We're not sure quite how bad it is yet, but with food poisoning he's bound to be out for a couple of days at least. Even then, his recovery could be slow.'

'We are *screwed*,' the team principal growled. 'I'm down five mechanics, we have backups on the way, but who knows what kind of speed they're going to be? I can't believe this. We were so close to winning the constructors' championship.'

'It will be okay. I'm good to step in as reserve.' Nina's mind worked furiously over the statistics and strategies they'd perfected recently. Their new star was good, but Apollo was still settling in. If he made a mistake in the first seat and didn't secure a third-place finish at the minimum, they'd lose the constructors' championship. If Nina took first seat and drove her very best...they still had a chance. But as she opened her mouth and began relaying her thoughts, the older man immediately scoffed.

'After that stunt you pulled in Spain? There's not a chance I'd put my faith in you, Roux. You lack the aggression required to drive in first. I won't clear it.'

His phone rang and he growled, taking the call and walking away.

Apollo was already suited up and preparing for the first practice session when Nina walked into the opposite end of the garage.

'Looks like you're driving with me, Roux,' he said, a brief attempt at a smile on his handsome face.

'I won't clear it, Falco.' The team principal appeared, still bellowing into his phone. His face sweaty and red. 'You think you can just call me up and demand I put your fiancée in my first seat? I'd rather walk.'

Nina frowned. Tristan? That was who was on the call?

'I mean it, Falco,' Jock cried. 'I'll leave.'

Whatever Tristan's reply was, the older man's face blanched and he threw his phone down on the ground with a growl, smashing the device to pieces.

'I support the decision to seat Nina first,' Apollo said matter-of-factly. 'We won't have to argue about it then.'

'You actually agree with that madman?' Jock bellowed. 'In my thirty years at this team, I have never heard such ridiculous—'

'I'd stop right there or you'll be fired, Jock.' Alain appeared behind them. 'Then we'll be down a team principal today as well as half our team.'

'Alain! I wasn't aware that you were back. Good, I

might get you to talk some sense into that man who took over our team.'

Alain moved to stand behind Nina, his hand upon her shoulder. 'I think you'll find that it's *our* team. As of today, our shares have been restored to us by Tristan Falco and I've been appointed as managing director once again. Myself and my sister have not agreed on many things, but the fact that she is the most qualified person here to lead this team today is not one that's up for debate.'

'Thank you, Alain,' Nina said, a lump in her throat. 'I know our contracts stated that Apollo was to be in first, and most of my experience so far has been in second…'

'You can do it,' Apollo said encouragingly. 'Even with my experience, we all know it was the plan for me to drive in second seat today, Nina. I've seen you instruct our strategy team on how to help Roberts win; you are undoubtedly the natural choice for first driver today.'

'Seems like you're getting your way again, *princess*.' Jock glowered.

'You know what? I've had enough of you,' Nina growled. 'If it's true that my shares are back…then I've been waiting a long time to say these words. Jock, you're fired.'

Nina's eyes widened as the team principal lunged towards her and her brother launched to her defence before shouting for security to remove the abusive old bat from the garage once and for all.

In the chaos that followed, Alain announced that he was going to be acting team principal for the day, a position that he'd hoped to wait until next season to assume after undergoing training while at the recovery centre. He didn't need training, of course, he'd grown up on the track just as she had. He'd never shown any aptitude for the driving side of things, but he had always had a way with people. She looked at him, seeing once again how vibrant and alive he looked, and she realised belatedly that she had Tristan to thank for all of it.

Tristan, the man who had allowed the world to paint him as a frivolous playboy, swiping up a team in a sport he had no knowledge of or interest in simply to avoid the destruction of a long-respected Elite One racing team. When all the while, he had actually been their saviour. Yes, he'd made mistakes along the way. But didn't everyone?

Closing her eyes, she leaned her head down upon a stack of tyres and took a deep breath, hoping and praying that all of her training would stand up as she attempted to pull off what was the most difficult feat of her entire career.

As she drove into her starting position on the grid, she looked up to the box where she hoped Tristan would be, even though he had no reason to stay for today's race. He'd done his part in launching the event and had participated in countless press calls. Now that the end of his role as team owner had arrived he could slip away without anyone knowing any differently.

As her eyes scanned the crowd of guests in the box, she felt her chest tighten with relief. He'd stayed. He stood head and shoulders above everyone else, his handsome features looking pinched and drawn. He was still here, standing guard in his brooding fallen-angel way, silently supporting her even after she'd rejected him and walked away.

She knew family wasn't supposed to give up on you, unlike her parents. Her aunt Lola had always said love meant always being there, even if you were fighting, even when you messed up. Real love was unconditional. She had never known that kind of love, she hadn't known how to accept it when he'd so bravely tried to make her see what he was offering to her.

But now…she wanted to try.

CHAPTER FIFTEEN

She'd done it.

Tristan almost burst with pride as he watched Nina take her third place upon the podium. The first podium of her career in Elite One and, judging by the calibre of her driving today, it would not be the last.

As well as winning third place, their team had sealed their win of the constructors' championship. Alain, looking awkward as ever, had to take the stage to accept the trophy for Falco Roux, which he did with an emotional cheer coming from the crowd. Tristan felt a maelstrom of emotion as he watched the siblings embrace, and he knew that if this was the only good thing that had come from his involvement in their lives, it would be enough.

He had been the one to suggest that Alain stepped back into management early now that he was well. But still, it hurt to know that he would not be the one to congratulate the woman he loved in person today. He was content to stand back and allow her to shine, enjoying the moment she'd thoroughly earned. She had an entire crowd of screaming fans waiting for her, press and experts all waiting to dissect her drive and hear her speak about the sport she was a true expert in. She was a superstar, and he was glad that the world was finally seeing it too.

Perhaps it was cowardly, but he had only intended to

stay long enough to see her take her place on that podium. Now that it was done, he needed to get away.

Walking away from the crowd, he took a shortcut through the long corridor that led behind the garages, unable to resist taking one last look into the world she'd shown him and made him fall for too. The Falco Roux garage was still lit up, rows upon rows of tyres and instruments shining in disarray as they'd all been dropped in the midst of their celebrations. He would never be near the scent of engine oil and not think of Nina Roux.

Sounds behind him caught his attention and he turned to see a familiar figure in the doorway. Her red racing suit was covered in liquid as though she'd been in heavy rain, her hair wet with celebratory champagne and plastered to her face. But the look in her eyes was what made him pause.

'You didn't leave.' She breathed heavily, as though she'd been running.

'I came to watch you race. I couldn't stay away. You're amazing and I can't believe I ever signed Apollo instead of you. Is that the only reason you chased me down here?'

'I didn't chase…' she began, and then shook her head. 'No, I told myself I wasn't going to fight you. I told myself it was time to be brave.'

'You're always brave,' he said huskily.

'Am I? Because you told me that you loved me and you told me that when you love someone, you grow and you change, and you choose to put eachother first. But I did the opposite of all that. I ran from your love. I was the coward.'

He dared to hope that what he was hearing was exactly what he thought it was, that she'd finally realised she could trust him with her heart. That he would always be there for her. But still he remained in place, not daring to touch her until he knew for sure. 'What are you saying, exactly, Nina?'

'I'm saying, I'm hopelessly in love with you, Tristan Falco. I couldn't stop loving you if I tried.'

Nina felt as though her heart were about to beat out of her chest as Tristan remained silent, his feet still planted firmly in the centre of the garage where he remained frozen in place. She had seen him in the crowd as she'd accepted her third-place trophy and as the traditional champagne bottles had been popped and sprayed around the place. It was a moment she had waited for her entire life and yet all she'd been able to think of was running to him. Not having Tristan in her life was like missing a limb.

'You love me?' he repeated.

'I love you so much,' she declared, allowing all of the emotion she felt to bleed into her voice without fear. She was done being afraid. 'I want a future with you, Tristan, or at the very least I want the hope of one. I want to be yours and I want you to be mine, if you'll still have me. You were right, love is about changing and growing and you make me want to grow. You see me and you make me want to be a better version of myself.'

He moved towards her in a flurry of motion, or perhaps she moved towards him. It all became a blur as they fell into one another's arms, mouths meeting in a riot of heat and relief and love... So much love.

After she was pretty sure all of the breath had been pulled from her lungs and her heart grew a couple of sizes once more, she pulled back and met his eyes.

'Do you forgive me for rejecting you and walking away?' she asked.

'Only if you forgive me for being an impossible fool. I tried to do my best to make good on everything, by encouraging Alain to take back control and returning the shares. But I know it's not enough. I should have told you the truth from the start.'

'It's enough,' she breathed, placing another kiss on his lips. 'You are enough, Tristan, more than enough. Too much really, by most people's standards, but I accept you just as you are. Flamboyant dress sense and all.'

'Perhaps my dress sense will rub off on you?' he teased. 'I won't lose hope just yet.'

'Let's not go that far, darling.' An idea occurring to her, Nina took a step back and looked around the floor. Finding exactly what she wanted, she smirked and dropped to one knee before him.

'What are you doing now?' He smiled, then froze as he realised what she held in her hand.

'I never want to wake up in a world where you're not by my side so… I guess I'm actually more traditional than I thought?' With an oversized wheel nut, Nina proposed to the man she loved.

It wasn't quite the rare black diamond that he had presented her with all those weeks ago, but it felt right. Just as it felt right when he lifted her up into his arms, shouting his acceptance as he twirled her in a circle.

'We're going to have to negotiate some new terms for our engagement, real ones this time,' Nina joked.

'No wedding until you win a driver's championship,' Tristan suggested.

'I accept.' She laughed. 'And no babies until I've won three.'

Tristan's eyes darkened, his hands pulling her closer as he breathed in her scent. 'Did you just tell me you want to have my babies, Nina Roux? Dear God... I'm barely keeping my hands off you as it is.'

'I do... But not for a while yet. I want to enjoy you all to myself for as long as I can.'

'It's okay, I'm not ready to hang up my playboy hat just yet either.' He laughed as her expression immediately turned incredulous. 'I mean that I have a new routine to perfect now. To prepare for. The playboy husband experience.'

'What exactly does a playboy husband do?' Nina asked breathlessly as her fiancé's lips began to wander scandalously low on her chest, and he unzipped her racing suit inch by inch as he lowered himself to his knees.

'He is scandalous, dissolute, utterly shocking,' he murmured against her belly button. 'He also seduces his wife in very inappropriate places.'

Nina smiled. 'Thank goodness for that.'

More passionate kissing ensued, and they might or might not have consummated their engagement up against a stack of tyres in the dark. To all intents and purposes it was the most romantic thing Nina could have ever hoped for. The perfect place for them to pledge their love to one another permanently.

EPILOGUE

NINA STARED AT her reflection in the floor-length mirror of the church vestry and fought the urge to smile. It was her wedding day, and not only was she excitedly awaiting the prospect of getting married... She was wearing white.

She hadn't set out for a traditional look when Tristan's mama had accompanied her shopping in Buenos Aires just two days ago when Tristan had finally agreed to elope with her. Well, he'd half agreed—hence why she presently stood in a church and not in a tiny Las Vegas chapel as she'd suggested.

She smiled to herself, remembering the exultant look on his face when she'd stepped down off her podium after winning her very first world championship right here at the Falco Aerodrome and immediately reminded him of the deal they'd made upon their official engagement four years before. He'd swung her around in a circle while the crowd whooped and cheered, unaware that they were witnessing the final taming of Argentina's wildest playboy. Today, they would become husband and wife in the same church where his mother had said her loving vows to Tristan's father and Agustin. Nothing in her life had ever felt more right than it did at this moment.

Tristan's mother stood nearby, fussing over a delicate lace veil and deftly securing it to a pair of discreet combs with her bejewelled hands. Dulce had asked if she would wear the veil she had worn on her wedding day to Tristan's father.

'I've been instructed to wait until this moment to give you another surprise from my son.' The woman's eyes sparkled with mischief, so like the charming rake she had raised.

'What on earth has he planned now?' Nina smiled wryly, watching with only a little trepidation as Dulce moved to retrieve a slim square box from her bag. The box was emblazoned with the Falco crown, the symbol that Tristan had brought back to glory as a worldwide status symbol as he worked tirelessly on various campaigns over the past few years.

'He said that you would understand, once you saw it.'

Nina held her breath as the box was opened and felt a wide smile take over her face as a familiar gold and sapphire tiara was revealed. The same tiara that she had worn on the night they had first officially met. The night that everything in her life had changed...and she had been utterly swept up in the storm that was Tristan Falco.

Her throat tightened with emotion as she helped Dulce position the delicate piece upon her head and watched with a sense of surreal awe as one of the world's greatest fashion icons primped and fussed with her veil until she was satisfied.

'Stunning,' Dulce whispered, placing a single kiss upon her cheek before quietly exiting to give Nina a few more moments alone. It didn't last very long however, as another knock sounded, this time Alain arriving to tell her that it was time to go.

She linked her arm through her brother's, breathing a deep sigh of relief that he had agreed to walk her down the aisle today, in lieu of her father. Neither of her parents had bothered to come. But she still had Alain in her life. He'd supported her when she chose to speak publicly about her experience of late-diagnosed autism the year before, just as she'd supported him when he decided to seek treatment for ADHD. They laughed as they walked and Alain made quiet jokes under his breath like he used to do when they were kids, trying to make her laugh, trying to make her break the character of the good society girl.

And she did laugh, without any worry of what the high-society Argentinian guests might think of their beloved playboy's unconventional bride. Because the moment her groom turned and his eyes met hers she knew that there could be nothing more right in this world.

Of all the people that Tristan Falco had imagined giving a speech on his wedding day, Alain Roux was not one of them. And yet here they were, grand tables filling the courtyard of his family's historic estate as Nina's brother recounted a mildly embarrassing story about the bride and groom in his usual entertaining style before wishing the new Mr and Mrs Falco health and happiness.

Tristan leaned across to kiss his wife while applause erupted around them and once again he felt an overwhelming urge to gather her into his arms and steal her away. Watching her walk down the aisle towards him had been overwhelming, but that was nothing compared to the feeling of finally sliding a wedding band onto her finger after four long years of waiting. She'd been worth every second.

When they stood up for their first dance, Nina had a mischievous sparkle in her eye. As he led her onto the dance floor he leaned down to whisper in her ear, 'I know that look, what on earth are you up to?'

'You're not the only one who has surprises up their sleeve,' she murmured before spinning herself out into a circle on the floor as the low hum of an Argentine tango sounded out from the band.

Tristan watched with wide eyes as his sultry wife clipped off the skirt of her wedding gown to reveal a more slim-fitting knee-length skirt beneath. She raised a brow in his direction before clapping her hands and beginning the slow sequence of moves that led the dance. The moves she had performed when he had tried to teach her all those years ago, much to the entertainment of their guests. It seemed she had been secretly taking lessons. His stomach tightened as he watched her sensual movements. She was quite literally dancing circles around him while he watched. It took a moment to remember that he was supposed to respond in the dance, and so he did, moving in and allowing her to lead him. After a few moments, Nina stepped in and murmured in his ear, 'Your turn.'

She bent at the waist, reaching her hand towards him for him to lead her this time. It was a beautiful reflection of their marriage, he realised. All the ebb and flow of the partnership they had built together over the past four years as he had supported her in her bid to become the first female Elite One champion. He had never been more proud than in the moment he had watched her lift that trophy high above her head, her eyes meeting his with triumph.

Now, as the dance came to an end and she spun into his arms, her body flush against his chest, he knew that he would always support her, no matter what she wanted to achieve. They championed one another, him supporting her and her doing the same for him as he'd brought his mother's company back to its former glory. Their relationship itself was a dance, an invigorating sequence of moves in tandem as they led one another to be the best version of themselves.

When all their guests had finally left, Tristan and Nina stayed in the dark of the courtyard hand in hand, looking up at the stars.

'What next?' She laughed, her head leaning back into his chest. 'We've done the championship and you've taken the fashion world by storm. Not to mention you finally nabbed me as your wife.'

'I nabbed you, did I?'

'Well, I suppose technically I'm the one who tamed the world's most untameable playboy, aren't I? But I suppose… Things might get a little boring around here if we don't up the challenges a little.'

'*Querida*, you couldn't bore me if you tried.'

'Tristan, I'm trying to tell you that I'm ready.'

Her meaning took a moment to sink in, and he frowned, looking down into her beautiful face. 'You're ready… For the next step?'

She knew he wanted children, and when she'd proposed to him she'd told him she wanted to win the championship three times first before becoming a mother. But…

'I've decided to take next season off to focus on growing the girls academy. And while I have some downtime… I think we could start our family. I find myself quite impatient to have your babies, Tristan Falco.'

'Dear God… That sentence from your lips… You're

going to give me a heart attack right here and we've only been married a few hours.'

'So dramatic. I have conditions, of course.'

'Ah, I should have guessed that this would be a contract negotiation.'

'I have my terms… We have to practise quite a lot first, so that I know you're up to the job.'

'Oh, I'm up to the job, I assure you. So I propose that we begin today, this exact moment, in fact.'

She laughed as he chased her inside, into their bedroom, spinning her until she fell backwards onto the bed and he proceeded to make good on that threat, proving once again that he was the best adventure she'd ever taken a chance on.

* * * * *

If Fast-Track Fiancé *left you wanting more,
then make sure you catch up on the first instalment of
The Fast-Track Billionaires' Club trilogy*
The Bump in Their Forbidden Reunion

*And why not explore these other
Amanda Cinelli stories?*

The Vows He Must Keep
Returning to Claim His Heir
Stolen in Her Wedding Gown
The Billionaire's Last-Minute Marriage
Pregnant in the Italian's Palazzo

Available now!

BILLION-DOLLAR DATING GAME

NATALIE ANDERSON

MILLS & BOON

CHAPTER ONE

Zane deMarco inhaled deep, stretched out long, and let the sauna's dry heat sharpen every sense. Their squash score was still a three-way tie after nine rounds and while they could go all day, it would make little difference.

'Are you going to reveal why you summoned us here at the crack of dawn on a holiday?' he asked the brooding man sitting along from him. 'Because if it was to break the tie and take the lead, that plan sure as hell backfired.'

Adam Courtney shot him a withering glance. Zane just grinned back. His old rowing rival from his brief university stint in the UK was as laser focused and hyper-competitive as ever. The fact that wild card Cade Landry had also shown his face so early in the day underscored the significance of their meeting. While he sometimes came to their eternally equal squash sessions, the lone wolf didn't stick round for any bro banter. But Zane knew why he'd lingered today. They *all* knew the reason. But he prompted Adam into the conversation anyway.

Adam pushed a button on the infrared sauna and sent the temperature soaring before answering. 'Helberg Holdings.'

Bingo.

Helberg Holdings was an old money conglomerate—media, jewellery, retail property, hotels, everything imaginable, and—frankly because of that overreach—down on its luck. Reed Helberg, the last of the Helberg dynasty, had died seven months ago, and without its formidable, all-controlling head, the entity was now vulnerable. If changes weren't made soon, the entire operation could implode and leave little to salvage. The best option was to break it apart and sell off the bits that still worked. Corporate raiders often got a bad rap, but Zane had overseen many successful rebuilds from the parts of previous companies he'd bought and broken up. And yes, he'd made plenty of money doing it. But this time was different. This time was personal.

'What about it?' Zane stretched lazily.

'You and Cade have both been buying up shares,' Adam gritted out.

'Him too?' Zane nodded towards Cade, who was taking his time to join them.

'Yes.'

Ah well, the game was afoot. But because of Reed Helberg, Zane had spent years literally broken. So Zane would be the one to break Reed's most treasured thing. That was fair, right?

But now he merely shrugged as Cade settled into the corner seat of the sauna. 'Well, it's highly leveraged, vulnerable and has lots of assets… What's not to like?'

Adam's gaze narrowed. 'An overinflated purchase price.'

'Scared it's gonna get too much for you?' Zane countered dryly.

Actually, that *was* a potential problem. Too many interested buyers meant trouble. Cade remained silent, but Zane noticed the loner's gaze briefly drop to the scars zigzagging up Zane's thigh. Zane stayed sprawled back and refused to cover the unsightly purple streaks. People saw damage and assumed weakness. They were wrong. Where there were scars, there was strength.

'I need you both to back off,' Adam said.

A frigid edge sliced into the sweltering atmosphere.

Zane didn't do deals with guys like Adam or Cade. They were too alike, too alone, frankly too obstinate. So they fished in their own ponds and kept their battles to the squash court. It was safest for everyone that way.

'Helberg?' A muscle in Cade's jaw flicked. 'Not happening...'

Zane slowly shook his head and shot Adam a mock sad expression. 'No can do.'

Helberg's destruction was his alone to enjoy and he would do whatever it took to eliminate the competition. But these two were sharp and he'd have to think creatively through this one.

'It's a once-in-a-lifetime opportunity, y'all,' Cade said.

No shit. Any other company and Zane might consider walking away, but Reed Helberg was the whole reason why Zane had scars on his skin and metal pinning his bones beneath it. Zane was going to enjoy ripping apart the thing Reed had been so vainglorious about. The thing he'd never thought Zane was good enough for. Carve and cull was the only way through.

Adam inhaled deeply. 'Then we have a problem.'

'Actually, we have *problems*. Plural.' Cade glowered from his corner.

'What the hell are you talking about?' Adam's frown mushroomed.

Cade stiffened. 'Clearly you don't read *Blush*.'

'The women's glamour magazine?' Adam asked incredulously. 'You read that?'

'No, I don't read it, but my PR consultant does. He just texted me,' Cade growled. 'Did y'all know we are the star players in their latest dumb article: "The Billionaire Bachelors Least Likely to Marry"? Apparently, we three have been tagged as the One-Date Wonders...the guys with the longest odds, and they've already started a tally on how many dates we'll have racked up by Labour Day.'

The *what*? Zane cocked his head, both disbelieving of and bamboozled by this unexpected diversion. 'You're kidding.'

Privacy wasn't assured once your bank balance hit a certain threshold, so yeah, sometimes they were on those tragic 'youngest billionaires' lists and occasionally some appalling clickbait list involving paparazzi pictures of them poolside, but this one was even more ick. 'Who I date is no one's business but mine.' Zane shook his head, brushing it off. 'And I'm not going to stop—' He was happily married to his work, thanks very much. And very happy to play the little time he took away from it. Work hard, play hard—balance was best, after all. '—I've no plans to settle down. Ever.'

'Neither do I,' Adam snapped.

Zane blinked at the identical frowns deepening on Adam's and Cade's faces. The intensity was interesting. And possibly useful.

'They're turning our sex lives into a joke,' Cade added after a moment. 'And getting a lot of traction. And that's not the kind of media attention I want for my business. Do you?'

Zane didn't give a damn if people were so bored they wanted to bash his private life for their own amusement, but it clearly bothered both Cade and Adam.

'Exactly how much traction are we talking about?' Zane drawled.

Cade tensed even more. 'The hashtag "onedatewonders" is the top trending topic in the US on most of the main apps today. That much traction. And just about every American female online seems to have an opinion now about our sex lives… We're basically the red meat at the centre of a social media feeding frenzy.'

Adam winced.

Yeah, #onedatewonders was a truly appalling hashtag.

'My PR team is freaking out about it,' Cade added. 'Personally, I don't give a damn what a bunch of clickbait junkies and their enablers think of my dating habits…but no way in hell am I letting anyone make me look like a jerk who can't keep his junk in his pants.'

'We need to find a way to shut it down,' Adam muttered grimly.

Zane rubbed his hand along his jaw and considered the reactions of his rivals. Despite his protests, this article had obviously hit Cade on a visceral level, and Adam looked even moodier than usual. People made mistakes when they were emotional and both these guys were zooming towards anger and outrage.

Zane didn't become intensely emotional about anything. On the rare occasion something slipped beneath his skin, he swiftly suppressed it, because after his father had walked out he'd had to 'stay strong.' After he'd realised his exhausted mother was struggling and secretly wanted him gone too, he'd learned not to 'be a bother.' When he was housebound recuperating for years he'd had to 'be quiet' so his overworked mother could rest...

He didn't show hurt, didn't cry, didn't complain. When Reed Helberg had humiliated him more than once, he hadn't so much as winced. Hell, when the first girl he'd fancied had hung him out to dry in front of her overly controlling father, he'd hid how stupidly much *that* had hurt him. And he'd vowed not to let *anyone* hurt him ever again. And besides all that, he'd spent years suppressing *physical* pain, which was a far tougher task than swallowing the mild embarrassment from this little internet flurry.

But perhaps he could direct Adam and Cade's obvious discomfort to his own advantage. Indeed, the answer to the magazine slur was obvious to him. If they weren't seen out with a series of women, then there would be no stupid tally and nothing for the trash columnists to report on. The question was whether Cade and Adam could cope with that constraint—was that, in fact, a prospect for a competition?

Zane deMarco thrived on competition. The tougher the better. It made winning all the sweeter.

'What if we take ourselves off the market?' he mused.

'Forget it.' Cade sounded horrified. 'No way am I *actually* getting hitched to shut this down.'

'Absolutely not.' Adam was even more appalled. 'It's out of the question.'

Zane bit back a chuckle. Yeah, both of them were too volatile and that was good. 'Did I say anything about getting hitched?' he countered, oh-so-mildly. 'This is a countdown, right? So why don't we stop the clock before it even starts. All we have to do is each date one woman—and one woman only—from now until Labour Day. Simple.'

Cade's jaw dropped. 'You're kidding. You actually want to pander to this garbage?'

'Not particularly, but I'm betting you two will break long before I do.' Zane watched them closely.

Cade's blue eyes glinted. 'I'll take that bet, because the last time I looked, you're a bigger serial dater than the both of us.'

Usually true, but also irrelevant. While generally sex was a healthy part of his life, more than half of his most recent dates had ended early and chastely. He was tired of the more-than-sexual expectations he didn't have the capacity to fulfil. But Zane would endure anything to get hold of this company, and what was a little discomfort or deprivation? He'd suffered far worse pain than having to sleep with just the one woman for a while. Besides which, it was only dating her, right? Not necessarily anything more.

'You don't even know what the stakes are.' Adam shot Cade an astounded look.

Zane let the moment hang. He liked playing all kinds of games because his favourite thing in the world was to *win*, and because he'd come from having nothing for so long, he'd never been afraid of going all in. His risks had paid off.

'My Helberg shares,' he said softly and watched them both stiffen.

Uh-huh. That had their attention. His amusement rippled across his face but beneath that facade he tensed. Winning Helberg Holdings was non-negotiable.

'Hold on a minute.' Cade leaned forward, frowning. 'You'd bet on Helberg? Are you serious?'

Deadly, actually. But he played up his carelessness. 'Sure. Why not?'

If Cade and Adam thought he wasn't all that serious, they wouldn't take him as a serious threat. He'd lull them, then strike. 'It's Independence Day today. What if we meet back here on Labour Day. Winner takes all accumulated shares and has an unimpeded run at Helberg.'

That gave them a couple of months. There was no way either Adam or Cade would date only one woman for all that time. Both were allergic to relationships, both exuded intensity and drive and both did not like being told what they could and couldn't do by anyone. Put people under pressure and they made mistakes. Meanwhile, it would give Zane room to finish his due diligence and finalise divestment plans for Helberg. Plus if they all backed off for now, it would hopefully stop the share price surge.

'Have you completely lost your mind?' Adam shook his head.

Zane shrugged. He enjoyed doing the absolute opposite of what anyone expected of him. It made a challenge all the sweeter when he succeeded.

'This *Blush* business is an annoyance, but I'm more interested in sorting out which of us gets Helberg. This is a good way to take you guys on and beat you both for once and all. Two birds, one stone.'

'It's nuts…' Cade stared at him. 'But it also makes sense.'

'It's ridiculous,' Adam shot them down crisply. 'Not only will it not work, it's also immoral. And think of the unwitting women we'd be dragging into it. Where's your integrity?'

Zane bit back a laugh. Apparently perfectly posh Englishman Adam was too straitlaced to think creatively. As far as Zane was concerned, there was no reason why the woman he chose to date for the duration should be either unwitting or indeed unwilling. Everything—indeed, every*one*—had a price. All he had to do was find a woman savvy enough to take the deal he was going to discreetly offer her. But Zane was hardly about to point that option out to all-but-aristocratic Adam.

Zane had hauled his way to the top of his particular tree all by himself—he'd had no family money, no hand-outs from anyone else, least of all old man Helberg. He'd done everything on his own and he always would. Taking Helberg apart piece by tarnished piece all by himself would be particularly satisfying.

'You got a better idea?' He let a sprinkle of saltiness out. 'Because the likelihood of us stepping out of each other's way just because you asked nicely is…*what*?'

Cade's rare low laugh sounded. 'Afraid you'll lose, Courtney?'

Adam dated the least of the three of them. Cade, on the other hand, was barely tamed, while Zane knew his own reputation was voracious, which meant—once he'd thought about it—Adam would believe he would win this thing. Easily.

Sure enough, a split second later Adam nodded. 'Not at all… Quite the opposite…'

Yeah, it seemed Adam had mentally resolved his own integrity issue, while Cade simply looked wolfishly determined. Fortunately, Zane was heading home this afternoon and there'd be zero chance of encountering temptation there. After a courtesy drop-in to his neighbour's Independence Day party, he'd take the rest of the weekend to consider who he was going to approach and how.

'So just to clarify,' Adam added stiffly. 'We date one woman each between now and Labour Day. Anyone caught dating more than one woman in that time relinquishes their claim on Helberg.'

'Right.' Zane nodded. 'I'm in.'

'You're on,' Cade agreed.

Adam sighed as he rolled his eyes. 'May the best man win…'

Zane smiled. The best man absolutely would.

CHAPTER TWO

THREE BLUE-EYED BILLIONAIRE bachelors walked into a health club...

Sounded like the start of a bad joke, right? Or a dream opportunity for someone inspired by *Blush* magazine's latest article questioning whether there was a woman alive who could secure more than one date with any of them. The One-Date Wonders themselves: Adam Courtney. Cade Landry. Zane deMarco.

For Skylar Bennet, it was neither funny nor a dream. It was a full-fledged nightmare. She froze in the cafe across the street, staring in horrified amazement as, within the space of two minutes, the three subjects of the tasteless article currently being quoted all over social media stalked in. Well, Adam and Cade stalked. Zane simply sauntered.

Typical.

Skylar drained her coffee and ordered another. She'd done her run and didn't have to get to the office immediately, so she'd wait to see them walk out again. It wasn't the first time she'd watched out a window hoping to see Zane deMarco, but she wasn't some tragic teen suffering from her first crush now.

It was Saturday—the Fourth of July in fact, so it was a long weekend as well, but those guys didn't holiday like normal people. They weren't rolling up to a gym for fun and fitness. Setting up deals was their sport and recreation because nothing mattered more to them than making money. But as much as these three had in common, it wasn't normal to see them *together*. They were *rivals*, not besties.

Maybe that article did have something to do with it. As gross as it was, it was also accurate—they were each ridiculously young to have achieved billionaire status and all those pictures proved they were unrepentantly active on the social scene. But she didn't know much about Adam and Cade other than what else had been written—British Adam was all aristocratic old money, while Cade had built his construction company into a billionaire business. But she knew more than enough about Zane deMarco. The man was avaricious and an annihilator and he did not give a damn about what anyone thought of him. Which is why Skylar was quite sure it wasn't that article drawing them together today—it was something far worse.

They were coming for Helberg Holdings. That company was more than her place of employment; it had changed her life. She'd been a beneficiary of the Helberg Foundation—awarded scholarships first for senior high school, then a full ride for her entire degree. She'd interned for them through her summer breaks and come to work full-time in the company headquarters here in Manhattan as soon as she'd graduated.

It was the plan her father had dreamed she'd follow—to be the first in her class, the first in his family to get a degree, to work in the city in a prestigious firm, to *excel*, and to show loyalty... The Helberg scholarships had enabled her to do exactly that.

She'd owed. She still did. Now, years later, she'd made her way onto the HR team, but since the untimely death of the CEO Reed Helberg seven months ago, whispers about a take-over had been growing. The optimists in the office wanted it to be bought by someone who'd restore the conglomerate to its former glory, but Skylar was afraid it would be ripped apart by some ruthless corporate raider.

Someone like Zane deMarco.

The jerk scooped up vulnerable companies, stripped and

sold their assets and ditched the rest. He had zero commitment. Which was exactly how he approached women as well—absolutely a 'one-date wonder,' he'd accumulated as many notches on his bedpost as he had dollars in the bank. But while he was all fun and charm on the outside, Skylar knew the truth. He didn't just have the arrogance of the successful—he was a *soulless* vessel who lived only to make cold, hard cash. He didn't truly care about anything—other than getting further along an endless path of acquisition and excess. In short, Skylar hated him. She had for years now.

It didn't help that he could kiss a woman like no one else. That once, so very briefly, almost a decade ago, *she'd* been his target. She'd fallen for his looks, his superficial charm... Fortunately, her father had intervened before she'd foolishly given Zane everything he'd wanted—the way so many others had since.

And of course he'd forgotten her and moved on to his next target—the same way he had with all the companies he'd shredded and the employees he'd left redundant. They couldn't be more different.

The irony was that they'd come from similar backgrounds. They'd lived in the same run-down apartment building in one of the few affordable housing complexes in Belhaven Bay, a picturesque village in the Hamptons, when they were kids. Sounded fancy, right? Wrong.

Growing up in one of the most famous and wealthiest areas in the world ought to be wonderful, but being a year-rounder was a vastly different experience to being a child of the rich and famous who dropped in only for weekends of the best weather. She and Zane had other things in common too— they'd both been raised by a single parent: Skylar by her dad, a caretaker, and Zane by his mum, a cleaner. They'd even gone to the same school until she'd won that scholarship to that boarding school upstate for her senior years. And unfortunately, she still remembered the quiet boy he'd been so very long ago. He'd found her not long after her mother had run off with another man. A few days later, a disbelieving Skylar had tried to find her—a naïve, heartbroken kid wandering down the road with no direction or plan. Zane had come across her a couple blocks over from their complex. She'd been crying— as pitiful as she'd been hopeful. He'd not said anything. He'd just taken a bit of raspberry candy from a packet in his pocket and handed it to her. He'd waited while she'd eaten it. While she'd calmed down. Then he'd walked her back to their build- ing, up the stairs, and left her at her door. They'd been *chil- dren* but he'd been her friend. Just for that moment. Because he'd roamed freely as a kid—some would say wildly—while his mother worked long hours. But from then on, Skylar had stayed inside, obeying her father's new rules.

Because she'd needed to be safe and he'd needed to know where she was at all times. She'd needed to be good and quiet and study hard. And she had. Because she'd not wanted her dad to disappear on her too.

Then Zane and his mother had been in an accident. He'd had to take a long time off school and hadn't roamed their block any more, and she'd hardly seen him at all.

It wasn't until the summer after her first year at that board- ing school when everything had changed. She'd been sixteen. Still processing her mother's absence, still pleasing her fa- ther—adhering to his strict lessons on loyalty and work ethic and not succumbing to distractions. She'd watched the world from the balcony as she'd studied. From her bedroom window in the evenings as she'd combed her hair. Late one night, she'd spotted Zane in the darkness across the courtyard. He'd been on the balcony of the two-bedroom unit that was a mirror of her own. He'd become something of a local legend by then—his jaw-droppingly elite academic performance overshadowed by rumours of some online financial success. But that night he'd looked moody and serious and honestly as lonely as she'd felt for years. He'd been wearing nothing but an old pair of shorts and unfortunately for her, in the shadow and gleam of that moonlit night he'd had the beauty of a brooding angel—tousled coal-coloured hair, sharp cheekbones, a sculpted torso. He'd leaned out with his arms wide on the railing and stared down at the courtyard as if he were Atlas himself with the world on his shoulders. Her heart hadn't just thumped painfully, it had flipped right over. She'd stepped back into the darkness of her own room but kept watching him for the full fifty minutes he was out there, and at one point he'd looked up, staring directly at her window, and even though it'd been dark and she'd known there was no way he could have seen her, she'd flushed.

From that night on she'd ached to see more of him—naively imagining they were kindred spirits, what with all those commonalities—and more of him she had then seen. It had become her habit to go for a run early in the mornings—not that she'd been good at it, but it'd been the one way of getting out that her father had allowed. She'd argued she needed to be fit to study well. To her surprise—and secret pleasure—she'd passed Zane on her way out a couple of times. He'd smiled at her. He had a captivating smile.

Then, on one of her last days home, as she'd come back from her run, she'd all but slammed into him as she'd turned into the stairwell on her side of the building. He'd steadied her and in the cool shade he'd smiled and his pale blue eyes had gleamed, and she'd felt energy emanating from him. Later, she'd learned it was around this time that he'd made his first million. All but overnight, so the story went. As a freaking teenager. Now she realised he'd wanted to celebrate in true playboy fashion—with a female conquest. A notch for his new belt. But back then, she'd thought his piercingly pale blue eyes had seen straight to her soul. Or at least, he'd noticed the movement of her mouth.

'What are you eating?' he'd asked.

It had been raspberry candy, of course. Her favourite and always her post-run self-reward.

'Got any to share?' he'd asked when she'd told him.

She'd shaken her head as she'd swallowed. 'That was my last piece.'

'Yeah?' he'd muttered huskily. 'Maybe I can still have a little taste.'

With that, he'd made his move. The kiss had been tentative at first. Soft. Gentle. Then it just changed. *She'd* changed. It was like a wildfire had exploded within her. She'd moaned, suddenly all the more breathless. She'd become so hot, so malleable in his arms. She'd have let him do anything. So *easy*. He'd lifted her up, surprising her with his strength as he'd pressed her against the wall with his lean body. But *she'd* been the one to curl her leg around his slim hips, welcoming him closer. She'd been the one to hold him *so* tightly, recklessly racing with him towards the precipice of something she hadn't understood but innately knew would be profound. She'd lost all track of time. Of everything. All she'd known was that she'd wanted that contact more than anything.

So she hadn't heard the heavy tread of her father coming down the stairs. She hadn't stopped kissing Zane back, clutching him closer, letting him touch—

For a time after, she'd tried to reassure herself that it would have looked worse than it actually was—after all, she'd already been flushed and breathless and sweaty from her run—but being caught pinned against the wall by a panting Zane, her father had thought her disarray was because Zane had manhandled her...

The scalding mortification of that moment still overcame her even now, years later. Even though her father was no longer alive.

'Get off her!'

She'd been paralysed. Her father had pulled Zane back and

shoved him from her. She'd slithered to the ground and said nothing to either her father or Zane as her father had suggested…assumed…*accused*.

She'd sunk back against that wall and watched the glittering passion in Zane's eyes morph into bitterness as she stayed silent in the face of her father's fury. And then even that bitterness had faded until he'd stood there, coolly and dispassionately enduring the endless onslaught of her father's rage.

'I don't care what money you've supposedly made. *Don't you dare* touch *my* daughter! *Don't you dare* help yourself—you'll never be good enough for her. You're a troublemaker, stay away!' Her father had berated him repeatedly before whirling to her. 'And *you*, get upstairs. *Don't you dare* squander the opportunities you've been given! *Don't you dare* ruin your future!'

He'd gone on and on and on. She'd been too stunned—too scared—too shamed to speak. She'd scuttled upstairs and hadn't dared leave the apartment again. Fortunately, it was only a few days before she'd had to return to school. She'd done so quietly and dutifully, repeatedly apologising to her still-disappointed father.

When he'd calmed down, when she'd finally summoned the courage, she tried to assure him Zane hadn't taken liberties, that she'd welcomed that kiss. But she hadn't said that right at the time.

And then her father had got angrier. *'Don't you dare let lust control you; don't you dare waste what you have on a boy who wants only one thing…'* It would, he'd lectured her, only lead her off the path into selfishness, into shirking responsibility. Disloyalty. After all, look at her mother—wasn't she the prime example of that?

Skylar had been devastated. She'd promised not to lose focus. She'd promised to make him proud again. There would be no boys—no lust. Not for years. Not—she hadn't realised at the time—really ever again.

When she'd returned the next holidays, Zane had left town and so had his mother, and a different family had lived in their apartment. She'd been glad. She'd tried hard not to follow word of Zane's success but it had been hard to avoid. He was the town's poster child. She'd seen the write-ups of the 'wunderkind' investor, seen the pictures of him at parties over in the UK even—always with a beautiful woman on his arm.

And the year after that she'd met him again. They'd both been guests at a formal graduation function of their old school. Even at eighteen she'd still felt awkward, wearing a thrift shop dress that was too big in the bust. Most dresses were still too big in the bust. She'd been nervously excited, knowing Zane was going to be there. Because despite everything, she'd never forgotten that kiss and at that point she'd not yet had another. At first she'd been too shy to look him in the eye; she'd forced her attention on being polite to Reed Helberg. The generous, old CEO rarely made appearances at events like that.

When she'd finally summoned the courage to glance over at Zane, he'd met her gaze for less than a second before coldly turning his back. She'd been flattened. He didn't talk directly to her. She'd noticed he'd not even politely applauded when she was announced as the Helberg Scholar—with a full ride to a prestigious university. He'd only deigned to shoot her a patronisingly sarcastic look as she'd sat back down, as if it were somehow disappointing to him that she'd accepted such an amazing offer. Anger had brewed in her then. But Zane hadn't bothered to look her way again. He'd spoken only briefly to Reed—and it was evident Zane hadn't thought much of him either. He'd been so rude he'd actually left before dessert, and on his way out he'd muttered to her beneath his breath.

'You're pathetic.'

His dismissal that night, his arrogant rudeness, had destroyed the remnants of her crush completely.

So, if she were an awful person, she'd whip out her phone

right now and post an anonymous tip on social media to let the single women of the world know exactly where the three billionaire baits could be found. By now they were probably in the sauna—as if it wasn't hot enough in Manhattan in July. But these men did everything to extremes, including how many women they dated.

Skylar had zero interest in securing a date with any of them, least of all Zane deMarco. She only wanted to know whether he was discussing Helberg Holdings with those other sharks, but short of sneaking into the gym changing rooms to eavesdrop she wasn't about to find out. But she was certain Zane would want Helberg—it was exactly the kind of prize that he liked. Big and sparkling, coveted by all. He liked to take such things and tear them apart. Just because he could.

But if Zane ripped Helberg to bits, as she knew he would, he'd ruin the hopes and futures of countless other kids like her who would benefit from a Helberg scholarship. Plus he'd also threaten the livelihoods of so many workers who'd been loyal to Helberg for decades, and Skylar simply couldn't stand for that.

A bunch of people dressed in red, white and blue burst into the cafe, wreathed in smiles and excitement. Skylar stilled, remembering how the rest of the country wasn't working today because they had feasts and parties to attend with family and friends.

Zane deMarco might not have much family but he liked to party harder than anyone—especially with all his female 'friends.'

She pulled out her phone and did a quick search to remind herself that indeed this was the one time of year that he sometimes returned—not to the enclave of groundskeepers, caretakers, cleaners and cooks, but to an elite annual party at an oceanfront summer residence that would be a permanent palace for anyone ordinary. Danielle Chapman's Independence Day party.

Skylar jumped off her seat, energy bursting as a plan formed. A year older than her, it had been Danielle's job to settle Skylar into that new school because she spent part of her summers on Long Island. Despite their vast differences, they'd actually got on well and Danielle's approval had spared Skylar from a lot of bullying. Danielle still spent every summer on the island. Her parties were exclusive and discreet. The few invitations she sent were coveted, but every year she sent Skylar one—ditto to her Halloween party upstate. It was a running joke between them that Skylar could never make either because of work. Danielle had been teasing Skylar about working too hard for years. But Skylar wasn't a party person and to tell the truth, seeing via socials that Zane had attended Danielle's most recent parties, she'd had all the more reason *not* to go. Not this year though.

Skylar shot the health club doors a final glance. She wasn't going to sit around waiting just to spot them in the distance and do nothing. She had to take *action*. She'd *go* to Danielle's party tonight. Zane would surely be there and the guy was *not* discreet. If she could get within earshot, it might give her a chance to find out for herself what his plans were. She whipped out her phone while she still had momentum.

'You're coming?' Danielle shrieked less than a minute later. 'Fantastic! You know the dress code is white—do you need something to wear? You'll stay the night out here? Do you need transport?'

Skylar laughed as she refused all Danielle's offers of additional help. It was enough for her to actually go; she liked her independence. And she held back from asking for confirmation that Zane would be there. It was a crazy long shot, but one she had to take.

CHAPTER THREE

JUST AFTER LUNCHTIME, Skylar boarded the crowded bus, hardly about to spend any of her savings by charting a helicopter like the other party guests would. Most of them didn't have to earn their own money. She used the hours to get on top of the work she'd not got to this morning. But as the bus neared her destination, her heart grew heavy. She hadn't been home since her father had passed unexpectedly two years ago. She'd packed up their old little apartment and not looked back. She'd just kept her head down at Helberg, knowing how proud her father had been of her achievements. Loyalty was everything—he'd drilled that into her over and over and she still felt the need to repay that debt. So she wasn't going to let Zane tear her company apart like it was nothing. Her colleagues were her family and they were stressed enough in the face of a difficult retail climate. But she'd seen Zane's stone-cold centre and she had to know his plans for sure.

'Wow.' Danielle greeted her with a wide smile and a huge hug. 'You look amazing.'

Yeah, her make-up, dress and shoes weren't exactly her usual sedate style. She'd had limited options, what with almost every store closed for the holiday. Having to wear white but not wanting to look *bridal* meant she'd had to take the silk dress that skimmed her figure a touch too close, plus had a high split to the side of the long skirt.

'And you're still rocking that high ponytail.' Danielle winked as she handed Skylar a cocktail.

Yeah, long hair tied up was still her thing. It wasn't exactly deliberate. She just never took the time off to get to the hairdressers often and it was easier to keep the length out of her face by either braid or ponytail.

Squaring her shoulders, she sallied forth into the party. She could do this.

Within ten minutes, she knew she'd made a mistake. There were too many people. While she could hold her own in a work meeting, this sort of socialising didn't come naturally. Attending that private school should have helped but in fact had only made her reticence worse. Her father had taught her that trust took a long time to build and was easily destroyed. She had to be careful. Maintaining relationships took a lot of effort, so she had few. Her work was her constant focus, which was why she'd do anything to save it—even engage with the destroyer himself. But as time ticked by, he didn't show and her discomfort increased.

Seeking space, she stepped outside. The lush green lawns leading to the beach were immaculately groomed and she wistfully thought of her father, who'd have been spotting the rare patch that needed work. She walked along the thick hedgerow that formed the side boundary to another palatial holiday home next door. There was a gap along the row and she turned into it, following the path before stopping, surprised to discover a secret garden before her—a rectangular space filled with mature fruit trees, a couple of sun loungers placed in their shade. Completely hidden from view of the houses, the stunning little sanctuary had obviously been here for decades.

She inhaled deep and relaxed properly for the first time in days. Tossing her small bag on the nearest lounger, she strolled beneath the shade of the pretty fruit trees, holding her long ponytail up high so she could feel the slight breeze on her back.

'What are you doing?' a low drawl sounded right behind her.

She spun, dropping her arm. 'What—'

She jerked to a halt, her hair pulling hard as she tried to step back. It took a blink before she realised her ponytail had caught on the low-slung branch above as she'd turned. Now she tried to shake it free with a nonchalant jerk of her head. She failed.

Ridiculous.

He was staring at her wide-eyed. *Him*—breaker of hearts, destroyer of moods, thief of peace. Zane deMarco himself.

'Now look what you…' She trailed off, mortified as she reached up blindly and tried to detangle the long strands caught above her.

Of all the people to startle her into a completely humiliating position… All she could hope now was that he'd not recognise her. The odds had to be in her favour given it had been years since the last time they'd crossed paths, and right now she was out of context, what with her heavy make-up and a slinkier-than-usual dress and please, please, please let him be so sated with so many women they'd all merged into one and he'd never remember the girl he'd once kissed in a cold stairwell early on a Saturday morning…

'You know the cherries aren't anywhere near ripe.' He stood three feet away, taking her in with a sweeping, sardonic gaze that went from her tangled hair to her silver-sandaled feet.

His attention made her very aware of her vulnerability—her raised arms made her dress cling even more to parts of her figure. Parts that all of a sudden tightened with pure chemical awareness. She dropped her hands to her sides with a slap and glared at him.

'What are you doing out here?' he repeated softly. 'Were you trying to find me?'

'Of course not,' she snapped. Even though she was here to do *exactly* that, it was still so arrogant of him to assume. 'I had no idea anyone was out here. I was just—' She broke off as she realised he was still looking her over in that slow, deliberate way, and it felt too *intimate*. Suddenly it didn't matter what she was doing or why she was here; she just needed to escape. ASAP. 'Are you going to help me or just stand there being entertained by my suffering?'

He moved closer. The light stubble on his jaw didn't mask the honed angles beneath and while his mouth was curved in an annoying smirk, his pale blue eyes gleamed with rapier-sharp scrutiny.

Skylar could meet that intense gaze for only so long before she had to lower her lashes. He was wearing black tailored trousers and a white dress shirt, which was unbuttoned at both the collar and sleeves. Indeed, those sleeves were rolled back, revealing strong, sinewy forearms. She gritted her teeth but still her traitorous pulse skipped every other beat as she remembered the strength in his arms. He was a jerk but her stupid body didn't seem to care. It was almost a decade ago, for heaven's sake. It was *not* yesterday.

'You're actually, seriously caught?' he asked sceptically.

'Obviously, or I'd have run away the second you appeared,' she muttered.

'Really?' He looked arrogantly disbelieving.

'Yes, really.'

'And somehow it's all my fault?' he murmured.

Quite. She'd seriously underestimated the impact of see-ing him again, and now here she was—*stuck*—but feeling that same insanity she'd felt every time she'd been in his pres-ence. Her tongue was tied, her mind was mince and prickly heat spread across her skin.

Summon anger.

Unfortunately, anger didn't show up. She simply stared into his striking eyes while thoughts of fallen angels and devilish temptations flitted in and out of her scattered brain. Seconds became centuries. Everything slowed as deep inside some-thing fizzed, bubbling higher and higher and hotter and hot-ter. She had to be ill. Surely. Sudden onset of a strange virus.

'Are you going to help me?' She eventually croaked out another request, because all he seemed to be doing was staring right back at her and standing as still as she was.

'I'm working out the best strategy to extract you from this disaster.'

'I thought you were meant to be a genius.'

His pale blue eyes lit and that was almost the end of her—spontaneous combustion imminent. She closed her eyes. She *couldn't* be feeling this. Nope. Not over Zane. Not again. She was *not* sixteen and full of impossible fantasy now.

She *knew* him—remember? She knew how cold he really was inside. How quickly, how easily he could walk away. He did not care about anything or anyone—

She dragged in a breath but was further intoxicated by the subtle scents of salt and musk and something a touch rougher. Whisky. Every sense ignited. Desperately she stood stock-still, held her breath and kept her eyes screwed shut.

'Skylar?' he murmured huskily. 'You still with me?'

Oh, *hell*. Her eyes flashed open. So did her jaw. Of course her hope that he wouldn't remember her would be futile. He probably had one of those eidetic memories with every minuscule detail of his life stored inside his annoyingly intelligent brain.

'What, did you think I didn't recognise you?' His eyes widened—almost revealing pique. 'Of course I recognised you…'

He raked his gaze down her yet again, taking in the delicate ribbon straps at the base of her neck. The halter-neck style meant she was unable to wear a bra beneath it—though to be fair she didn't really need a bra. But as his gaze swept down her, she felt her breasts respond again as if his glance were actually a stroke. Infuriated with herself, she willed her gaze to be more of a slap back. But when he lifted his focus back to her eyes, his smile merely widened from smirk to blindingly gorgeous.

'Just as you recognise me,' he added.

Well duh, of course she did. He was currently wallpapering the internet—one billionaire catch of the day. But okay, yes, it was because she'd spent most of her adult life trying to forget him.

Such things were impossible.

'We lived in the same apartment complex as kids,' he said conversationally as he stepped closer.

She struggled to retain her composure, glad he'd opted for that detail, not the fact they'd once been smashed together, frantically kissing against the wall of said apartment complex. Maybe he'd forgotten that had even happened. She could only hope. 'That's a long time ago now.'

He nodded and reached above her head. 'It doesn't exist any more.'

She took a quick, sharp breath. She'd not been back to their village since her father had passed. She hadn't known the building had been demolished. 'A lot has changed.'

'A lot certainly has,' he agreed with that mocking edge.

He'd been handsome then and he was stunning now. It was severely unfair for one person to get everything—extreme brains and extreme beauty. And she was just like every other woman who came close to him—unable to resist drinking in the sight of his sleek, fit body as he ran his fingers along the length of her hair, trying to smooth it free from the branch. She quelled her shiver but now her pulse thundered. This was way too intimate.

'Your ponytail is very long,' he said. 'Is it all your own?'

'What?' She jerked and her hair tightened again. 'Of course it's mine.'

He laughed beneath his breath. Her mood sharpened. Retaliation was required.

'I've thought you'd manage this more quickly,' she murmured saltily. 'Given you're supposed to be good with your hands.'

He stilled, mere millimetres away from her. Skylar took a second to replay what she'd just said and realised how stupid it was. How incendiary. How easily it would be interpreted as a tragic attempt at flirtation. But before she could backpedal he leaned closer still and resumed his effort to detangle her.

'Oh, I'm very good with my hands,' he drawled softly right near her ear. 'And slow is better, don't you agree?'

No, she did *not* agree. Because the century-length seconds had slowed even more and she wasn't coping.

'Oh, yeah,' he muttered into the thickened silence. 'I should have remembered that you prefer things fast...'

She couldn't reply and he bent to look into her face. There was that mockery in his eyes, but there was heat too—heat that made that fizzing inside even more intense. If she were normal, she'd laugh this off with some flippant comment. But she wasn't normal. She couldn't think of anything flippant. She couldn't think of anything at all except—

'Just hurry up and finish,' she whispered, unable to believe what both her brain and body wanted.

'Wow,' he breathed back. 'There's a first.'

She clenched her fists and battled to hold herself back. 'You're not used to your attentions being unwanted?'

His smile of disbelief spread wider. 'But you're the one who asked me to help,' he pointed out. 'I'm being gentlemanly here, rescuing you from the evil clutches of a cherry tree.'

She couldn't laugh. Quicksilver, not blood, flowed in her veins. Handsome in pictures, devastating in the flesh, Zane deMarco embodied sensual vitality, and every breath, every glance, every moment basking in his attention sent Skylar further along the path towards total brainlessness.

His dilating pupils were the only movement he made. 'It really bothers you that I'm this close?'

Dynamite, meet detonator. His mere proximity provided the shock wave to ignite something within her that had long been—well—dead. He wasn't just hard to handle, he was impossible to ignore, and unfathomably that ancient crush just...

resurged. Even when she knew what a callous lump of a heart he had, her body didn't care. Her body simply sizzled.

He suddenly moved. She felt loosening at her scalp and his fingers finally ran the full length of her hair and when they hit the end her ponytail fell back to rest against the bared skin of her back.

'There you go—free of me at last. Quick, get away while you can,' he jeered huskily. Bitterness glittered in his eyes. 'There's no one here to rescue you this time. You'd better run inside for safety.'

That was what she'd done almost a decade ago. Run inside and shut the curtains and not peeked out.

But she still couldn't move. She watched that flicker in his eyes and the sardonic curve of his full lips and decided she *wouldn't* give him the satisfaction of running scared. Because when she'd run all those years ago it hadn't been from him.

In truth, right now she was more scared of herself. But she'd come here for information, and while this was hardly the ideal interaction, at least she'd made contact. And suddenly there was an imp within that simply spoke for her.

'Oh, no.' She flicked her hand through her hair and the swish of her ponytail basically hit him in the nose. 'I'm not going anywhere. That would be far too easy for you.'

'You're here to make things hard for me?' Zane jammed his tingling hands into his pockets. He was hard already in a shockingly instant reaction to this unexpected encounter. He hadn't been going to bother with Danielle's party. He'd flown up later than intended and been late to cut across the garden, and as he had he'd glimpsed a nymph in the orchard and investigated only to find—

Skylar Bennet.

Hers was a face from the past that he preferred to keep well behind him, and he'd certainly not expected to see her here and looking like this. Not all glossy hair, glossy lips, glossy dress…not the perfectly polite, dutifully docile, completely irritating swot he knew Skylar was.

So he could do nothing but stare. The white silk clung to her slender curves, and a high split in the skirt teased flashes of skin while a thin ribbon at her neck secured the dress. He wanted to tug on the ends and watch it all slip from her silky-looking skin. He wanted to see the secrets beneath. He wanted to free her hair and feel it trail and tease his skin—and all but whip him in the face again.

Of course, the truth was he'd wanted all that since he'd been eighteen and guiltily watching her comb her hair at her window across the courtyard and up one floor from his. And he'd not been allowed then, had he? Her father had informed him he'd never, ever be good enough for her. And yeah, he certainly wouldn't be good enough in that man's eyes now.

Only now here she was in front of him again. He'd not expected her to be so tartly defensive. She'd verbally lashed him like a little wild creature caught in the bushes. Except she wasn't so little. Not in the good places. He'd reacted. So had she. Sexual tension had taken command of them both.

'Maybe I am,' she huskily countered.

Sexual tension was *definitely* still in charge. His muscles bunched as he watched the tilt of her chin and the antagonism build in her eyes.

She'd grown up in that third-floor apartment opposite his. A pretty, petite brunette with the biggest brown eyes he'd ever seen. He'd struggled with his own issues back then—all that time it had taken to heal after the accident, the risky moves he'd been making with his online trading platform, desperately trying to make money to get out of there, but she'd been a constant in the background. A fellow battler on the block. Another only child of a solo parent. She'd been better than him though—she'd been *good*. She'd been so intensely focused on her studies she'd won one of Reed Helberg's prestigious scholarships.

And she'd gone.

But the shy, pretty girl he'd occasionally seen had come back from her fancy new boarding school for the holidays and somehow been completely different. She'd sat on her balcony in the shade and studied all damned day, only moving to make her father meals or fetch his drinks when he returned from work. The only time Zane saw her leave that apartment was to go for a morning run. A new routine. He'd seen her smile and heard her soft laughter as she'd chatted to her father. They'd seemed close. And Zane had been so smitten, he'd loitered in the courtyard at her run time like a lovesick fool. And one morning, for just a few stolen moments, he'd tasted her.

Before she'd turned her back and betrayed him.

He'd not seen her again before she'd gone back to school and then he'd left town. They'd been at that stupid dinner at his old school where he'd been guest speaker a couple years later. He'd been flattered by the invite and had said yes. He'd not made that mistake again. Reed Helberg had been there and Skylar had been so perfect and polite. She'd not even looked at Zane; everything had been about Reed. He'd been infuriated—because of her desperation to please, right? She'd won what he'd been denied but his irritation hadn't been because of that. He'd hated that demure demeanour—that her docility was so underpinned by anxiety. Wide-eyed and terrified by the supposed importance of the old man who'd dominated the dinner conversation. Those stupid scholarships might supposedly be life-changing, but in Zane's opinion, the price paid by the winner was too high. It was all so wretchedly *controlling*.

But now Skylar Bennet was entirely grown-up and all alone and apparently here to make things hard for him. Well, she'd succeeded.

'So you did come here to see me,' he said, feeling visceral pleasure at the thought.

She stared at him—basically breathing fire. His recklessness surged as he watched the enmity battle the interest bur-

geoning in her deep brown eyes. He wanted to turn that gleam
into sleepy satisfaction. He lost track of everything else. Where
he was going. Why. What he was meant to do and not do…
none of it mattered. Because he could see only her and right
now he wanted nothing but her.

That old desire slammed back into him. He'd wanted her
so much back then—with all the ardour of inexperience and
youth. She'd been tantalisingly close, yet so out of bounds.
Maybe that was why it was back so fiercely now. She'd been
his first crush—wholly forbidden fruit.

'You don't usually come to this party.' His throat tightened.
He'd liked touching her hair. It was long, silky, fragrant, and
he battled the sharp urge to release it from that tight band now.

She stiffened as he stepped closer.

He suppressed his smile with difficulty. It was harder to
suppress everything around her. 'You still don't party much?
Ever the hard worker, Skylar?'

She was quiet and dutiful while he wasn't. Maybe it was
the simple, strong magnetism of polar opposites, because she
couldn't seem to take a step from him. Nor could he from her.
The defiance in her brown eyes deepened.

'You've not bothered to pay attention to the dress code,
I see,' she said coolly. 'At least I've made the effort to do as
asked.'

'Of course you have,' he murmured insolently. 'I bet you always do as you're asked…' He couldn't resist stepping closer.
'Like a good girl.'

Her eyes narrowed.

'You always were so *obedient*,' he growled, scrambling to
stop the racing thoughts rising from his own damned words.
'*Such* a pleaser.'

God, he wanted her to please him. And he wouldn't just
please her back. He'd destroy her.

Because all those years ago she'd gone up in flames in his
arms. He'd almost lost his footing she'd been so passionate—

she'd wanted him every bit as much as he'd wanted her. But she'd not defended him when her father had thought the worst of him. How she'd silently abandoned him as they'd faced her father's wrath and rejection. He couldn't forgive her for that. But nor could he forget that *she'd* been the one rubbing against him in the most arousing of ways. *She'd* been the one moaning. *She'd* been the one shaking. It had taken every ounce of his utterly limited experience back then to try to slow them down. Because it had been a conflagration. And he was so close to every brain cell burning up again now.

'While you're a taker,' she replied tartly.

He smiled wolfishly, enjoying her attack. 'You think?' Spreading his hands wide in innocence, he shot her a look. 'But tell me, how can I wear all white when I'm prone to getting a little dirty?'

Her eyes widened and twin spots of colour deepened in her cheeks. He was unrepentant. She was the one who'd started this—even if that earlier innuendo had been unintentional. But they had chemistry and it wouldn't be curbed. Zane was all for fireworks now they were adults. Fireworks were fun.

'Or maybe it's just that you think the rules don't apply to you,' she said.

'Rules?' He faux shivered, as if she'd raised a horrifying spectre.

His little nemesis rolled her eyes. 'You won't ever do what others ask of you,' she said with soft precision. 'You're too arrogant.'

Every rule jumped out the window.

'You think?' he breathed. 'Why don't you find out for yourself?' He was a millimetre from her pretty face, willing her to take what he was really offering. 'Go on, Skylar. Ask me anything. *I dare you.*'

CHAPTER FOUR

OH, SHE'D DARE...

But she didn't. Old habits were hard to break. She just had to back away slowly. Take the exit via the beach.

'You can't go yet,' he said softly.

'Why not?' She glared at him.

'You really have to ask?'

A moment of searing tension strung her out before she shook her head sceptically. While she was thinking wildly inappropriate things about him, he was merely toying with her. That was what he did. 'Oh, please.'

He stood very, very still—his hands still in his pockets—as a faint flush coloured his sculpted cheeks. He was insanely handsome but he didn't mean anything in this moment. He could turn his charm off and on like a switch.

'I didn't get a thank-you,' he said eventually.

'You'd be satisfied with a mere thank-you?'

'Yeah, no. You're right. Actions do speak louder than words.'

What kind of *actions* was he thinking of? She glared at him. 'You want a ticker tape parade for acting like a decent human?'

'Maybe you might offer to get me a drink,' he said.

'You're thirsty?'

His smile appeared. 'You have to agree it's very hot out here.'

She shot him another withering look, but she was the one withering inside. *Run.*

'Still no thank-you?' he said after a moment. 'When I rescued you so gallantly?' He tut-tutted. 'You do intrigue me, Skylar.'

'Am I supposed to be pleased about that?' She folded her arms across her chest and wished for inches.

'You're saying you're not?' His grin widened. 'But maybe you're not *quite* as polite as you've always appeared.' His eyes gleamed. 'Maybe you sometimes like to get dirty too. In fact, I'm sure you do.'

Her breath stalled. She couldn't answer that.

'Thanks or not, I'm glad I was here to help,' he added. 'Your hair is stunning. It would be devastating if it were damaged.'

Devastating? She felt an absurd pleasure that he liked her hair. And it *was* absurd, because she also knew this was just another of his lines. 'You really can't stop yourself, can you?'

'Stop myself from what?'

'Flirting.'

The corner of his lush mouth curved. 'You think this is me flirting?'

Die. Again. Just die.

He walked so close that she had to step back. And she kept stepping until the backs of her legs hit the sun lounger. That's when she was forced to stop. But he didn't stop. Not until he was less than a breath apart from her.

'You definitely weren't at this party last year,' he said softly. 'You're *never* at these sorts of parties.'

She tossed her head. 'What makes you so sure?'

His voice dropped. 'I'd have noticed.'

Her temperature rose. She dragged in a searing breath. 'No you wouldn't—'

He reached out and gently flicked a wisp of hair from her face. His hand landed on her waist when he lowered it.

'What are you doing?' she stammered.

He smiled indulgently, his blue gaze intent on her. 'This is me flirting.'

'This isn't flirting, this is just you…crowding me.'

'Too close?' he breathed. 'Shall I step back?'

His ice blue gaze locked on her for a long moment. She was toe-curlingly hot and she couldn't possibly be wanting what she was thinking. She was supposed to be here to ask him about Helberg—only suddenly she didn't want to think about any of that. Suddenly she didn't want to think about anything at all.

'I don't think you want me to step back,' he whispered. 'I think you want me to stay right where I am.' He cocked his head. 'I think you want other things as well. So let me dare you again, Skylar…*ask me*.'

She swallowed. She should shut this down right now but she simply couldn't, such was his potency. 'You get what *you* want far too easily,' she muttered feebly.

'And?' He slid that hand around her waist, his broad palm spread wide and flat on her back. The heat and strength of him through the thin silk was both arousing and oddly *reassuring*…

She'd been here before and once more she couldn't move. He was the biggest tease and she was falling for it—letting him all over again—because yeah, just like that, she was a *yes*.

'Do you want me to walk away?' he challenged her huskily.

But he was serious. She realised that with one word from her, he would leave. He would not look back. Once again, it would be like this moment had never ever happened.

And suddenly she couldn't speak. She couldn't lie and send him from her. Because this was every unfinished fantasy she'd ever had. And she was furious about it.

At university *years* later, she'd tried to find this fire with someone else. She'd let another guy kiss her. It had left her cold. She'd kissed a different one. Same deal. She'd wondered if maybe her father catching her had caused some shame that she needed time to get over. It had been a relief to think that. A relief not to try anything more with anyone else ever.

But now it destroyed something in her to realise that it wasn't that at all. Because she still responded to *Zane*. Right here. Right now. She was aroused. And maybe that wouldn't happen with anyone else while *he* was still in her system. How hideous that he was the only man who she responded to in this insanely intense way. That had to be fixed.

In this second, what happened with Helberg Holdings was irrelevant. There was no one around to interrupt them. No one to tell her *not* to dare...

She needed to get over this stupid hang-up. And maybe that was by having what she wanted from him. As galling as it might be to add herself to his list of conquests, maybe she'd be free of her fixation on him at last.

'Stop teasing me,' she snapped jerkily. 'So far you're all talk.'

Surprise flashed in his eyes, followed swiftly by a flare of satisfaction. Both were engulfed in the blue-black heat of engorged pupils. He didn't wait for her to change her mind. His hand at her back firmed, pushing her close so they were suddenly belly to belly and he'd proven he wasn't all tease. He promised very real passion. She gasped as he anchored her to his hard body and as she did, he lowered his head.

'Will you taste of raspberry candy this time, Skylar?'

She shook her head. She'd not had raspberry candy in years—it was too associated with him. 'I prefer lemon.'

'Right,' he muttered. 'Apparently you've become a little acid drop.'

Taking total advantage of her parted lips, he kissed her— deeply, intimately, endlessly.

Boom. Combustion of epic proportions.

She threw her arms around his neck and held on, tangling her tongue with his, pressing her pelvis closer to his. Power surged and she was out of control all over again. But he didn't press his forehead on hers and croon her name beneath his breath this time. His hands didn't tremble as he ran them down her arms. He just demanded her response—and devoured her.

But one thing remained the same. She felt wanted. Absolutely, utterly *wanted*. And she wanted him right back. Wholly sexually, right?

Wholly unbearably.

He pressed her closer still, grinding her body against his. She had no idea how long they were plastered to each other, frantically kissing. It was an inferno in seconds, every kiss better and better until her whole body quaked with desperation.

Of *course* he was a complete philanderer. Good for all those women who'd enjoyed this experience. She wasn't going to deny herself just to teach him a lesson he was never going to care about. She was going to take what she wanted. And that was this. Him. Now. Nothing else mattered. The kissing went on—hotter, more erotic, more hungry. She wriggled, helplessly aching and restless. Until he suddenly tore his lips from hers.

'Don't you want to know what I want?' he growled breathlessly.

This *should* be a two-way thing, but now he'd found that split in her skirt and his fingers were sliding up her leg—skin on skin—and she was so overwhelmed, so afraid of him stopping, she didn't want to admit how much this suddenly mattered.

'Do you think I care?' she asked.

He laughed, and the vibrations resonated deep in her belly and turned her on even more.

'Oh, I know you care,' he teased, and kissed her again as if it were all reward. 'Bleeding-heart little pleaser like you can't help *caring*.'

She leaned back, letting her pelvis grind harder against his even as she glared at him. 'For the record, I do *not* care about *you*.'

'You think you dislike me as much as I dislike you?' But his hand hit her panties as he taunted her. His fingers twisted. With total strength, he tore the lace so he could target her… *there*. 'You annoy the hell out of me, Skylar,' he growled.

But his fingers teased, skilful, utterly intimate little strokes that matched the magic he worked with his mouth as he pressed lush kisses across her face and neck. She began to tremble, and that's when he leaned closer still. His whisper was hot, his lips brushing just beneath her earlobe on that ultra-sensitive skin of her neck. 'So I want to see you crumble.'

His blistering focus—his irritation with his own attention on her—pulsated within her. Deeply. Their antagonism was real and couldn't be resolved. The fact was she didn't like him. And he didn't like her.

'Then make me,' she dared.

'It'll be my damned pleasure.' He lowered his lips that last millimetre back to her skin and licked his way down to the neckline. 'There's no one around to stop me now. And I know you won't.'

Skylar shivered, breathless and hot as he kissed beyond and below—all the way to her breast. He didn't care about the silk. He sucked on her taut nipple straight through it as his fingers twisted and slid right inside her.

She came. Hard. Bucking her hips, she writhed on his hand and arched her back so he could mouth more of her breast. She was greedy. Fortunately, so was he.

His arm was an iron rod at her back, but even so, she barely remained upright. He lowered her with a rough laugh, straight onto the sun lounger behind her, and followed her.

'Oh, you do like it fast,' he muttered. 'Even faster than I'd expected.'

Bliss pulsated in rivulets down her body but that cord of sexual tension wasn't yet severed. 'You're a supercilious jerk, you know that?'

He nuzzled his way back up her neck. 'And you're a sanctimonious swot.' He reared up and looked into her eyes. 'So what? We're still going to have sex.'

And there it was. She stilled, staring up into his eyes and seeing the intent. The invitation. The opportunity of a lifetime.

His pelvis dug into hers so she had no doubts about whether he really wanted this. But she registered his hesitation—his query. If she were her normal self, she'd say *no* instantly. But she wasn't just tempted nor just curious—she was so unbearably turned on there wasn't time to think about it. 'Of course we are,' she snapped. 'Just hurry the hell up!'

His laugh this time was low and exultant and he dropped back down to kiss her—pure reward, pure tease.

'Not *so* fast, this time.' He reached up and freed her ponytail from the tight elastic. He ran his hand through the thick length of her hair in an intensely intimate caress. It felt like he was worshipping her. But surely not—it was just that he was pure hedonist. A sensualist who enjoyed all touch. And right now, so did she.

'You've changed, Skylar Bennet,' he muttered as he pulled at the ribbons of her halter neck.

For the first time nerves fluttered. 'Not so much, I'm as f-flat-chested as ever...'

He glanced up, wide-eyed but laughing.

'Wouldn't want you to be disappointed.' She flushed with annoyance at the self-conscious wail that had escaped her before she could stop it. But the man had had a million lovers.

'Not gonna be,' he said. 'Vexed by your mouth, maybe. Never, ever disappointed by your body.'

The silk finally slid, exposing her breasts. He just stared and she felt him take in a deep breath and harden even more against her. To her total mortification, as he pressed closer, she just came all over again. Shivers of sensual bliss shook her.

'Hell, Skylar...' he hissed. 'Should've known you'd be exceptional in everything you do.'

She was too far gone in her bliss bubble to be able to answer. But he thought she was exceptional?

'Don't think you're done,' he whispered. 'Not done yet. Not without me.'

He rose to his knees and reached into his pocket. He had protection with him. Other than a quick feeling of relief, she didn't give that fact a second thought. There was no time for thinking. Only feeling. Moving. Teasing with a kind of anger that came from someplace she didn't really understand. But she suddenly wanted him to feel this as urgently as she.

He didn't bother stripping entirely. He just unfastened his trousers and yanked his boxers down enough to roll on the condom. There was no time to get her completely free of her dress, so he just slid her skirt up. Her panties were little more than shredded lace on a waistband and were no obstacle at all.

He paused for a moment, his hand flat on her lower belly, and shook his head as he stared at her. 'Skylar—'

She growled and shifted restlessly beneath him and with a groan he just kissed her. A second later, his full weight was on her and it was everything. He grabbed her thigh with his big hand and lifted her leg over his hip to make more space for him. And then he was there. She shuddered as he breached her virgin body with his.

'Hell,' he choked. 'I'm gonna—' He broke off with a groan and gritted his teeth. Lodged hard and deep inside her, his muscles bunched beneath her hands. 'I want—' He broke off again. 'You—'

He was so breathless, panting hard as if he faced a battle he knew he couldn't win. His struggle for control snapped hers. Heat surged, chasing away the tiny pinch of pain that had halted her breath when he'd first pushed inside her. She grabbed his hips, suddenly hungry for more, and writhed beneath him. She desperately needed him to move.

'Damn it, Skylar!' he roared. 'You're not making me—'

He pulled right out of her and she moaned at the loss in agonised frustration. But he half laughed before drawing in several steadying breaths.

'*My* pace, princess,' he finally said as he held her fast and slowly reclaimed his place deep inside her.

There was no pinch this time—only a sensation so intense that she could scarcely sigh as he leisurely rolled his hips and slid fractionally deeper with each powerful thrust.

'That's it,' he muttered. 'Stay with me now.'

Oh, she was with him—imprisoned in his embrace, impaled on his shaft—it was the best torture ever. With slow decadence he moved within her. The pull and drag of the friction between them was the most exquisite sensation of her life. She'd always felt so awkward around others that any kind of physical intimacy had felt impossible. But this with him was simply *effortless*. And so exciting. Which was also *so* annoying.

'I hate you,' she muttered breathlessly even as she clutched him closer, instinctively arching her hips to meet his over and over in this dance.

Humour-laced passion glittered in his eyes. 'Want me to hurry up and finish?'

She helplessly mumbled a meaningless denial. She sighed and stirred, matching his moves with the answering arch of her hips. It was fun. And good. And now she really did want it faster. And harder. And more all over again.

His choked laughter was followed by an explicit curse. She slid her hand into his hair and kissed him. His hands tightened and his movements roughened, his possession deepened even more. She broke free and gasped and as her orgasm rushed upon her, she realised he too had finally lost it.

There was no kissing in those last frantic moments. Only his harsh whispers—his intentions of dirty and deep possession savagely and repeatedly sworn. It was so hot that she shook in ecstasy all over again.

The last thing she heard was her name—uttered as if it were a curse as he came hard inside her.

CHAPTER FIVE

'SKYLAR?'

Lost in a sensorial haze, Skylar kept her eyes closed as she breathed in the balmy air, savouring the sultry scents of salt and heat and musk. She'd just had sex. For the first time. Outside in a garden, mere metres from a gathering of some of the most rich and powerful people in the country. Sex with Zane deMarco in fact. The guy she loved to hate. And as he was still holding her, still inside her, there was no escaping that reality.

But she didn't *want* to escape. She wanted to stay right here, for good. Because even though he was heavy, she was somehow floating in a rapturous state unlike anything she'd known. She felt weightless and lax and utterly relaxed and she didn't want it to end.

'Skylar?'

There was a tone in his voice that she didn't recognise. Opening her eyes, she saw he'd eased up onto his elbows and was staring down at her. The haze she'd been enmeshed in slowly dispersed and in her reluctant return to reality, a top-to-toe tremble racked her body.

'You're cold,' he said gruffly.

That hadn't been a shiver but an aftershock of epic proportions. Hardly surprising given the intense experience her nervous system had just endured. She'd gone from first intimate touch to triple orgasm in minutes. Searing, sweet minutes that she ached to savour. She still didn't want it to be over.

But too carefully, too swiftly, he levered himself off her and stood. He wasn't smiling any more. There wasn't any of that smooth tease she'd expect—in fact, he looked as awkward as she felt as he turned away to haul up his trousers.

Did he regret this already? Doubts flurried in. She'd been inexperienced. Maybe it hadn't been all that for him.

Her heart was still thundering as she sat up and awkwardly swung her legs to stand. She'd lost some coordination and the crumpled silk dress that had been bunched around her waist now slid to the grass as she half stumbled to her feet.

Great. Now she was fully naked—aside from the high-heeled sandals that made little difference in getting her any-where near his height. Zane bent and retrieved her dress from the ground before she could think to beat him to it.

He frowned and gave it a shake and frowned. 'I don't know how we got grass stains…' He lifted it higher so he could see it more clearly in the fading light. 'Not grass. Blood.'

Horrified, Skylar bent her head, letting her hair hide her face and half her super-sensitive body while she took a deep breath.

But Zane spoke again before she could. 'You have your pe-riod? Do you need me to get you some—'

'I'm fine. It's fine. I'm not— I don't need anything.' Except a magic wand with which to vanish. Instantly. Only they didn't exist so she was going to have to bone up and deal with the reality. Bluntly. Honestly. Matter-of-factly. The man was so comfortable around women that he thought nothing of dis-cussing something she found deeply personal.

'But—'

'I was a virgin,' she blurted. 'Don't worry about it.'

'A what?' He stared at her and crushed the dress in his hands. 'A *what*?'

She licked her lips nervously. 'First-timer. Let's forget it.'

'You were a virgin?' He snatched a breath and repeated it again. 'A *virgin*?'

Her annoyance returned. Which was good. 'Say it again, you might understand it next time.'

'A… You…' He drew in another breath. 'I've never taken anyone's virginity.' He stared down at her grimly.

'I guess there's a first for everything.' She winced.

He dropped her dress back to the ground and ran his hand through his hair a couple times. 'You shouldn't have—what were you *thinking*?'

'I wasn't. Obviously. Same as you.' She cleared her throat. 'If it's such an issue, just forget it ever happened.'

'Forget?' He threw her an astounded look, which morphed to furious in a nanosecond.

She wasn't sure why he was suddenly so angry. But as he stalked towards her, Skylar held her stance, crossing her arms but wincing inwardly at her nudity. He stopped three feet away, shrugged off his shirt and held it out to her.

'Put it on,' he ordered after a moment.

At her continued hesitation he grew more grim. 'Do you really want to walk back through that party with all those people in a crumpled, stained dress and have absolutely everyone know exactly what we've been doing?'

She snatched the shirt from his hand and slid her arms into the sleeves. It was still warm from his body and it hung to her mid-thigh and it smelt of him and she shivered again. His jaw sharpened but he said nothing more.

She bent and picked up her bag. 'I'll—'

'Come with me.' His grip on her wrist was firm.

'Come with you *where*?' she demanded curtly. 'I'm not going through that party like this *either*.'

'Come with me to a "where" with privacy. A shower. Food.

Drink.' He muttered beneath his breath. 'And more damned clothes.'

He led her through that garden to a different gap in the hedge, then walked up the path to the palatial house next door.

'We can't just walk into someone else's house,' she whispered, scandalised as he boldly led her up the path.

'We're not. We've been on my property this whole time.'

'What?'

'That orchard is on my side of the boundary and this is my house.'

She yanked her arm free of his hold and whirled to stare at him. 'Since when is this *your* house?'

He simply sidestepped around her. 'Since a month ago.'

Once more she wished for the magic vanishing wand.

He opened the door with a singular touch to a small tech pad. The house was stunning. Comfortable and homely. The furnishings cosy and somehow not what she would've expected from Zane deMarco, ruthless corporate raider. But Zane de-Marco, as a teen, housebound while recovering from injury, might have wanted something exactly this comfortable.

He was watching her sardonically. 'I bought it furnished.'

Right. Of course. This was someone else's sense of happiness and intimacy. He was corporate raider Zane now, through and through.

'Come on.'

He didn't seem able to look at her for long. Her self-consciousness grew. She probably looked a sight. Loose, her hair hung to just below her buttocks and was no doubt tangled. His white shirt was smudged and creased and also hung to below her buttocks. But it was only because of her lack of clothes that she was still here, grudgingly going along with his suggestions.

He led the way down the hallway and up the stairs and she followed him mutely. He walked her into a gorgeous bedroom.

'You need to have a shower,' he grated. 'Get dressed. Warm.'

Huh, she was boiling already.

'Wait here a moment.'

It was less than a minute before he was back and handing her a bundle of sweats. She took them from him but he paused. He stared at her for a long, long moment. The heat that had overwhelmed her so instantly earlier now resurged. For a split second she hoped he was about to tumble her to the bed they were standing beside.

'I'll take the other shower,' he said tightly. 'Don't even think about vanishing on me.'

He turned his back on her and stomped out so quickly her head spun.

It was one of those showers that had nozzles pointing in every direction that gave her a whole-body massage effect. It was the second-most sensual experience of her life. She lost track of time again before coming back to herself and turning the water off hurriedly.

She needed to get out of here. She'd get changed. Get back to her little motel. Get space to get her head around everything. Because she'd royally screwed up. Yet she couldn't quite regret it.

She plaited her hair to keep it out of the way and pulled on the sweatpants. They were so big she had to roll the waist over several times. They were definitely his. And definitely turning her on. Too hot to bother with the sweatshirt he'd put on the pile, she slid on the white T-shirt. It hung like a dress so she knotted the hem, but it made little difference. He'd swamped her in his clothes—hiding her few curves. She couldn't look less sexy and yet her sensual awareness of him couldn't be higher.

She'd had sex with Zane deMarco. Fantastic. Unforgettable. Fiery sex. And all she could think was that she wanted more. Right now in fact. But he clearly didn't because he hadn't been able to get away from her fast enough. Which was mortifying. Wasn't he supposed to be some insatiable playboy?

That's when she finally remembered just who and what he was. Mr One-Date Wonder. The man took what he wanted and moved on and she was such a fool for forgetting for so long tonight.

Red alert, red alert, red alert.

Zane paced in the kitchen. What the *hell* had just happened? And *how* had that just happened? Yeah, he liked sex and honestly got it easy enough, but that was the fastest he'd gone from saying hi to being horizontal. It had been the merest of minutes. And with Skylar Bennet? Petite, perfect student Skylar?

The one he'd wanted long ago and not been allowed. The one who'd said nothing as her father had torn shreds off him— rejecting him as so many others bloody had. Even when he'd just made his first million.

So tonight, when he'd seen her looking at him with those judging eyes, it had all come flooding back and something had snapped. He'd wanted to best her. He'd wanted to win. And he had. In fact he'd just won her *virginity* beneath his damned cherry tree!

And how the hell had *she* still been a virgin? Because honestly, thinking back on that encounter when they were teens, he'd figured she was about the only woman he'd ever met who might have a sex drive to match his…she'd gone up in flames *so* damned quick. But apparently, she'd never gone all the way? What the *hell*? How could he have been so wrong? Had she been saving it for someone? But that didn't make sense when she'd just gone headlong into hedonism with him in seconds. And why hadn't she said anything—warned him? Because that hadn't been the gentle initiation he'd have given her had he known. That had been fast and physical and he was *furious* with her for taking that risk with him. He did not want to think that he might have hurt her.

But the fact was he hadn't even had the restraint or patience to bring her the extra few paces into his house and to privacy and clean sheets on an actual bed and with a whole night ahead of them. There'd been nothing but desperate urgency on a damned narrow sun lounger. He'd had to have her then and there and she'd been five steps ahead of him the whole way...

It had been his hottest moment in months, years—ever— and he wanted it again. Now. The second he'd got her inside his house he'd got hard all over again. He'd had to gruffly hustle her into the guest wing and go take an ice-cold shower. It hadn't worked. He still wanted her. He would give almost anything to linger over her in his big bed right now.

Except she didn't like him. And he didn't like her. And this had been one *massive* mistake.

He stopped pacing and leaned against the counter, staring out at the ocean though it was barely visible now under the night sky. But all he saw was her heart-shaped face and deep brown eyes. Not to mention those plump lips that could go full pout—the sort you could just sink into. And then there was the dimple. It didn't show with a polite smile, nor a restrained smile. But it did with a satisfied post-orgasmic smile. His body went hard as a rock all over again. He reckoned the dimple would show with laughter too. Part of him really wanted to test that theory. But he clenched his fists and summoned restraint. There couldn't be any of that now.

Because he'd finally remembered all the stupid plans he'd made today and this was the *worst* timing imaginable. He wasn't supposed to be fooling around at all let alone with someone horrifyingly innocent. Someone who he didn't even *like*...

But the second he'd seen her in that perfect white silk number he'd forgotten everything. Including that bloody bet.

He'd screwed up. Royally.

* * *

Skylar cautiously ventured through the immaculate house that screamed sultry summer energy. It was the perfect place to laze at the beach and indulge in long sensual nights. A heavenly holiday destination, and it honestly just made her angry with him all over again, for buying something so damned perfect that he probably was going to sell in mere months.

She paused on the threshold of the kitchen. He was leaning on the counter, looking out the window, his arms stretched wide in an echo of that night all those years ago when she'd seen him on his balcony. He looked as lonely. But he must've caught sight of her movement because he suddenly turned and his expression smoothed as he walked towards her.

'Are you okay?' he asked with soft intensity.

An unfamiliar emotion clogged her throat.

He walked closer still—until he could take her face in his firm hands so she couldn't look away from him. Couldn't avoid answering him.

'Are. You. Okay?' His pale blue eyes glittered with fire.

For another second she was unable to utter a thing. She swallowed—hard—as she realised the source of his concern. He didn't want to have hurt her. 'Yes, I'm okay.'

In fact she was far better than okay. And she was melting because he was so close and she wanted his mouth on hers again. She wanted *everything* all over again and his concern only made her attraction to him stronger. But he released her and stepped back.

Desolate, she watched him walk away. She didn't want this to be over. Yeah, she was *that* tragic. But he'd moved on while she'd lost sight of everything—of why she'd even come here tonight and what it was she *truly* wanted. Suddenly she was mad with herself for losing her aptitude, her capability. She was no less than he—she didn't need to be *cosseted*.

'Are you?' she called after him sharply.

He paused and glanced back. 'What?'

She walked over to where he stood frozen in the centre of the kitchen. 'Are *you* okay?'

His eyes widened. 'Of course.'

He looked shocked she'd asked.

'Because I didn't mean to give you a fright,' she added calmly. 'And I wanted what happened between us.'

'Right. You know I had worked that one out…' He frowned at her. 'But what I'm not sure about is why you really came to that party in the first place.'

It was her turn to freeze. It all came back—Helberg. Her colleagues, their future. Indeed, her career—the one she'd worked so hard for. The company she desperately wanted to be saved was teetering on the brink of destruction and the man wielding the sword was now standing right in front of her.

'I can't stay the night here.' She glanced away from him.

'I've not asked you to.'

'I'll call a car.'

'The likelihood of you getting any kind of taxi tonight is nil and you know it. I'll take you anywhere you want once we've talked.'

'There's nothing to talk about.'

'Sure there is.' He watched her closely. 'What did you *really* want from me tonight, Skylar?'

Her heart stopped, then pounded faster than ever. This was not how it was supposed to go at all. She'd meant to find out all she could about his plans for Helberg—not find out all about his performance in bed.

And he knew, somehow, that there was more to her appearance tonight. So she might as well just ask him now. Straight-out. She had literally nothing left to lose. 'I wanted to find out your plans for Helberg.'

He stilled. 'What?'

She'd surprised him. 'I know you're interested,' she said firmly.

'Indeed I am,' he answered too smoothly. 'Very much.'

'In *Helberg*,' she said primly, because he was prevaricating now and she wasn't falling for his false charm. 'I don't know what you're planning with those guys but I know it won't be good. Not for the company, its customers or its employees.'

He stepped closer. 'What guys?'

'I saw you this morning. In Manhattan. At that health club.'

He was visibly taken aback. 'You saw me with Cade and Adam?' His jaw tightened. 'Were you spying on me?'

'Of course not.' She was offended. 'I was getting a coffee on my way to work. The cafe isn't far from the office.'

'The *Helberg* office? Don't tell me you're *still* involved with them?' He gaped at her. 'Do they actually pay you now or are you still one of their interns?'

'Of course they pay me now,' she said stiffly, outraged.

'Well, I hope they it's a lot given you were headed there first thing on a Saturday.'

'There's a lot to be done.'

'Certainly is.' He frowned at her. 'Have you ever worked anywhere else?'

She glared at him, not seeing the relevance.

'Loyalty at the cost of your own career?' He shook his head dolefully. 'You really are far too much of a pleaser.'

'So what are your plans?' she asked determinedly. 'I don't think you three were there talking about that article in *Blush*.'

'You've seen *that*?' He was taken aback all over again.

'Hard to miss if you have a phone,' she said.

He leaned back against the bench and folded his arms, watching her acutely. 'Why don't you think we were talking about that?'

'Because you don't care what anyone says or does or thinks about you.'

There was a moment of total silence. A moment in which the world seemed to shrink as he stared right into her soul with those ice blue eyes.

'You think you know me, Skylar?' he asked softly.

'You're saying you do give a damn?' she countered.

He stared at her a second longer than released a pent-up breath. 'I like being my own person. It's liberating. It enables me to make the decisions I want to make. I'm not held back by obligations to others. Unlike you.'

'You think I've been held back?'

'Absolutely.'

'Caring—giving a damn about others and what they may or may not think has never held me back. And fulfilling a duty—repaying a debt—is important.'

'It's stifling,' he dismissed her.

She stepped up to him, toe-to-toe, in her bare feet. 'Helberg shouldn't be ripped apart by a bunch of sharks.'

'A management buy-out isn't going to happen,' he said bluntly. 'Is that what you're hoping for?'

It was exactly what she would have hoped for once, but the current management had proven themselves incompetent and it wasn't going to happen. She needed a better buyer.

'You're right, of course,' Zane suddenly said. 'We're all interested in acquiring Helberg. Which is why you came to this party. Why you sought me out tonight. Are you *that* concerned about your job that you offered yourself as a virgin sacrifice?' His smile wasn't kind. 'Should have negotiated terms first, darling.'

'I was no sacrifice and I didn't tangle myself in that tree deliberately.'

'So what was your original plan in coming here tonight?'

She didn't know. She was an idiot. She'd never really had the confidence nor skill to pull this off. It had been the most ill-conceived plan ever. Employment contracts she could do, but taking on Zane deMarco?

He seemed to take a little pity on her. 'I'm not working with Cade or Adam on this,' he said. 'We each want it for our own reasons. Fortunately we've worked out a way to settle which one of us is going to get it.'

'Really?' She was sceptical. 'You're such arrogant control freaks I'm astounded that you've found a way to do that.'

The smile that slowly creased his face was devilish. 'Well, we billionaires tend to nail creativity.'

'Oh?' She wasn't going to inappropriate places in her head again.

'Yeah.' He watched her closely. 'We've made it the prize of a bet.'

'A *bet*?' She gaped. 'What are the terms?'

CHAPTER SIX

ZANE DREW A sharp breath and brazened it out. 'We did actually discuss that article this morning. The guys don't like the attention it's bringing to business so we've made a bet to date only one woman over summer.'

'And that's, what—a challenge for you?' she asked caustically.

Amusement rippled within him. He liked sparring with this grown-up, salty Skylar. 'Very, as it so happens.'

A storm gathered in her eyes. 'You're seriously deciding about the fate of a company and all its employees by betting about your *sex lives*?'

'*Dating* lives,' he corrected her facetiously.

And actually it was a *disaster*, because he wasn't going to be able to go anywhere without being photographed alongside someone. He needed a force field around him so no unintentional contact could be misinterpreted.

'No way was this Adam Courtney's idea,' Skylar analysed quickly.

'He only agreed because he thinks he can easily win,' Zane conceded with a grin.

'And *Cade* thinks he can beat you.' Skylar studied him. 'Only a bunch of jerks could sort out a business decision based on their sex lives.'

He felt heat rise even though he was wearing only a thin T-shirt and shorts. 'No one should be writing any stupid articles about our sex lives. We're entitled to privacy as much as anyone else. There's nothing wrong with enjoying the company of other adults and we shouldn't have to moderate our behaviour because of some judgmental hack journalist.'

'Yet you've created a bet requiring you to do exactly that,' she pointed out.

He gritted his teeth. 'It was a vehicle to settle the dispute.'

'It was a whim.' She watched him. 'It was *you* who suggested it, wasn't it. The one *they* think is least likely to succeed.'

Yeah, that too.

'You really enjoy acting on the spur of the moment,' she said. 'You like spontaneity.'

He felt the edge of spontaneity now, heaven help him. 'And you don't?'

'Not…often. No.' She coloured slightly. 'Are you going to keep your vow?'

'I keep my word. Yes. I'm allowed one woman for the duration.'

'*Allowed* one woman,' she echoed. 'Gosh, how magnanimous of you. It's just so marvellous that one lucky female doesn't get to miss out on your attentions.'

He laughed lightly at her false gushiness. She was right, of course, it was ridiculous. 'Glad you agree given the female is you.'

'What?'

'We slept together after the timer had started.'

She stared at him. 'Which means…'

'Which means you're the only woman I'll be sleeping with for the next two months.'

She just kept staring at him.

He leaned forward and waved a hand in front of her eyes. 'Why, Skylar, are you so ecstatic that you've gone catatonic?'

She finally blinked. 'What if I don't want to sleep with you?'

His smile widened. 'Oh, sweetheart, we both know that's not the case.'

Her whole face radiated irritation. 'You're the most arrogant prat on the face of the earth.'

'Yeah, but you still want me. You like what I do to you,' he said boldly. 'I mean, you gave me your virginity in less than twenty minutes.'

And how *that* was possible he was still trying to figure out. This was Skylar—passionate, fiery Skylar. How had she gone all this time without sex?

'We've already established that I wasn't thinking at the time.'

'And who's to say there won't be another incident where you find yourself "not thinking"?'

'Me,' she said. 'I'm here to say there won't.' She folded her arms and glared at him. 'I enjoyed myself. But I don't actually like you.'

He shrugged. 'Who needs like when there's lust?'

'Not happening.'

But she was flushed and he was so drawn to her flame.

He'd meant to play this stupid bet out slow. Find someone suitable who he could trust to play it discreetly with him. No one had seen him with Skylar tonight, so in theory he could ask her to keep this quiet and still make an arrangement with someone else as he'd originally intended. But he couldn't lie. He wanted to win honestly. Which meant he was stuck with her. And that wasn't quite as terrible as he'd first thought. Because her reactions to him now were endlessly entertaining.

So this had just become a game within a game.

He knew she was a pleaser and insanely loyal—to everyone but him, that was. So he was going to have to convince her by some other means.

'It's not looking good for you, is it?' she said. 'Less than a day since you made your stupid bet.'

'You think I can't control myself?'

'Obviously not,' she said drolly. 'I'm astonished you suggested this when they'll all think you're the one least likely to succeed...' She squinted. 'Which was the point for you. Proving people wrong.'

'You're right.' He aimed for contrition. 'I really need your help.'

She shot him the most deadly look ever. 'You're asking for my help now?'

He couldn't resist aggravating her. Apparently it was an uncontrollable urge where she was concerned. 'If I'm seen with you, then that will stop other women from approaching me.'

'Is that a problem for you?'

'That article has had an impact already. Many messages.'

'How *awful*.' She pressed her hand to her chest in a gesture of mock empathy.

'I know. Would you believe I've even been stalked at a party? This random woman was lurking in my private garden pretending to be caught on a tree branch.'

'Really.' She gritted her teeth. 'So now you want us to fake date?'

'No. You can just be my personal bodyguard. Protect me from the *other* bodies. We don't have to hold hands or kiss in public or anything. It can be purely platonic if you want.'

She stared at him like he was nuts. Which he was.

'Can't you just not go out? You can't possibly stay at home?' she asked. 'Not date at all? Be single like a normal person?'

'I don't think so, no.' There seriously was a bunch of messages. Not that he'd prove it to her, because she'd accuse him of arrogance all over again, and he needed a break from the salty edge of her tongue. Otherwise, he'd end up silencing her with his, and that would be unwise. 'Don't worry. I won't do anything you don't want me to,' he assured her. 'People will see us and assume what they want to assume. It's usually the worst. Or the best, depending on your perspective. Whatever. It'll keep the heat off me.'

Skylar tried to calm down, not be stupidly flattered and actually say yes. This whole thing was vintage Zane deMarco outrageousness. 'This is all about you. What's in it for me?'

His smile came slow and wicked. 'Whatever you want.'

'Well now, there's an offer.' She paused for dramatic effect then batted her lashes at him. 'Back off Helberg.'

'Anything but *that*.' He shook his head. 'No point in the bet at all if I just give it up because you asked.' He stepped closer. 'Seeing you're still working for Helberg and they're obviously not paying you enough, I'll pay you.'

'I do *not* want your money,' she said stiffly.

He chuckled. Of course he'd only offered that to wind her up.

'I'm a danger to you,' she said softly. 'If they found out about this…' She began to smile. 'You *need* me.'

He stiffened. 'I don't *need* anyone.'

'Well, I certainly don't *need* to help you. Surely I'm better off seeing you date other people so either Cade or Adam could win. They might have better plans for Helberg.'

A fiery glint lit his eyes. 'They'll be *vastly* worse.'

She'd waved a red rag in front of a bull and it felt good.

He was a danger to *her*. She just had to play this game well. She felt a shiver of anticipation at the prospect of pitting her wits against his.

'Better the devil you know, surely. And you do know me.' He paused and added softly, 'Even better now.'

Well, she definitely knew him better than she knew either Cade or Adam or indeed any other man. And he was too close again. Making her brain operate too slowly. 'I want time.'

He nodded, coming closer still. 'For what?'

'Not that,' she muttered. She was not sleeping with him again. That had been a mistake. A marvellous but utterly unrepeatable mistake.

'Then for what?' he asked innocently.

'I want to show you Helberg. What it was, what it is and what it could be.'

'Like the Ghost of Christmas Past?' He shook his head slowly. 'You want to humanise me? Too late, Skylar.'

She held firm. 'Time.'

'You do realise that I'll use everything you show me as part of my acquisition preparation.'

'Of course you will, but I don't consider it a risk because I won't be showing you anything confidential. But I'll get you inside the company corridors, which is closer than you've been in a while, right?'

His expression shuttered. 'Skylar—'

'Don't patronise me.' She stood in front of him. 'You break companies up.'

'Yes. So they survive in some form.'

'Do they, though?' she challenged. 'More often than not companies go under once they've been stripped of their assets.'

'Helberg is old and unwieldy. Reed overstretched and his model is no longer commercially viable. Think of it as lifesaving surgery. We cut out the rot—the parts of the company not performing.'

'And sell that rot to someone else?'

'Sure. One person's rot is another person's treasure...'

'And a guy like you gets rich on the quick sale. But you leave little more than a skeleton that has no chance of longterm survival.' She lifted her chin. 'I think I can prove to you that it's a company worth holding together.'

Her loyalty meant she couldn't stand by and see it destroyed. Because of her colleagues and the values the company had stood for. Helberg had done good for others for generations.

Now she had nothing left to lose and she had to try. Was he as soulless as she'd thought—or was there an echo of that kind boy who'd shared his candy with a crying kid still inside him?

But he was still. Silent. Unemotional. Uncaring.

Skylar's heart sank. She had no chance of convincing either Cade or Adam given she didn't even know them. So in spite of everything, Zane was actually *her* best bet. She needed *him* to win, so she would help him.

She straightened. 'I'll be seen with you once a week so you still have a chance with your stupid bet. In return, once a week, you come with me on a visit to Helberg. That's my offer. Take it or leave it.'

He didn't answer. Still didn't move. But she saw the flicker in his eyes.

'Come to the office next week,' she said. 'I'll text you with a time that's convenient.'

'What if it's not convenient for me?' he muttered huskily.

She shrugged. 'It's your choice. You want to be seen with me then you'll make it convenient. I'm not the one trapped in a stupid bet.'

'You know you won't change my mind, Skylar.'

Probably not, but she had to try. And she grudgingly respected that he was trying to warn her. But she had an in with him, and one thing that Skylar had always had was hope. So she smiled at him. 'We'll see, won't we?'

CHAPTER SEVEN

AT 8:00 A.M. on Monday, Zane deMarco finally admitted he had a productivity problem. The concentration catastrophe otherwise known as Skylar Bennet was lodged in his head—in his body too—hell, she'd seemingly invaded him on a cellular level and he had so *many* questions.

Not that any of the answers were truly his business. He shouldn't be distracted by Skylar Bennet's lack of a sex life. He should be more concerned by his *own* complete loss of control. The smile she'd shot him when she'd realised she had a little power? The dimple had surfaced and he'd had to summon every ounce of restraint not to lose it and haul her straight back into his arms.

He had fun with his lovers, yes, but he'd never been in an incident where the drive to have a woman had been so overpowering. Okay, he'd felt it one other time. With her. Which was deeply annoying. And this had only happened now because of that back then, right? It was some sort of warped want for the one he'd been told he couldn't have.

He'd barely slept on Saturday night. Sure, he slept badly at the best of times, sometimes troubled by twinges in his leg, sometimes just restless as hell. But knowing she was under the same roof had rendered sleep impossible. For hours he'd battled the urge to stalk to her bedroom. Hours cursing himself for his impatience.

He'd taken her too fast and it had been over too soon.

Sunday morning had been nothing short of awkward, which frankly was another foreign situation. Usually he'd slide from a one-nighter by sending them off with his chauffeur and a smile. But yesterday he'd driven Skylar himself. He'd taken her to the small motel so she could collect her things, then insisted she share his helicopter back to Manhattan. He couldn't watch her board that painfully slow bus. Once they'd made it back to the city, he'd insisted on driving her to her apartment. And yeah, it'd been entirely to suit his own ends. He'd wanted to know where she lived. He'd wanted to extend the time they shared even though it was torture. And the fact that she'd so clearly wanted to *refuse* all those offers had been deliciously amusing. Because she knew that he'd seen her reluctance—and so she'd accepted his offer at every turn. Which was even more delicious torture. They'd barely spoken. She'd appeared lost in thought. He'd just been battling his incredibly basic urges. The hottest of highlights from those moments in the orchard had flicked through his mind the whole time. Even now, only one thought in five was actually relevant to business; the rest were not safe for work.

It was also because of that stupid bet, right?

Cursing the whole stupid idea, he went online and skimmed the magazine and saw there was an update to the article already. They'd loaded a photo of Adam taken only last night. And they'd added a *tally*.

It looked a typical Courtney Collection event—glamorous and elite, and Adam was with society model Annabel St James no less. Zane copied the picture into a text and tapped out a quick caption.

Could do worse for the summer! ;)

He winced at the weak banter but he was incapable of coming up with anything better. Grimly he realised the poll that had been started was the worst thing possible. Was *any* photo of him standing next to any woman going to count? Surely not. He glanced at the photo of Adam—there was clear contact between the man and his date. There was nothing on Cade yet. Nothing on Zane either, but that wasn't surprising. Danielle's Independence Day party was renowned for its privacy protections for her guests.

Why had he told Skylar about the bet? Pillow talk totally wasn't his thing. But he'd enjoyed being brutally honest with her—and he'd wanted to shock her. Because she'd shocked him. But no one knew about the bet other than Adam and Cade. Skylar could make them far more of a laughing stock than the original article had if she went public. Which meant he was forced to keep her close.

Anticipation tore through him. He could keep her very close. He could turn that judgment in her eyes to surrender again. Because her judgment pinched in a way that the judgment of anyone else didn't. Maybe it was because she knew the shitty apartment building he'd grown up in, the underfunded school. Because it had been her building, her school too...

She knew more about him than almost anyone—despite the fact that in all those years they'd spoken only a handful of times.

But she'd also betrayed him. That one time they'd touched, they'd been caught and she'd let him take the blame. So of all people not to give a damn about, Skylar ought to be top of his list. And he didn't give a damn, he just wanted...what? Aside from the obvious.

He wanted a little *honesty*.

She'd said she didn't want to have sex with him again but that wasn't true. He'd bet that when it came to it, she wouldn't be able to control herself any more than he could. But she didn't *want* to want him. Which was different. So he'd respect her rule. If he had to be celibate for the rest of the summer, he would. Purely to confound her. Even if it was going to kill him.

But he'd torment her in other ways. He'd spar with her. Provoke her. Because when he didn't hold back, she bit. *That's* how she was different now. She wasn't silently watching any more. She snapped back. He wanted more and that he *could* have. Hell, maybe he'd even provoke her sensuality—just a little. But even so, what little honour remained in him dictated he be honest about his intentions regarding Helberg. He'd told her up front that her plan was going to fail. Apparently that wasn't going to stop her from trying. Though if she thought he was going to sit around waiting for her summons, she had another thing coming.

Zane didn't wait for anyone any more. Certainly not Skylar Bennet. He'd done that once before, and he wasn't being burned by her again.

He cleared his schedule, cancelled meetings and postponed delivery dates for reports from his stunned underlings.

At nine on Monday morning, Zane deMarco walked through the atrium of Helberg Holdings and threw the blinking receptionist a wide smile.

'I'm here to see Skylar Bennet,' he said suavely. 'She's expecting me.'

Skylar's jaw ached from gritting her teeth so hard in the ten seconds it took for the elevator to take her from the fifth floor down to the atrium.

He was here. Unexpected. Uninvited. Wasn't that just typical of the man, to try to throw her off her game?

She was already off. She'd barely slept in the last forty-eight hours as she'd struggled to process what she'd done with Zane. And the only regret she could summon was that it had been only the once.

She was angrier than ever with him. Why him? Why *only*

him? It was a chemical catastrophe. Why hadn't she met anyone else she wanted any of that with? It was horrifically unfair.

Because it had been so, so good and it was all she could think about. The delicious aches in her body reminded her with every step of the intimacy, and heaven help her, all she wanted was a repeat. With *him*. Which was appalling. She hated him. They were polar opposites and they wanted wildly different things. And she'd gone her whole life without needing sex so why did she have all these nymphomaniac urges now?

Because it had been so, so good.

But after that shocking conversation when he'd told her about that *bet*, he'd politely led her back to that immaculate bedroom with its enormous beautiful bed. That she'd not slept a wink in. The next morning, he'd offered her a stunning breakfast of French pastries and fruit. She'd opted for black coffee. He'd stuck by her side all the way back to Manhattan and she'd struggled to stay calm the entire time. Her nervous system was caught in a cycle of chaos. It was the most appalling attraction. But thank goodness she'd had enough nous to block any idea of them sleeping together again, because *he* clearly wasn't interested in anything more than her 'help' in winning that ridiculous bet. She shouldn't have offered to assist him. She should've left him to stew in his mess. She should tell that magazine about their outrageousness and humiliate them all.

The problem was Helberg. It was more than her job—it was her whole life. Yes, as a student, it had been her safe place—she'd interned in the various departments during her varsity holidays. Then she'd come to live and work full-time in Manhattan. She'd worked *hard*. Her father had been so proud and she'd begun saving to get him into a better home—because he'd worked hard for her for years. She'd slowly got to know some colleagues, cared about them. And she'd kept working hard—because that's what you had to do to remain valued. Needed. Wanted.

When her father had passed, she'd buried herself deeper in her work. It was what he'd have wanted. He'd be devastated to see the company go under. She had nothing much outside of it. So she had to stop it from happening. And Zane was her one and only access point to the elite power brokers.

She spotted him the second the elevator doors slid open. Hard to miss him given he was leaning against the pillar opposite and looking appallingly gorgeous. Apparently he'd slept well, given he was such a vision of vitality. That charming smile curved his lips but the ice blue eyes were sharp. Her nerves tightened. Her lower belly basically burst into flames.

She gritted her teeth harder, feeling as if she'd just run down the twenty flights of stairs instead of taking the lift. It took everything to keep her chin up and her gaze locked on him as she walked over.

'What are you doing here?' she asked through a forced smile, aware that everyone in the atrium was watching.

He straightened and stepped closer, staring right into her eyes, and his smile deepened in intimacy. 'You promised to show me *everything.*'

Skylar stalled, needing a second to snatch a breath. His ability to imply innuendo in every other comment was impressive. And annoying. Because for all that huskiness, he didn't mean it. He truly was a one-date wonder.

'I told you I'd text you a suitable time,' she said crisply.

'I didn't get where I am today by waiting—'

'No,' she interrupted firmly. 'You just turn up when *you* like and take what *you* want.'

He cocked his head ever so slightly and that arrogant charm lit his eyes, but she was determined not to be swayed by it.

'I apologise for misunderstanding.' His smile was shamelessly *un*apologetic. 'Naturally I assumed you'd mean first thing Monday morning given saving Helberg from my evil plans is surely your highest priority.'

'Right.'

He leaned close—too close—and dropped his voice even lower. 'Saturday night for our date, by the way. I'll pick you up from your apartment. I have the address locked in.'

Skylar was aware of the receptionist hovering—watching, listening—and the other people in the atrium all not-so-surreptitiously staring. She needed to get him somewhere private because he was putting on a show. She just needed to remember that it *was* a show and there was no need for her body to react as if his flirtations were real.

'Of course.' She held her stance and smiled super politely. 'If you'll follow me.'

'Gladly,' he said so meekly that she just glared at him.

He remained silent in the elevator while she was too steamed to speak. She briskly walked to one of the meeting rooms on the executive floor. A million people milled in the corridor. Yes, word was out and everyone was out to see for themselves that Zane deMarco was here. And definitely wondering why. Hopefully her boss wasn't going to ask any difficult questions later. The perils of her plan presented themselves in rapid succession. She would never show Zane anything commercially sensitive—never jeopardise her own career or Helberg's reputation. Plus regulatory bodies might get involved—their bet was dodgy enough, surely?

'Second thoughts, Skylar?' he murmured as she closed the door behind him.

How could he read her mind?

'Don't worry.' He dominated the space in the room. 'I won't ask you to do anything you're uncomfortable with.'

Her body heated even more. More innuendo that he probably didn't mean. He was only out to tip her off balance. He talked up a game, but he wasn't really playing. His desire for Helberg was no joke.

'What's your role here these days?' he asked.

'People and culture.'

'HR? You?'

His obvious surprise annoyed her. 'You think I'm not good with people?'

He definitely wanted to throw her off but she wasn't going to let him. In fact, she was going to make him pay for his arrogance and entitlement. He really assumed she'd drop everything to accommodate him. The man needed a lesson. He was about to get it.

She smiled at him. 'If you'll wait here a moment, I'll make arrangements for this morning's information session.'

His eyes widened. 'Sure.'

She left him in the room and stalked to her own office. She couldn't believe he wanted to break up a massive company with such a prestigious history. The Helberg brand had been around for more than a century and was renowned. The dynasty had engaged in a wide variety of philanthropic endeavours in many ways. But yes, in recent years, some of Reed Helberg's decisions had raised questions in the boardroom. Some divisions had struggled. But that was still no reason to break it up completely.

Zane deMarco just had a thing for a sledgehammer. She couldn't understand how he could so easily destroy what others had taken so long to build. Why didn't he respect their effort? She needed to show him some of the people he'd be hurting.

She picked up her phone. Three minutes later, she went back into the meeting room. As she approached, she noted his was expression was cool but his gaze watchful. She couldn't resist stepping just a little too close—as he'd done to her. It was an absurdly strong satisfaction when he tensed and she heard his sharp intake of breath.

'Bernie is going to show you from the ground level the kind of systems Helberg has,' she said.

'Systems?'

'Heating and ventilation, sprinkler systems.'

He took a beat. 'Are you talking about building maintenance?'

'Helberg constructs and services all its own buildings.' She smiled at him. 'Here's Bernie now.'

Bernie was almost seventy. Super hardworking and loyal and he refused to retire. He was damned good at his job. And he was talkative. Very talkative. A fact she appreciated. She didn't think Zane would.

'If you'll come with me, Mr deMarco,' Bernie said jovially.

She saw Zane's mouth thin but he didn't demur. It was only when Skylar didn't move with them that he turned back to her.

'Are you not coming on the tour, Skylar?' he asked silkily.

'Sadly I've another appointment.'

'More important than me?'

She simply smiled.

Three hours later, she paced the meeting room back and forth and back and forth. What was taking so long? She'd expected Bernie to keep him busy for a while, but not for *this* amount of time. It was the worst idea she'd ever had. She hadn't got any work done herself and she'd probably have infuriated him with this time waster of a meeting. Yet she couldn't help inwardly chuckling at the thought of immaculately suited and booted Zane wandering through the pump room and maintenance tunnels.

Maybe he'd left the building without saying goodbye— given up on the whole thing. Disappointment hit hard at that thought—she wanted that date more than she was willing to admit. She was weak.

Half an hour later she swallowed her pride and went down to the basement to investigate what had happened. Bernie's office door was wide open and she heard voices, then laughter. Stepping through, she saw the old man was leaning back in his chair, beaming, and there were takeout coffee cups and bagel and donut wrappers littering the desk. Skylar's mouth watered. Zane was in the seat beside Bernie—he'd pulled it round so the two men were side by side. He'd removed his jacket and tie and his sleeves were rolled up and she couldn't stand to look at his arms. Like Bernie, he was laughing.

He glanced up as she appeared and his gaze brightened. 'Oh, Skylar!' He smiled at her wickedly and raised his half-eaten donut to her in a mock salute. 'Were you waiting for us? Have Bernie and I lost track of time?'

'A little.' She smiled through gritted teeth. 'It's probably time we let Bernie get back to it, I'm sure he has things he needs to attend to—'

'Not at all,' Bernie interjected. 'It's been a pleasure to have you here, Zane. Come back anytime.'

'Thanks, Bernie.' Zane shot Skylar a sideways look. 'I'll be sure to do that.'

Oh, *please*. Skylar watched as Zane took his time to stand and take his jacket from the back of the chair. He and Bernie shook hands and Zane was intolerably genuine in his thanks. Of course Zane had charmed the man and now they were BFFs for life.

Turning, he licked a little sugar from his lip and batted his lashes at her. 'Where next, Skylar?'

'I'll see you to reception,' Skylar muttered.

'Afraid I won't find my way on my own?' His smile widened. 'You trust me that little?'

She pushed open the door to the stairwell. It was one flight of stairs. *One*. But as she got to the landing, Zane stopped two steps below her.

'Is something wrong?' she asked when he didn't move.

He was looking directly into her eyes. She should have taken him to the elevator.

'I'm curious. Do you really believe that that experience would make me want to keep this company intact?'

That 'experience'? She frowned and moved to the edge of the top step to see his expression. Had he been faking that friendliness with Bernie? Good to know. But she was disappointed in him. 'Wasn't it worth your precious time?' she asked sarcastically. 'Well, too bad. You deserved it because you don't value other people's time. I figured why not waste some of yours?'

'I value your time,' he said softly. 'Most of all I value the time we *share*, together.'

Every muscle tensed. She was *not* going to be taken in by him. 'Does that sort of line actually work?'

But she was flustered. *Really* flustered.

'It's not a line,' he said simply. 'It's the truth.'

'Stop—'

'And you're wrong, by the way,' he interrupted. '*I'm* not the one wasting my time here. This morning's session with Bernie was extremely worthwhile. He's a very nice guy.'

That disappointment melted and she softened towards him. 'Yes. I'd trust him with my life. He's been here for ever.'

'Yeah.' He climbed one step so he was closer. 'He told me a lot about you.'

'He…*what*?' Skylar's breath stalled. 'What did he tell you?'

'Lots. You're first in, last out. You know everyone by name—'

'I work in HR. It would be bad if I didn't—'

'Care too much? I really don't get why you're still working here,' he said. 'You're bright. You work hard. You could've been VP at some other company already. Instead you're sidetracked taking on all the projects no one else wants. Bernie said you leap to help anyone who asks. That it's too easy for you to say yes and you find it impossible to say no. Which is so ironic when apparently it's the reverse in the rest of your life.'

She gaped.

'Do you still feel like you owe the company something?' he pressed her. 'Loyalty can last only so long. You should have moved on right after your internship. This company is merely a machine that will chew you up till there's nothing left. It doesn't value *you*.'

'You're wrong,' she whispered.

'I think you already know I'm not.' He lifted her braid and resettled it over her shoulder.

'Don't toy with me,' she whispered.

'Is that what you think I'm doing?' He shook his head and smiled. 'You're the one who won't let me get past on the stairs. *You're* the one standing too close...'

She mirrored his gentle shake of the head. 'You're the one inappropriately touching me. Go find someone else to sleep with.'

'Can't. You know I've made a vow not to sleep around for a couple of months.'

'I still can't fathom why you'd suggest something so obviously counter to your nature,' she muttered tartly. 'Sleeping around is as essential to your existence as breathing.'

He put his hand around her waist and pulled so she almost teetered on the edge of the top step. 'Go harder on me,' he smiled wolfishly. 'I like it when you don't hold back. Just be prepared for the same in return.'

It was dynamite again. And yes—she wanted to best him in so many ways.

A door slammed in the stairwell above them. Skylar stepped back at the same time as he dropped his arm. She stalked ahead, leading him back into the atrium but super aware of how close he was behind her and how much she'd wanted him closer still.

'You've played your first card regarding Helberg, time to pay up with a *very* high-profile date,' he said calmly. 'Be ready.'

'How formal?' she choked.

'I'll be in black tie.'

So she was going to need a dress. Not slinky. Not white. She'd find something that covered her from top to toe. An enormous sack, perhaps.

Thankfully the atrium was emptier than it had been when he'd arrived this morning. She saw him glance up at the large portrait of Reed Helberg that hung above the exit and his smile evaporated.

'You okay?' she asked curiously.

He stiffened. 'Of course.'

She didn't believe him. 'You never liked him. Why?'

He kept his gaze on the painting. 'What makes you think that?'

'You clashed the night you came back and did that speech at school.' The night he'd told her she was pathetic. 'Something must have happened to make you want to destroy his legacy so badly.'

'This isn't revenge, Skylar,' he scoffed, but his smile didn't reach his eyes. 'This is just business. Their numbers no longer add up—surely you've looked, you must see it. Nothing lasts. Not even old money.'

No, judging by the look in his eyes a second ago, there was more to it than that. 'You don't care what others think *now*, but I think you cared about *him*. About what *he* thought.'

He remained silent, his expression blank. But for once that told her something. Adrenalin pooled inside her as she realised she was right. 'How you feel about Helberg—about Reed—is *personal*. He's different.'

And if she could understand what it was that bothered Zane about Reed, then she might be able to find a solution—an alternative ending to the one he was pushing for. But Zane wasn't looking at the portrait any more. He was looking at her.

'Why do you look so pleased about that?' he growled.

'Because it shows someone can get through your defences.'
Her heart pounded but she couldn't help but be honest with
him. 'Someone can actually get to you.'

His lips twisted into a rueful smile. 'No, Skylar.'

'No?' It didn't look that way to her.

'Not any more,' he added softly.

But someone once had—*Helberg*. How and in what way?
He clearly wasn't about to tell her, which also meant that Zane
still felt strongly about him. And in turn, that meant he still
felt, full stop. So maybe she had more of a chance than she'd
originally thought, because there was something of a heart
still inside him.

'I think I can make you change your mind,' she whispered.

'It's a good thing you've got time to adjust to failure.' Zane
brushed her cheekbone with the lightest stroke of his fingertip. 'You won't take it so hard.'

CHAPTER EIGHT

ZANE STRAIGHTENED HIS TIE, swept his hand through his hair and stalked out to the waiting car. He'd been irritable all week. The days had dragged as he'd gone straight from home to work and back again, not setting a foot anywhere else so he wouldn't inadvertently be 'seen' with someone. He'd been counting down the hours until he got his driver to take him back to her apartment. Skylar Bennet was still a catastrophe.

'Take a couple turns around the block,' he muttered to his driver when he paused outside her apartment building. 'I'll message when ready.'

His muscles twitched. He'd run up all seventy-odd stairs in his condo tower earlier today but even that hadn't been enough to use up his excess energy.

He pushed the button and she buzzed him up. By the time he'd climbed to the second floor she'd opened her door and was visible in the frame. For the first time all week, he stood stock still.

'Is this on the mark?' She sounded nervous but looked defiant.

Oh, it was on the mark. Very, *very* on the mark—if the mark was his libido. The silver slip dress skimmed her slim frame. Her glossy hair fell sleekly to the curve of her bottom. Her skin was radiant and those deep brown eyes of hers were huge. 'I've worn heels so I won't look stupidly short next to you.'

He liked her height. He remembered pressing her against

him in the garden and wrapping her leg around his waist. He wanted that again.

She frowned in the face of his silence. 'I rented a couple alternatives if it isn't…'

He struggled to rein in the direction of his thoughts. 'How very diligent of you, Skylar.'

'I like to do a good job.' She straightened.

'I know you do.' He stepped past her into her apartment. That she thought of this as a 'job' irritated him. 'We're going to a film premiere. A thriller, I believe. You can hold my hand in the scary bits if you like.'

He moved deeper into her apartment and discovered it was tiny. Which was a problem. He couldn't trust himself to touch her—not even offering a socially polite kiss on her cheek. Getting that close to her was impossible—he actually feared he'd lose control and caveman toss her onto her own bed. He'd take her fully clothed first, then he'd rip the beautiful dress from her and have her all over again. Naked. And then again. And yes, he was going out of his mind.

'There'll be lots of cameras at a film premiere.' She closed the door behind him.

'Yes. We'll walk the red carpet. Pose in front of the press pen.'

'Press pen?' She sounded aghast. 'You're kidding.'

He focused on the apartment. The absolute lack of space. There wasn't even a kitchen. Just a sink and a microwave.

Her low mumble reached him. 'What's the worst they're going to say…' she muttered. 'Probably that I'm not pretty enough to be seen with you.'

He turned.

'And that I'm not from the right sort of society.' She fiddled with the strap of her purse. 'Will they pry into my past? How detail oriented are these people?'

Very, unfortunately. He had a lot of money and stupidly that made people interested.

'You want to back out, Skylar?' he asked, though he really didn't want to.

'Not at all. I can handle this.' But she didn't look as certain as she sounded. 'It's not like I have a past to be worried about.'

'If you worry what someone thinks, that gives them power over you. You get distracted wondering about their reactions, which means you can't make a clean decision on your own. Like your dress tonight. No one else's opinion should matter. Only yours. If you're comfortable, if you like the dress—'

'So not even your opinion matters?' she interrupted.

'No. It doesn't.'

She cared too much. Always had. Seeking approval. He remembered her silence. Her dutiful manner to her father. And he was suddenly reluctant to expose her to that online commentary. The magazine was bad enough, but worse were those trolls who hid behind anonymous screens and keyboards and spouted cruel words for the malevolent fun of it. The thought of them had never bothered him before but now he was concerned for her sake. She was about to lose her privacy—paying a steep price for what? Nothing. Because there was *zero* chance of him changing his mind on breaking up Helberg. A bitter taste rose in the back of his throat. *Guilt.* But he couldn't tell her what had really happened between him and Helberg and the immediate aftermath of that excruciating meeting when he'd been a child. He'd never spoken of it—or of the accident after—with anyone. Not even his mother. He kept that shit well buried where it couldn't bother him and it would never see the light of day.

But here she was, wondering why he wanted Helberg so much. Acute enough to know there was something more than business about it. And perhaps he could explain just *some* of it. Because there was that greedy part of him, the part that liked to win. That part didn't want to quit this game. Not yet. Besides which, he reassured himself, she looked stunning. No online troll could ever say otherwise. 'Skylar, you could wear anything and—'

'Please don't flatter—'

'I'm *not*.' He gritted his teeth to stop himself *showing* rather than telling her how much of a freaking goddess she was. 'You're beautiful. Your dress showcases the fact.'

'I thought you didn't like me.'

'Right. But I still think you're sexy.'

There were two other dresses hanging from the door that he presumed led to the bathroom. One was midnight blue, the other was short and a bold red. His mouth dried. He wanted to see her in both. Yeah, he'd suddenly turned into some warlord who wanted his woman to try them on and twirl before him. He'd sit on that too-small sofa, legs sprawled apart, hard as a rock, and watch her like some totally erotic movie montage moment. That was *definitely* the premiere he'd prefer tonight.

'We should go.' She snapped her clutch purse. 'My apartment isn't really big enough for us both.'

He forced a smile. 'You don't want to move somewhere a little bigger?'

'It's close to work.'

Which was seemingly her one and only priority. His irritation resurged. 'And that's all that matters?'

Why did she still work there like a loyal little angel full of optimism and misplaced hope? Because she liked the people she worked with. That had been the main thing he'd learned from Bernie. Her loyalty to them—the way she went the extra mile. Didn't say no. Still a pleaser then—to those she felt she owed or something. Irritation rippled. She shouldn't spend her life repaying debts no one else bothered with. Why waste her time when it was clearly crumbling? She was good. She knew her numbers. Surely she could recognise that it was too late to turn that massive ship around. The iceberg was imminent and Helberg was going to sink.

'It's close to some good restaurants too,' she said.

'Oh?' He watched her sceptically. She wouldn't go to any. He bet she started early at the office and stayed late and probably lived on snacks and cereal.

'Yes, I have a good relationship with the Thai restaurant one block over. They deliver.'

Deliver. Right.

She tilted her chin at him. 'It's close to the park too.'

Yeah, he'd noticed the worn shoes at the front door. 'You still run?'

She nodded, colour rising in her cheeks. The room went silent. She was remembering that morning. Same as him. He couldn't ask her about it. Couldn't think about it.

'Every day.' She cleared her throat. 'And a group run on Saturdays.'

'Such a strict schedule,' he teased weakly. 'No such thing as spontaneity in your life—'

'That was last week.'

And never to be repeated. Yeah, he got it. He forced himself to look away from her again. It was a petite apartment for a petite person and perfectly set up just for her. Everything was neat and just so. Her bed was on a mezzanine level with the lowest of ceilings so he'd hit his head if he were up there and on top—

He tore his gaze away, not letting himself finish that thought. 'You're right, we really should go.'

Unfortunately the drive didn't take all that long.

'Right...' Skylar drew in a steadying breath as they approached the theatre. 'You need me to smile? Look adoringly at you?'

Her speech had quickened, risen. She was nervous. He hadn't seen her at parties in all these years. He got that she hadn't gone out when she was young because of her father, but why hadn't she since she'd left home? Why still so very alone and seemingly isolated aside from work friends—at least one of whom was almost three times her age?

He didn't want her 'performing' to any script of his. Didn't want to have any control over what she did…though of course he'd made her come here tonight with him, hadn't he?

'You never have to smile,' he said shortly. 'Not if you don't want to. Look as moody as you like. I'm not asking you to fake anything for me. Tonight we're merely companions.'

But that wasn't entirely true. They were enemies. With chemistry.

The red carpet walk wasn't long but it was crowded. In the photo pen ahead the photographers were calling loudly to the film stars.

'What do you think of the hero?' He jerked his chin towards the buff guy posing with quite a stunning selection of angular jaw expressions.

'Gonna ditch me for him if you get the chance?' He was half curious as to whether the blond Adonis type was for her.

She rose on tiptoe to study the actor for a moment and Zane actually felt a stab of—

'Maybe…' She turned and lifted her face to his, batting her lashes coyly.

'Don't believe you,' he whispered in her ear. 'He's not arrogant enough for you.'

That dimple appeared and then her giggle sounded. 'True.'

He couldn't wipe the smile from his own face. He pulled her close to guide her through the crowd. And then, greedy man that he was, he kept his arm around her, faking nothing.

He had no idea what happened in the movie. He was too distracted thinking about her. Smelling the soft scent of her hair. As the house lights came on in the theatre, he wrapped his arm around her waist again—purely to guide her back through those crowds again.

'What now?' she asked quietly. 'Is there an after party?'

'Yes. You want to go to it?'

Skylar hesitated, unsure how to answer. She didn't want this night to end, but she didn't want to be around all those other people and have everyone watching because she didn't want their physical contact to be purely performative. 'Do you?'

'I'm not saying.' He shot her a tantalising smile. 'I dare *you* to make the decision, Skylar. You don't need to please me or answer however you think that I want you to. Do what *you* want.'

Her pulse quickened. He'd *dared* her again. She was sure it was deliberate. Because that day her father had demanded the opposite over and over again—*Don't you dare...*

What she *wanted* was to be alone with him. They'd not had enough time alone *together*. Belatedly she realised that this movie was his version of Bernie. The lack of time together *alone* was a deliberate choice. This really was only about being seen with the same woman in public. He wouldn't be with her at all if it weren't for that stupid bet of his. He'd had his actual 'one-date wonder' with her and this was only for show.

'I was merely being polite,' she muttered. 'These dates are your nights and what we do on them is your call.'

He stared down at her and that intensity in his eyes sharpened. She couldn't move as she replayed her own tragic innuendo again. It'd honestly just slipped out—as if her subconscious determinedly sent him the invitation before she could think. But his wordless response—just that look in his eyes—made her toes curl.

Only he said nothing. He was good at that when he wanted to be. Saying nothing and walking away.

'I should go home.' But she ached for an alternative. And

then she was mortified to be so bowled over by the charm he turned on anyone at any time.

He pulled his phone from his jacket pocket. 'I'll call the car.'

He kept his phone out and scrolled through some messages on the drive. She had little to say anyway, too busy battling her disappointment at his easy acquiescence.

Stupid hormones. They'd been triggered by their one-night stand last week and she needed to turn them back off. Urgently. She thought about the guys at university she'd kissed. The invitations at work that she'd turned down. People had stopped asking. Probably said she was frigid and honestly she was glad. It had made it easier. She'd wanted to focus only on work. And she had. Until now. Anger bubbled inside of her. But it wasn't just that—hunger clawed. That old drive to be near *him*. Life was cruel. Why was it that the one guy who turned her on was an irritating playboy who only wanted one woman once?

Finally his driver pulled up outside her apartment and she forced a polite farewell for Zane. 'Thanks for tonight, I enjoyed it more than I thought I would.'

His sardonic smile flashed. 'Even the press pen?'

'Oh, no, that was hideous. I probably have my eyes closed in every photo.'

'You don't.' He held up his phone to her.

'They're out there already?' She leaned closer to study the pictures. For a moment she was stunned. Her eyes weren't closed—she was too busy gazing up at him. It made her wince. This 'date' *was* fake, but her interest in him couldn't be more obvious. She channelled her embarrassment into annoyance. 'Don't you *hate* this? It's such an invasion of your privacy.'

'Generally I don't bother looking. It's meaningless. But in this case, it's how I'm going to win that bet.'

The damned bet. Helberg, the reason for it all. 'Why do you want Helberg so badly? I don't believe you'd make such a sacrifice for just *any* company—'

'You think my spending time with you is some kind of a sacrifice?' he interrupted, the pale blue of his eyes suddenly fiery.

She froze, caught in the flames.

'Did you know you have this cute dimple in your left cheek?' he said quietly. 'See it here?' He pointed to one of the pictures. 'It doesn't appear when you smile politely. Only when you giggle. I'm glad I made you giggle then.'

Embarrassed, she lifted her hand to her mouth.

'And your immediate response is to hide it,' he scoffed. 'Why is that?'

But *he* was the one hiding—completely avoiding answering her question about Helberg. Again. Which was infuriating.

'While your immediate response when faced with a difficult conversation is to distract your way out of it with flattery and flirtation. Or else you just go silent.' She glared up at him. 'You don't want to tell me the truth.'

He stared at her for a long moment. 'All right, I'll tell you about Reed Helberg if you answer *my* questions.'

'About what?'

He shook his head. 'That's my offer. Take it or leave it.'

'Everything is a game to you.'

'Not a game. A deal. In fact, this is a *bargain* because it's so easy. It's merely some answers to some questions—how difficult can that be?'

'Well, it seems to be very difficult for you.' She watched him suspiciously. 'You have to be honest about you and Reed.'

There was the smallest hesitation. 'Sure, I'll be honest if you are.'

Oddly enough, she actually enjoyed being brutally honest with him and not bothering with the cautious politeness she always maintained around everyone else. 'Fine. Tell me what happened with Reed.' The man had a summer residence not far from the same town as them. A compound that had been in his family for generations. He liked to offer the scholarships to the kids of the local school. 'He must've thought you were amazing. Offered you the scholarship to end all scholarships.'

Zane hesitated again. Shadows flickered in his eyes and his features sharpened. That's when the penny dropped. He'd been a student at her high school for all his schooling years. She'd assumed it was because of his injuries—he'd needed to remain at home. And then he'd not gone on to university because he'd already made his fortune.

'Didn't he offer you one?' she whispered.

'Clever, Skylar,' he muttered steadily. 'I wasn't good enough.'

Never could *that* be true. Never ever. Zane was a genius. And he'd had that shocking injury in the car accident that he'd fought back so strongly from. He'd shown strength and courage as well as intelligence. Whereas she'd worked so awfully hard just to be good enough for consideration.

'How is that possible?' she asked.

He chuckled but the bitterness touched her. 'I guess I wasn't the right kind of polite, malleable student who he could wheel out in front of guests to make him look good. He was pure egotist.'

Malleable? Well, the last thing Zane was, was malleable. He was his own person. A maverick who seemed to take little seriously—aside from making millions. 'You were too much of a threat—'

'My own ego was,' he said. 'I made my first million when I was still at school—'

'But learning from home for half that time—'

'Right.' He blinked, disconcerted for a second. 'Fool that I was, I wanted him to admit he'd been wrong about me. I was young and egotistical enough to feel pleased about the invitation to speak at the gala but Reed couldn't have been more dismissive. Told me it was easy enough to make money. The real test was whether I'd be able to keep it. That he wasn't a betting man but he was *sure* I'd fail.'

She stilled. Reed had rejected him. Repeatedly.

But now Zane smiled in reminiscence. 'I'd had no idea you were going to be there, but you were that year's scholar. As beautiful as ever. As well behaved as always. You wouldn't even look at me.'

She felt her skin heat. Truth was, she'd not been able to meet his eyes initially because she'd not known what to say. The last time she'd seen him had been when her father had physically pulled them apart. She'd been *mortified*. By her father. By her own silence. But Zane himself had said nothing—he'd just stalked off. And he'd stalked off from the dinner that night too. But he'd muttered as he'd passed her.

'I believe you called me pathetic,' she said.

He nodded. 'It wasn't polite of me. But you were.'

That stung. 'For being grateful?'

He drew in a deep breath.

She waited.

'It was *your* brain that got your grades,' he finally said. 'Your work. You never needed that scholarship.'

He was wrong but she couldn't tell him about the pressure her father had put on her—that both the school and varsity scholarships had provided something of a necessary escape. She felt too disloyal to her father to even think it, but sometimes she'd been caught between the contrary needs to please him and to have breathing space of her own...

'I was just someone to take your annoyance out on,' she muttered.

He shook his head. 'I was pissed off that night but even more so when I saw you.' His gaze roved over her face, settling on her eyes. 'You were the perfect little protégée.'

'We can't *all* make our first million while we're still in our teens.' She frowned, turning her thoughts back to what Zane had told her. There had to be something more personal beyond his desire to prove himself to Reed Helberg.

'Is that it?' she challenged him. 'He didn't like you, so now you want to wreck his legacy?' It didn't make sense. Not when Zane himself admitted he didn't give a damn about what anyone thought. 'I know you. *You're* not that pathetic. What aren't you telling me?'

His eyes widened. 'Those are the basic facts. Now it's my turn for questions.'

She glared at him. He glared right back. Tension pulled the silence to screaming point—until Skylar felt forced to duck his gaze.

'What do you want to know?' she growled.

'Why do you have so little fun?'

Her focus shot right back to his face. 'Fun?'

'You're twenty-six and you were a virgin. What about boyfriends?'

'Seriously?' She shot an embarrassed glance towards the driver.

'He can't hear—'

'You can ask me anything and you just want to know about my previous relationships?'

'So you've had them?' He leaned closer, eyebrows arching. 'Had they all taken a purity pledge or something?'

'There's no "they,"' she growled. 'There's been nothing and no one. Literally nothing.'

'No relationships at all?'

She shook her head.

He stilled. 'You don't go out dancing? Not to bars or parties? You're not on any dating apps?'

She kept shaking her head.

'I get that you might not want a relationship, but don't you want—?'

'Casual sex?' she interrupted. 'No.'

'Yet that's what you had with me the other night,' he muttered. 'And you enjoyed it.'

'Yes.' But she couldn't have it again. It wasn't anything like she'd thought it would be. It had been hot and intense and honestly, all the damn stars had burst in the sky. She hated how wonderful it had been.

'Don't you want to experience that again? If not with me, then...' He cleared his throat. 'Someone else?'

Her blood quickened. That was the problem. *Never* with someone else. It was only he who made her inner siren emerge. Not that she'd admit that—he'd take too much egotistical pleasure from it. 'Relationships. Affairs,' she mumbled. 'All that stuff...it's too much effort.'

'Effort?' He shot her a startled look. 'It didn't take much effort from either of us the other night.'

Right. Again. 'That was just...'

She tightened her grip on her clutch purse. She didn't want to analyse this.

His gaze narrowed. 'You put so much effort into your work, you obviously think *that* effort is worth it.'

'Of course.'

'But you don't think what happened the other night is worth a little more *effort*?'

Sometimes the best defence was offence. 'I don't think *you're* in any real position to talk to me about making an effort.'

He laughed. 'Meaning?'

'You constantly acquire big only to then discard almost everything,' she said. 'Isn't it exhausting?'

'Are we talking about women here or—'

'Buying companies.' After all, that was his real passion. 'Breaking them up. Selling the best parts off in packages and letting the rest decay. Don't *you* ever want to put long-term *effort* into one of them? You're all about quick returns and moving on to the next project. Surely there's no real satisfaction in such fast turnover?'

'I'm very satisfied with my returns,' he said smugly. 'My talent is spotting the acquisition. Helberg is obvious—so obvious that I've got serious competition for it. Other acquisitions aren't always as clear-cut.'

'You like finding those ones best. Spotting the treasure before others see it. You like getting to them first...' She inhaled deep, pleased she was back to being annoyed with him. He was so annoyingly confident and capable. He was all cream—rising to the top in everything, all the time.

'You don't know *me*, Skylar.'

'I know plenty,' she scoffed. 'You were literally the poster boy at our old school.'

'And of course you paid close attention to some poster—to everything you were taught,' he drawled. 'Such a *good* student. You think you see everything? Perception and reality are often two very different things. Won't you consider that maybe you're misinformed?'

'Then *educate* me,' she snapped. 'Properly.'

His pupils flared.

She wanted him to *school* her. *Badly.* Being this close to him was torture. But being closer still was as effortless as breathing—was bliss. She ached for that. She stared at his mouth hovering just above hers. Seconds became centuries again and it took her too long to realise that he was speaking. It was the softest, most strained of whispers.

'I think you'd better go inside, Skylar.'

CHAPTER NINE

'YOU WANT ME to meet you where?' Zane asked haughtily but bit back a smile at the same time.

'Montague's. The jewellers on Fifth Avenue,' she said smugly. 'You know the one.'

'Yeah, I know.' He also knew she was biting back her laugh too.

She thought she could make today's Helberg reconnaissance mission his worst nightmare. But she couldn't be more wrong, because he'd been dreaming about seeing her again for days. Good, hot dreams. Which—now he stopped to consider it— were nightmares, given he was only supposed to look at and not touch the very precious treasure that was Skylar Bennet. Oh, but she was the perfect jewel with which to decorate his bed. That he'd been warned off all those years ago only made him want her more now she'd crossed his path again. Her father wasn't there to protect her now. And she didn't need him. She could protect herself. She wasn't silent with him. Wasn't well behaved. She was spirited and sarcastic as hell and he relished it so much he couldn't resist provoking her more. Because she couldn't seem to stop herself reacting to him. Which was good. It made them even.

'Ever been inside?' she followed up too innocently.

'You know I haven't.'

'Actually, I wouldn't have picked that,' she countered breezily. 'Don't you buy sparkling goodbye gifts for all those women you date?'

'No. I don't pay them off with trinkets and baubles.'

'You just leave them broken-hearted?'

'Empty-handed,' he corrected coolly. 'Because they don't need recompense for spending time with me.'

'Because they're just so very, very lucky already?' Her laughter was soft but he was certain the dimple was out.

'As well *you* know,' he purred. 'Why this jewellery store?' He prolonged the conversation because this date was still too many hours away and he liked hearing her voice. He'd missed it all week. Wednesday hadn't come quick enough. 'It doesn't even have the Helberg name.'

'Because it's only still in existence *because* of Helberg. Because they bought it into the family.'

'You think Helberg is a family?' His smile faded. 'Skylar, you know you don't have to repay the chance Reed gave you with your absolute soul—'

'And I'm not. It isn't just about the scholarship. And yes, Helberg Holdings is family. It's nice to feel needed there and valued for the things I do.'

'You ought to feel needed and valued *regardless* of what you do,' he growled. 'You ought to be needed and valued just for being you.'

There was a moment of silence down the phone.

'Did you get hit on the head?' she asked.

He'd taken a hit of some kind, apparently. But he laughed, relieved that she'd gone for a joke because he really didn't know where that had come from either. He'd go to her damned jewellery store and now he understood her motivation it made sense that her modus operandi regarding Helberg was the human connection. She wanted him to meet more of *her* work family. She didn't want him to break them up.

'Who are you going to fob me off onto this time?' he muttered, still unable to end the call.

'The jeweller.'

'Thrilling. Anyone else?'

'The sales manager. They're both lovely. They both have a lot to share.'

'Can't wait.' The sad fact was that wasn't even a lie.

Montague's was the high-end manufacturing jewellery arm of the business that Adam Courtenay was most interested in. No surprise there, given jewels were already Adam's family deal. But this was a flagship store—all exquisite space, gleaming luxury and not a price tag in sight. Zane grimaced as he looked around the plush premises three hours after he'd hung up on Skylar.

'Is the sight of all the engagement rings giving you hives?' She stole up beside him and chuckled.

Glancing down, he saw the amusement dancing in her eyes. Her dimple appeared the second he smiled back at her. He had to freeze and process the urge to haul her close and kiss her hello. He'd kiss her until she was breathless and begging for more. Then for mercy. Because he would tease her to the edge and back over and over again. Torment her the way she was tormenting him right now. Night after night he thought about her and what he'd do the second he had another chance.

He couldn't believe he'd squandered that opportunity. He'd been a fool. A teen all over again. So fast. Far too fast. The fire had consumed them both. And it wasn't enough. He gritted his teeth. She was a crush from his teen years. She should mean nothing now. But that old ache was back. She'd been the only one he *couldn't* have. The only one he'd become bitter about. So maybe she was the only one who he was going to need to have more than once.

'Come on,' she said.

She was too bright-eyed. Too trusting. Guilt rose in a tsunami-like wave this time. He hadn't told her everything that had happened between him and Reed. But he hadn't exactly reneged on his deal with her—he'd told her some, just not *all* of the truth. Which wasn't cheating. Some wounds cut too deep to be exposed. But she'd guessed there had to be more. And he needed distraction from this already.

'You don't wear jewellery.' He cocked his head and teased her. 'Is such adornment too much *effort*?'

'Do *you* wear any?' She bit right back as he'd known she would.

'I like a good watch.' He shrugged.

Her eyes widened in faux awe. 'So you know when it's time to leave?'

He smiled appreciatively. This was what he needed—for her to spar with him, not stand by silently. He'd known—even all those years ago—that she'd have smart things to say. And he liked that she wasn't afraid to call him out. The wealthier he'd become, the more people said yes around him. The less they challenged or argued. They started to treat everything he said as immutable law. Which was rubbish. It was also—frankly—boring. Skylar was fresh.

'I sometimes wear rings too,' he said.

'To ward off evil spirits? Or all those women setting themselves at you?'

'For fun.' He moved closer, unable to stop himself. 'Which apparently is a foreign concept for you.' He brushed the backs of his fingers lightly against her cheekbone, then swept wider, noting the tiny holes in her earlobes. 'Let's look at the earrings.'

'Zane—'

'You have a graceful neck.' He had no qualms whatsoever about hijacking her expedition and thwarting her. 'You should wear long earrings to show it off.' He moved to the cabinet before she could attempt to argue more. He was aware of her watching as he assessed the collection. The ruby and diamond drops caught his attention immediately. Red definitely had to be her colour—as striking and sensual as she was. 'Can we have a closer look at those, please.'

The assistant couldn't move fast enough.

'Zane—'

'Beautiful, don't you think?' He was seriously enjoying himself.

She stared round-eyed at him and then finally at the glittering jewels he held towards her. 'They'll get caught in my hair,' she said dismissively.

'You wear your hair up more often than not. Try them on.'

'I can't—'

'It's no problem, I'm sure.' Zane smiled at the assistant, who hurried to nod.

He turned his focus back to Skylar. A hint of smokiness clouded her eyes. He knew she was tempted, which was *super* interesting—yeah, she was a sensualist who liked nice things. She just didn't let herself indulge very often. Why was she so damned studious—so restrained—even after all this time? Even after her father had passed? The guy had been controlling and overprotective. She'd basically been under house arrest. She'd gone to school. She'd gone for her runs in the mornings. And that was it.

Zane had been housebound because of his injuries. He'd worked hard to get strong enough to leave. But Skylar had sat studying on her balcony for hours—silently watching the world, seemingly unbothered by her father's controls. And even after she'd left home, even after her father had died... she'd stayed as self-contained. Indeed, as the rubies gleamed prettily in the light, she didn't move. *Why?*

'We'll take them,' he said to the assistant without lifting his gaze from Skylar.

His smile widened as he saw her jaw tense. He knew her drilled-deep manners and good behaviour stopped her from arguing with him in front of the entire store. He stepped up to the counter and completed the transaction.

To his astonishment, that's when Skylar suddenly spoke up.

'Don't box them.' She smiled at the assistant. 'I'll wear them out.'

The assistant's eyes widened but she hustled. Zane was simply speechless as within less than a minute Skylar stood adorned with rubies and diamonds dangling from her ears, and he couldn't take his gaze off her gleaming eyes.

'You can buy them but the second I take them out I'm giving them back to you,' she murmured the moment the assistant left them, clearly well trained to know when to leave her customers to consider their other options.

'Sure.' He shrugged. 'No matter.'

'What are you going to do with them then? Wear them yourself? Give them to someone else?'

The edge in her voice pressed on his pleasure nerve because it sounded a little like jealousy. 'I'm going to look at them and think of you. Often.'

She shook her head. 'And why would you want to do that?'

'Well, I already think of you often—'

'Don't,' she breathed suddenly.

He stopped doing everything instantly—moving, breathing. Hell, even his heart stopped for a second.

'Don't flirt with me,' she finished so very softly. 'I'm doing what you want already—I'll be your companion in public. You don't have to…'

'Be honest?' He watched her intently.

He'd known the gift would bother her and yeah, that was partly why he'd given it to her. But he'd also wanted to see her in those earrings really badly and he just couldn't not buy them. And yeah, he liked this. Her challenging him. When she pushed. She was the only person to look at him with undisguised irritation at times.

But now she stepped back and instinctively he reached for her hand and stopped her. 'You don't ever treat yourself at the shops? Or ever let someone else treat you a little?'

Her eyes flashed. 'Dropping however many thousand you've just dropped isn't some *little* treat.'

Right. Good point. 'You're awfully serious, Skylar. You never do anything just for the heck of it?'

'You know I don't. Well, almost never.' She shot him a look. 'It's the way I was raised.'

He nodded his head slowly because he knew that was accurate. 'Your dad didn't let you wear any jewellery.'

She stiffened. 'We couldn't afford it. We needed other things—you know, like food.'

No. It wasn't only the money. It was her overprotective, controlling dad. 'He didn't let you do lots of things.'

It hung between them yet again. Zane had been too stunned—and yes, too hurt—to ever stop and deeply consider why she'd been so silent. Why she'd turned and run. He'd just felt rejected twice over. The best moment he'd ever experienced had devolved into a nightmare in less than a second. She'd not defended him—not admitted that she'd been as much to 'blame' as he. Zane had actually loitered in the grounds the day after, hoping to catch her on her run. She'd not appeared. And now—far too late—he wondered how scared she'd been of her father. Had he punished her?

Zane had never heard shouting, or seen any evidence of it. He'd thought the man had just been overprotective as hell of his beautiful daughter.

'You didn't rebel even once you left home? Didn't spoil yourself with your first proper pay?' Zane asked her now. 'Or are you still obeying the rules he set for you back then—putting his wishes ahead of your own desires.'

She stiffened. 'My father wanted the best for me and I knew how tough it was for him dealing with me on his own. But you're not entirely wrong. He was strict. Protective. He wanted me to prioritise my studies and then my career.'

'You weren't allowed out.' His anger stirred. 'You were *never* allowed to go out. You were always there.'

It rippled again. That memory.

'But your ears are pierced,' he said slowly. 'So when did he let that happen?'

'My mother took me not long before she left.'

Another memory flashed—one from far further back. When she'd been a little girl and he'd given her his last piece of candy because she'd been crying because her mother had gone.

'Dad had a fit,' she added softly. 'When she left he threw all her jewellery away.'

'She didn't take it with her?'

'She didn't take anything. She left it all.'

Including her daughter.

'He didn't think you might want it?'

'She left with another man and never looked back. I guess he thought it was tainted. He threw away my earrings too.'

Yeah, her dad had tried to control the one thing he'd had left. 'He wouldn't let you do anything.' He looked at her. 'No earrings. No dates. No fun.'

'Actually, most of that was really *my* choice.' She stepped close and her brown eyes bore into him. 'At first I thought if I were really, really good, then she might come back.' She still spoke softly but somehow that made her rising emotion all the more audible. 'And then I started to worry that if I wasn't really good, *he* might leave as well.'

Zane stood very still, inwardly stuffing down the pain that had risen so sharply. He'd felt that desperate desire to hold on to someone—to somehow make them stay. But his dad hadn't wanted him from the start.

And Zane had been hard on his mother. Because where Skylar had been obedient, it had taken him a while to get on board. He'd been endlessly curious. A wandering child, who'd made his mother's life difficult.

'So yes, I was good. I worked hard. And of course I did what I was told.'

Including obeying her dad when he'd yelled at her for kissing him. She'd been what, sixteen?

'That's why that scholarship was so important,' she said. 'It was an acceptable escape.'

Right. He sighed. And yet it still seemed to him that she hadn't escaped all that much. She was still living in such a constrained way. Like a nun.

'I don't blame you for wanting the scholarship,' he said huskily. 'I blame Helberg for using it to control people. To make them bow and scrape before him. It was a power trip for him.'

Skylar tried to regain control of her emotions. She'd just told Zane far too much that was too personal. But bow and scrape? Her interview with old man Helberg hadn't been like that. 'His foundation gave lots of people like me an out. You did it all on your own. Most of us ordinary people can't.'

She gently fingered the cool stones dangling from her ears. She'd started wearing earrings again a few years ago. Just little studs, nothing like these stunning things. But they didn't even feel that heavy. She liked the sensuality and the sparkle and the sway when she tilted her head. She liked the way Zane's gaze tracked them when she did. The way it lingered on her skin. She could almost feel it.

'But I bet your father was proud of you,' he said huskily.

Oh, yes. He had been. She'd been so studious and careful and yes, eager to please. But she'd got to Helberg HQ and not really made the moves she'd thought she would. And that wasn't because she hadn't worked hard. But her father had wanted her to stay. To keep trying. And once he'd gone, staying there seemed to matter all the more. She'd promised her father, and for him there was nothing worse than someone breaking their promise. She'd never wanted to let him down in the way her mother had.

'Skylar—'

'I didn't tell you that to make you pity me or whatever. But maybe you're right about my treat-free existence,' she breathed out. 'I've been focused on my work for a long time. So have you.'

'In many ways we're not so dissimilar.' He nodded, all serious.

But she laughed because he'd definitely had his treats along the way. 'I'm nothing like you.'

All those parties he'd gone to? They hadn't affected his business success at all. Maybe she should have gone to some.

He tilted his head and a speculative gleam entered his eyes. 'You came to that Independence Day party to try to see me. What was your approach going to be?'

She flicked her hand carelessly, covering up her own cluelessness. 'I hadn't worked out the finer details.'

'You were willing to use a social situation to pursue a business interest.' He leaned close. 'Which means you and I are not so very different after all.'

'There's a vast difference between a tasteless bet and just hoping to bump into someone.'

'You wanted to bump into me.' His grin flashed wickedly. 'You definitely met your goal there.'

Skylar threw him a withering glance but the next second giggled. It felt good to giggle. Even better when he laughed with her.

She glanced around and realised the jewellery store staff were keeping their distance but also keeping their eyes on them. They'd been ensconced in this corner, intimately talking in low voices for a good ten minutes. Oh well—that was probably good for Zane's bet.

But she straightened. 'Right, you're here to meet the jeweller, remember? He's worked here for sixty years.'

'He's not ready for a nice relaxing retirement?' Zane winked at her.

For the next thirty minutes she watched as he chatted with the jeweller, listening to the history of the place. The joy he found in his work. The pride. The capital funding from Helberg that had enabled their expansion. The jeweller and the manager both gazed up at him, clearly delighted to meet him. It was his smile. Everyone fell for it. Even her.

But when they finally stepped out onto the summer pavement he shook his head at her. 'You brought me to one of the most successful subsidiaries. It's been in the stable only a decade and doesn't even bear the Helberg name. What was the point?'

To make him uncomfortable. Of course, that hadn't worked. He'd flipped it on her the second he'd spotted those earrings.

She was failing already—only two weeks in. And it wasn't even a surprise because deep inside she was worried he was right about Helberg Holdings. Something had to happen with it.

Zane was only indulging her in these visits and the truth was she wanted him to indulge her in another way altogether. *Educate me. Properly.*

The command she'd issued the other night circled in her head. Tempting her. The ache inside sharpened—the appetite she couldn't suppress any more. She should have all the treats she'd missed out on for so long. The physical ones. All she'd done all her life was work. Learn. Study. Stay safe. Stay focused. She'd missed out on a lot of fun. And he was the perfect person to help, right? Because he'd worked too. But he'd become far more successful than she *and* he'd had a lot of fun along the way. He really knew how. Which meant he could teach her many things. And there was no way her heart would be endangered—she still didn't actually like him all that much, right? And his heart was in no danger at all given he didn't have one…

'You have the weirdest look on your face,' he said, looking down at her.

She raised her eyebrows. 'What kind of look?'

'Cunning. Like a fox. Pretty fox.'

It was the only time in her life she'd ever been called a fox. She quite liked it.

'I don't trust it,' he added.

She chuckled. 'Shocker. You don't trust anyone.'

'Fair.' He smiled. 'You don't trust me either.'

'Not entirely true, actually. I trust you to be honest with me. You've been pretty blunt thus far.'

'Hmm. That's true. As have you. Tell me what you're thinking.'

'That I'm no longer a virgin but I'm still inexperienced in bed.'

Such raw shock pinched his features that she bit back a laugh.

His fingertips touched a spot on her left cheek. 'You should always laugh when you feel the urge. Don't hold back, Skylar.'

'Well, I've still no experience in an actual bed, have I?' Heat trammelled through her and she inadvertently swayed towards him before catching herself and straightening.

'And that's what you want? More experience. In bed. With me.'

'Right,' she breathed huskily. 'You're skilled.'

'I can't decide if I'm honoured or offended.'

'You're honoured. We both know that. We also both know you're going to agree.' And she was crossing both fingers behind her back and hoping like crazy she was right.

'I am?'

'You can't resist a game.'

'Is that what this is?'

'You can consider it a challenge if you like.' Her temperature soared but she pushed on lightly. 'For me this is a learning journey.'

'A learning journey?' He started to laugh. 'Wow, that's so HR of you. Will you want to set some goals? Get a performance appraisal afterwards?'

'That's really not a bad idea—'

'Flow chart? Bonus points for creativity?'

'For all sorts of things.' She nodded.

'No.' He shook his head. 'No, no, no.'

She died inside. 'You're declining my offer?'

'I'm declining the flow chart and bullet points.' He stepped right into her space and put his hand gently on her shoulder. 'This can't be business between us. This is play.'

'Surely you like a game to have rules?' She instinctively knew she needed them.

'Don't you realise how much I hate rules?'

'There have to be *some* boundaries.' For safety—to protect her heart, right?

'Tell me something.' He ran his thumb gently back and forth across her lower lip in the softest, most sensual of touches. 'Why are you suddenly willing to make the effort?'

Her legs barely held her up as relief then arousal slammed into her. 'There's not much effort required for this.' The truth just spilled from her.

His eyebrows shot up. 'Why, Skylar, how you flatter me.'

She closed her eyes briefly and summoned the shell of strength she was going to need. 'There's no effort because this isn't a *relationship*. It's an *arrangement*.' She opened her eyes and gazed right into his. 'And to be frank, it's all about me.'

His lips twitched. 'What you want. And I get nothing?'

'You need for nothing, you've already made that clear,' she pointed out with a tiny shrug. 'But you enjoy a release every now and then and right now you can't because of that bet.'

'Every now and then…'

'Do you always repeat what people say to you?'

'Only when it's weird.'

Crushed, she flinched.

He put his other hand on her other shoulder, holding her firmly in place. 'No. Don't back out now. Tell me how you want this to work.'

He'd inched closer, and when he was closer, everything was easier.

'It's very straightforward,' she muttered. 'On your public date nights, we sleep together before I go home.'

His fingers tightened fractionally. 'So you're revising our original agreement.'

'You revise deals all the time. It's a normal part of business.'

'Right.' He huffed a breath. 'Well, revision works both ways. You want an amendment, then I get one too.'

She hesitated and looked at him warily. 'What amendment do you want?'

'You've sprung this on me. I need a little time to figure it out. I'll let you know.'

She shook her head. He was quick, he could come up with something here and now. 'I can't agree if I don't know the details.'

'You're going to *have* to trust me—more than just being honest.' He suddenly smiled. 'That's the real challenge, isn't it.'

'As if it isn't for you?'

Ignoring the passers-by on the street, he stepped in even closer and lowered his head towards hers. The intimacy seared—it might as well only be the two of them in the world. She was certain he was about to kiss her—indeed, as he spoke, his lips almost, almost brushed hers.

'You want your learning journey, Skylar? All you have to do is say yes.'

CHAPTER TEN

SKYLAR STRUGGLED TO BREATHE. Her pretty rented dress was short. She had only a thin slip beneath it and a tiny scrap of silk beneath that. But she was still too hot and she couldn't release enough of her nervous energy either. She'd said yes, of course, but this wasn't the straight-to-bed evening she'd secretly been aching for. He'd brought her to dinner at one of those restaurants that you needed to book a year in advance. Unless you were a young billionaire with half the internet following your every move. Then you could just walk in and be given the best table. And waste a whole lot of time. All she wanted was to be alone with him. In bed. Now that she'd said yes, Skylar was appallingly impatient.

'You want to share some mini plates?' he muttered.

She nodded. 'You pick.'

She watched him study the menu. It took an age—and all she did was note how his dark shirt and trousers emphasised his handsome features. He was stunningly good-looking. But it was the gleam in his eyes and the twitch at the corner of his mouth that got her the most.

He was good-humoured. And a tease.

Eventually the dishes he'd selected arrived—plate after plate of small snacks. So many plates. She nibbled to be polite. To pass the too slowly ticking time. To her surprise, he picked as little as she did, before he suddenly pushed his plate away and vehemently sighed. She arched her eyebrows at him.

'I'm not hungry,' he growled in answer.

'Then why did you order all this food?' She gestured at the laden table.

He rolled his shoulders. 'I was trying to distract myself.'

'From…?'

He shot her a sizzling look.

'We didn't need to come out to dinner,' she said quietly.

He released another massive sigh. 'Yes, we did.'

She'd forgotten about the public aspect to their dates. 'Well, now what?' she asked, seeing as dinner was done for them both. 'Should we go to a club?'

'No.'

'You don't want to go dancing?'

'I really want to dance with you,' he ground out. 'Just not in public.'

'Aren't we supposed to be seen in public? Aren't we here right now for the photos that waiter is surreptitiously taking?'

'No,' he contradicted her shortly. 'We're here to slow down.'

'To…*what*?'

He shot her another of those smouldering looks. 'You know once we start, we're like a runaway train. So out of control.'

'Yes,' she breathed. *Exactly*. That was the bit she liked best, actually.

'So we need to slow down,' he muttered.

'Why—'

'Because you deserve more than a quick—'

'I like quick,' she interrupted.

He closed his eyes. 'Not helping, Skylar.'

Good. 'Haven't I waited long enough?'

He gazed at her fiercely—a picture of hungry, virile man. 'All the more reason to slow down and do this properly.'

She really didn't want this whole slow approach. 'I said yes, you don't need to woo me with dinner.'

He paused. 'Maybe I'm ensuring you have adequate fuel on board.'

'I already have more energy than I know what to do with,' she said. 'I can hardly sit still.'

'*Damn it*, Skylar.' But his smile suddenly flashed.

She couldn't resist provoking him a little more. 'You just don't believe in boring Saturday nights at home.'

He gaped at her for a moment. 'This one isn't going to be boring.'

He stood up, tossed a sheaf of cash on the table and jerked his head towards the exit. 'If you don't want more of a scene, move now.'

Skylar grabbed her purse and half skipped to keep up with him. Delighted.

But then the chauffeur didn't drive fast enough for her. She was aware of Zane watching her, that half smile on his face, but keeping his damned distance the entire ride.

Finally they turned into the basement parking lots of one of the needle-thin, super-tall, billionaire tower blocks on the southern edge of Central Park. The chauffeur held the door for them then Zane led her to the elevator and punched several numbers on the keypad. Moments later, they stepped into the elevator. Unable to resist, she looked up at him, met his wild gaze.

But he shook his head. 'No. Not yet.'

They whizzed skywards in the smooth, silent lift. The second the doors opened, Zane stepped forward. For a split second she watched him—a tall silhouette against floor-to-ceiling windows. Her pulse trebled its tempo. She drew a steadying breath and followed.

'Your apartment is incredible,' she said. It was like a palace in the sky. The city and Central Park stretched below them for miles. 'The view is amazing. So is the one from your Belhaven beach house.'

'Yeah,' he said. 'I've been to beautiful beaches all around the world—the Mediterranean, the Caribbean, Hawaii, off the coast of Australia, but none of them beat that one.'

'Because it's home.' She zipped and unzipped her little purse, desperately burning just a smidge of the energy that had been firing around her body for days. 'I've never been to any other beaches. Never been overseas. Not even out of state.'

'Not ever?'

'No.' She paced, taking in other details with hyper-awareness. There was a vast computer screen set-up in the place others might have as a dining area. There was a stunning open plan kitchen. Intricately woven rugs on the beautiful wooden flooring. Glancing back, she saw he'd not moved from the window. He was as still as before, still just staring at her.

'What's wrong with you?' she teased. 'Are you glued to the floor?'

'Apparently.'

The strain in his voice emboldened her and she walked back to where he stood. 'What should I do?'

He released a deep sigh and shook his head again. 'I'm not going to teach you how to please me.'

She paused. She'd kind of thought that was the point.

'You need to learn to please yourself.' He reached into his pocket and pulled out a foil strip of condoms and held them out to her. 'Do what you want. How you want. You need to figure out what you want and what you like.'

She still didn't quite understand.

'Tonight you're taking the lead,' he added with a mocking grin.

And that was not what she wanted. At all. She just wanted him to sweep her back into that fiery caldron—to seduce her. Completely. She had no idea how or where to begin.

He watched her for another moment and that smile softened. 'Okay, look, given your inexperience, I'm gonna assume you've never seen a naked man before. Shall I strip for you?'

'Well.' She took the protection and gripped it ridiculously tightly. 'You did say you wanted to dance.'

'You want me to put some music on?'

'No,' she snapped. 'No more time wasting. Strip. Do it now.'

He chuckled delightedly but began unbuttoning his shirt. Slowly. One button after another, captivating her as his skin was revealed. His chest was gorgeous—broad, muscled, a smattering of hair that trailed down...

Her fingertips tingled. He tossed the shirt to the floor, then his hands went to his belt.

'Look. Touch. Don't touch,' he muttered, holding her gaze as he worked the buckle. Then the button. The zipper. 'Dance with me. Whatever you want. However fast. However slow. Your choice.' He shoved down his trousers and stepped out of them.

She drew in a sharp breath.

'You know I was in a car accident,' he said ruefully. 'It was probably on that stupid poster about me at school.'

It hadn't been on the poster, but she knew—though not any personal details. She'd never seen scars like this. His thigh was like patchwork. 'You studied from home while you recovered.'

'Rehab took a long time. There are a few metal pins. I set off airport security alarms—'

He set off every alarm—*warning, dangerously charming man ahead.* 'So basically you're bionic now.'

'It doesn't hinder my performance if that's what you're worried about.'

'I'm not worried.' She stepped closer. 'But I don't think I want a *performance*.'

'Right.' He shoved down his boxers.

Skylar stared. Super-hot and super...stunned. Just stunned.

'Skylar?'

'Mmmm?'

'Did you run this morning?' he asked, slowly walking towards her.

'Of course,' she answered on auto. 'I haven't missed a Saturday-morning run in more than two years.'

'Impressive.'

Yeah, that wasn't what was impressive here. He was completely, beautifully naked.

'It makes you feel good?'

'Yes,' she mumbled. She couldn't take her eyes off his body—his smooth olive skin, the sleek muscles, the rippling abs, the slim hips, the...

'Why don't we find out what else makes you feel good.'

'Okay.' She paused. 'You're really...'

'Turned on?'

He was. He very much was. And she was *so* hot. 'It's been a full two weeks since we... That's not what you're used to. Of course you must be feeling frustrated,' she muttered.

'It's you I want to feel.'

She shook her head. He was a virile man, that was all.

He huffed a little laugh. 'How can you not believe me?' He drew in a deep breath. 'Seeing is believing. *Feeling* for yourself might be even better.'

Oh. 'You want me to—'

'Do whatever you want with me,' he said with exaggerated patience. 'Any time you like. I'm clearly *ready* for whatever, whenever you are.'

He certainly was. Skylar inhaled another deep breath and released it slowly, determined to get a hold of herself. This was an *opportunity* and she was going to make the most of it.

'You're saying I can do anything?' she asked innocently, lifting her chin. 'You want a safe word?'

His jaw dropped.

'*Stop* should suffice, don't you think?' she added.

He just stayed there staring at her. She smiled happily. She'd rendered him speechless. There was a first. Confidence trickled into her veins. There was no denying he was hot for her. Which was really, really good.

'Do you think you could sit down?' she muttered. 'You're too tall for me to—'

'Chair? Sofa? Bed?'

Bed was too far away. 'Sofa.'

He took position in the centre of the large sofa and looked up at her as she stood in front of him, his cheeks slightly flushed. She'd spent so long watching for him—*waiting*—and now he was before her, naked. Willing to do whatever she wanted. She really didn't know where to start.

But then…then, she did. She knew what she wanted. She stepped forward and straddled him, a knee either side of his thighs. Right on his lap. His lips parted but he said nothing. She smiled and put the packet of protection beside them. It was time to touch. Just the lightest brush of her fingertips down his chest. Goose bumps lifted on his skin. His nipples tightened. Unable to resist the urge, she leaned forward and licked one.

'Okay, Skylar.' He stretched his arms wide along the back of the sofa and gripped the leather in his fists. 'Okay.' His breathing shortened. 'This is your game, sweetheart…you take the lead. I'm not…not going to interfere.'

She smiled, unsure if he was telling her that again or reminding himself of his mission. And frankly, she still *wanted* him to interfere. So maybe she was going to have to make him. She glided her hands further over his hot, fit body. Couldn't resist leaning closer, breathing in his heat and scent, trailing her fingertips up the side of his neck to his jaw.

'You smell nice,' she murmured. 'And you've shaved.'

'Yeah,' he muttered. 'Thought I ought to in case you wanted me to kiss you in some…uh…sensitive areas.'

She stared into his eyes, her brain shorting at the image he'd just put in her head. 'I appreciate your consideration.'

He swallowed. Hard. 'I was happy to make the effort for you.'

Oh. He was tricky. She slid her hand back down his chest and felt the thump of his heart. It was fast and his skin was more than warm to the touch now—a sheen of sweat glistened on him. She slid her hand lower. 'Are you okay?'

'Actually, I'm not sure my lungs are working properly,' he muttered. 'It's getting quite hard to breathe.'

Pleasure and power surged. Even if it were only right now and only physical, he *wanted* her. A lot. 'You might need a little mouth-to-mouth?'

'You think it might help?' His smile lifted.

She chuckled too, a different kind of warmth adding to her molten temperature. She pressed her mouth gently to his. It rushed back on her—this silken, sudden delight, and she remembered the total pleasure of tangling like this with him. The heat they generated together.

Detonation all over again. Suddenly there was no restraint within her. Her touch firmed, teasing, testing—getting to know the indentations of his body—the firm muscle stretched over long bones. Then she swept lower, seeking out his most sensitive areas—stroking, teasing, *tasting*.

'You've done some research, Skylar?' he growled, his hips lifting beneath her ministrations.

She flushed and glanced up at him because yeah, she had. 'I might've read a few articles in the last couple of days.'

He groaned and his head fell back against the sofa. 'I…uh… appreciate your studious preparation.'

She almost purred under his praise but in moments was lost in her exploration of him. He was beautiful, and the freedom to discover every inch of him was too delicious.

'I like it when you play with me. Skylar—' He broke off on another groan.

She moved faster, stroking him with two hands and then taking him deep into her mouth…ever so slowly.

'Jeez, Skylar.' He tensed beneath her.

Yeah. This was *hot*.

'Two more strokes,' he growled, suddenly impatient. 'Two more…'

She gave him one. And then stalled, lifting her face to watch his reaction. His eyes flashed open and he gazed down at her. His pupils were blown, his cheeks flushed.

'Oh.' His breath hissed but he smiled like a feral wolf. 'Is that how it is?'

'Yeah,' she breathed. 'That's how it is.'

She wanted to torture him—the very best kind of torture.

He closed his eyes, the strained agony of being this close to ecstasy made him so damned handsome. 'You realise you'll get it back three-fold.'

'Fantastic.' The only problem was that she was close too. So hot. So close. And she wanted to come. She ran her hands along his arms, still stretched wide along the sofa, and gripped his wrists and tried to tug them. 'I need you.'

'Need me to what?' he baited, resisting her attempts to make him move.

'You know,' she breathed. 'Please.'

'Touch you? Kiss you?'

'Do *everything* to me,' she muttered.

He moved, gripping her waist to take him with her as he simply slid from the sofa to the floor. She toppled to the side, easing off his lap to roll onto her back.

She gazed up at him, feeling hedonistic and hot. 'Kiss every inch of me,' she muttered, finally getting the hang of making her wishes known. 'Every inch.'

His smile was utterly wolfish. 'My appetite has returned and I'm ravenous, Skylar. So I might do more than kiss.'

'Sounds good.'

He lavished her with licks and nips, touches. Her nipples ached, tight and needy, while deep in her core she melted. She reached for him and he pushed her with his big hands, sliding them down her body to hold her squirming thighs apart. He kissed the tops of her inner thighs, kissed her more intimately than that. She closed her eyes, loving the sensations he gave her. 'More.'

He paused. She whimpered. She didn't want him to tease her now. She just wanted him. *'Zane...'*

He must've heard her plea because he filled her with his fingers and sucked right where she was so sensitive.

She came. Hard. But even as she moaned helplessly, she asked again and arched, utterly open before him. 'More. I want you *with* me.'

He took only a moment to prepare and then was back. 'Skylar.'

She curled her arm around his neck to keep him close to her, looking into his beautiful eyes. He pressed close. Yes. This was what she wanted. What she'd always want. Zane with her. His body moving within hers. She wrapped her leg around his hip and got grabby, gasping as she worked to get closer to him still. His hands firmed, holding her so he could grind.

'You want me as deep as it gets?' he growled.

'Yes. Deep.' She shuddered. 'Really deep.'

He worked harder, pushing into a rhythm that was fierce and fast and everything. She shook, her eyes closing as her tension burst and a white-hot orgasm hit. This was it. This was the best feeling of her whole damned life.

When she could finally open her eyes again, she found him holding her, watching her, still breathing hard.

'That was...' He shook his head almost helplessly.

'Awesome. Just awesome.' She would never move again.

'Yeah.' Zane released her slowly and rose to his feet. 'Back in a sec.'

It was no time before he was back. He bent and handed her a glass. She sipped without querying the contents, then spluttered on a laugh.

'Is this electrolytes?' She held the glass up to the light. *'Seriously?'*

'You need them. I sure do. And if our recovery is fast, then we can carry on. So drink up.'

She was very glad to know they would be carrying on. So she drained the glass.

He inclined his head and chuckled. 'Full marks, sweetheart. You really are stellar.'

'Full marks to you too.' She laughed as his eyebrows lifted. 'What, you don't think you should get graded because you're the more experienced one?' She batted her lashes at him. 'Have you not heard of three-sixty assessments?'

'I'll give you three-sixty.'

She yelped and giggled as he pulled her back against him and she felt his laughter rumble in his chest.

Getting him to upskill her education was best idea she'd ever had.

'I should get going,' she mumbled a couple of hours later.

'You what?' Zane questioned with full authority. 'Class isn't over, Skylar. I thought you were a diligent student. The sort who puts in *lots* of extra hours. The kind who pulls all-nighters in fact.' He rolled out of his massive bed and threw her a T-shirt. 'You just need more sustenance.'

'Not more electrolytes,' she moaned.

'Definitely something a little more substantial.'

She didn't argue with him. She didn't want to leave. After the electrolytes, he'd carried her to his shower. Helped her bathe—thoroughly—then carried her to his bed. She quite appreciated all the carrying. She appreciated the attentions in his bed even more.

Now she followed him to the kitchen, and while he pulled things from the cupboards, she sneaked peeks at the shelves. 'You use all these fancy ingredients?'

'I have a chef on call. He's here most afternoons to make my dinner and prep breakfast and lunch that I just have to assemble. But I can cook for myself when I need to.'

'And what do you cook?' She watched as he took a pan from a drawer and got a stick of butter from the fridge.

'Protein pancakes.'

'Protein?' She giggled.

'I had them for dinner almost every night. I still love them.' He got busy with a couple bowls, eggs, flour and a whisk.

Skylar got busy watching.

'When you're in recovery, you need the best nutrition you can get,' he lectured her with a laugh.

He had been in recovery for a while with that leg injury.

'Four operations,' he said. 'I know you're wondering.'

These weren't box pancakes. These were made from scratch and were thick, fluffy and enormous.

'These are really good.'

'Why are you so surprised?' he asked with mild outrage. 'I told you I made them all the time when I was growing up.'

'Your mother's recipe?'

'No.' He glanced at the fridge. 'She worked late.'

'So you made them for her too?' She just knew he had. 'They're so good.'

'I have a far wider assortment of toppings now.' He placed a pack of strawberries on the counter. Then a bottle of maple syrup. A can of whipped cream. A bottle of caramel sauce, another of chocolate. He looked at the array and then looked at her with that wicked gleam in his eyes. 'What do you think? You like any of these?'

His playfulness stoked her own. 'I like all of them.'

His smile widened. 'You have an adventurous appetite, Skylar?'

'It seems that I do.' She ran her fingers down the cool can of cream and shot him a wicked smile. 'Adventurous *and* voracious.'

Zane watched her sleep. Yeah, it was weird of him to do it but he really didn't want to wake her. He was too busy feeling smug. She was in such a deep sleep. He'd not just satisfied her—repeatedly—he'd exhausted her. And she'd exhausted him. This morning, he'd woken the latest he had in *years*. Yet he wasn't entirely satisfied. He wanted to see her indulge in more—of all the sorts of thing she'd decided were too much 'effort.' Having fun. Treating herself. Holidays. Finding a new job even?

Because it struck him that she'd stalled. And it bothered him. Even though it shouldn't. It was her life, not any business of his to interfere in. But they could have some more fun together. They could do that right now. Well, as soon as she woke.

And when she finally stirred, he didn't give her time to feel awkward. He'd keep this as effortless as possible.

'Come on. Let's go to the local market and get brunch,' he ordered.

'Brunch?' Her eyes gleamed but then immediately dimmed. 'I can't wear that dress at this time of day.'

'I've got something you—'

'I'm not wearing your sweatpants again.'

He chuckled. Yeah. 'Not those.' He handed her the bag he'd retrieved from the lift.

She pulled out the jeans, the tee, and shot him quite the stunned look. 'When did you get these?'

'They were delivered a few minutes ago.' Because he'd predicted the problem. 'Want to shower before getting dressed?'

That look turned sultry. 'Want to join me?'

'Absolutely.'

It was another hour before they were dressed and headed towards the elevator.

'I guess this way you can get morning-after photos,' she said thoughtfully.

Zane hesitated, his finger hovering above the button to summon the elevator. That hadn't occurred to him and certainly hadn't been the reason he'd suggested they go out. 'Does that bother you? We can always order in if you'd rather.'

'I don't mind the photos or the speculation.' She shrugged airily. '*Not* caring what others think is the other thing I'm learning from you.'

CHAPTER ELEVEN

SKYLAR TOSSED AND TURNED. It was well after midnight and she couldn't sleep a wink. She'd finally be seeing Zane again tomorrow—taking him on their next Helberg visit. Though secretly she wished it was Saturday tomorrow. Another date night. Last Saturday should have been enough. It wasn't. Even though it had bled into Sunday. She was losing sight of her goal, prioritising the pleasure he could give her instead. Maybe her father was right—lust led you from the path and into self-ishness. All the more reason to sate that lust, then, right? Because it would ease eventually, surely.

Her phone rang. She glanced at the caller ID and answered before thinking better of it.

'It's me.'

'Yeah.' She was glad he couldn't see the smile on her face. 'What do you want?'

'I was thinking about you.'

'So you decided to phone and wake me up?'

'You weren't asleep anyway. You answered too quickly and you sound wide-awake and breathless. Why are you breathless?'

She gritted her teeth to stop herself laughing. 'What were you thinking about me?'

'Everything and then some.'

She could hear *his* smile. 'Oh?'

'I've been thinking about some things we didn't cover the other night.'

'Oh?' she squeaked.

'I've bet you've never had phone sex either, huh,' he purred.

'Um—'

'Think about where you'd want me to touch you if I were there now,' he said softly.

She'd spent every night this week thinking about that. Which was why she was wide-awake now.

'Skylar?'

'Mmm-hmm?'

'Touch there,' he muttered.

Her toes curled. 'Zane…'

'I dare you.'

Heat burned through her because he hadn't needed to dare, she already was. 'What about you?'

'I'm already there. I've got myself in hand and every time you sigh, I stroke.'

'Oh…'

'Yeah…like that.'

'Ohh…' She dragged in a breath. 'Faster?'

'If you want—'

She wanted. So much. 'Tell me more,' she breathed.

He muttered. Low. Hot. Dirty.

'Ohh… I… *Zane*…' As she dragged in a deep breath of recovery, she heard his groan. She flushed with pleasure again.

'Want to hear some of my other ideas?' he drawled.

'I think you should write them down,' she whispered, broken yet burning all over again.

'Bullet points?'

'Yeah. Works for me.'

His laughter was low. 'See you tomorrow, Skylar. Sweet dreams.'

Her dreams were anything but sweet.

* * *

'We're going to one of the distribution warehouses in New Jersey.' She couldn't quite look him in the eye after that phone call last night. And she knew he knew it. He looked so amused. So smug.

'Let's go in my car,' he said. 'It's a long drive.'

'Yes,' she said primly. 'How ever will we fill the time?'

She shouldn't have been so transparent. Definitely shouldn't have blurred the boundaries between their meetings about the business and their dates. But it was too late. She watched him press the button to close the privacy screen the second they were both belted in the back of the car. Then he turned, leaning above her, retribution glinting in his eyes. 'You're a temptress, Skylar Bennet.'

She stared at him.

'You drive me crazy,' he muttered. 'Make me forget everything but what I want to do with you.'

That was the only balm on the burn searing through her—that he felt this intense drive to touch her every bit as much as she ached for it. 'And what's that?'

He kept her pinned in his gaze. She waited. His hand slid up her thigh and under the hem of her skirt. He wasn't even touching her skin to skin—hadn't slid those tormenting fingers beneath her panties. But the slow circles, the skating tips of his fingers were enough to pull her into the furnace… He wove the fingers of his other hand into her braid and kept her head tilted towards him. The smallest sinful smile curved his lips. She knew what he wanted. To watch her—this close—as he made her lose control with the gentlest, lightest of touches. Such torment. Because she knew his strength and she wanted all of him—full power. Her breathing shortened, she spread her legs, she tilted her chin. She wanted his kiss. She wanted him to lose control too, wanted him *with* her in this.

'Let go, beautiful. I'm here. I've got you,' he breathed. His blue eyes gleamed—provocative, possessive, protective. Giving her almost everything she wanted.

She sank, shuddering under the waves of bliss as they washed through her. Breathing out deeply, she looked back up into his eyes—saw the glint of satisfaction in his eyes, the strain of desire in the firm hold of his mouth.

She wanted more. Of course she wanted more. She could never concentrate now. Not on anything else until she'd made him feel the same.

The flicker of amusement in his face told her he knew. 'One, nil,' he smugly muttered.

'You're keeping a tally?' She rolled her eyes. 'Of course you're keeping a tally.'

This was all a game to him. It could be to her too, couldn't it? But with no rules at all now. The man did not play fair and there was nothing she couldn't try with him.

'What can I say, I like numbers.' He shrugged. 'You like them too. You know we have so much more in common than just our hometown. You're as competitive as I am. As focused. As driven.'

'You think?' She liked that he saw her as an equal. As a worthy competitor. She leaned across him.

He stiffened. 'What are you doing?'

She leaned a little lower. 'Evening the score.'

It took Zane for ever to realise that the car had stopped. Good thing the rear windows were tinted. Her 'evening the score' had felled him. He'd hauled her close to finally kiss her. Once he'd started, he couldn't stop. He'd kept kissing her and it had culminated in this—the complete loss of time, control, composure. Her crisp—so very HR—blouse was untucked and creased, most of the buttons undone. Her skin was flushed, her lips puffy. Her eyes were huge. Dishevelled and dazed, there was no hiding what she'd been doing. While he was just hot. So hot. And not just his shirt but his trousers were undone. He had the horrifying thought that his hunger for her was never going to end.

He pulled back from her and coughed. 'I don't think either of us are in any state to meet people.'

'No,' she agreed. 'We're just here to see property anyway. It's a site expansion.'

Zane ran his hand through his hair and tried to summon a speck of concentration. Property was Cade's interest. Whether this was the piece the guy was after, he didn't know.

'Why a blank site?' He glanced out the window. 'There's nothing here, Skylar. What are we doing?'

'It was metaphorical. I was hoping you can see the potential.'

He hated that this deal was between them. He wanted to forget about it so he could focus on seeing out this fling. Educating her in so many other ways.

'You can't, can you?' she said quietly. 'Because you're so stuck on the fact that the old boss didn't give you a scholarship? Hell, Zane. It wasn't like you needed it. You'd achieved more by the time you were twenty than he personally had.'

He could tell her the rest of his history with Reed. How truly life-changing his meeting with the man had been. How devastating. Maybe then she would understand. But he'd never told anyone all of that. Never discussed it even with his mother. And she'd been there. He didn't think he physically could. You kept your pain to yourself. You didn't complain.

'You really can't forgive and forget?' She waved at the bare plot. 'It could be a blank state. Start afresh. Rebuild it. You could do that. You could do anything.'

No, he couldn't. Not with this. 'It's going to happen anyway, Skylar. If not me then it'll be some other entity.'

Skylar was failing on several levels. To convince him. And to keep this 'arrangement' from sliding into something that meant more to her.

Maybe he was right about Helberg but she'd worked her whole life to get to where she was—and if she wasn't here, then…where? She'd been on this one path her whole life. Not daring to deviate from the plan put in place by her father so long ago. She didn't know what she was going to do going forward if it all ended—and she didn't like that uncertainty.

'You get out of HQ and come to empty plots of land quite often?' he asked her.

'I like getting about to see people on other sites. It makes me feel more connected to everyone within the company.'

'Because it's lonely in your office going from project to project?'

'I like people.'

'Yeah, I know all about how you help everyone, Bernie told me.'

'You don't think I should care about people, only profit?'

'Without profit, those people you like don't have jobs,' he said. 'That's the rapidly approaching possibility for half of Helberg's employees. Sure, some divisions are doing well, but some definitely aren't. Study the numbers, Skylar. I know you can see this.'

As much as she didn't want to admit it, parts were bloated and ineffectual. Divisions could be run better. Hell, she knew that better than anyone. She'd seen the senior management and their time wasting.

'Decent management might be able to turn it around,' she said obstinately.

'You don't think Reed Helberg was decent?'

'Do you really have no respect for him at all? He built a massive company. He did good in the community.'

'He *inherited* a successful company and proceeded to run it into the ground by focusing on expansion into luxury brands with little relevance to core business. He did limited charitable acts to buy praise and goodwill. To be seen as someone outstanding. But he was a selfish egotist. You know he was hardly in the office in recent years.'

She didn't want to admit that Zane might be right on that either. She'd hardly seen Reed in the office. She'd heard that in the last months he cantankerously called in with instructions and commands that sent shivers through the finance department.

'It's still worth having someone come in and try.' She drew in a breath. 'People have invested more than their time in Helberg. They've invested their money.' She tried to make him understand. 'The old employees share scheme encouraged them to invest—it was considered a sign of loyalty.'

He stilled. 'Did you invest?'

She shook her head. 'That scheme was closed to new employees a few years ago. But some of the long-timers did. Now the share price has dropped and those loans aren't repaid and...'

He inhaled deeply, cursed beneath his breath. 'Bernie?'

She nodded.

'Skylar,' he said quietly. 'Isn't that all the more reason to let someone come in and liquidate where necessary and lift the price of assets to the best possible?'

'People will lose their jobs.'

'People are made redundant every day. We'll do our best but the alternative is that it goes under completely and everyone loses their jobs.' He looked at her. 'You can't guarantee security, Skylar.'

Yeah. She knew that. She just didn't want to. And she still wished someone would try.

Zane drew a deep breath into his lungs, trying not to get distracted by her beauty again. But she came alive when she talked about her colleagues. She cared about those people passionately—her work family. And right now she made such a different picture to the wide-eyed girl he remembered silently watching the world from the top floor. The girl who'd all but crawled inside his shirt when he'd stolen a kiss from her.

He wanted another kiss now.

He liked to ensure his lovers were satisfied but his desire to satisfy *her* was on another level. He didn't just want her satisfied. He wanted her total surrender. He wanted her eyes glowing and her skin flushed and her as out of control as ever. With him. It was insane. Was it really just that interrupted kiss? That they'd not burned out their chemistry at the time, and her father's rejection had ignited another determination within him? Did he want Skylar this much because he'd been told in no uncertain terms that he couldn't have her?

But now he could. Was. Would some more. So he would get over it, right?

Because he had no intention of ever settling down. Of ever hurting a child the way he had been. Because he'd have no kids. Ever. No commitment.

He just needed to rid himself of this fixation on her. And he was sick of meeting her in offices or shops or seeing factory floors. Maybe he'd show her how spectacularly the division of assets could work in a company's favour.

'I've thought of my amendment to our arrangement,' he said huskily.

Her eyes widened.

'I don't want a date this Saturday.'

Her jaw dropped pleasingly.

'I want a whole weekend,' he added quickly. 'A long weekend. Away.'

'Where?'

'It's a surprise. But there's relevance to our business as well.'

He almost had her. Then he saw the shadows flitter in. 'I can't take time off work—'

'You worked on the last long weekend. I bet you have far

too many holidays accrued. We'll fly out Friday morning, fly back Monday night.'

He'd known she'd worry about work.

They'd have whole days and nights together. He would have his fill of her. He would get control of his own mind again. Dial it back for the duration of the time they'd be dating. Because this was only a game. That was all. And this weekend would be just the thing to get it back under control.

'Would it be public?'

'No.'

'That means several days with nothing on that website.'

'No problem. We've given them enough for now.'

She shook her head. 'I can't make those arrangements that quickly. I can't just abandon all my projects. I've got too much work to do.'

He understood and respected that even though his body rebelled. 'Then we'll have a quiet weekend this weekend so you can get ahead and clear the decks. We'll go the weekend after.'

She looked tempted. But also strangely wary. 'So we won't have a date this Saturday?'

'Are you worried you're missing out?' He felt a ridiculous warmth bloom in his chest.

'No, it would be convenient, actually. I'm just concerned about your ability to have a boring night at home all alone.'

'I guess I can manage it just this once.'

CHAPTER TWELVE

SHE WASN'T MISSING HIM. Nope. And she certainly was *not* feeling disappointed there was no date tonight. She was in a good space. She'd had a good week. Great, actually. She'd been working round the clock, getting reports written. Achieving with a capital *A*. She was still working even now. Some might call it a boring Saturday night at home but she was satisfied...

Yeah, right. Of course she wasn't. She was edgy. It took everything to keep herself on track and not check her phone every five minutes in case he'd messaged.

There'd been eight messages this week—for the record. Silly comments that made her smile. A stupid meme. A copy of the latest photo of them together, which, to her shame, she'd saved as her wallpaper. And yes, she knew this arrangement wasn't a relationship, but she couldn't help herself. She was staring at it when she realised someone was pushing her buzzer. And not releasing it.

'Let me in,' he growled the second she hit the intercom.

The big bad wolf himself. She listened to his rapid thudding feet as he ran up the stairs and inwardly marvelled at his fitness given the mauling his leg must have had to be so scored with surgical scars.

'I thought you didn't want a date this week.' But she held the door open for him.

And he held a bag that smelt delicious.

'Thai.' He put it on her table. 'I was betting you hadn't had dinner.'

She recognised the sticker on the brown bag. He'd found her favourite. Her mouth watered. Then she looked at him and her mouth watered more. There was stubble on his jaw, slight shadows beneath his eyes.

'You look tired,' she said softly. He looked fit for bed.

'I've been burning the candle to get some work done. Had to travel a bit.' He frowned. 'While you look fresh as a daisy.'

She didn't feel like a daisy. She felt like a firecracker—filled with wild, endless energy that couldn't get release without ignition. But the spark had arrived and that familiar fizzing inside had begun.

'Have you got your work done?' He opened the bags and lifted out a couple of containers.

'Pretty much.' She grabbed a couple of forks. 'At least, enough of it done to be able to get away.'

Oddly, his frown deepened. 'No problems concentrating?'

'I can block everything out when I need to.'

But now she realised she was famished. She reached for the first container instead of him. But he didn't take the fork she'd put on the table for him.

'You're not having any?'

'I already ate.'

She wasn't sorry—all the more for her. 'You chose well.' She licked her lips.

'Uh-huh.' A self-mocking smile curved his lips and then he groaned. 'I should probably—'

'Lie down on the bed,' she said.

His eyes widened.

'I mean, you barely fit in here,' she explained as if it was simple. But she couldn't hold back a playful smile. 'Lying down will probably be the most comfortable place for you in here.'

'Comfortable.' He released a low huff of laughter.

Good. She much preferred it when he smiled.

'I didn't come here for—'

'Yeah, you did,' she said. 'And I'm quite okay with it.'

He toed off his shoes and vaulted up there. She shimmied out of her shorts and tee.

He opened his arms and sighed as she worked her way up his body—loosening his clothes as she went.

'You like appreciation.' She trailed her fingertips across his skin. 'Thanks for dinner,' she breathed.

'You had three bites.'

'I'll have more later. I'm hungry for dessert now.'

Zane had fallen asleep mere moments after she'd ravished him. Stayed asleep for hours. The minx was a fast learner.

He'd wanted to make sure she'd had least had dinner. There was no actual kitchen in her place and he felt hungry at the mere thought of that, and yeah, he knew she ordered in, but he was also sure than sometimes she got too buried in her work to remember. So he'd brought some to her. Turned out *he'd* been the dinner. And he was not complaining.

He *was* surprisingly comfortable in her tiny space, even though, when he stretched right out, his feet hung off the end of her mattress. So he curled up, spooning her. He appreciated the underperforming air-conditioning unit even if it was noisy. It was a calm cocoon in the middle of the sleepless city. He'd been sleepless all week in his quiet, perfectly air-controlled palace.

'Where are you taking me this week?' he asked when she finally stirred as the dawn sun pierced the gap in the curtains. 'You haven't sent an email appointment for my calendar.'

She sighed. 'I don't think I'm going to take you anywhere this week.'

'No?' He shifted and rolled her onto her back so he could

see her face. 'You don't want me to meet some logistics operators? Some assistants on the shop floor at the grocery store?'

She shook her head a little glumly. 'I don't think there's much point.'

'You…' He was actually lost for words. She'd given up on trying to convince him to resuscitate Helberg? That meant he'd won. It didn't feel like it. Because he didn't want her to lose her fight.

Her mouth twisted. 'You're going to do whatever you're going to do. What I say isn't going to make a shred of difference.'

That was true, but it wasn't enough. He wanted to prove to her that his plans made good business sense. He wanted her to agree, to admit he was *right*—

His whole body went cold. 'What does this mean for our deal?'

If there was nothing in this for her any more, she might end it early.

She laughed bitterly. 'Nothing matters more than the bet.'

No, that wasn't it. He wanted the time with her. It couldn't be over yet. They had too much fuel still to burn through.

'I should leave you, so you lose the bet,' she said. 'But it seems I've caught some of your selfishness. My balance is off. You've pointed that out to me.' She looked right into his eyes. 'I still want to further my education with you.'

Immense relief hit. 'That isn't selfish. That's smart.'

Now her lashes lowered. 'I don't think I've been all that smart.'

'What? How so?'

'I've somehow sleepwalked into a life that I didn't plan.' She bowed her head. 'Dad died so unexpectedly.'

Zane swallowed. He didn't much like her father but he got that Skylar had adored him. 'What happened?'

'I was here but I went home most weekends. Worked on the

bus both ways so I could hang out with him. I was saving for a new place. I wanted him to have an actual house, you know? His own little bit of land. He wanted that too. Was still working three jobs. And one day, his heart…'

'I'm sorry, Skylar.'

'You know what it's like to lose your dad.'

He shook his head. 'I never had him to begin with.'

The man hadn't wanted to be tied down with the burden of an overactive kid. He'd left when Zane was three. His mother had struggled financially until she could get him into school.

'I think I was lost after he died…he'd been so…'

Authoritarian? Zane bit back his judgment of the man Skylar had loved. And obeyed to the letter.

'I didn't go home again after he'd gone. I couldn't. I buried my grief by being busy at work. I guess I transferred all that loyalty to Helberg…not Reed, the company. I needed to feel indispensable. But I think I also needed the structure it gave me. The familiar discipline and purpose. Rules, you know? Rules to keep you safe. Praise for performing. Doing an excellent job for everyone but myself.' She bowed her head. 'I'm really tragic.'

Zane didn't know what to say. The old man had been crazy protective and she was sweet and kind and obedient—but spirited beneath. She had a lot of spirit. She'd been stuck up on that balcony like some damned Rapunzel. And Zane hadn't been good enough to be anywhere near her.

Don't you dare…

She was loyal to her father. That was admirable, right?

'You're not tragic.' Zane sighed. 'Maybe he was afraid of losing you. Maybe that's why he held the reins he had on you so tightly. He'd lost his wife and he didn't want to lose you too.'

'He never would have lost me.'

'You'd never have fallen in love? Got married and moved towns?' Zane stilled inside, not wanting to hear her answer.

She never would have picked a lover over the wishes of her father.

The past shimmered between them. A moment that should have been nothing. That they should be able to laugh about now. But he couldn't even bring himself to mention it aloud.

'I would have stayed near. I would have done anything...'

Yeah. That old bitterness rippled through him. Even though part of him understood it. Totally. 'You were scared of losing him too. You clung to the things that worked for you both to make you feel secure. He was strict and you were studious. But you don't owe anyone anything now. You've got those savings from your hard work. Your *effort*. But maybe you were so busy putting all your effort into the work you didn't have the energy to explore your own hopes and dreams. Your needs. You do have needs, Skylar.'

Skylar pressed her cheek against her cool pillow. 'You mean I'm a repressed nympho.' She felt hot and prickly inside.

'You should have your own dreams. You should just do what you want, Skylar.'

The trouble was those 'needs' had only turned up the same time as he had. Just as they had when they were teenagers. Before she'd gone back to that boarding school and he'd gone to make it big in the city.

And they were worsening. She needed them to ease off and this conversation really wasn't helping. 'For someone who doesn't like relationships, you're quite the analyst.'

'I'm at a distance and able to observe more dispassionately, I guess.' He cleared his throat.

He was *definitely* at a distance. Deliberately. He kept secrets. Fair enough. She usually did too—by circumstance. There wasn't someone around who she'd talk this personal with. But he was easy to talk to. She'd just told him too much.

That pale blue of his eyes had all but disappeared now and she stared into the depths of his pupils.

'I just want to see you do whatever the hell *you* want,' he said gruffly.

That was how *he* lived. Doing what he wanted. With whomever he wanted.

She'd loved her father but he'd wanted her to be 'good'— by *his* definition. *Don't you dare*...run off and abandon all responsibility. Don't leave him in the lurch. Alone. Like her mother had left them both.

But he'd never encouraged her to be *brave*. He'd never given her alternatives to consider. It had been *his* way...and she'd never had the chance to figure out what she truly wanted to reach for.

She needed to—not just regarding her career, but her personal life as well. Because how she'd been living all these years wasn't enough. She'd lived so long with pressure to succeed, to please her dad, to please her bosses, her colleagues. Working all the hours. But that had been to avoid other parts of life. These last couple of weeks had shown her this, and she was hungry for a lot more. But she had only until Labour Day with Zane. She couldn't think beyond that. So for now, there was the one fantasy she could fulfil. 'I want this weekend away.'

CHAPTER THIRTEEN

JUST AFTER LUNCHTIME on Friday, Skylar passed Bernie on her way down the stairs. He noted her bag and the jacket she'd slung over her shoulder and smiled broadly.

'You're leaving early?' he asked.

For the first time ever. She smiled shyly as she nodded. 'Have a great weekend, Bernie.'

At the airport she drew a breath as Zane introduced her to the liveried crew lined up to greet them in the luxury private lounge. He joked with the pilots, who teased him right back— which made her curious.

'You travel with this crew often?' she asked as they boarded the plush ten-seater cabin, though they were the only passengers on board.

'Whenever I can. They're good. This private charter airline was a spin-off from a large acquisition I made a few years ago.' He took the seat opposite hers. 'They've tripled in size since then. Naturally they love me.'

'So this is your one asset-stripping success story.'

He shot her that smug look. 'One of many, Skylar.'

'You really believe in what you do?'

He cocked his head and a serious gleam entered his expression. 'Yeah, I do. Nothing lasts for ever. Companies come and go—fortune smiles on them one year, then a storm hits. Being able to adapt is a skill not all CEOs have. They don't see the squall coming, they can't course-correct quickly enough.'

'So you lighten their load so they can move faster again?'

'And be agile, yes.'

As much as it galled, she actually believed him. She'd done what he'd told her to the other day. She'd looked at the numbers. Closely. And he was right. She just hadn't wanted to see what it really meant. And even now she still hoped that a massive overhaul wouldn't mean total destruction.

She'd not wanted to think of Zane as a good guy in any way, but that was because of her pride, wasn't it? She'd let their past cloud her judgment of his business practice. She'd disliked his successes—in every arena. Hell, maybe she was jealous. But he was successful for a reason. Some companies actually welcomed his interest—*wanted* him to come in and tell them how to streamline and refocus their businesses.

And if she were honest with herself, it wasn't that galling any more.

She went for an unsubtle subject change. 'How long is the flight?'

He stretched back in his seat and shot her a come-hither look. 'Long enough to give you a very in-depth lesson on the pleasures of the Mile High Club.'

'Does a private jet even count?' she challenged huskily.

'Why, Skylar.' He smirked. 'Do you want the thrill of the crowds on commercial? Are you a closet exhibitionist?'

Apparently she was many things around him. Mostly, she was free—to say what she really thought and do what she really wanted. Because he didn't really care what she thought of him, right? He played up to her little sledges of him but underneath he didn't give a damn. He was purely himself. Although to be fair, she had to admit he was a good listener. She'd talked too much lately but he'd been quietly supportive. And he'd listened to her all those years ago when her mother had left and she'd been sad.

He'd not said anything then either. Just silently offered a

few moments of companionship. And a little something sweet as distraction.

He could be kind, in a quiet, understated way. But that silence was also frustrating.

Yet she could ask him for things without worry. He'd tease her about it, but he'd deliver. She knew if she ever asked him to screw her on board a plane alongside hundreds of other passengers, he would. With flair. And yes, that thought had her hot.

There were no 'set lessons' in bed with him. No plan. There was just exploration, discovery, and every experience she had with him was different. And delightful.

On paper, this ought to be the perfect 'benefits' arrangement. She should just keep on enjoying it. Trouble was, it was a little *too* perfect. She was enjoying it all a little *too* much. And he'd made her realise all that she *had* been missing out on. It was a lot—and she wondered what more there was. But in a matter of weeks, this game would be over. Her skin chilled. She gritted her teeth—halting the discomforting direction of her thoughts. She had to forget the future. She had to make the most of it now.

'When does the lesson begin, before or after take-off?' she asked.

'You know it's already started.'

Their plane landed an hour before sundown. A waiting car took them to a stunning villa situated right on a beach. Private and spacious, it showcased stunning views of wide blue skies. Skylar gazed in awe at the powdery pale pink beach and the teal water. It was so transparent that she could see shells and fish and singular grains of that gorgeous sand. The air was balmy and evocative.

'Want to shower and change, then food?' he murmured.

'Yes.'

The bedroom had crisp white linen, an oversize soaking

tub and yet more of those stunning views. She stepped into the dress she'd bought specially during the lunch break she'd actually taken two days ago. The floral organza had a deep vee neckline and fitted bodice that then flared into a floor-length skirt, which had a thigh-high split. She didn't bother with shoes. She was relaxed and hedonistic and living in this moment. Only this moment. Because it was the sexiest of summer nights.

She found Zane down by the water's edge, trousers rolled up and paddling in the shallows. He watched as she walked across the powdery sand to meet him and she felt a hot pride when she saw the colour run beneath his skin.

'Nice dress,' he muttered. 'Nice earrings.'

'I made a little effort.' She hitched her skirt and flashed the tiny silk briefs that were the exact shade of the dress.

His eyes actually glazed over. 'And I very much appreciate...'

She paused a couple of feet away, watching him with a coy smile. 'Are you speechless?'

He just lunged for her.

It was another hour before they got to the charcuterie board the discreet staff had left for them. Afterwards, Skylar lay in his arms and listened to the water and let him take her to the stars. Again.

'Come on, Sleeping Beauty.'

'What?' Skylar rolled onto her side with a moan that deepened into a complete groan when she saw he was fully dressed and standing beside the bed with his hands behind his back. '*Why* are you waking me so early?'

'Because it's Saturday morning, and don't you run three miles every Saturday morning?'

She blinked at him. 'What?'

'There's a group run. Local park. Not far from here.'

Her pulse picked up. 'But I didn't bring my gear.'

He pulled a hand from behind his back and showed her a shoe box. Her brand. Her size.

She gaped at him. 'How did you—'

He whipped out his other hand, dangling a large bag. 'I've got shorts, tee, socks as well.'

'You saw my size at my apartment?'

He shook both box and bag. 'Come on, you don't want to miss it seeing I've gone to all this *effort*.'

He was teasing but this *was* a big effort.

'You have a really big brain, don't you? Big memory.' She took the purchases from him.

'Well, I wasn't sure about underwear.'

'I can make it work.' She chuckled and took the shoes from the box. 'Are you going to run too?'

'Absolutely not.' He turned. 'I'll go find you some electrolytes for after.'

She smiled as she pulled out the shorts and tank he'd got her. He'd even noticed her passion for neon colours.

She hesitated. 'Why did you do this?'

'Because you haven't missed a run in more than two years and I'm not being the reason for you to break your Saturday-morning streak.'

She stared at him, somewhat taken aback.

'I don't want to stand in the way of things that are important to you. Running is important to you.'

Warmth bloomed in her chest. 'You realise I'm not fast or anything. Like not at all. To be honest I only started running because it was the one way I could get dad to let me out. I took my time—went slow and enjoyed the outdoors.'

His expression turned tender.

'But I'm still slow,' she whispered, a little embarrassed. 'Like, seriously middle to the back of the pack.'

'Thank goodness.' He huffed out an exaggerated sigh of

relief. 'It was getting stressful, you being excellent in every bloody thing you do. No way I can compete.'

'Please.' She chuckled at that. '*You* excel at everything.'

He was a natural genius. She'd had to work so hard to get grades half as good as his. But he'd had to work hard too— to overcome his injuries and rebuild his physical strength. So in that they were similar—determined, driven, disciplined.

He winked at her. 'Why, thank you.'

'Ugh.' She gave him a playful shove. 'You were fishing for compliments.'

'And you delivered. Beautifully.' He pressed a quick kiss to her pouting mouth. 'Get ready.'

Zane couldn't wipe the smile from his face as he watched Skylar join the throng of people similarly clad in brightly co-loured, dry-wicking tops and shorts. Her smile was infectious, all full-dimpled delight. The couple standing near her smiled back. In seconds she was engaged in conversation, her head cocked as she listened and nodded. She might feel awkward but she was interested in others. She was nice. Curious. Kind.

He'd not considered that watching her run would be arous-ing. But she was beautiful with her ponytail streaming out behind her, colour in her cheeks and a wide smile on her face as she pushed for a sprint finish alongside some random sep-tuagenarian—totally in her happy place. Zane gripped her water bottle. His chest felt tight, as if he were the one who'd been running—a marathon or more.

She crossed the line smack bang in the middle of the pack— tying with the old guy—just as she'd predicted, but he couldn't help clapping and cheering as if she'd just won Boston. She waved bye to the couple she'd chatted with at the start line, then wove her way through the milling crowd to him. He scooped her into his arms and kissed her.

'I'm all sweaty.' She wriggled in embarrassment but he didn't release her.

'Yeah.' He didn't care. But he stepped back and pulled a couple wrapped pieces of candy from his pocket and offered them to her. 'Raspberry or lemon?'

She looked at the candy in his palm and then up into his eyes. He knew she was remembering that moment in the stairwell so long ago. He was too. And he thought he knew which she'd pick.

'Raspberry.'

Right. The real favourite. Satisfaction and sweet, steamy memory swept over him. 'We'd barely spoken before that afternoon and you just melted in my arms,' he muttered. He'd never forgotten it.

Skylar rocked onto her toes in her new trainers. She'd not expected him to mention that. Certainly not now. But she wanted to hear what he had to say about it.

'You were so beautiful,' he added. 'So hot.'

'So were you.' But then she remembered how badly that moment had ended. She ought to say something now. Apologise for not saying anything then. Her father had been so awful. But before she could say more, he slung his arm around her waist and squeezed.

'Let's go back to the hotel and I'll give you a rub down.'

'Now, there's an offer,' she breathed, both aroused and disappointed.

She wanted to talk about that moment with him. She wanted to work it through. But now he had that charmingly wicked smile on his face and she put that raspberry candy into her mouth. Because *he* didn't open up—that was how he rolled.

'There'll be pancakes, strawberries and cream too,' he drawled. 'And coffee.'

'Stop it.' She pouted at him. 'Or I'll end up falling in like with you.'

He laughed. 'An arrogant prat like me? Impossible.'

But Skylar almost choked on the last of her candy. Because she did like him. She actually, truly did. She wasn't supposed to. The fact that she *didn't* like him was what was meant to have protected her. Because this only about sex. About getting him out of her system for good so she could move forward and be more…normal. Maybe meet another man. But now *that* prospect was horrifying. She didn't *want* anyone else. She never had.

But this was nothing more than a *game* to Zane. He didn't want a relationship. He indulged only in fun *physical* intimacy—he'd been with a heap of women in the past. And she knew it was never emotional. Because he didn't open up. Sure, he'd listened to her prattle on about her past some, offered the smallest of responses. But then he redirected. Hell, he hadn't even mentioned the total bawling out her father had given them both that day just now. Which bothered her so much but she didn't know what to do about it.

Flustered by her inner chaos, she opted for redirection herself. 'What I *really* like is the beach.'

'Then let's go.'

'You want to go on the water?' he called as she walked over the beautiful sand in a scarlet bikini more than an hour later. 'I'll paddle. You'll be tired from your run. You can spot the fish.'

He'd prepped a two-seater ocean kayak with snorkels, masks and flippers on board, plus a stash of water and snacks. As excited as a kid on her first-ever outdoor experience, she scrambled into the front seat and eagerly pointed out all the pretty fish and coral she spotted.

'You didn't do this much even though we grew up near one of the best beaches in the country, did you?' he teased.

'You didn't either,' she pointed out—pausing to see if he'd talk more about back then.

But he just pointed out a turtle she'd missed.

An hour passed as he paddled them along the reef and from cove to cove. Warmed by the sun and tempted by the sea, she precariously clambered upright and dived into the water to cool off. Getting back on board wasn't quite as easy for her to manage. He watched, laughing at her, until in the end he hauled her back with one strong pull. Then he turned the kayak back towards their beach. She saw the sun had passed its zenith. Time was slipping by too quickly. She carried the snorkels and watched him haul the kayak beyond the waterline ahead of her.

'You're bleeding.' She dropped the gear and grabbed his hand.

'It's nothing.' He tried to curl his hand into a fist. 'Just a blister. Go ahead and tease me about having soft hands not used to real hard work.'

But Skylar held his hand in both of hers and forensically inspected it. It wasn't a blister but a deep cut on the inside of his thumb.

'Why didn't you say something?' She fetched a towel and pressed it against the wound. 'You're really hurt.' She lifted the towel but the gash immediately refilled with blood. 'You should have told me. I would have helped.'

'I didn't need your help. Besides, you were enjoying yourself—'

'At your expense—'

'It's not that bad.' He laughed. 'Just a scratch.'

'It's not a scratch, you're *bleeding*.' She applied more pressure on the wound and glared as he winced. 'You know I would have helped if you'd asked. You didn't have to suffer in silence.'

His smile faded. 'Are you seriously mad with me about this?'

'You hold back. *Everything.*'

'What?' His eyebrows shot up. 'You cannot accuse me of holding back in bed.'

'I mean your feelings.'

He stiffened. 'I don't—'

'Have feelings? Right. You're a robot. Who bleeds. You could talk to me, you know. About anything. I wouldn't mind. But you won't. You can't even express a little literal pain to me, let alone anything actually—' She broke off as she registered his shuttered expression.

She'd gone off. And now she was mortified. She stalked up the beach to the villa, fossicked for a sticking plaster in the small first-aid kit she always had in her pack, then turned back to find him right behind her. She handed the plaster to him.

'I won't offer to put it on for you,' she said. 'Heaven forbid you let someone tend to your wounds.'

He took the plaster meekly. 'Thank you.'

She watched him ruin one plaster. Handed him another. Watched him ruin that one too. Which gave her time to think. To realise her mistake. He didn't talk to her about anything deeply private because he didn't *want* to. Because, as she well knew, this wasn't a relationship. It was an arrangement. And while she might've spoken to him about stuff, that didn't mean he then had to do the same. Talking had been her choice. *Not* talking was his. She had to respect that.

'You do it,' he said gruffly when she tried to hand him a fourth plaster. 'It's too awkward a position for me to manage.'

He sat on the edge of the bed and she knelt to wrap the plaster around his thumb with quick, matter-of-fact ease.

He cleared his throat. 'You think I'm…'

'I think you're okay,' she said softly. Biggest understatement ever. 'I think you're kind. And I think…' She trailed off and shook her head. 'It doesn't really matter what I think.'

Zane gazed down at her. Speechless. Because what she thought did matter to him. And that realisation made him motionless as well as speechless. It shouldn't matter. Until this second, he would've argued it didn't…but it really did. This wasn't like their flirt-tipped verbal swordplay. Or a caustic analysis of their differing views on Helberg. This challenge went deeper.

She was bothered by his silence. And that bothered him.

That first night in his orchard, he hadn't much cared at all—he'd thought it had been his chance to assuage their out-of-control chemistry. And that chance had been extended. He still didn't really *care* though, right? But he was *concerned*.

Surely not saying anything about a stupid small cut that he'd barely noticed was a problem? He'd wanted her to have a good time out there on the reef. Hell, he'd been having a good time. Even with that little bit of pain—it was a little price to pay for the pleasure of seeing her entranced by the sea life.

But now that nothing of a wound throbbed like his thumb had been sliced off completely. Worse, an ache pressed inside him and he couldn't pinpoint the source. He'd put up with physical pain in his leg for years but this was different. He needed to soothe it. Soothe them both. *Silence* them both.

Because talking was pointless. It was action that mattered. Always.

He cupped her face and held her so she couldn't slip away from him and kissed her gently. Then a little less gently, and he leaned back so he could watch that smoky surrender enter her eyes. Then he kissed her everywhere.

And said nothing.

CHAPTER FOURTEEN

SKYLAR STRETCHED OUT her warm, achy muscles. It had been
another magical night of tease and sensuality… She blinked
drowsily and realised the morning was only *almost* perfect.
Zane wasn't lying beside her. She sat up. He was probably taking an early-morning swim. Which was fine. A little space
was probably good.

Relax and enjoy it.

But her nerves were brittle and she suddenly felt a wave
of warning. She tried to push the panic away—not ruin this
moment by panicking about everything ending. Labour Day
was a while away and she was here *now*, she could settle for
this. It was already more than she'd ever had.

She got out of bed and shrugged on a silk robe. Glancing
out the window, she saw he wasn't in the pool. She wandered
from the bedroom into the lounge to check the beach view.
That's when she registered the softly playing music. She followed the sound—upstairs. Once she hit the second floor she
stopped at the open door, unable to believe her eyes. There
were tall windows with even more expansive views over that
amazing teal water, but Skylar's attention was completely absorbed by Zane. Wearing only boxers, he was seated at a sleek
piano. She watched the muscles rippling across his back as
he played. Still and silent, she listened until the last note had
faded. And when it had? That's when she lost it.

'Are you *kidding* me?' She stalked towards him. 'Of all the—'

'What?' Startled, he spun and lifted his hands like she was pointing a gun at him. 'Did I wake you? I was playing softly. I didn't think you'd be able to hear from the bed.'

She walked towards him. 'I can't believe *you* were really playing that.'

'Who else would it have been?' He grinned.

'A paid professional?' she muttered. 'Like you're not already...'

'Already what?'

'Attractive enough. Gorgeous face. Fit body. Successful.'

His eyes widened. But he joked, 'Don't forget outrageously wealthy.'

'Right, should have put that first. Let's not forget wickedly amusing...a foil to mask the moodiness of a lost soul.'

'Just irresistible, right?'

'Right. And now you're a ridiculously talented musician as well.' She shook her head. 'I think I hate you.'

'You think? You're not sure? You were definite before. So that's definitely progress.'

She shook her head. 'You don't want me to like you.'

'Touché.' He smiled, almost contrite. 'Didn't you notice the music room in my penthouse?'

'I don't think we've made it into your music room.'

'Right.' He chuckled again. 'Another lesson.'

'Seriously.' She was so grumpy with him. 'Is there *nothing* you can't do?'

He pulled a wry face. 'Express my feelings, apparently.'

She sighed and walked towards him. 'I shouldn't have said all that yesterday. I was just tired. You don't have to share anything if you don't want to. Not to me. Or anyone. Or anything.'

'We're spending a lot of time together,' he said slowly. 'I guess it's inevitable we'd be curious about more than...'

'What turns each other on,' she said.

She followed his gaze down to his hands. The plaster on

his thumb was still in place. Obviously no hindrance to his performance.

'I've been playing since I was a kid,' he said.

She shook her head. 'I call BS. We lived in the same apartment building for years. Was there even room for a piano in your place? *Surely* I would've heard you practice.'

'Not when I had an old second-hand electronic keyboard and tinny headphones. No one else heard anything.'

Her heart twisted. If she didn't know this, then she didn't really know him at all. 'But when did you have *time*? You were so busy getting strong again. Then doing all your online trading things all while acing your studies... How is it possible that you got so good at this?'

He half swivelled back to the piano and played an arpeggio with one hand. 'When my leg ached I'd go through my scales.'

'Distraction?' She perched on the piano stool next to him, unable to resist the need to be nearer to him. To touch.

'Discipline. It kept me focused. My leg hurt all the time. I had several operations through my teens. Eventually it became like a meditation. A place to go to when I needed respite from everything else that was going on.'

She paused, processing all that. It was about the most he'd ever told her about his life. But one thing leapt out at her. 'So you need respite now?'

He hesitated. 'I guess.' He pressed down the keys. 'I couldn't sleep.'

Skylar made herself stay silent. If he wanted her to know *why* he'd been unable to rest, he would tell her. She wasn't going to ask. But it killed her not to.

He nudged her shoulder with his. 'I can see you holding back your questions.'

She smiled and opted for an easy one. 'Please don't tell me you composed that piece.'

He laughed. 'No, that was Debussy.' He glanced at her. 'French composer.'

'I know who Debussy was.'

'Yeah. Of course you do. Brains as well as beauty.'

Not *so* clever. Stupid actually. Stupidly falling for the man she'd once thought she hated. The crush who'd crushed her. The one she couldn't physically resist. And when his stupid bet was over, he would destroy the one constant she had left in her life. Her job. The one she wasn't sure she even wanted any more. He would walk out of her life. And she wouldn't know what to do with herself. She didn't know what to do with herself right now. But she knew for sure he had a soul. No one who could play like that didn't.

'You worked so hard. It really matters to you, doesn't it?' he said quietly.

'Helberg changed my life.' And she wasn't sure it had been for the better any more. But she'd never dreamed a different route. She'd promised her father she'd follow the path he'd outlined—to a better life, right? And if she didn't, she'd end up alone. Only that's where she was anyway, for all her loyalty and duty.

'Yeah,' he muttered. 'He changed mine too.'

Glancing up, she saw bleakness in his eyes. 'Zane—'

'I want you to understand,' he interrupted her before she told him he didn't have to tell her anything. He knew he didn't have to tell her but right now it mattered that she not think him completely shallow and pettily vindictive. He needed her to know. He couldn't hold it down any more.

'You know I went for one of his scholarships. I imagine the process didn't change over the years—you would have had an interview with the great man himself too, right?'

She nodded. 'I was so nervous.'

'Because you'd been told it was such a life-changing opportunity.'

'Yes.' She stared at him.

'I was too young to really appreciate that. Too self-involved. I just wanted to read the things that interested me. I didn't have anything to say to that blustery man and I didn't care. So I came across as a sullen smart-ass.'

'Surely he would have seen through that—'

'Perhaps. But he wanted performers. Articulate and polite and full of adulation. *Don't you know how to smile, boy?* He just wanted someone who'd smile when he was told to, who'd make Reed Helberg look good.'

'How old were you?'

'Eleven.'

Her eyes widened. 'That's so much younger than—' She took a breath. 'I was fifteen when I got a scholarship to that boarding school.'

'They took you on a tour to get your hopes up, right?'

'Yeah. It was huge. All those playing fields and…' Something dawned in her eyes. 'You didn't want to go,' she guessed softly. 'You didn't *want* to win it.'

Yeah, he'd always known she was smart.

'Leave the beach? Home?' He shook his head. 'And I saw those other boys there. I think you'd call them arrogant prats. Entitled and lacking in empathy.'

'Not all of them were like that. At least not all the time.'

'Right. Because you made so many friends there?'

She stared at him. 'Okay, I'll admit Danielle's about the only one.'

'Yeah.' He played another chord. 'Reed's rejection was instant and brutal, and on the long drive home my mother grew increasingly upset.'

'She must've been disappointed for you.'

Zane stopped playing for a moment while he pushed back the pain he'd long tried to hold down. He didn't want to tell her this, but nor did he want her thinking it was only out of shallow spitefulness that he wanted Helberg. It cut so much deeper than money.

'I didn't understand how much she wanted me to go away to that school.' He cleared his throat. 'I was too much, I guess. A scamp of a small boy. In trouble when I was bored—which was all the time in school. The teachers accelerated me but I was still a problem. She didn't have the energy to cope with me.'

He'd been too young to understand just how hard she worked. How tired she must have been dealing with him. Because he hadn't been easy. 'She was in tears. And she lost it. She shouted at me for...' *Everything*. He swallowed. 'She missed the traffic light.'

'That was when you had the accident? On your way back?'

He'd taken the brunt—pinned in the car while his mother had been able walk free. And then everything was worse. So much worse. 'I became even more of a burden.'

Medical bills. Constant hospital appointments. And no fancy boarding school to give her any respite from him.

'Zane—'

'I'd failed.' So he'd never failed again. He didn't lose. Ever. He worked and worked and worked until he won. Once he'd decided on a target, that was it. 'She was upset because of me. Distracted because of me. If I hadn't failed that interview, it wouldn't have happened. The accident was—'

'An *accident*,' Skylar said firmly. 'If anything, your mother could have taken a moment to calm down before driving.'

'We had to get home quickly because she had to get to work. It wasn't her fault.'

'Okay,' Skylar said. 'But it certainly wasn't yours either.'

He shook his head. He'd never forgotten his mother's distress. He'd never wanted to make her—or anyone—that upset again. Not with his failings. Or his demands.

'My grandfather came and stayed briefly. He told me I needed to keep it together. Not bother her. She already had to work hard enough and now there were my medical bills on top of everything. I had to be strong.'

'What about your father? Did he ever help?'

Zane looked at her. 'My mere existence was too much for him. He cleared off when I was three.'

He'd worked hard. He'd absorbed the pain. Learned to be quiet about it. Then worked to get stronger. He'd suppressed everything—including his own emotion—to protect his mother because he knew he'd let her down. He'd cost her the freedom that scholarship would have given her. And he'd learned to damn well smile and mask it all. *Without* Helberg.

'I smiled and acted like nothing ever touched me. Nothing ever bothered me. Nothing ever *hurt*. I can hide hurt, Skylar.' It had become habit.

'Yes.' She looked troubled. Almost guilty.

That moment in the stairwell just after her father had found them flashed before him. When she'd stood silently, letting him take the blame. Letting him be verbally abused. Not speaking up.

He'd hidden his hurt then too. Because he *had* been hurt. The best moment of his life till then had turned atrocious in seconds. He pushed it away and pivoted to what should have been his main point all along.

'I never forgot, never *forgave* Reed Helberg. He made a snap judgment and didn't change his mind about me no matter what I did from then on. I know his opinion shouldn't matter yet it always did.' Zane had channelled his anger towards Helberg. It had been easiest to. 'No one person should have that much power over some kid's life. Why choose just *one* lucky recipient? Why change only one student's life?' The man had been so damned wealthy—until he'd begun to run his company into the ground with a series of bad choices. 'What about all the others? Why not lift the performance of the whole damn school instead of scooping out that one stellar student and sending them somewhere supposedly better.'

Skylar stared at his hands. 'You're the anonymous donor behind the new gym at our old school.'

He shot her surprised look. 'You know there's a new gym?'

'I'm still on the email list for the newsletter.'

'Of course you are.' He blinked.

'What about the new science lab?'

'That too,' he mumbled. 'And the music room.'

'Anything else? A library?'

'A physical rehab centre at the health clinic in town,' he muttered. 'For kids and people who need to rebuild strength after accidents like mine.'

'And that's anonymous too?'

He had to drop his gaze from hers. 'I call in there sometimes. But I don't want my name over anything. It's not about me.'

'So you make out like everything's a bit of a joke. That you don't care. But you donate to all those charity things. Just not publicly.'

'I don't want people to come to me so desperate for my support that they'll do almost anything I want.' A ripple of guilt went down his spine.

'You don't let anyone get that close,' she said softly. 'You've never trusted anyone with the truth of how you actually feel. You didn't take comfort from your family.'

'I didn't need comfort,' he said. 'I could take care of myself.'

'*Everyone* needs comfort.'

'No, they don't.'

'Right, that's why you support a rehab clinic for kids. Why you go visit them and encourage them. Because they don't need comfort.'

'That's different.'

'Why? Because they're not as tough as you? Not as capable?'

'They're far braver than I ever was.'

'Yet you say you didn't need comfort.'

He rolled his shoulders. 'Don't, Skylar.'

'I'm not judging you, Zane.'

'No?'

'No.' She sighed. 'We all do our best, but we all screw up sometimes. And most of us admit we need help sometimes. But not you. You won't ever stop or ask for help. Or take a step back and say, *I'm tired.*'

'I'm tired.' He paused. 'Of this conversation.'

He didn't know why he'd thought it would be a good idea to start this. Why it would help in any way at all. Because now she was looking at him with soft sadness in her eyes and he did not want her pity. He didn't want her feeling *that* for him.

'Where's your mother now?' she asked.

'Florida. Fiercely independent. Won't retire even though I bought her a condo and made arrangements. She cancelled them. She doesn't touch the account I opened for her.'

He wanted to take care of her and she wouldn't let him and it rubbed everything that was raw inside and now he *really* regretted saying everything he had in the last half hour.

'Maybe she feels like she doesn't deserve your help because of what happened.'

'*I* caused that crash.'

'It was an *accident.*'

'*Stop.*'

'You're invoking your safe word when we're just talking?'

Yeah. Because he didn't talk. He shouldn't have said any of this to her.

'So you do everything good quietly. And everything wicked with a smile.'

'I make the tiniest of differences,' he growled. 'And I'm no saint. I bought the house of my dreams on the beach that I love and I have my Manhattan penthouse with a spectacular view. And you know I like my personal pleasures too.' He drew in a sharp breath. 'Money and power corrupts. Who's to say it hasn't corrupted me?'

'Because you know what it is to be desperate and you wouldn't take advantage of anyone in that state.'

'No?' He looked at her bitterly. 'Wouldn't I take advantage of someone desperately wanting to convince me to do something about something they cared about?'

'You haven't taken advantage of *me*.' She looked put out.

'I'm not so sure about that.'

He'd been pleased to find her literally caught in his orchard and needing his help. He'd been pleased that she couldn't get away. For a moment there, he'd even toyed with the fanciful idea of not helping her, so she'd be trapped in his garden for always. Because that old chemistry had flared. And then he'd used that stupid bet—all but engineered her loyalty to the company to spend more time with him. Because she'd always been in the back of his mind. The one he couldn't have. The one he wanted more than any other. And he didn't know what he felt worse about—engineering their fling, or the fact that he *still* wanted her so badly.

'*I'm* the one who pushed for us to sleep together again,' she said. 'I asked. I took. Don't act as if it were all your idea.'

Yeah, but she just wanted some 'experience.' He'd not been good enough for her back then. He'd been a *distraction*. Maybe that's all he was now too. Because even more important to her was her desire to save Helberg. Once this bet was done, she'd continue with her workaholic ways without him. The thought of all that reality bit hard. *Unsatisfied*. He was still *so* unsatisfied.

'Kiss me then,' he muttered gruffly. 'If that's what you want.'

She lifted his hand from the keys and pressed her lips to that raw spot on the inside of his thumb. The small thing that still hurt.

Her touch was too gentle and it wasn't enough. He was still greedy. He slipped his hands around her and drew her onto his lap. He would take this now. Only now.

And then they would be done.

CHAPTER FIFTEEN

ZANE'S MOOD DROPPED like a stone when he realised it was early and he was alone. They were flying back to Manhattan tonight and he really didn't want to have woken alone at this hour. They'd spent most of yesterday in bed after that time at the piano. It still hadn't been enough. And now she was gone. He went hunting for her. Found her in the lounge. She'd positioned a wide armchair to catch the first rays of the sun.

'You're working?' He checked his stride when he saw her laptop. 'I thought you'd got everything done before we left.'

He hadn't realised she'd brought her computer. Admittedly he'd brought his but he hadn't opened it. Hell, he hadn't *remembered* he had it till now. But here she was, up at stupid o'clock working—mentally back in Manhattan already, and was he actually feeling jealous that her attention was elsewhere?

He gritted his teeth at the bitter irony. Usually he was the one too busy to be sociable over breakfast—the one avoiding extended intimacy with a conveniently timed meeting. But not now. Now he wanted her back in his bed. Warm and willing and fully focused on him.

'I'm just doing a favour for Avery,' she muttered. Her gaze remained trained on the screen in front of her.

Zane was the one who didn't get distracted—he didn't prioritise a lover over work, but today *Skylar* wasn't. Because work was totally her priority. As it should be his.

They clearly felt differently. Hell, he actually *felt*—and not good. The realisation that she wasn't as into this thing between them as he was, was sharply—what? Painful? Suddenly he was pissed on several levels.

'She's in logistics,' Skylar added, oblivious to the tornado brewing inside him. 'Such a sweetheart. One of her kids is really into distance running. Way faster than me.'

His overly possessive outrage worsened. Of course she knew all this about the woman and her family—she was gently curious and she remembered everything. That one-to-one kindness of hers was genuine. But it was also universal. Belatedly he bitterly realised that her listening to him yesterday morning hadn't been anything special to *her*—she did that for *all* of her work associates. But for him it had been decidedly unique.

He felt exposed. And even though he'd told her all he had about Helberg, she still wanted that damned company to be rescued. She was doing work for the bloody thing right now and he knew it was irrational of him to be angry about that, but he was. And dealing with it, he *wasn't*.

His old pain hadn't affected her view of the company at all. Because she still cared about all the people she worked with. *They* mattered to her more than anything *he'd* shared with her. And that was fair enough. He was nothing more than a deal to her.

Except he was bothered. Badly.

And nothing soothed it this time. Not the swim he had with her when she'd finally finished. Not the leisurely lunch they shared. Not the last few hours they'd spent in that magnificent bed—he'd carried her there, determined to have her attention solely on him. And he'd succeeded.

Only then he realised the extent of his mistake.

He didn't do this. He didn't spend night after night with one woman and certainly didn't go on holiday with her. He didn't laze about, talking of too much that was too private. He'd never let anyone get to him like this—God, didn't it serve him right to be finally interested in a woman only to find she wasn't really interested in him.

But she was beneath his skin—and there was part of him wanting her to *stay*. His heart pounded. He couldn't let her get any deeper.

The fact was they were *never* going to agree on what ought to be done with Helberg. Nothing had changed there. Nor would it. So this whole game they had going—and it *was*, he reminded himself, a game—was pointless. No point in continuing the arrangement. Because he was angry. And uncomfortable—he'd told her too much.

The demise of Helberg would devastate her. There was no disentangling how this whole mess had begun. He'd wanted her—now he'd had her he wanted more. But she just wanted to protect Helberg, and getting some sexual experience had merely been a bonus on the side.

So this whole situation was only going to worsen in every way.

There was only one option left to him. And he couldn't get back to Manhattan quickly enough.

Bitterly—weakly—he stalled until the last few minutes when his driver was en route to her tiny apartment.

'You're free of any obligation to me, the deal's off,' he said quietly.

She twisted in her seat. Her expression confused. 'What does that mean?'

'You don't need to be my date any more. It's not necessary.'

Her eyes widened. 'Has something happened with Helberg? Someone else made an offer?'

Right. Of course her first thought was about the company. Not him.

He shook his head. 'I've reconsidered my position,' he said coolly. 'I can just stop dating for the rest of the time and still win Helberg. As long as I'm not seen with another date then I'm still in it.'

He didn't know what he was going to do about the stupid bet. Right now he just needed space from her.

'You don't want to go on any more dates with me?'

Bingo. 'It's not fair of me to hold you to the bargain when you've already conceded.'

Skylar could hardly hear over the thundering of her pulse in her ears but it sounded a lot like he was ending their deal early. Way too early. She needlessly fiddled with her bag, needing a reason not to look into his eyes. 'How noble of you to want to play fair.'

She'd known it would end but she'd thought she had a few more weeks. Labour Day, right?

'I don't want to hurt—'

'You haven't,' she interrupted him quickly. 'This was always a temporary thing.'

'I know,' he clipped. 'I meant about dismantling Helberg. I can't change my view on what needs to be done there.'

'Right. Of course.' She released a tight breath. 'To be honest, I knew that.'

He hadn't changed. But to her horror, she realised *she* had. Not in regard to Helberg—in regard to *him*. She didn't want this fling to end early. Because spending all this time with him—getting to know him properly, beyond the chemistry that had blinded her for so long—had changed her.

She hadn't known that terrible accident had occurred right after his awful scholarship interview. That he'd been so young, a wary, too-intelligent boy who hadn't wanted to leave his home. A boy who'd already been rejected by his own father and who then realised that his mother too didn't seem to want him around. Skylar knew how deep, how irrevocable that kind of hurt was. To have a parent who wasn't interested. Who left.

No wonder he'd blamed Reed Helberg—because it was far

easier to hate him for it all than to put it on his parents, who she knew he still loved.

She totally understood that feeling. Unlike him, she'd wanted to escape—only she hadn't. Not even now. She still worked for that complete pressure.

Her father had humiliated Zane that crazy afternoon when they'd kissed so passionately in the stairwell. But she'd said nothing—she'd just stood there and let Zane take all the blame. It might've stung at the time but it wouldn't have bothered Zane the same as the others. He probably laughed about it— if he ever thought of it at all. And he had what he wanted now—his success and that beautiful home on the beach. But he was very, very alone. That was how he wanted it—or so he proclaimed. But now she knew the scars on his thigh weren't anywhere as deep as the ones inside.

'Why was it okay for us to be together this weekend but not for longer?' she couldn't stop herself from asking. 'What's changed?'

He shook his head. 'Nothing's changed. That's the point.'

But he should have people in his life—for longer than the few nights he allowed.

'You might have a lonely few weeks,' she muttered. 'Not dating anyone.'

'I think I can handle it,' he muttered dismissively.

But he didn't *have* to. Her heart pounded harder. 'You don't want company?' She tried to keep it light. But she was angry with him for waiting until the last possible moment to tell her. To give her no time to process or to argue. But it slipped out anyway. 'You don't think we could just keep on seeing each other like this?' She could handle a bit longer. It was only sex after all. An affair that she didn't want to be over yet.

'No.' He stared just beyond her, slightly pale given the last few days in the sun.

No. Instant, flat rejection.

'I don't want to,' he added.

As if she hadn't got the memo already.

It hurt so much more than it should. *Stupid, Skylar.* This was only a game and apparently for him it was no longer fun. Was he *bored*? After all, they'd had a few more dates than one.

She shouldn't have asked. She'd sounded pathetic and needy. She forced a smile to cover up and was so, so glad the chauffeur had pulled up outside of her apartment. 'Sure. Of course.' She opened the door and as she scrambled to get out of the car, she muttered, 'I guess you're going to be busy.'

CHAPTER SIXTEEN

ZANE STOOD ALONGSIDE GRACE, unable to sling his arm around her shoulder like they'd agreed. He'd managed to stand with his hand hovering at her back on their way into the restaurant and he knew the photos had been uploaded directly to socials. Even so, he'd endured dinner with her at the restaurant just below the rooftop bar they were now heading to for the final part of the evening. He'd hated every second but he was determined to see it through. There would be more photos taken at the bar, which would ensure there would be no doubt—Zane deMarco was back to his one-date wonder ways.

'At least *try* to smile,' Grace murmured as they moved past the next photographer.

Tonight's event was a frivolous summer celebration. No worthy high society charity do, this was a vibrant night offering excess and excitement and some new EP from some famous music producer. One that high-profile influencers posted live on their social media accounts. All pumping music, vibrant lights, short dresses, tight shirts, sparkles and skin…pure festival vibe. The rooftop club and bar was packed while the famous DJ dropped his best beats.

Zane shot his senior analyst a rueful look. 'Thanks for this. I'm going to push off shortly.'

Grace didn't even try to convince him to change his mind. 'Thanks for getting me in here. I've always wanted to see this bar.'

'Enjoy.' He knew she'd be fine—she was on track for a fantastic night. Whereas he was officially over people and parties. He wanted nothing more than to be alone. He'd pay his driver triple time and go back to the beach tonight. He might have to take a bottle of whisky with him.

But he couldn't resist a moment to check the stunning view of the Hudson River and the city lights, but three steps along he came face-to-face with Cade Landry.

'Hey.' Zane braced.

'Who's that?' Cade jerked his head towards Grace, currently stalking her way through to the dance floor. 'I thought you were seeing some petite brunette who works at Helberg.' Cade's eyes narrowed. 'Which is pretty interesting, given everything.'

'Didn't work out,' Zane said shortly.

'No?' Cade lifted his glass with a smirk. 'That isn't her heading towards us right now?'

Zane whirled and scanned the balcony, instantly spotting her petite frame amongst the revellers.

He'd died and gone to hell.

The scarlet minidress stopped his heart. The look in her eyes ripped it from his chest. Five days since he'd seen her. Five interminable days and endlessly restless nights.

She'd not been in touch and he'd been doing everything to keep himself distracted and not succumb to the temptation of calling her. He'd left the city for a couple of nights just to stop himself. It was while he was away then that he'd made this plan. Because he needed to be clear of *everything* she was associated with.

Quickly he turned back to Cade. 'I'm out of the bet. I don't want Helberg. You and Adam carry on without me.'

Cade's jaw dropped. 'You're—'

'Done. I've dated two women since the bet started. There'll be more in the next few days. I'm out. Completely.'

He didn't explain further. He just had to get away. From Skylar. From trying to explain it to *her* without…he didn't know what.

He pushed through the crowds and got to the elevator, hitting the buttons to get him down. Out. Away. The lift didn't come and the tightness in his chest worsened. He'd take the stairs. He weaved through the crowds again, no relief from that image of her in his mind, and as he turned the corner she was there. Right in his path, as if she'd just been waiting for him all along.

'Why are you running away so early?' she said.

Because he couldn't stand seeing her. Especially not in that scarlet minidress. The long sleeves and high neck were made of something see-through while a silk slip the same colour covered her best bits beneath—but only just. It was playful and provocative as hell. Her hair was in that high ponytail and his ruby earrings sparkled in the light. But it was her eyes he really couldn't handle seeing. Not the gleaming anger in them.

Why was *she* angry? *He* was the angry one.

'What about your date?' she asked over the top of the thudding music. 'Are you just going to leave her alone here?'

His chest tightened even more. She was concerned for his *date*? She wasn't jealous at all—not even the *slightest*?

'She's fine,' he said tightly. Grace wouldn't be at all bothered that he'd vanished. He desperately needed to get to the beach and down that bottle of whisky. Maybe two.

'Are you deliberately throwing the bet with a fake date?' Skylar stood right in front of him and she was taller because she was wearing high heels the colour of her dress.

He gritted his teeth. He did not want to answer that question.

'Don't you want Helberg any more?' She followed up.

Of course she'd ask about Helberg. It really was her priority. And of course that was exactly why he'd decided to step back from it completely. And of course tonight's bloody date was fake. 'Right.'

Her eyes widened. 'Why not?' She drew a sharp breath. 'What's changed?'

'The price,' he muttered harshly. 'Pushing up. It's one I can no longer pay.'

'You've decided it's going to cost you too much?'

'Something like that.' He didn't want to talk about this. He didn't want her to know the truth. So he fudged. 'There are safer investment options.'

'Safer,' she echoed.

Why had he ever wanted the stupid company—why had it mattered so much that he be that one to break it apart? He couldn't remember why he'd felt that so intensely any more. Everything had been superseded by something else. Some*one*. And she was just staring at him now, her brown eyes deep and doubtful and angry.

'I don't care about what happened with Helberg any more,' he growled. 'That's so long ago now. Maybe I can even thank him for motivating me to succeed. I probably wouldn't have had that fire without his…damned judgment.'

She was still for a second and he tensed up even more.

'So you've made peace with it?' She blinked slowly. 'Good for you.'

It wasn't 'good.' He simply had no choice. Even though he knew she was only interested in him physically, he couldn't be the one to break Helberg up. It would still happen, but at least it wouldn't be him. It wasn't that he cared about the stupid company—he cared too much for her. And while she'd finally acknowledged the problems with the company, she still didn't want it to happen. And he didn't want to be the one to cause her that hurt.

Irritated with his weakness for her, his control slipped. 'Why are you here tonight? This isn't your scene.' He cleared his throat as a fierce glint flashed in her eyes. 'How did you even get in?'

She didn't move. For a moment he didn't think she'd heard him.

'You should leave.' He wanted to leave. 'It's over between us, Skylar.' He had to remind himself. 'I've moved on.'

Her lips slowly curved. 'You think I came here tonight to see you?'

Hadn't she? 'You're wearing the earrings I gave you.' His voice rose as his rage rose, because she looked stunning—make-up, jewellery, the things she'd never bothered with before. Was she here to meet other *men*? 'You've made an *effort—*'

'Yeah, I did,' she snapped. 'I made an effort. For *me*.'

The music was beating so loudly Skylar couldn't be sure he'd even heard her, but it didn't matter. She turned and took her shredded heart and turned on her heel while she could remain upright. She needed to breathe. Just breathe. Just for a moment. Because in this instant she couldn't keep it together, not for a second longer. And she needed to.

He'd *crushed* her. Blindly she walked—missing the exit, just heading to another part of the balcony bar. She'd seen his arrival at that restaurant with the tall blonde on her social media. It had popped up practically in real time. The strangest ice-cold rage had overcome her. She'd dressed, jumped in a cab and stalked with fierce confidence straight past the security guys at the door, who'd just waived her through. She'd had to see for herself if he was throwing the bet or if that date was *real*. Yet finding out it was fake hadn't given her any relief, because seeing him again had ripped the barely formed scab from a wound she'd not acknowledged was so damned *deep*. She missed him. She wanted him. So very much.

She made it ten paces before stopping. It didn't make sense. *None* of it made sense to her. What *was* he doing? Why? Was he really over a lifetime of anger? She needed to understand properly. Turning, she retraced her steps.

He was standing where she'd left him. His head was bowed

as he leaned against the pillar and his expression almost yanked her already battered heart out of her chest.

'Zane...' she whispered.

He jerked his head up, somehow hearing her, and that haunted expression was instantly wiped. 'What are you doing?' he said harshly.

'What are *you* doing?' She glared at him. 'You're at a fabulous club with a stunning, beautiful woman and you look freaking miserable. Answer me honestly—are you okay?'

He stared at her. Stunned. And said nothing.

'No?' She stepped up close to him. 'You know what I think? I think you've spent your life suppressing your own needs and protecting people from your true feelings.'

Exactly the same as she had. She'd been so good for so long. She'd done everything expected of her—and more—for her whole damned life. Even when she no longer actually had to. And it was enough already.

'You think I suppressed my needs around *you*?' he mocked harshly.

'I'm not talking about sex.' She breathed hard. 'At least, not *only* sex.'

He stared at her.

'You ended this with me before you needed to because what, you actually opened up for five minutes? You got uncomfortable with that?' She shook her head. 'The thing is, you've got more to offer a woman than you think.'

'Skylar—'

'I get that you don't want *me*. I get that.' She stretched up as tall as she could and spoke furiously, right in his ear. 'I thought you were totally cold beneath that playboy exterior. That superficial charm masked an empty shell. That you took things apart because you're not whole and you can't stand to see other things complete.'

His nostrils flared.

'But you're not,' she said huskily. 'You brought me my favourite food, remembered the things I like to do. You supported me in my one hobby...that wasn't all part of the game. That was *you*. You're a caring, kind guy. You have more than great sex to offer someone, you know? You should have a person in your life.'

She really wanted to be that person, and while she could accept his decision that she wasn't, she desperately hoped he might change his mind. That he might be hiding so much more—same as she.

But he just stared down at her. 'I thought you said I was an arrogant prat,' he said roughly.

She rocked back onto her heels. 'The fact is you know me better than anyone else, but I know *you* too. I know how you can hide hurt, Zane. You even *told* me how good you are at it. I think you're afraid, and I don't blame you because you took some rough blows when we were young. But you can't hide it for ever. It'll rise,' she said, her voice catching. 'Eventually it'll become impossible to ignore. And all the partying in the world, all the money you can make, won't be distraction enough. And when you finally realise that maybe you *do* have the courage to face it, and let someone in, it might just be too late.'

He still didn't move. The man was ice. He wanted to stay that way. And it was too late for *her* already. Her shredded heart broke right in two. She blinked, furious with her loss of emotional control in the face of his rigidity. But that's where they were different now, right? She *let* herself feel. He still didn't.

'You should go home,' he said gruffly.

'Screw that.' She lifted her chin with a defiant sniff, determined to mask up again. 'I'm going dancing.'

CHAPTER SEVENTEEN

JEALOUSY STORMED THROUGH Zane at the thought of her on a dance floor with someone else. He made himself walk. Away. Not go caveman and scoop her up and storm out of there with her hanging upside down and screaming over his shoulder. Much as he wanted to.

This possessiveness was intolerable. He instructed his driver to floor it and keep driving. He didn't want to go back to his penthouse. It was tainted with memories of her. As was the beach house. But he needed to go somewhere. A momentary stop at a liquor store helped…eventually. Hours later, he was where he needed to be. Alone and by the ocean and more than halfway through a bottle of whisky.

Not that he felt any better for it.

He tossed the bottle off the balcony, irritated. He didn't do this. He never drank alone. Never tried to numb pain with substance abuse. He endured—and he could handle this too, right? This was nothing.

But it wasn't nothing. It was agony. And it was awful.

This was the thing he couldn't do. *Relationships*. Fun, yes. For sure. But that had become a hollow satisfaction, whereas his satisfaction with Skylar was anything but hollow. It was everything.

But she didn't want a relationship either. She didn't want to make that *effort*. Sex was 'easy' with him and all she'd wanted was the experience he could offer. The 'learning' she'd not had for years for whatever unfathomable reason. And he was a safe choice because he didn't want relationships either—he was a one-date wonder after all...

Except maybe now he wasn't.

And the bitter irony was he meant little more than nothing to her. It was only Helberg she held in her heart. For her father. That was why she'd come looking for him. And he'd used it, hadn't he, to manipulate her into his little game. Because having sex with her the once hadn't been enough.

Heaven knew he would never have enough.

Groaning, he stumbled downstairs to the cabinet and abandoned his noble attempts to endure pain. He couldn't do it any more. He needed an anaesthetic and whisky was the only available option.

Hours later, his head was absolutely killing him. So was his heart. Every damn beat reverberated the pain around his body. It *sucked*.

He stood beneath the shower and flicked it to cold. He leaned against the wall and closed his eyes and endured the freezing temperatures. Regretting everything.

Pure self-inflicted punishment. His relentless thoughts of Skylar only made it worse. They'd tumbled into lust the second they'd had the chance. Both back when they were both teens and again when he'd found her in his garden. Both times they'd barely spoken before the chemistry between them had instantly exploded—out of control and unstoppable.

Her father had broken them apart and torn strips off him.

'Don't you dare mess with my daughter!'

'Don't you dare...'

The strict old man had repeated that phrase to *Skylar* over and over that day. And she hadn't, had she? She'd not dared deviate again from the path her father had set out for her. The narrow path of academic excellence, loyalty to the benefactor that was Helberg.

He got it. He really did. He'd wanted to protect his mother for years, suppressing the anger inside him because he couldn't be honest with her. He hadn't been able to tell her he didn't want to go to that damned school. Hadn't been able to tell her he was hurting. How badly he hurt for years with that injury—because he'd not wanted to make her feel worse. Because he'd not wanted to cause her more trouble.

As an adult he'd rationalised it all. He'd known his mother had been exhausted, working hard at two jobs—that she'd thought that scholarship would be best for him because she'd believed she couldn't meet his needs. But she'd not asked him if it were what he wanted. Equally, he'd not said.

And he'd been so alone for so long. Because he'd gone the opposite way to Skylar—he'd gone for hedonism. Using temporary pleasure to wash away the pain but keeping it short, meaningless, keeping himself safe. Anything more took too much *effort*.

Only it didn't take any effort with Skylar. So easily he could laugh with her. And he'd told her truths he'd barely been able to face himself. He could tease her and play sexy little games that he loved. Only with her.

Because it was *her*. He'd had such a crush on her back then. He'd wanted her so much. But he was completely in love with her now. Not that he'd told her. No. He'd turned his back on her. Because she scared the hell out of him.

He wasn't good enough, right? And hearing that again? *Losing* her? He couldn't tolerate that. Which was why he was here now, indulging in a futile attempt to wash away a hangover of epic proportions.

Maybe she had wanted to speak up for him that morning all those years ago, but she'd been too shocked, too scared. Hell, it had only been a moment—they'd hardly spoken. He'd been blown away by the intensity—maybe she had too. And she'd have been terrified of her father.

Zane had turned his back and walked—had to—stung by them both.

But Skylar had been stuck. Had to stay for so much more of the same. And she'd become such a people pleaser. She put everyone else first. *Everyone.* Her father. Her colleagues. A whole damn company. She'd not stopped to consider what it was *she* really wanted…she'd just stayed on that damn treadmill that she'd been set on because she thought she had to.

And she'd tried to please him too, hadn't she? Was it only because he'd plucked at her too-soft heartstrings in Bermuda— telling her about the accident?

No, it had been for so much longer than that. She'd barely known him at the beginning of the bet business because he kept all his cards close. But she'd known enough about him to be aware that he liked games. That he didn't want a *relationship*. So she'd, what, made a play that she thought he could tolerate?

But after Bermuda, when he'd ended their deal, she'd asked if they could keep seeing each other anyway. Then at the bar last night she'd suggested he needed people in his life. But she'd not expressly suggested herself. Had that been because she'd been afraid of asking outright—afraid of his rejection? Did she want something more with him?

Hope soared. Because *he* was the only man she'd ever let touch her. She'd let *him* in. Actions, not words, right? And it wasn't solely about 'education.'

But while she'd played with him, while she'd been confident enough to take something of what she wanted, she'd still put *his* wishes ahead of her own.

She'd asked him if he was okay. She'd wanted him to say what he really felt…but he hadn't shared that part of himself with her. He'd not told her his truth. Because he still believed that he wasn't what she wanted, that he wasn't best for her. He'd assumed it was all only about Helberg for her. What if he'd been wrong about that?

Had she done exactly what he did? Had she hid her hurt—not admitted her feelings—not said what she really felt, or what *she* really wanted…?

And by staying silent, Zane hadn't let her make her own informed choice about their future. He'd made it for her by pushing her away. In all that assumption, he'd pushed her into the same place she'd been with her father.

Silenced.

He'd been selfish. And controlling. And yeah, a complete coward.

He growled, letting the icy water stream over his face.

Enough of that already!

CHAPTER EIGHTEEN

THE DANCING PHASE lasted about forty minutes. She didn't want to dance with anyone but him. Didn't want to dance without him at all. Her feet hurt, her heart bled, her eyes watered. Infuriated, she went home and threw herself into work. That phase lasted about five minutes.

She didn't want to work like this any more. And, she accepted, she didn't *have* to.

She didn't get out of bed the next day. She slept. She thought. And yes, she cried. In her weakest moments she looked online. Zane's tally on that stupid website hadn't increased. It had stopped at two and there were no more pictures of him dining or dancing with another woman last night. But it was only a matter of time though, right?

Because it was over between them. He wasn't going to wake up and realise he was in love with her…the way she was in love with him.

Yeah, she could admit that now—to herself at least. And she'd sort of told him last night, in a tragically weird way, trying to convince him he needed someone in his life.

Of course she'd meant herself. And of course he'd stood like a stone.

But while he didn't feel the same, she couldn't believe what they'd shared was *nothing*. They had a real connection—more than their shared past, more than the undeniable sexual chemistry. He just didn't want it to last. And fine. But that didn't stop her holding her breath, hoping and wishing. Checking her phone. But no matter how long she stared at it, he didn't message her.

She couldn't—and wouldn't—wait for ever. *She* had to move forward too. But it would be in a different way to him. She'd worked so hard and been so loyal to everyone else *but* herself for too long. She'd not blossomed in all these years—she'd been blinkered.

She needed time away to figure out and focus on the things she *could* attain—*other* than Zane himself. And there was much—the travel she'd not done. She needed to explore all the other beaches, see all the other amazing buildings in the world. And she could—because she had money saved. All that money to buy her father a better house and she hadn't been able to because he'd passed too soon. All the money sitting there because she'd not spoiled herself. Not gone anywhere.

Then there were the job opportunities she'd not explored—heck, maybe she'd go for a whole career change. She owed it to herself to reach for the life she wanted. The one she'd not taken true hold of... She could get excited about that. She could make something more for herself. And she would be okay.

She picked up her phone and adjusted some settings so there'd be no point in looking forlornly at it any more.

And on Monday morning it was time to move.

It was appallingly easy for them to accept her resignation. For her to gather the few personal things she had in her desk. She didn't even need a box. Then she got on the bus heading east, the route familiar and slow. She'd do her farewell tour.

And then she'd be free.

Zane waited at reception, his back turned to that portrait of Reed Helberg. Cleared his throat. Checked his watch. Adjusted his collar. Ignored the dagger looks the receptionist shot him every other interminable second. It was Bernie who finally appeared. Zane saw his face and was hit by a bad really feeling.

'Where is she?' Zane asked as soon as Bernie was within earshot.

She'd blocked his number. When he'd tried calling her from an alternate phone she still hadn't picked up. He'd gone to her apartment and she wasn't home. Not during the day. Not late at night. She wasn't around.

'She's finished up. Gone away.'

'Gone *where*?'

Surely not. It was only Tuesday. She wouldn't walk out on her job without giving due notice. That wasn't Skylar's way. But maybe she'd really wanted to get away.

While that was terrifying, it also fuelled him. Because it meant she was upset. And not all about her job.

The old guy looked at him with total disappointment in his eyes. 'I think she leaves the country in a couple of days.'

Zane had to take a moment. 'So where is she now? You really don't know?'

'No. I'm sorry.'

Zane believed him. Because while she considered these guys family, she didn't open up to them. It was like she was still shut away in her room upstairs, looking out the window at the world. Still lonely.

He spent an hour wondering where the one place she'd go before leaving the country for a while might be. And then it was obvious.

He drove himself—tearing back down the very road he'd driven only the day before. Back to Belhaven Bay. He drove past the site where their old building complex had been. He went to the beach. He went to the cafe. It was only when he happened to drive past the cemetery on his way to their old school that he slammed on the brakes. He'd almost missed her sitting on that park bench in the middle of the memorial gardens.

He took in a couple of steadying breaths before getting out of the car. He had to be so careful. She wanted to travel and he refused to stand in the way of her doing something she really wanted for herself. But he didn't want her to leave without being honest with her. He owed her that. He owed himself too. So he would control himself here. But at least she would know she was loved. That she meant so very much to him.

And he would accept whatever happened.

She glanced up when he approached. Paled. Her hair was in a messy ponytail and her eyes red-rimmed.

'You've left Helberg,' he said.

'I have a lot of holidays owed so I was able to leave with immediate effect,' she said. 'I'm going to travel. Sit on some other beaches. Run at some other parks. Figure out what I really want in my future.'

He nodded. 'That sounds great.'

She stood but didn't move closer, just hesitated with her arms wrapped around her waist. 'What are you doing here?'

'I...uh... I wanted to tell you...' His throat was scratchy and he swallowed, finding it almost impossible to speak.

But she waited silently. He appreciated her patience. And he would make this effort. Always.

He cleared his throat. 'I was here over the weekend. Came late on Saturday night...' He'd run away and drowned his sorrows. It hadn't worked. 'That's not what I came here to tell you though.'

'No?'

'You're a loyal person, Skylar. You put other people first all the time. Their needs. You should dare to be free, Skylar. Dare to do whatever you want.'

She lost a little colour. 'You want me to be happy.'

'Yes.'

'You want me to do what *I* want.'

'Yes. Exactly.' His heart pounded. 'I want the best for you.'

She stared at him. 'Why?'

He was actually trembling inside. This beautiful woman who he'd wanted for so long, the woman he'd finally truly got to know. The woman he'd completely fallen for. Was standing in front of him and about to leave.

'You were right,' he coughed. 'I don't just hide hurt, Skylar. I hide all my feelings. And that's not fair of me.'

'Okay.'

He twisted up inside. 'That's just it. I'm not okay.'

Skylar could hold herself together for only so long. She didn't want to interrupt him—didn't want him to ever stop talking in that gentle way—but at the same time she couldn't stand to see him. He was heartbreakingly gorgeous.

'I'm not okay,' he whispered again. 'Not without you.'

The echo of her pulse in her eardrums was deafening. She willed him to say more. Or to move—to step forward and pull her into his arms. She would take that. She would take anything.

But he suddenly covered his face with his hands. 'I'm so scared of having you and losing you. I want you so much. In my life. Always. But I don't want to—' He broke off and looked skywards and swore. 'I'm screwing this up, Skylar.'

'Why are you here?'

He drew in a harsh breath. 'I don't want to confuse you. I don't want to stand in your way. I don't want to hold you back from anything, ever. I don't want to say this and have it have any sway over your decisions because that's what you do for the people in your life… But also, I think I have to say this, Skylar.'

So many things he didn't want if he… 'Say what?'

His hands dropped. 'I love you.'

'What?' She stared at him, not wanting to move or breathe. She just wanted a replay of what he'd just said. Had he said—

'I ended our agreement after Bermuda because I was uncomfortable. I know we strike sparks when we get within ten feet of each other, but I need you to know that this became so much more than that for me. More than some fun game. More than unfinished business from a lifetime ago.'

'How much more?'

'Everything more.' He remained frozen, so far away. 'That's what I meant by "I love you." Like completely, utterly, totally, I am in love with you.'

She had to put her hand on the back of the park bench for balance. 'You what?'

'It's you, it's always been you.'

'But—'

'I know there've been other women.' He looked awkward. 'And I know it sounds bad, but none of them meant anything much.'

She understood, actually. 'You didn't let them get near enough to matter.'

Because this brilliant, strong, kind man didn't think he was worthy of someone—his father had left him, his mother had struggled to cope with him alone, he'd been rejected by the most powerful man in town, and he'd been crushed—literally. So he'd suppressed so much. His pain. His needs. He'd rebuilt himself—but there was still that little bit broken inside.

'You matter,' he said softly. 'Always have. I watched you… you came back from that school and you were different.'

A smile escaped. 'You mean I'd been through puberty?'

He chuckled softly. 'Not just that, you were so…serene and focused and I wanted to talk to you. I should have talked to you. But I got near and…' He lifted his shoulders.

They were on that runaway train together.

'And you don't think *you're* the best thing ever to walk back into my life?'

His pale blue eyes widened.

He'd been a handful of a boy. He was a handful of a man. And she loved him for it. Because he was gold—through and through.

'I mean it,' she said. 'I know I'm a pleaser. I want people to like me—to need me—that's true. But I could be me around you. Free. Maybe at the start I thought it didn't matter because it was only a game, but now it matters more than anything. *You* matter more than anything,' she whispered. 'And I'm so, so sorry.'

'Why?' He paled. 'For what? What are—'

'I should have said something that day Dad caught us. I just stood there and let him berate you, let him chase you off, let him think you were pushy when I should have spoken up and stopped him.'

'Oh.' He released a massive sigh. 'No.' He shook his head gently. 'We both did what we had to, to be safe. In here.' He pressed his hand to his chest. 'I don't blame you for that.'

'But I hurt you.' She realised it now.

So had her dad. He'd made him feel unworthy. It had been another blow in that pile-on he'd felt.

His shoulders lifted. 'You were hurt too. And, sweetheart, we were kids.' He smiled sadly. 'Far too young to be able to handle something this big.'

Skylar trembled. This was that big for him too? Overwhelming and all-encompassing and wonderful…and terrifying. But now he was here. He'd come after her.

'You came to see him?' Zane gestured towards her father's grave.

'To tell him I've left Helberg.' She nodded and gazed at her father's small headstone. 'You know he never dated anyone or anything after my mother left. He was so self-contained and he encouraged me to be the same—that just the two of us was all we needed. I guess he thought it was safe.' She looked back up at Zane and saw the intensity in his eyes.

'He didn't think I was good enough for you,' he muttered.

'In his view, *no one* would have been good enough for me,' she said. 'But it wasn't his choice.'

She drank in Zane's stance—he was so focused on her. He listened. He cared. He loved her. And she needed to make him understand that she loved him right back. So much.

Emboldened, she stepped closer to him. 'This is *my* life and my choice. And I don't want to be alone.'

Zane's eyes flashed.

'I want a relationship, not a fling.' Her voice both rose and shook. 'I want one love for a lifetime. I want a home. And I want a family. Children. And a dog. Two, actually.'

'What else?' he muttered huskily.

'I want to travel and see all the things I've not seen yet.' She blinked but through the tears she saw he'd stepped closer still.

'Sounds amazing. Is there more? What else do you want?'

Blinking again, she saw the vitality just bursting from him—his expression both light and hard and so very focused. Her courage overflowed, because his feelings were undeniable and so very obvious.

'You,' she said simply. 'With me. I want us to do it all together.'

'I would love to. I would love to do all that with you, Skylar.' He opened his arms and she just toppled into them.

'All that. All that and so much more.' He caught and held her tightly. 'But I don't want to stop you discovering everything else you want. I don't want to cramp your style—'

'You could *never*. You're the one who encourages me into some really creative things.' Her teary laugh was muffled against his chest. 'I want you *with* me.'

'Okay then.'

She felt his deep sigh.

'Always,' he whispered.

Yeah. That's what she wanted.

Drawing back but still holding Zane's hand tightly, she turned to face her father's grave. 'I love you, Daddy,' she whispered. 'And I know you loved me and I know you wanted to keep me safe. But I know you were hurt and you worried a little too much and held me a little too tight.' She told him what she'd been too young and too scared to say so long ago. 'But Zane's a good man. I love him and he loves me and we're going to be okay.' She drew in a shaky breath. 'We're going to have it all.'

Zane didn't let go of her hand the entire car ride—releasing her only to get out of the car and round to her door. Then he wrapped his arm around her waist and led her into the house, up the stairs, straight to his bedroom.

'I love you,' he said before she could breathe. 'I love you.'

He kissed her and told her over and over. She had no idea how they got naked, how they got into the bed. All she knew was that they were together—naked and entwined, and he was loving her with his words and his body and his spirit. And he was hers—really and truly hers.

Hours later, she stood wrapped in the top sheet, looking out at the stunning view of the garden and the beach beyond. 'I love it here,' she breathed.

He wound his arm around her from behind. 'Plenty of room for our kids and the dogs to roam free, don't you think? We can watch them playing from the balcony up here.'

She nodded, leaning back against him. 'That would make this great view unbeatable.'

'Yeah.'

And that was exactly what it did.

CHAPTER NINETEEN

Three years later

DANIELLE CHAPMAN'S ANNUAL Fourth of July party was in
full swing. The beat of music and the bubble of chatter wafted
through the still summer night, easily reaching the ears of the
woman lying on the sun lounger that was artfully placed beneath an old cherry tree, hidden by the thick hedge that formed
the boundary between the two vast beachfront properties.

Skylar wasn't wearing white, because she wasn't going to
the party at all—she was in a scarlet bikini and, despite the
rapid approach of dusk, she was still feeling hot. She was also
feeling huge. She heard the clink of ice and glanced up to see
her husband walking towards her balancing two tall glasses
of she didn't know what, but she knew it would be delicious.

Actually, it was her bare-chested husband who was delicious. Clad only in beach shorts and sandals, every muscle
was on display. She felt hotter still.

'Something you need, Skylar?' Zane chuckled and set the
glasses down on the small table that had been dragged near
the lounger long ago.

'You know me too well,' she muttered.

He ran a fingertip over her lower lip. 'Pregnancy makes
you very hungry.'

'It does,' she purred. 'I need a *lot* of attention.'

This was their favourite place to be alone together. Where

they'd spent many lazy summer afternoons, dozing, reading, making love...

The first year they'd travelled lots. They'd both walked away from Helberg, but Skylar had been beyond touched to learn Zane had offered Bernie and the other older employees a guarantee on their Helberg investment in case things went bad. Bernie had since retired, his pension fund intact.

Zane had cut back on the hours he'd worked and reprioritised. They'd married in this very garden only a few months in—the two of them standing in the trees with only Danielle as witness. Danielle who'd been astounded and then enchanted to learn of their history and delighted to be part of their very private celebration.

At the end of that first year, Skylar had discovered she was pregnant. They'd not been trying, but they'd not been *not* trying...and it had happened quicker than either of them had imagined it would. They'd been ecstatic. Eight months later her impatient son had arrived. He had his father's eyes and demanding nature and she adored him.

Right now he was inside their home cuddled up with the puppy, being read to by his doting grandmother, who was tasked with keeping him awake just long enough to catch a glimpse of the fireworks from Danielle's party.

Zane had asked Skylar to come with him to visit his mother not long after that day by her father's grave. It had been awkward between mother and son at first. Skylar had chattered to fill the gaps, but slowly things had got easier and both Zane and his mother had talked through some of the tough times in their past. She'd finally retired and even let Zane help her. Now she visited often. It gave Zane no end of pleasure to see his mother relaxed and able to enjoy spending time with their small, inquisitive boy. They were all looking forward to the arrival of his little sister—due in four months' time.

'What attention would you *particularly* like?' Zane rested his hands either side of her and bent over her.

She just wanted all of him. Now. She curled her arms around his neck and tugged him so he toppled down to her.

'Careful,' he grunted. 'I don't want to crush you.'

She slipped from beneath him, giving him a nudge so he rolled onto his back. In seconds she straddled him and greedily worked the waistband of his shorts down. But he was busy too. He released her hair from its ponytail first—as he so often liked to do. Then he tugged the strings of her bikini top until they became dangerously loose, but didn't go further.

'Are you playing with me?' she asked archly as she teased him every bit as much.

'Is this a game?' He batted his lashes wickedly. 'Or is this a *race*?'

'Oh, it's a game,' she whispered.

'No, it's a race,' he whispered right back before snatching the bikini from her and cupping her breasts in both hands.

She shuddered as his thumbs teased her sensitive tips. But she shook her head and worked her hands that bit harder.

'I like watching you come first,' he growled. 'Then I like watching you come again.'

'Come *with* me or I'll turn my back and then you won't see my face.'

His wicked smile broadened and he swept his hands over her belly and below. 'Reverse cowgirl is always acceptable,' he drawled. 'I can touch you where you like it most. And I love it when you scream and whip your hair in my face.'

She flushed and giggled at the same time. Next second she gasped. *'Zane!'*

He felled her. Every time. He rose up and wrapped his arms around her to hold her close, kissing her as he finally filled her and succumbed to the sparks between them. She clung, quivering as she welcomed him back to her heart. They moved fast yet gentle—playful and passionate—until they were out of control and shaking in ecstasy together.

'I love you,' he panted.

This was the race he liked to win—to say it first in the mornings, to say it the most. To mean it always.

But it was no game really. Skylar held his handsome face in her hands and gazed right into his eyes. 'I love you too.'

His smile was stunning—so satisfied and smug and yet full of wonder that she'd said it still. They'd given each other the family they both craved. The security they both needed. All the love they'd secretly longed for. And it all just kept growing.

She kissed him. Fireworks whistled and burst above them, filling the sky with sound and colour before fading all too quickly.

But Zane and Skylar made their own fireworks. And they always would.

* * * * *

Did you fall head over heels for
Billion-Dollar Dating Game?

Then you're sure to adore the other instalments in the
Billion-Dollar Bet trilogy,
coming soon.

And while you wait, why not dive into
these other Natalie Anderson stories?

Carrying Her Boss's Christmas Baby
The Boss's Stolen Bride
Impossible Heir for the King
Back to Claim His Crown
My One-Night Heir

Available now!

COMING SOON!

We really hope you enjoyed reading this book.
If you're looking for more romance
be sure to head to the shops when
new books are available on

Thursday 26th September

To see which titles are coming soon, please visit
millsandboon.co.uk/nextmonth

MILLS & BOON

MILLS & BOON®

Coming next month

ITALIAN BABY SHOCK
Jackie Ashenden

'I'm so sorry,' Lark said quickly as the phone vibrated again. 'But I really need to get this. It's my daughter's nanny.' She bent to pick the phone up off the table, turning as she looked down at it.

He could see the screen over her shoulder. On it was a photo of a baby, a little girl dressed in pink. She had a cloud of soft, rose-gold curls and blue, blue eyes.

It was a singular colour that rose-gold, as was the intense blue of her eyes. He'd never met anyone else who'd had hair that hue apart from his mother. And as for that blue…

That was Donati blue. Two hundred years ago the Donatis had been patrons of a painter who'd created a paint colour in their honor. And that's what he'd called it.

Cesare went very still as everything in him slowed down. Everything except his brain, which was now working overtime. Going back over that night. Going over everything.

Because if there was one thing he knew, it was that the baby in that photo was his daughter.

Continue reading
ITALIAN BABY SHOCK
Jackie Ashenden

Available next month
millsandboon.co.uk

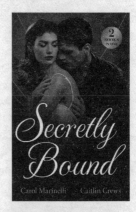
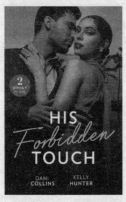
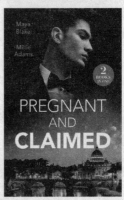

LET'S TALK
Romance

For exclusive extracts, competitions and special offers, find us online:

f MillsandBoon

X @MillsandBoon

⊙ @MillsandBoonUK

♪ @MillsandBoonUK

Get in touch on 01413 063 232

For all the latest titles coming soon, visit
millsandboon.co.uk/nextmonth

afterglow BOOKS

Afterglow Books is a trend-led, trope-filled list of books with diverse, authentic and relatable characters, a wide array of voices and representations, plus real world trials and tribulations. Featuring all the tropes you could possibly want (think small-town settings, fake relationships, grumpy vs sunshine, enemies to lovers) and all with a generous dose of spice in every story.

@millsandboonuk
@millsandboonuk
afterglowbooks.co.uk

#AfterglowBooks

For all the latest book news, exclusive content and giveaways scan the QR code below to sign up to the Afterglow newsletter:

SCAN ME